"Go to Hell, Braddock!"

"I won't go to hell, or anywhere else! And I won't stand by and watch while you let the Triple X die because you're too damn stubborn to accept my help."

"Why, you ..." Rachel hauled back her arm and swung.

Sin stopped her fist with his hand and pulled her off balance, catching her as she fell across the desk and against his chest. Both his arms went around her, and he held her there.

Rachel was shocked to find herself in Sin's arms. "Let go of me, you bastard!" she demanded and pushed against him. The strength of his arms surprised her as she struggled to free herself.

Sin felt the heat of her fury in the way she fought against him. He pulled her across the top of the desk, sending a wood paper-box and the ledger crashing to the floor, and set her on her feet in front of him. She'd grabbed his shoulders as she slid across the desk, and with her arms up, he found himself flush with the voluptuous curves of her body. Reason left him, and before she could react, he slid one hand down to the firm curve of her buttocks and pulled her even tighter against him. Her head came up in surprise, and as she opened her mouth to protest, his lips took hers possessively, demanding a response....

ROSEBUD

FAYE ADAMS

POCKET BOOKS

New York   London   Toronto   Sydney   Tokyo   Singapore

An *Original* Publication of POCKET BOOKS

POCKET BOOKS, a division of Simon & Schuster Inc.
1230 Avenue of the Americas, New York, NY 10020

ISBN: 0-671-88298-8

First Pocket Books printing May 1994

10 9 8 7 6 5 4 3 2 1

POCKET and colophon are registered trademarks of
Simon & Schuster Inc.

Cover art by Elaine Gignilliat

Printed in the U.S.A.

To Lydia and Robert Adams,
grandparents who helped make my
life special

1

Rachel knew that the hot August sun and skin-scorching wind, blowing sand across the plain in blasts, could make a cowboy's nerves scream in pain at the slightest turn in the saddle. Even so, as her cool green eyes surveyed a crew of her ranch hands working on a break in a corral fence, she couldn't keep from adjusting her seat. The creak of saddle leather and answering movement of discomfort from the horse beneath her caused her to squint from the painful sensation similar to sandpaper on raw flesh.

"Sorry, Roux, I can't seem to keep my mind on business today."

She once more glanced at the men. They were working hard, and perspiration stained their shirts in dark triangles. Lowering the brim of her hat by tipping her head slightly to hide her face, she smiled to herself. These were good men. Men who respected her. She raised her view once more. Well, she thought, at least they respect my position as boss.

Once in a while one of them would glance in her direction. She made a stoic but beautiful picture sitting astride Roux, the big chestnut gelding her father had given her. Sometimes a new hand, usually young and full of himself, would try to start up a romance with Rachel. They never knew she was tempted. Her strong exterior and firm refusals soon cooled even the hottest pursuer. They would have been very surprised to know that their aloof boss-lady had many less than ladylike thoughts of her own while watching them at work. As it was, they accepted their place and hers, ranch hands and boss.

She shifted again in the saddle, an inner restlessness making it impossible for her to sit still. Roux shifted with her from one foot to another, sensing her nervousness. Flexing her shoulder blades as a trickle of perspiration ran down her back, she took off a leather glove by biting the fingers one at a time. She wiped the sweat from her brow with it and slapped it against her thigh raising the dust there.

"Damn it, Roux, let's go swimming." She pulled slightly on the reins but Roux turned almost without guidance. It seemed that he understood what she said because he took off at a trot in the direction of the creek.

When they could see that Rachel was almost out of sight several of the men straightened from their work and took off their sweat-soaked shirts.

Jace straightened and stretched his back as he watched her ride toward the distant hillock. He could feel the beginnings of desire rising within him and bent to his work to quell the stirrings.

A spindly young cowboy with sparrow-sharp blue eyes couldn't resist goading Jace. "You think she went t' the creek, Jace?"

Not sure what was coming, he responded. "Yeah, Ben, I think she went to the creek."

"You think she swims nak'd?" The sparkle in his eyes showed that he hoped he was causing some trouble.

Jace knew that Rachel did in fact swim in the nude, but he wasn't ready yet to share just how he knew.

"Ben," another voice warned.

"Aw Hank, I'm jest funnin 'im."

2

"You just get back to work. It's too hot to horse around now."

Ben did what he was told. Hank was the ranch foreman and despite his age of well past sixty he was hardly ever crossed. Hank knew something of the history of Miss Rachel and Jace, but he minded his own business and thought others should do likewise. He figured that nature usually ran its course and would here too. Besides, Miss Rachel never acted like she wanted anyone interfering in her business and 'til she asked him for advice he wouldn't give any.

Removing his hat and wiping the sweat away with his sleeve, he scanned the horizon for Rachel. No sign of her, but he frowned at what he did see there.

"Boys, there's dust on the horizon. I'm headed for the house. I'll fire if I need you."

Rachel reached the shaded swimming hole. It was a place in Leaver Creek that wound around on itself and created a perfect spot, deep, wide, and right now, most important, cool. Rachel swung a leg over Roux's head and landed on the soft ground with both feet at once. Her boot heels sank into the dirt, leaving deep impressions. She looked overhead through the leafy roof created by the many willow trees growing in this spot and was appreciative of the shade.

As she dropped the reins, ground-tethering Roux, she thought about how Leaver Creek was the life blood of the Triple X. Fed by high mountain streams, it never went dry. Even during the worst summer droughts it flowed freely, full of cool, life-saving water.

Stripping took only seconds and she was soon swimming the breadth of the hole. The water felt like fingers caressing her nude form; she dove deeply under the surface and shuddered as the water moved between her legs. She could feel the muscles relaxing as she swam and the nervous edge that had accompanied her movements all day began to vanish. Swimming to the edge she pulled herself up and lay on the grassy bank. The wind that ripped across the open prairie was but a breeze here in this secluded area and goose bumps rose on her bare skin.

"This is helping, Roux." The big horse pawed the ground as she spoke.

She sat up and curled her arms around her knees.

"Roux, I'm twenty-seven years old today."

Roux snorted and tore a fresh hunk of grass from the bank.

"I know, so what? That's what I keep telling myself but I can't get over this feeling that something's about to happen. Maybe it has something to do with Pa's death." The shadow of a frown darkened her face as she thought about her recent loss.

Speckles of sunlight on the red coat of the horse shone like copper pennies as he bobbed his head.

Shaking off her momentary sadness she stood and looked at her reflection in the water. "Twenty-seven isn't old."

The woman looking back at her was far from old. Deep red, almost burgundy, hair circled her head and fell in wet curls nearly to her hips. Strong shoulders and arms were in good proportion to her small waist, and long straight legs supported her frame. Turning sideways and putting her hands under her breasts for support she examined the feminine side of her figure.

"I don't look too bad, do I?"

The peaks of her breasts were hard from the cold swim, and her stomach was firm from a lifetime of hard work.

"I may not be the prettiest woman in town, but I bet I could raise a man's ... interest." She smiled a little.

Roux snorted, and with nerves tuned to changes in the air, Rachel knew something was wrong. Heedless of her nudity she stepped to Roux's side and pulled her rifle from the saddle and waited. It took only a second to discover the change. Dust in the direction of the house. Looking to the sky for the time, she tried to guess who could be on their way to the ranch.

"It's too early for Tish to be home from school."

Putting the rifle back on the saddle she reached for her clothes.

"These are going to feel terrible," she muttered.

She had planned on drying in a sunny spot before dressing so the abundance of dust caught in the fabric wouldn't turn to mud on her skin. Now, with this unexpected interruption, her plans had gone awry. Grimacing with every move, she pulled on the offensive garments.

"This better be something important, Roux," she nearly growled as she swung up into the saddle and headed for the house.

The farther she rode the more uncomfortable she became, and the more the unsuspecting visitor was going to suffer for it.

The ride had been a long one, and now as he reached the house he was wondering if it had been worth it. Sin sat in the carriage and surveyed his surroundings. The house, though large, was neither attractive nor impressive in any way. It was in bad need of a good coat of paint and perhaps some minor repairs as the porch seemed to sag a little. The barn and other outbuildings seemed in good repair, though, making the house seem even more run down in contrast.

Removing his black felt hat and looking to the upstairs windows where tattered lace curtains hung, he remembered all the tattered curtains, torn wallpaper, ragged carpets, burned homes, piles of rubble, disfigured bodies . . . the more he thought the worse it got.

Memories, some too painful to dwell on, flooded his mind. He remembered those days he'd lain in the Northern army prison hospital, recovering from a severe shoulder wound. Somewhere in that dim region between life and death, he'd wished, at times, he would die so he wouldn't have to listen to the cries of the soldiers around him as limbs were sawed from their bodies with no anaesthetic. He hadn't known such Hell existed on Earth, couldn't comprehend the cruelty he witnessed. Some of

the doctors had tried to be kind, but most of the order-
lies inflicted pain on their Confederate patients when
asked for comfort. So he learned to suffer in silence.
When ants crawled under his bandage he'd gritted his
teeth until a sympathetic doctor walked by.

Infection ran rampant through the hospital and each
day he'd seen his fellow soldiers, some of them from
his own company, hauled out on wooden stretchers and
dumped in a line or pile, awaiting some sort of burial.
He, himself, had suffered the ravages of fever and chills
for two weeks before the doctors announced he was recovered enough to be put with the prison population.
That's where he'd discovered the real Hell began.

Lying on the damp floor of a cell, in the stench of
human excretion, with only a threadbare woolen blanket
to keep him warm, he'd vowed to survive this nightmare.
He ate every disgusting thing thrown through the bars
of his cell, not that there was much, and too often he
lay shivering in the cold while his stomach twisted with
hunger. But he was one of the lucky ones. He was an
officer and therefore afforded the luxury of a private
cell. The regular soldiers had to fight not only the cold,
confinement, and the cruelty of the guards, but each
other for food and warmth. He would often listen to
their brawls, helpless to stop them, and hear the guards
jeering and taunting as one man overpowered another.

The only thing that kept him going during this time
were the thoughts of freedom and home. The faces of
loved ones that floated above him at night. The letter,
tattered and months old, he'd received from Bessie, his
fiancée. He could recite its contents in his sleep but he
read and reread it, needing to feel some contact with
reality. She was sorry to tell him of his father's stroke
and following illness, but she was waiting for him. He
felt such a desire to get back home that he'd have done
anything to be free. Bessie was waiting and his father
needed him.

Then the day came when he was pulled roughly from
his cell and brought to the commander's office. He re-

membered the way Commander Wilson had turned up his nose at the smell of him when he walked into the room. He supposed he did stink, but he didn't care. He just wanted to know why he'd been summoned. Then he'd seen his old friend, John Wright.

John was a banker like himself. They'd met in college many years before and had maintained their friendship, even through the war. Now John was here to help him. When he'd heard about Sin's capture he'd begun contacting friends in the government to obtain his release. There was just one condition. He must give his word not to rejoin the Southern army. Captain Braddock had a reputation. He was too good a leader, too strong an adversary to be allowed to return to the fighting.

He remembered how it had stuck in his craw to agree to such a bargain. His pride and loyalty battled with his common sense. Then he thought about his father, needing him, and Bessie, waiting. He struck the bargain and was released.

"Let me know how and where you are?" John had asked as they'd parted. He'd thought it was a strange request at the time, but when he'd finally returned home he'd realized that John had already known what he had yet to see for himself. Devastation.

Everything that had kept him alive in that prison camp was gone. Everything. His father had been dead for months and their home and bank bombed and burned. Then he'd gone looking for Bessie. A neighbor told him where to find her. Sitting on her grave, he'd begun to cry. He cried for the first time he could remember, cried as nothing of the horror of the war or prison could make him do.

As he walked back from the cemetery a former employee, and friend, had met him on the street. "I've been saving these for you, if you ever came back," he'd said as he handed him a packet of papers. "It's all I could save from the bank. It burned so quickly." Sin remembered the man had such a dazed, blank expression. It was an expression he would grow to hate as the next few months passed.

The one thing he'd found in the papers that gave him hope for a future was a contract. The reason he was now here in Texas. A long shot. But also a chance.

He rubbed a hand over his eyes and, looking once more at the house, he decided it wasn't so bad after all. The war was nearly over and this ranch was all he had left. He wondered how Miss Walker was going to take to the idea of him becoming a partner in ownership of her ranch.

He pulled his pocket watch from its place in his vest and checked the time. Nearly one o'clock, almost time for her afternoon nap if she followed the same schedule of other southern ladies. Of course this was Texas, and so far he'd learned from his travel across it that things in Texas were different from anywhere else he'd ever been. Still, a woman was a woman. With that thought he looked down at his dusty clothes. He didn't look the way he would have liked to meet her but he hoped she would understand. He stepped down from the buggy and began brushing the dust from his suit.

"Mister, what's your business here?" Rachel demanded as she rode from behind the house.

His surprise at the question, so blunt, coming from a woman astride a horse and carrying a rifle, kept him from answering for just a moment too long. The rifle pointed straight up just long enough to shoot one round of warning then leveled on him.

"I asked you a question, and I don't usually have to ask one twice."

Swallowing, he said, "I've come to see a Miss Rachel Walker about some business."

"You've found her. State your business." Rachel looked him over carefully and quickly as she waited. He was tall and had thick black hair. She could see that he was wearing an expensive suit, but it had known better days. She sized up his frame and found him not lacking in masculinity, but wondered if his shoulders were as broad as they appeared to be or if it was a tailor's trick.

She could see that he too was doing a little examining of his own and stiffened slightly, remembering her sodden appearance.

Sin was not a man easily stunned, but this time he was nearly speechless. "I, I'm sorry. I didn't ..." He couldn't get over the sight of her. She sat straight in the saddle like a man, and her green eyes watched every move he made, making no ladylike attempt at averting her gaze when meeting his or from examining his body as her curiosity dictated. Long, wet hair wove itself around her body interestingly, and it surprised him even more to notice that water had soaked through the man's shirt she was wearing to reveal the voluptuous curves of her breasts. Yet embarrassment was not the emotion he was reading in those green eyes.

"Miss Walker, my name is Sinclaire Braddock. I was a member of the board at the Braddock Bank." He paused as if waiting for a reply. He got none.

"Perhaps, if you were to dismount so we could talk."

"Mister Braddock, my father taught me to never give up the advantage and so far you've said nothing to show me that you're not just some deserter trying to rob me." She remained on Roux with the barrel of the rifle pointed at his chest.

He thought for a moment. She was right. He had ridden in with no forewarning. These were hard times, and even though Texas wasn't actively involved in the war, he supposed she had seen her share of deserters. It was amazing the way a crisis brought out the true colors of a man.

"My apologies, Miss Walker. You are correct. Let me remove my coat and show you that I carry no weapon. I have a rifle and some pistols in the carriage, but I will leave them there. I'm sure you agree, a man would be a fool to travel without some protection."

She watched as he took off the coat and was pleased to see that it contained no padding. Her eyes scanned his body again. The coat had been hiding not only broad shoulders but a strong chest and narrow waist and hips.

He noticed her gaze and was surprised by so bold a stare. No lady had ever looked at him in this manner. Only whores looked at a man like this, but Rachel was no whore. He could tell that by looking at her. But was she a lady? He forced his thoughts from a growing stiffness inside his trousers and back to the business he'd come for.

"Miss Walker, I have a contract here that was signed by your father."

"My father? You know that he died a month ago?" It was painful for her to speak of his death, but she refused to let this stranger see her pain and raised her chin a bit.

"Yes, that's why I'm here."

"And you say that he signed a contract. What kind of contract?"

He didn't want to have to discuss an important business matter at gunpoint. "Perhaps we could . . ."

"Perhaps we could nothing, Mr. Braddock, is it? What kind of contract?" Her eyes narrowed slightly.

He waited only a moment before he decided he'd better give her an answer. "Your father borrowed money from my bank, using this ranch as collateral. He never repaid it." He stopped there, letting her fill in the rest.

Rachel digested what he'd just told her. "Mr. Braddock, you're a liar." She waited.

Sin stiffened. No man called him a liar and got away with it. This woman, but for the evidence of abundant femininity pushing against the wet shirt, acted like a man and seemed to expect to be treated as one. Perhaps she didn't understand the results calling a man a liar could achieve. No, the rifle's aim had pinpointed on his heart and her eyes watched his, reading him the way a gunfighter would. She didn't move a muscle. It seemed that she didn't even blink, and he noticed that the big horse beneath her read her thoughts and froze too. He decided to take her very seriously. This woman would shoot him as soon as look at him, and he hadn't come this far to die in the dirt of property he didn't even own ... yet.

"You got a problem here, Miss Walker?" Hank stepped from behind the corner of the house. His gun was not pulled, but Sin could see that his hand was poised just above it. "I saw the dust and decided to ride up and see who was coming to call."

Rachel's eyes never left Sin's. "No real problem, but I'm glad you're here. Stick around for a while." She swung her right leg over Roux's neck and jumped to the ground, the rifle never changing its aim.

"I just called this ... gentleman a liar, and I'm waiting to see what he does about it."

"Yes'm." Hank stood where he was. "If the boys heard the shot they'll be comin.' "

"Let 'em come."

Sin's black eyes burned with the rage he felt. It galled him to be at such a disadvantage. He was not a man to back down from a fight, but this was a very rare situation. He'd never been called a liar by a woman before, at least not by one willing to settle the question with a gunfight. His eyes narrowed as he thought about his position.

Rachel watched his every move. She saw his eyes change as he sized up the situation. She could see the muscles working in his cheeks as he gritted his teeth, and she could sense the tightness of muscles in his arms as he clenched his fists. She knew by instinct that if he'd had a gun at that moment, she would have had to kill him.

Just then he surprised her by relaxing.

"Miss Walker, although I'm not a liar and don't like being called one, I'm not in a position to do much about it except prove you wrong. If you'll let me show you the contract your father signed, I'm sure we can get this misunderstanding cleared up."

It was her turn to size up the situation. The longer she stood in the sun, the more uncomfortable she became. The mud between her skin and clothes was quickly drying to a crusty mold, and even though she didn't trust this stranger, the opportunity to get out of the sun for a moment was tempting.

"All right, Mr. Braddock, I'll look at your papers. On the porch." She gestured with the rifle.

Sin moved toward the porch but kept his eyes on Rachel.

As she followed she called over her shoulder. "Keep an eye on him, Hank."

"Yes'm."

Sin stiffened slightly. Being watched this way was frustrating. The one saving thought was that soon, very soon this man, Hank, and all the other hands would be working for him.

"Okay, Mr. Braddock, show me this . . . contract."

Lifting his coat, he reached into its inside pocket and pulled out a thick envelope of buff-colored paper.

After making sure Hank was watching Braddock, Rachel put her rifle down behind her, out of his reach, and took the envelope from him.

"May I sit down?" Sin asked, not because he needed to but because he hoped to create a more relaxed atmosphere for what was sure to come.

She looked at him and couldn't help but respond in a physical way to his good looks, but somehow she felt like he was setting her up for something. She nodded her approval.

Sin lowered his long frame onto one of two weathered ladder-backed chairs that graced the porch. He noticed that when he did, Hank repositioned himself at the other end of the porch to keep him in view. He smiled to himself. A good man, he thought.

The sound of riders coming fast told them the crew had heard the shot she'd fired earlier. Horses, snorting in the heat, ground to a halt at their riders' commands. Sin could feel six pairs of eyes on him and didn't like the hot seat. Several had drawn their guns and a big man with unruly brown hair had an especially concerned look on his face when he asked Rachel if everything was all right.

"Yes, Jace, Mr. Braddock here says he has some business with me."

"The shot?"

"It took him a little too long to tell me what kind of business."

Ben snickered and spat a stream of tobacco juice at his horse's feet. "Hell, I told you fellers Miss Rachel could take care o' herself."

A warning look from Hank told Ben he'd said enough.

Rachel opened the envelope and pulled out a bundle of neatly folded papers. When she opened them she saw the letterhead of the Braddock Bank. The man said he was on the board there, but anyone could forge documents. She read on. As she did, she had to lower her weight to the railing of the porch. The papers had the ring of truth, but she couldn't believe her father had done this. She tried to swallow but her throat was too dry. She turned to the last page and looked for her father's signature. It was there. Hyram Walker always put his brand and the ranch name after his signature. Three x's with the middle x small. XxX. Rachel knew that the middle x was for her. When her father started the ranch there had been one X. When he married he'd added a second. When Rachel was born he added the third small x between the two others for her. He'd told her that was where she'd stay, safe in the middle. She didn't feel safe now. This man had come to change her world. She stood up and dropped the papers on Sin's lap.

"Mr. Braddock, get off my land." She spoke almost in a whisper, and the men couldn't hear her.

Sin hadn't known what to expect. Perhaps tears and temper tantrums. But that was before he'd met Rachel Walker. She was not an average woman, given to emotional outbursts. He picked up the papers, stood and looked down into her green eyes.

"Miss Walker, you read the contract . . ."

"And I don't believe it."

"You saw the signature and mark."

"A forgery. Mr. Braddock, you are not only a liar but a thief as well. You're trying to steal my ranch, and I'll be damned if I'll let you do it." She stared hard into his eyes.

The men still couldn't hear what was being said, but they could see the stiffness of Rachel's back and feel the tension between the two.

"Now, Mr. Braddock, get the hell off my land."

This was more than he could take. He could see the cold rage in the depths of those emerald eyes, and the strength of emotion was so overpowering that he took a step toward her. It was then he heard the cocking of the guns and knew he was coming very close to death this day. He backed away from her slowly, picked up his coat from the chair and turned back to face her.

"Your father had a copy of this contract. I'm sure you could find it if you looked." He walked toward the steps, then turned back again. "The war has taken everything I had. This contract is all that's left."

"Then you have nothing."

"Miss Walker, I'm not going to give up. This is a legal document and I'll be back, with the sheriff if necessary."

As Rachel watched him ride away her anger grew in her stomach until it threatened to cause her to scream out in rage. Hank told the men to get back to work, then stayed on the porch with Rachel until Braddock was out of sight.

"Thanks, Hank." Her voice was choked with all that she was feeling, but he pretended not to notice.

"Yes'm." He would think a lot about what he'd overheard today, but he'd keep it to himself. It didn't hurt a man to hang on to a little bit of information awhile. He rubbed a hand across rough gray whiskers. "I best be getting on back to work myself." She nodded at him like she hadn't quite heard what he'd said.

Rachel continued to stay on the porch long after the dust from Sin's carriage lay still in the ruts of the road.

She was no longer aware of the dirt on her skin or the sticky feeling of wet hair on her back. If the contract that Sinclaire Braddock possessed was valid, her whole life was threatened. He'd said that her father had a copy of the papers and she knew she should go in and look for them, but she was afraid she'd succeed. She hadn't gone through her father's things very well, simply because it was still too painful, but now she'd have to. She just couldn't make herself get up and go into the house to look. She almost laughed at herself. She, whose lifestyle dictated that she be afraid of nothing, was afraid to look for a packet of papers.

She must have sat there a long time because it wasn't until the sound of laughter and childish voices caught her attention that she looked up from her deep thoughts.

"Tish!" She ran from the porch to pull her daughter's giggling body from the wagon that brought her home from school in town. "How's my little girl?" she asked while tickling the child. The greatest joy in her life was this little girl and it never ceased to amaze her that no matter how bleak things looked, a smile and a kiss from a wiggly daughter could make things easier to take.

"I'm fine, Mama, Billy swallowed a frog in school today and the teacher said that it would make him sick, and we all waited but he didn't get sick, but I almost did when he swallowed it, but it wasn't a very big one ..."

"Whoa, slow down a little. You have to breathe, don't you?"

"Oh, Mama," she turned to wave to her friends as they rode away, "of course I breathe. Everything has to breathe, except the frog Billy swallowed." She started to giggle all over again. "I have to go tell Lena." She threw her arms around Rachel's throat and almost choked her with the force of her hug.

"Okay, I think she's probably starting dinner now, and making my surprise birthday cake."

"Mama, you weren't supposed to know about it." Tish scolded her mother with her little hands on her hips.

"With you two whispering around the house for the

last two weeks? How was I not going to know? But we won't let Lena know that I'm not surprised. It'll be our secret, okay?"

Thrilled to be part of another secret, Tish clapped her hands together and rapidly nodded her head in agreement. She then turned and ran toward the house. Just as she was about to go through the door, she turned back to Rachel. "I almost forgot to ask you. Did you have a nice day today, Mama?"

2

Rachel's birthday dinner had been wonderful. The two women, exchanging knowing glances, enjoyed the 'surprise party' through the wonder of the child. But now she faced the closed doors of her father's office. She'd known this moment would come, when she'd have to face all the memories held trapped in that tiny, cluttered room. She'd hoped she could put it off until she was emotionally ready. Today's events were forcing her to do this too soon.

Her hand held the old brass doorknob for a moment before opening the door. How many times had she entered this room to see her father sitting at his desk? How many times had she forgotten what she'd come to ask him because he'd begun teasing her before she even got halfway into the room? Her father, her friend. And now one month after his death she still couldn't believe he was gone.

She turned the knob and slowly pushed open the door. "You should be here, Pa. I need you," she whispered as she scanned the darkened room. For a moment she couldn't swallow. The smell of his tobacco assaulted her nostrils. He'd always smoked a horrible brand and she'd complained about it often. Now it smelled better than Lena's dinner had two hours before.

"Damn you, Braddock." She brushed a stray tear from the corner of her mouth and let her anger carry her into the room. "If it weren't for your lies I wouldn't have to do this now."

Circling the desk she sat in her father's chair, the hair on the back of her neck raising as she did. The leather had molded to fit him after years of use and now it was much like sitting in his lap. She forced herself to clear her throat and began going through the desk drawers.

Grain orders, horse and cattle records, whiskey orders for the Rosebud, everything seemed in order. She hadn't balanced the books in the month since Hyram's death but that had been his responsibility, one she knew she'd have to take over now. Letters from relatives in Georgia caught her eye. It was a small bundle and she put it on top of the desk to take to her room and read later. Nothing in the desk said anything about any contract with Mr. Sinclaire Braddock. She felt a triumphant swelling in her breast. Tomorrow she would tell Mr. Braddock to go straight to hell.

She leaned back in her father's chair and closed her eyes. She could see him in her mind and feel him in this room. A small thin man with rangy features and a quick smile. She remembered how strong he was, his thinness disguising the iron in his arms. She remembered when he gave her Roux. She was fifteen and had just started to fill out. He'd told her then she'd be boss one day, and that being a woman, and a real looker, it was going to be hard and that she'd need a big horse to look down on the men from. "Keep 'em lookin' up to ya, gal." He'd blushed a little then and finished, "Don't never let 'em look down on ya. Ya know what I mean?"

She'd known. He'd said an awful lot in those few words. She knew exactly how he'd felt about things and the warmth in her chest grew when she remembered that he'd never once acted disappointed in her when she'd told him she was pregnant and not getting married. He never even asked who the father was. He'd just trusted her judgment and stood by her in her decision. She knew there had been times when some of the townsfolk let him know what they thought of his "bad" daughter, but he'd never held his head down nor come home telling her tales of their disapproval. He hadn't cared whether they approved or not and neither had she. She smiled when she thought about it. The fact that they hadn't cared one whit about the town's opinion probably irritated them more than her pregnancy ever had.

She didn't know exactly how long she sat there remembering, but she started to doze off and realized it was time to go to bed. She had a full day tomorrow. She got up and headed toward the door, then remembered the letters from her relatives. As she turned back, something caught her eye. The coat rack behind the far edge of the desk still carried her father's long work coat. Sticking out of the side pocket was the corner of what looked like an envelope. She tried to remember the last time he'd worn it, her mind racing as she crossed the room. Tentatively, she pulled the envelope from the pocket. Her hands were shaking as she opened it and removed the papers. Tears blurred her vision and bile rose up in her throat as she read. No, Pa! No! her mind was shouting. Don't you know what you've done? How could you do this to me? How could you leave me like this? Damn you, Pa. How could you do this?

The red glow from Sin's cigar was the only light in the small room he'd taken over the saloon. The noises from below filtered through the thin floorboards, making it impossible to sleep. Not that he would have been able to, anyway. The day had not turned out the way he'd expected at all.

Actually it was Rachel that hadn't turned out the way he'd expected. He'd never met a woman like her. He'd have been able to deal with another woman's crying and temper tantrums. He'd even hoped Miss Walker would be a little grateful for a man to step in and take over now that her father had died. But he had no idea how to deal with the cold fury in those emerald eyes. As he thought about the way she looked at him, inspecting him as she would livestock, he once again felt the familiar stirrings he'd experienced earlier that day.

Bessie had never made him feel this way. He'd always felt like he needed to protect her. Whenever she let him kiss her trembling lips, he'd curbed his baser instincts, knowing she would be horrified by the things his body was capable of. He'd often wondered what their wedding night would be like. He had worried that he would hurt her, she was so fragile. Now he would never know. His dear, sweet Bessie. Gone.

Now there was Rachel. She was not fragile. She did not need him. And he was taking half of everything she owned. He knew she'd fight him every step of the way, but he couldn't let her win. The law was on his side and he knew how to fight too.

Standing up and stretching, he dropped the butt of the cigar on the wood floor and stepped on it. Going to the window he looked out on the street. Mesa City was not a large town, but he could feel it was a good one. One he'd like to become a part of. The only thing standing in his way was a strong and incredibly beautiful woman who at this very moment was probably wishing he would die a horrible death before morning.

A loud crash from below announced a barfight and urged him into leaving the stuffy room. Downstairs he asked a willing-looking girl if there was anyplace to get a quiet drink, and he emphasized quiet.

"Sure, Mister," she purred, pushing her ample breasts against his arm. "My room's quiet."

Not even tempted, he tipped his hat. "Thanks anyway, maybe some other time."

"Swell, if I'm still here," she pouted.

"A chance I'll have to take."

"Then you might as well go to the Rosebud."

"Rosebud?"

"A little bar at the edge of town. They don't have no

girls. That's why it's so quiet, nothing to fight over."
With that she caught the eye of a big cowboy and saun-
tered over, using her breasts as bait once again.

Sin stepped out of the saloon and felt no fresh air.
The August nights were no cooler than the days, just
darker. He had no idea which end of town the girl
meant, but a walk would do him good. If he found the
Rosebud, fine. If he didn't, there'd be plenty of time in
the future.

Rachel's deep, dusky voice filled the quiet of the
Rosebud. The song she was singing was about unre-
quited love, a favorite topic for cowboys on the range.
The crowd listening was mostly regulars who came for
a drink and conversation. She never knew that they also
came in hopes of hearing her sing. She had a talent she
never realized. She just sang when she needed to. Whenever she was too sad or too happy to sleep. Tonight it
was the former. After finding the papers in her father's
coat she'd cried until she had no tears left. Then she'd
washed her face and headed for the Rosebud.

She signaled Vera, her bartender, to get her another
drink. Rachel took her whiskey neat, and though she
could hold her liquor well, she rarely drank much at the
bar. Her mother hadn't approved of drinking, but her
father had told her that since she would someday own
the Rosebud, along with the ranch, she should be well
instructed in the art of drinking. Tonight she'd needed
a drink. In fact, she'd needed several and was feeling
the effects in her limbs. She was enjoying the sensation
of her nerves relaxing and the tension dissipating.

"You sure you ain't had enough, girl?" Vera asked
her as she handed her the whiskey.

"I'm sure, Vera." Rachel put her arm around the
older woman's shoulders. "Sometimes only a strong
drink can get a woman through the night."

"Or a strong man."

"Show me one of those and I just might take you up
on that." Rachel grinned. "Trouble is, if you find one

with a strong back, they've got a weak brain, and if they're smart, too, they've got no feelings. No, Vera, I think I'll stick to the whiskey. At least whiskey doesn't lie to you or let you down. It is what it is right up front. You know you're going to get sick if you get too full of it. With a man you don't know that 'til you're layin down hurt'n."

Vera could tell by the way she was talking that Rachel had had too much to drink and it worried her. Rachel was always so strong. And she was always kind of quiet, a little like a man herself. She guessed that was why her men respected her so much. She didn't prattle on about nothing the way most women did.

Vera knew what men liked about women. She'd been a whore most of her life. Now she was too old and a man wouldn't pay to sleep with her anymore, but she was a good bartender. Rachel had hired Vera three years earlier and since then she'd come to care about her like a daughter, although Rachel didn't let herself get too close to too many people.

"Miss Rachel, I think you best be gettin' on home now. It's awful late. Don't you have to work tomorrow?"

"Yes, I have a lot to do tomorrow." Her brow furrowed at the thought of Sinclaire Braddock and the coming day. "I think I'll sing one more song before I go."

She adjusted her guitar and watched the swishing hem of Vera's long burgundy brocade skirt as it brushed the floor with her leaving. People in the bar quieted their talk to listen to Rachel's sad voice fill the room. They could see she was troubled, but none knew how to reach out to her so they just listened. Her song started out soft, and each person in the room felt the vibrations of the guitar strings as she played. The hairs on the backs of necks stood up as they were touched by the timbre of her voice. Sinclaire Braddock was equally moved from where he watched in a dark corner.

He'd come in while Rachel was talking to an old woman with hair dyed the color of stale carrots. He'd been surprised to see Rachel in a bar and even more surprised to hear someone make a remark about her owning it. Did that mean that he owned it too? He'd have to check into the titles and deeds to the ranch. But right now Rachel's voice was touching him, moving across his body like soft fingers. He was unable to move. He didn't want to. He wanted to sit here and listen to her sing all night. He felt a powerful force coming from her. An energy that seemed directed at him even though she didn't know he was there. It seemed everyone felt the same way because no one around him moved. And yet, her eyes were looking directly at him. Had she seen him in the dark? No, she wasn't looking at him, just in his direction. Then without warning her song was over. People began talking again and Rachel was once more conversing with the old woman. He watched her go behind the bar and check the cash drawer, and then go through a door to a back room. He decided to wait a while to see if she would sing again. Rachel was almost home before he realized she'd gone out the back way.

Rachel scanned the horizon as she rode Roux the next morning. She knew Mr. Braddock would show up sometime that day so she kept one eye open for the dust of a rider. Her head was throbbing dully as it had since she'd awakened, and that, combined with the heat and the prospect of his arrival, had put her in a foul mood. She'd already given hell to a couple of her men and had the rest walking lightly around her.

"Hank, make sure this section of fence gets mended before noon."

"Yes'm."

She turned Roux in the direction of the barns. There were some horses being broken today. Maybe she'd ride over and take a look at how they were doing.

She could hear the shouts and laughter of the men long before she could make out individuals. They were trying to break a little mare and were laughing at the man trying to do the job. As she got closer she could see it was Jace. She frowned as she watched him strain against the animal and wondered whatever possessed her to hire him when he came riding back into her life six months ago.

"Aw, come on, Jace. Sweet-talk her a little," one man shouted.

"Sure, and if that don't work, give her a little kiss." The men guffawed loudly at that one.

Normally she would have joined them in their fun, but today was different. Today she had too big a problem on her mind. She'd thought she'd suffered her worst the day her father died. She'd shot the horse that had thrown him to his death, but it hadn't helped how she felt. Today she didn't know what to do to stop the worry. With Hyram dead she still had the ranch and the Rosebud. If Sinclaire Braddock got his way . . .

She knew she'd have Pete Bigley check the contract for validity, but then, if need be, she'd have to deal with Braddock.

"Howdy, Miss Rachel."

"Howdy, Stoker. Having trouble with the mare?"

Stifling a chuckle, he tried to answer with a straight face. "Well, Jace seems to be."

"Is that true, Jace?" she asked him directly.

Stoker, a good hand for nearly ten years, looked at Rachel in surprise. She wasn't following the joke. Something was wrong.

Jace had the mare secured with a rope around her neck, and although he was far from mounting her, he didn't want to look incompetent to Rachel.

"I'm doing all right, Miss Rachel." He turned glaring eyes to Stoker. "We were just having some fun."

"All right then, I'll be on my way to the house if you need me." She turned Roux away and they watched her go.

As soon as she was out of hearing distance, they started to discuss what was bothering her.

"You think she's sick?" Stoker asked.

The general belief was that she looked fine. A little tired maybe, but not sick.

"You know anything, Jace?"

"Why should I?" he asked defensively.

"Oh, I don't know. Maybe 'cos you'd like to know," Willie, a younger man, answered.

"I'd make you eat those words if I didn't have my hands full of this horse."

"I was counting on that," laughed Willie, and was joined by the other hands.

Jace grinned. "Here, Stoker. You take over. I need a break." He took off his gloves and walked to the fence.

Jace watched Rachel leave and wondered what was bothering her. He was curious about the man that rode in yesterday, but no one knew what he'd wanted. In the old days he'd have asked her what the problem was, but that was a long time ago and things had changed. Rachel had changed. She was hard now. She was no longer the smiling young woman who'd let him make love to her in the tall grass by Leaver Creek, or crept out to dance with him in the moonlight. Now, he was just one of the hired hands. And he had to admit that he didn't like it.

When Sin entered the sheriff's office that morning it was after he'd had a good breakfast in the Shady Place Restaurant next to the Wagonwheel Hotel and Saloon. He knew this was going to be a long day, and a full stomach was what he needed to get going. The Shady Place also boasted serving the best coffee in town, and Sin had to agree after consuming nearly a pot by himself.

Sheriff Jamison looked up from a desk containing more dust than paperwork.

"Can I help you, son?"

Sin smiled to himself. He hadn't been called 'son' in a long time. He was in the second half of his thirties and given how many young men in the South had died in the war or were still fighting it, he'd begun to consider himself quite old.

"Yessir, I think you can." He took the contract from his coat pocket and laid it on the desk in front of the sheriff. "If you'll read over these papers, I think you'll see my problem."

The sheriff eyed him a little suspiciously for a moment. He was wearing a little fancier clothes than was usual for these parts, and his gun was tied down to his thigh, which could spell trouble. Then again, most of the cowboys in the area did too. He picked up the bundle.

"Very well, son. I'll look them over. You have a seat." He gestured to a ladder-back chair leaning against the wall opposite the desk.

Sin pulled up the chair and sat to wait while the papers were read. He crossed his long legs ankle to knee and his eyes scanned the office, a wood stove in the corner of the room, an empty wood box, gun rack on the wall, not locked, and a file cabinet. The walls also sported Wanted posters of men supposedly seen in the area. He noticed that most of them were wanted for desertion from one army or the other. He wondered how many had actually deserted and how many were just missing in action, lying in some ditch somewhere, rotting, unidentified.

A long, low whistle from across the desk brought his attention back to the sheriff.

"Have you shown these to Rachel?"

"Yessir. That's why I'm here. I was warned off at gunpoint yesterday by her and her crew."

The sheriff took off his hat and rubbed his forehead with the back of his hand. He let out a low chuckle.

"Well, I ain't surprised, son. Hell, what surprises me is that you're not dead."

"I did feel like I came close a time or two. Mind if I smoke?" He took out a cigar and offered one to the sheriff. He took it and Sin lit them both.

"You see, Sheriff, I don't have anything left except this chance at the Triple X. I'm not a thief. I'm not trying to take something that's not rightfully mine. I intend to work hard and make the best of a bad situation. I know Miss Walker's not going to like this, but there's not a whole lot she can do about it."

"She could kill you."

Sin could see that he wasn't altogether joking with what he said.

"Yes, she could do that. But now that I've come to you, and if you'll ride out there with me today, she'll have to be real careful if she does. If I come to any untimely and suspicious end in the near future, you'd have to suspect her of something. I only spoke to her yesterday for a short while and I could see she was a lot of things, but she didn't strike me as being stupid."

"No, she isn't stupid. Stubborn, independent, willful, and more beautiful than she deserves to be, but she's not stupid. In fact, she's smarter than most men I know."

"You sound like you're just a little bit in love with her." Sin smiled at the older man.

"At my age? Well, maybe I am, just a little. I'll go with you today, just to make sure she doesn't shoot you on sight. Then you're on your own. I'm real curious how this is all gonna turn out."

The ride out to the Triple X was long and hot. Although it was still morning, the sun was making everything pale in its way. Wavering mirages floated above the land like shining ghosts.

"You know, son, this is crazy. The more I think about it, the more I don't believe it will work. Why don't you sell your half of the ranch back to Rachel and just go on home?"

They'd been riding in silence for quite a while, both men obviously wrestling with their own thoughts. Sin pulled his horse to a stop and turned to face the sheriff as he spoke.

"Because I have no home to go back to." A guarded shutter fell across his eyes as he remembered again the loss he'd suffered because of the war. "Sheriff, you are looking at a man with nothing but the clothes on his back and a piece of paper in his pocket that gives him one last chance in this world."

"That chance is a slim one. Rachel's not going to give up without a fight."

"I realized that yesterday while looking down the barrel of her rifle." The guarded expression seemed to lift a little. "But like I said, it's the only chance I've got."

He turned his horse and smiled as they started out again. "Besides, she just might like me once she gets to know me."

From the front porch Rachel saw the riders coming. She recognized instantly the tall dark frame of Sinclaire Braddock, her enemy. She also knew the shorter, thicker build of Frank Jamison.

"So, Mr. Braddock. You did bring the sheriff," she muttered under her breath.

She'd been sitting on the porch for nearly an hour, and she was tired of waiting for what was coming. She'd thought long and hard about this turn of events. It seemed that it was something she couldn't avoid entirely, but perhaps this Mr. Braddock could be dissuaded from staying around too long. Perhaps he could be bought off. She hadn't thought about that yesterday, but maybe that was all he wanted in the first place. She had the heel of one boot hooked over the railing and brought it down when they got a little closer, sticking her thumbs in her front belt loops as she did. It seemed like an eternity, yet not long enough, before they were stopped in front of her. She stood.

Emerald green eyes locked with black and the time passed in a silent battle.

"Miss Rachel, mind if we get down and water the horses?" Frank's voice called a truce for a moment.

"I don't mind if *you* get down, but Mr. Braddock there can go straight to hell."

"Now, Rachel, I've seen the papers this young fella's carrying, and I'm sure they're legal."

Rachel and Sin's eyes locked again, sending a warning down her spine, a warning she ignored. "I just wonder what the circumstances were when my father signed them."

"Also purely legal." Sin's voice had a cold cutting edge when he spoke. "Someday, when you're in a more hospitable mood and not telling me to go to hell, I'll be happy to explain it."

"Explain it now."

Ignoring her demand, he dismounted and began to untie his bedroll.

"I said, explain it to me now, Mr. Braddock."

He turned and faced her squarely. "I am your partner, your equal partner, not your ranch hand, and I do not take orders from you or anyone else on this place."

Rachel stood still, but every nerve in her body was screaming out with hatred. She longed to kill this man, wanted to see him in the sights of her rifle or feel her finger squeeze down slowly on the hammer of her Colt. Her eyelids lowered perceptibly, and unconsciously her right hand hovered over her gun.

"Does Lena have any of that coffee cake I love so much?" Sheriff Jamison nearly shouted to break the tension between the two.

Rachel let out her breath slowly and looked at Frank.

"Yes, I think she does." She glanced back at Braddock and saw him watching her every move. He had taken a defensive stance. He'd known what she was thinking. She had the sudden and uncomfortable feeling that they'd just touched in some way, and she didn't like it.

"Come on, Frank, let's go inside, and I'll get Lena to cut the cake and pour some coffee." She couldn't force herself to invite Braddock, but she knew he'd follow.

Once inside, Sin let his bedroll drop to the floor by the front door. He saw Rachel flinch slightly when he did. She's one tough lady, he thought. I've got to find a way to get through to her that this doesn't have to be all bad. He watched her walking in front of him and the sheriff and was hypnotized by the way her dark hair played with her hips as she moved. He remembered the way she had looked the day before, with her wet clothing clinging to every curve of her very feminine form. The tightness these thoughts were causing made him bring himself up short. Braddock, you fool, he told himself, the lady despises you and everything you're trying to do. Don't complicate matters by being attracted to her too.

As they entered the dining room, a short round Mexican woman appeared through another door, wiping flour from her hands with a towel. She had a white apron tied around her ample middle, nearly covering the cotton skirt and peasant blouse she was wearing.

"*Señor* Jamison, it is so good to see you again," she exclaimed.

"Hello, Lena, how's the best cook in the county?"

"Oh, *señor,* you tease." But she was smiling. "What can I get for you, Miss Rachel? Oh, we have a guest." She saw Sin behind the sheriff.

"Not exactly a guest." Sin spoke up before Rachel got the chance. "I am Miss Rachel's new partner, and I am certainly looking forward to some of this wonderful cooking I'm hearing about." He smiled warmly down into the older woman's eyes.

Lena's shared an inviting smile of her own. *"Gracias, señor."*

"De nada, señora."

"Lena, bring us some coffee and cake." Rachel's abrupt order surprised everyone in the room. She was never rude to her people. She gave them hell when they deserved it, but she was never rude and especially not to Lena, who was more like family than anyone else.

Lena's eyes lowered with hurt and Rachel felt the knife of remorse twist in her breast.

"Here, I'll help you." She took Lena by the arm and guided her back to the kitchen.

"Lena, I'm sorry I spoke to you that way. I've just got a lot on my mind."

"*Sí,* a new partner. When did this happen?"

"Yesterday. He rode in with papers claiming half the ranch."

"But this cannot be true."

"I'm afraid it is. I found copies of the same papers in Pa's office last night. It seems he borrowed money from Mr. Braddock's bank and gave half the ranch as collateral. The money wasn't paid back by the given date so Braddock's come to claim his part of the ranch." She shook her head. "I just can't believe Pa didn't tell me about it."

"It sounds like there's nothing you can do about it, honey."

"Like hell there's not. My parents' blood and sweat went into making this ranch what it is. My hands have bled and my back ached with the hours I've worked on this land during my lifetime. My parents are buried on this land. And now this man comes in here with a little piece of paper saying that he gets half of everything. Half of my life? He's done nothing to deserve any of this, and I'm going to do anything and everything to stop him from keeping any part of it."

"What can you do?"

"I'm not sure, but I'll think of something."

Lena watched Rachel's face as she spoke. These were not good feelings she was having. Things in life didn't always turn out the way you wanted, and as her dear mama had told her many times, the Lord works in mysterious ways. She must think of a way to help Miss Rachel. She would watch the way things went for a while, and she would pray about it. Maybe in her prayers she would find an answer.

"You go back out there and keep them ... the sheriff, company while I get the refreshments." She pushed Rachel toward the door before she could protest.

A tense half hour later Rachel was standing shoulder to shoulder on the porch watching the sheriff mount to leave.

"It was nice seeing you again, Rachel."

"Likewise, Frank. Don't stay away so long next time.

Lena looks forward to your visits." She was shading her eyes with her hand.

"Sheriff," Sin spoke up. "It was nice meeting you, and I hope to see you again real soon."

Frank grinned from ear to ear as he got the double meaning of Sin's remark. "I'm sure you will, son. I'm sure you will." He then raised his hand in farewell and turned his horse away for the long trip back to town.

Rachel abruptly left the porch and went into the house and through the kitchen. She kicked open the screen door and headed out across the yard. Sin followed. There were things they needed to discuss.

"Miss Walker, wait a minute."

She didn't listen to him. She continued walking toward a small corral where he could see the big chestnut she'd been riding the day before standing under the shade of a large willow. Her strides were purposeful and each step kicked up a little puff of dust.

She could hear him behind her, the rustle of the smooth black fabric of his suit as he moved, the same one he'd worn yesterday. This fact reinforced her belief that he was just some sort of gold digger. She opened the gate and took her gloves off the gatepost where she'd left them. Pulling them on with jerky, angry movements, she stuck one foot in the stirrup and then swung herself up into the saddle. As she was about to ride through the open gate, he grabbed Roux's bit.

"Miss Walker, Rachel. Where should I stow my gear?"

She could hear the tension in his voice and see the way his muscles strained at his suit in an effort to remain calm. Even looking down on him from atop Roux she could see he was a big man, and she was a little startled at the ease with which he held Roux still when the horse rolled his eyes and tried to pull away.

"I hear the Lucky Seven Ranch is looking for hands. They're about forty miles from here. Why don't you try there?" she nearly shouted as she tried to free the bit from his grasp.

Sin reached up and wrenched the reins from her hands with a vicious jerk. Roux calmed immediately.

"I'm staying, Rachel. There's not a damned thing you can do about it. Now where do I sleep?"

She looked at him with eyelids lowered.

"The bunkhouse."

"Is that where you sleep?"

"Of course not."

"I'll sleep where you sleep."

For just a second the vision of being in the same bed with him flashed through her mind, and her breath caught in her throat. It had been so long since she'd lain with a man. . . .

"How many times do I have to tell you I'll not be relegated to the status of one of the hands? I'll stay in the house. Now will you tell me which room, or do I have to go poking around on my own?"

Rachel looked up then and saw Lena watching from the summer room on the back of the house.

"Lena!" she shouted. Sin let go of the reins and she began to walk Roux toward the house. "Show Mr. Braddock to the guest room. I'm going to go check a break in the fence, then meet Tish's wagon. I'll see you later."

"*Sí,* Miss Rachel. As you wish."

"Tish?" Sin looked at Rachel.

"My daughter."

"Your daughter?" Somehow, the possibility that Rachel had children never crossed his mind. "I didn't know you were married."

"I'm not." Then, anticipating his thoughts, "Never was."

Roux turned on command, and she rode away with her back straight and her face devoid of emotion.

3

Tish, honey." Rachel removed her hat and rubbed her hand across her eyes and forehead. "There's something I need to tell you."

"Yes, Mama?" She sat in the shade of a big willow near Leaver Creek. Her mother had let her take off her shoes and stockings, and her toes were now wriggling in the edge current of the water. She could tell her mother was upset about something. She'd been excited when she'd seen her riding up on Roux when she was halfway home from school, but something was wrong. It was like when grandpa died, and her mother tried not to cry when she told her. It had made her stomach hurt then, and she was starting to be afraid that same way now.

"Something's happened, Tish, and I don't know how to explain it."

Tish curled her toes up real tight as if to squeeze out the water between them and tried to tighten her stomach for what was sure to come.

"A man's come to live with us. His name is Sinclaire Braddock." Rachel found she had difficulty even saying his name. She was standing next to Roux, looking toward the house, wondering what he was doing there. She turned and looked at Tish. She looked so little sitting there in the grass with her tiny hands clasped tightly in her lap. Her head was down and a tear was rolling silently down her cheek.

"Tish?" She dropped Roux's reins and crossed quickly to kneel beside her daughter.

Tish threw her arms round her mother's neck and held on tight.

"Darling, what's the matter?"

"I'm scared, Mama."

"Scared of what?" She tried to smooth the child's hair back where her pink bonnet had fallen off, but Tish's head was buried too close to her neck.

"What you're going to tell me. I know when you're upset, Mama. You look sad today and your eyes are far away, like when you told me grandpa went to heaven."

"Oh, Tish, my darling Letisha. Don't be afraid. Nobody went to heaven. Everyone's fine." She pulled Tish slightly away from her to look into her moist brown eyes. "I promise."

The child sat back a bit and tried to wipe her tears away with the back of her hand. "Then why are you sad?"

She could only remember her mother being sad once in her life and that had been about grandpa. Her mother was always happy, not like some of her friends' mothers that lived in town, ladies with stern faces, starched aprons, and clean hands. Those ladies never rode horses like her mother did, and they didn't know how to shoot guns or rope cows. Those ladies were different from her mother, and sometimes she felt like some of those ladies didn't like her mother very much. She didn't understand it very well, but she finally decided it was probably because they were jealous. Rachel got to go outside all day, and they had to stay in their houses. Anyway, she knew her mother was wonderful and loved her more than anything in the whole world.

"I'm sorry for being sad and scaring you, my darling, but I do have something to tell you, and I don't know how to do it."

"Just tell me."

Rachel looked into the stark honesty of those eyes, and her breath caught in her throat. Just tell her. She made it sound so simple. This would never be simple.

"Mr. Sinclaire Braddock has come to live with us ..." She stopped, not knowing how to go on.

Tish put her hand under Rachel's chin and raised her face to hers. "Why?"

She hadn't even realized she'd lowered her gaze. "Well, in a way grandpa gave him half of our ranch."

A frown crossed the youngster's brow as she tried to understand what she'd been told. "Which half did he give him?"

If it hadn't been so serious to her, Rachel would have laughed at Tish's simplistic way of looking at things, as if someone had taken a map of the ranch and drawn a line down the middle and said, now this half's yours and this half's ours.

"He owns half of everything, Tish. Sort of the way you and I both own your horse, Poco."

Again the wait, while Tish absorbed the information. "Does he own half of Roux?"

"No!" The answer burst angrily from Rachel's lips before she could stop it. "I'm sorry, honey. I didn't mean to sound so cross."

"Then he doesn't own half of Poco either," Tish announced defiantly with her hands placed stubbornly on her hips.

Rachel smiled softly and took her daughter in her arms and hugged her tightly, falling back with her into the cool grass.

Mother and daughter lay in each other's arms for a long while, looking up through the speckled roof of leaves and listening to the quiet sounds around them, the soft trickling of water as Leaver Creek turned in this shady place, the muffled thud as Roux tore grass roots from their stronghold in the damp soil. All these peaceful, familiar noises were soothing but couldn't stop the burning anger in Rachel's chest against the man that threatened her world.

"What does he look like, Mama?"

She thought about it for a moment. She had to admit that he was very attractive and under other circumstances she might have considered ... no. "He's tall and dark ... and you'll see soon enough. Let's get going."

As she walked Roux back to the house, Tish's question kept surfacing in her mind like a sentence written on her eyelids she'd see every time she blinked. What does he look like? What does he look like? What does he look like? Even Roux's footsteps seemed to echo the same phrase over and over.

She kept seeing black eyes staring angrily down into her's, eyes as black as coal ... Stop it, Rachel. Those eyes only make him more dangerous.

"Mmmm. I can smell dinner. I love it when Lena makes steak, tortillas, and beans. Let me down, Mama. I want to run the rest of the way." Tish was wriggling so much she would have fallen if Rachel hadn't held on to her. They were very near the house so she let her slide to the ground.

"Don't you get in Lena's way!" she called after the already running child.

She thought for just a moment that Tish might run into Braddock. She didn't want that to happen until she had a chance to introduce them, but then she dismissed the thought. He didn't strike her as the type of man that would hang around a kitchen and that would be where Tish was, following Lena like a shadow and asking a million and one questions about whatever she was making for dinner.

"Roux, what am I going to do?" she asked the big horse quietly, while brushing him down a few moments later in the barn. Roux shifted from one foot to the other and snorted into his bag of oats and molasses. "I can't let him take what's mine, even if the law's on his side."

"Excuse me, Rachel."

Rachel jumped at the voice, so deep had she been in her thoughts. "Yes, Jace?" She could see he was holding a saddle. He was probably on his way to the tack room. "What can I do for you?"

He shifted the weight of the heavy saddle, and his eyes narrowed slightly. He again wondered how she could be so cool.

She could feel his eyes taking in every detail of her appearance and straightened a little. He'd meant so much to her at one time. But then he'd left. Disappeared for years without so much as a single letter. He never even wrote to his parents, and now they were both dead and their ranch in ruin.

Everything that had happened between them, and all the time in between should have kept her from hiring him when he rode in, but when he'd asked for a job she couldn't turn him down. She'd looked into those too familiar brown eyes, remembered when she'd called him "Coop," a shortened version of his last name, and given in. She'd been mentally kicking herself ever since. She also had to make sure that the soft spot she'd felt when hiring him didn't carry over into other things. She looked him over and admitted that his broad shoulders and strong arms looked very inviting at times, but she'd played that game with him once already and lost. A person only has to get hit by lightning one time to know it's a bad idea to go playing around in a storm, and Jace had been one hefty bolt of lightning.

Jace watched the play of emotions cross her face and wondered what she was thinking. He'd hoped when he came back and found she'd never married that there was some way of renewing what they'd had, but other than a moment when she agreed to give him a job, she'd shown him no more than the same cool courtesy she gave all the hands. His eyes narrowed even more. If she'd been holding a grudge against him for all these years, why had she given him a job? And why would she be holding a grudge when as soon as he'd left, she'd taken up with some drifter and had a baby? She couldn't blame him for that, could she? He couldn't figure her out but he knew one thing for certain. He didn't like the way things were between them now, and somehow he was going to change it.

"Rachel ..." He took a step toward her then remembered the heavy saddle he was holding. He also realized he was dirty and smelled of sweat and horseflesh. "I just needed to put this away but I was wondering if maybe later, after I have a bath," he smiled, "you might meet me somewhere to talk?"

She knew this was coming. She'd seen the way he had been looking at her lately and had tried to think of a way to make him understand how she felt. She had no intention of ever picking up where they left off. Damn it! Why had she hired him? Maybe she should just fire him. But no, when he'd asked her for work he told her he had nowhere else to go, nothing left. The same thing Braddock had said the day before. Why was it all of a sudden her responsibility to take care of people at the end of their ropes? She clenched her fists and set her jaw. "No, Jace. I don't think so. Good night." She turned her back on his rather startled expression, led Roux to his stall, and left the barn.

Jace threw the saddle onto the dirt floor and watched her as she headed toward the house. His features darkened. Why couldn't anything in his life ever be easy?

It was later than usual and Rachel was feeling guilty about making dinner wait. As she went up the steps to the back porch she thought she heard voices. Frowning, she removed her hat and unbuckled her gunbelt. She hung both on their pegs by the door and proceeded into the kitchen. The sight that met her stopped her cold. There, sitting on Braddock's lap, with flour up to her elbows, was a very happy, giggling, Tish. Lena was bent over the table trying to help her make a tortilla and laughing at her attempt. Braddock was smiling, stark white teeth in contrast with dark skin, and he seemed not to care a bit that he was quickly becoming covered with the white powder.

"Tish!" Her voice broke the happy scene.

Tish's brown eyes looked startled. "Yes, Mama?"

She wanted to shout. She wanted to jerk her daughter off that man's lap. She wanted to slap Braddock across that stupid smile and force him to leave her house. But she could see that her anger was frightening Tish, so she did none of those things.

"Wash up for dinner. I'm sure it's ready?" She looked accusingly at Lena.

"*Sí*, Miss Rachel. It's ready." Then a little tag, "It's been ready." As if to say, we had to find something to do while we waited.

Rachel's fingers rubbed her temples. Maybe it was just her imagination. Lena would never be sarcastic with her.

"Then let's eat." She crossed the kitchen and went through the swinging door to the dining room.

"She's a tough woman." Sin addressed Lena quietly so Tish, who was now washing her hands by the pump, wouldn't hear.

"*Sí, señor*, she has had to be." She picked up the tattered tortilla Tish had made.

Sin took her hand and forced her to meet his gaze. "I'd like to help her, Lena."

"*Sí*, and yourself a little maybe too, I think." She took her hand away, and he could see she didn't trust him. He supposed he couldn't blame her.

Dinner was a quiet affair. There would have been no talking at all if Tish hadn't been there asking the kinds of questions children ask that demand answers. Like, why did Mr. Baker in town shave off his beard and look like a different person, and why did God make birds fly and not cats.

Sin watched Rachel answer these questions and several more with the wisdom that he assumed came with motherhood. He wondered if Bessie would have handled the question of why dogs had lots of puppies and people only had one baby at a time with such ease. He saw that

Rachel answered her honestly without giving her too much information to swallow. But other than these exchanges, no words were spoken. Rachel didn't even look at him, and he saw her rub her temples several times during the meal. As Lena brought in dessert, he decided it was time to start involving himself in things.

"Since tomorrow is Saturday, it might be a good time for me to meet the men."

"Why would tomorrow being Saturday make any difference?"

He raised one brow as a premonition passed through him. "I just thought . . ."

"You just thought that it was the weekend and since you're used to keeping city hours that we'd all be laying around doing nothing. This is a ranch, Mr. Braddock. We work six and seven days a week. In other words, we work when there's work to be done. Obviously you're ignorant of this fact and probably ignorant of a lot more about ranching. It seems to me that if you're so set on taking half my property, you'd at least have obtained some working knowledge before you moved in. I will suggest once again that you leave."

Sin listened to her speech, and anger and resentment welled up in his breast. It was true that he had little knowledge of the workings of a cattle ranch, but he did know business and, damn it, this was a business. He looked over at Tish. Her large eyes were watching him, waiting for some reaction. His desire to make Rachel listen to him, to force her to understand how much he needed this chance in life was going to have to wait. He couldn't play out that kind of scene in front of a child. He stood and placed his napkin on his plate.

"I'm staying, Rachel. Now if you will excuse me." He nodded at Tish and Lena, who still stood with dessert in her hands, and left the room.

They watched him leave. Rachel saw the taut muscles in his cheeks and the way his fists were clenched, saw the long deliberate strides he took and the way his strong legs consumed the distance to the door. She found she was holding her breath.

"Miss Rachel, do you want some pie?"

"What? No, thank you, Lena. I'll just get some coffee and go out on the front porch, thank you."

"I want some pie, Lena. Lots!"

Rachel heard this as she entered the kitchen. She leaned on the counter with both hands for a moment and had to ask again. "Why, Pa?"

Sitting on the porch in the dark was peaceful for her. She'd tucked Tish in about an hour earlier and these quiet moments were a great respite after this hard day. She knew that somehow she was going to have to get rid of Mr. Sinclaire Braddock. He seemed so determined to stay that short of killing him she didn't know how to get him to go. She was sure there was a loophole in that contract. She'd read the paper, so had the sheriff, but they might have missed something. She had to have Pete look it over. He might find something. If there was no way out, she'd offer to buy him out. It was a last resort, an acknowledgment that his claim was valid, but if it was what she had to do to get rid of him, so be it.

She'd left the contract on her father's desk. She didn't relish going back in there but it couldn't be helped. She knew she was going to have to face going through all his papers very soon, especially since Braddock's startling arrival, as there were cattle contracts to be met and grain orders to make out. Taking a deep breath, she put her feet squarely on the floor and stood. Tonight was the night.

The house was dark except for lamplight shining into the hall from the dining room. As she crossed to her father's office she was perplexed to see light coming from under the door. Puzzlement turned to cold rage when she opened the door and found Braddock sitting at her father's desk going through his ledgers.

"What the hell are you doing here!"

"Going over these ledgers, and I've found . . ."

"Get out! How dare you come in here? This is my father's office!" She was now standing over him.

He could see the fury in those green eyes, but she had to be told about what he'd found. "Rachel, calm down. This is important."

Important? How could he think anything was important enough for him to violate this room, her father's memory? Tears were burning at the edges of her eyes, and she felt as though she would choke from the anger.

"Get out of his chair, you son of a bitch!" She instinctively reached for her gun, only to find she wasn't wearing it.

Sin saw this reflexive move, and his dark eyes opened wide at her intentions. Christ, this woman is going to kill me yet! he thought.

Frustration as Rachel had never known it surged through her body. She could barely see and her only thought was to get rid of this man. Looking wildly around the room for something to help her, her gaze fell on her father's gun cabinet.

Sin saw this the same time she did. They both lunged for the cabinet, Rachel bent on murder, Sin intent on saving his own life. His hand covered hers on the latch and their bodies hit the door with such force that its glass pane shattered, shooting tiny shards of glass into their clothing. Sin felt a dagger of glass tear its way through his shirtsleeve and into the flesh of his arm. Rachel saw blood coming from the back of her own hand but still struggled against the weight of Sin's body.

"Rachel, stop this!" He was surprised at her strength as she fought back, but nature had seen to it long ago that she would lose this fight. He grabbed her hands and turned her to face him. Her eyes were wild and her breath was coming in ragged spasms.

"I won't let you kill me." He shook her hard once and tightened his hold on her.

She tried to bring her knee up to where it would do the most harm, but he avoided that and shoved one of his legs between hers, pinning her against the broken cabinet. She stopped struggling but her breath was still coming in gasps.

He looked down into her face. Their bodies were so close he could feel her heart beating. Her breasts were pressed against his chest, and it could have been his imagination, but he would have sworn he felt her nipples harden against him. His body's answering response was swift and sure, and he pressed himself against her even harder.

A tiny flame sparked in Rachel's eyes as she felt what his body was doing. She could feel the muscles of his chest against hers, his strong thigh between her legs. Heat welled up in her middle and she experienced a rush of sexual need that was nearly overpowering. Then sanity returned. Somewhere a voice screamed. Not this man!

"Let go of me!" She tried to jerk free.

"Only if you calm down." Sin was quickly regaining control of his body.

She looked straight into his black eyes. "I won't shoot you, but I want you out of this room."

"Rachel, there are things we need to discuss. Things I found in those ledgers that are vital to the survival of this ranch." He was releasing his hold on her slowly, testing her.

She straightened as she felt him letting go. Instinctively, she touched the cut on her hand and winced at the pain when she discovered the glass was still there, protruding from the wound.

"Let me see."

"No, I'll take care of it myself." She bent her head to examine it closer, then crossed to hold it under the desk lamp.

Sin watched her as she pulled the glass from her hand and found himself admiring her in an odd way. He could see she was in pain by the way her muscles jerked, but not a sound did she utter. With the glass removed, the cut began bleeding freely.

"Here." Sin offered her his handkerchief.

Reluctantly she took it and wrapped it around her hand, but she couldn't bring herself to thank him.

"Will you leave now?" she asked.

"I told you I'm staying."

"I mean this room."

"Can I take the ledgers with me? And will you discuss them with me tomorrow?"

"Maybe." She looked at the broken glass on the floor and saw the blood on his shirt. "Maybe I'll talk to you tomorrow. Right now I've got to clean up this mess, and you need to tend to that."

He looked down at his arm and was surprised at the amount of blood soaking the sleeve. He pulled the torn fabric apart and looked at the angry cut on his arm.

"It's not bad. Just a scratch," he lied, then picked up the ledgers and headed toward the door. "Do you want me to send Lena in to help you?" He knew she'd refuse his help.

"No, she already went to bed."

"Good night, Rachel."

She didn't answer, and he knew as he left the room that this was going to be a long night for both of them.

The gray light of dawn found Rachel sitting at the small desk in her room. She'd slept fitfully for a few hours sometime during the middle of the night, and now she watched morning creeping slowly across the fields and buildings of her ranch through the bedroom window.

She'd played last night's scene with Braddock over and over in her mind and still couldn't deal with the emotions it brought forth. She was angry with herself for letting him take the ledgers. She hadn't even gone over them since her father's death.

Noises in the kitchen told her that Lena was up starting breakfast for the men. Rachel winced a little as she stood. Last night's battle had left her feeling sore all over. She poured water from a pitcher to the wash bowl and started her morning routine. She wanted to get started for town and Pete's office before Braddock got up.

Sin could hear the morning noises too and wondered if Rachel was awake yet. Somehow he was sure she was. During the long sleepless night he'd tried to justify his instant attraction for Rachel as a simple case of lust, but he knew there was more to it than that. He couldn't help but admire her. He just wished things didn't seem so hopeless.

"Damn it," he muttered under his breath. Reaching to the foot of the bed he pulled up the last ledger that Hyram Walker had made entries in. He'd studied it again and again throughout the night.

"Patriotic fool," he whispered. He'd gone over the figures and no matter how he tried to make the sum come out differently, the bottom line was that Rachel, this ranch, and now he were nearly broke. They had just enough money left to make maybe one more payroll. Something had to be done quickly to save the situation. He shook his head and dropped the book back onto the bed. He ran his hands through his thick black hair. "How am I going to get her to listen?"

As Sin entered the large dining hall at the back of the house where the men were eating, he met Lena and asked her where Rachel was.

"She went to town. You want some coffee, Mr. Braddock?"

"Yes, thank you, Lena." He was angry and frustrated at Rachel's actions. "Damn it," he muttered.

"Mister, you got a problem?"

Sin turned to see all the men staring at him. Hank, the older man he remembered from the other day, had asked the question. He looked from face to face, trying to read whether Rachel had explained anything yet. The blank, curious stares told him that she hadn't. He recognized several faces from the first day he'd come out, but most were strangers. He held out his hand to Hank.

"No problem. I'm Sinclaire Braddock, Rachel's new partner."

"Holy shit!" sputtered Ben from across the room.

Jace choked on his coffee, and a dark frown lowered his brow.

Hank took Sin's hand warily. "Ya don't mind if I hear that from Rachel before I take it as gospel, do ya?"

Sin smiled down at him. "Don't mind a bit. Do you know when she'll be back?"

"Probably not till tonight. She gave us our orders before she left."

His anger with Rachel grew, but right now was not the time to show it. "Mind if I sit down?"

"Not at all."

Lena came in with the coffeepot and brought him a cup. As she poured refills he checked out the men she served. A young man with bright blue eyes kept grinning into his coffee cup as though he knew something no one else did. Next to him, at the end of the table, a big man—about thirty, he'd guess—was watching him with a dark scowl on his face. Every so often the younger man would elbow the bigger one, and the scowl would deepen. Something to keep my eye on, he thought.

"You boys going to laze around all morning?" Hank spoke up as he stood. "We got work to do."

Grumbled agreement filled the room as the men left the table. Guns were strapped on and hats donned. Sin felt dozens of eyes on him but no one spoke to him. They, too, seemed to be waiting for the okay from Rachel.

"Mind if I tag along with you?" he directed to Hank.

"You haven't eaten yet."

"I've missed meals before. Hasn't killed me yet." He remembered the army prison.

"You gonna work or watch?" Hank asked.

Sin smiled. "Probably a little of both."

Hank grinned back. "Well then, come on."

Sin's day was long, hot, and hard. In the morning he helped put up a new section of fence on the corral they'd been working on, and in the afternoon he broke several horses. The men were pleased with his proficiency at the latter. He told them he'd done it once or twice before but didn't elaborate. He didn't think they'd be impressed that he'd helped raise thoroughbreds on his father's plantation as a young man. The fact that it was all gone now left nothing to discuss. Perhaps he just wasn't ready to talk about it with anyone. His family's destruction was still too open a wound.

"Don't tell me there's nothing I can do."

"I'm sorry, Rachel. This is a legally binding contract."

Rachel sat on a hard leather chair, looking across a huge walnut desk that completely dwarfed the small man behind it. Bright sunlight pierced the dusty room through the open drapes at the window. Perspiration glistened like jewels on the man's balding head as he laid the contract on his desk and looked back up at Rachel.

"But there's got to be a loophole somewhere. Some way for me to get out of this."

Pete could see she was upset by the way her hands clutched the arms of the chair. Rachel was an intimidating woman. He hated to have to tell her she was powerless to do anything about this contract. Also, he didn't envy Sinclaire Braddock. He felt certain Mr. Braddock had no idea the kind of woman Rachel was. He adjusted the glasses on his nose and shuffled the papers before him.

"Well now, Rachel," he cleared his throat, "I'm sorry. There are no loopholes." He could see her grip on the chair tighten. "It's a very straightforward contract. A loan was made with fifty percent ownership of the ranch as collateral. The loan wasn't repaid by the due date; therefore, Mr. Braddock has every right to make his claim."

He could tell by the grim set of Rachel's mouth and the blue in her nails that she wasn't taking this well. "It could have been worse. You father could have committed the entire ownership and given Mr. Braddock the right to claim it all."

Rachel slammed her hands against his desk as she

stood. "If he'd tried that I'd have shot him and left him for the vultures." She grabbed the contract from his desk. "I may still do just that!" As she headed toward the door she turned and fixed him with those green eyes. "Send me your bill, Pete." Then she was gone.

"Yes, Rachel," Pete whispered into the silence left by Rachel's absence.

Rachel could feel Sin's angry black eyes on her when she entered the room. The men also watched her for some sign of what was going on. She realized it had been a mistake to leave that morning without saying something to them, especially Hank. She looked at Sin and noticed he was wearing dirty work clothes similar to the hands'. Had he actually spent the day working with them? And what did he tell them?

"How'd it go today, Hank?" Rachel asked, while buttering a hot roll.

Hank watched her closely. "Just fine, Miss Rachel." He felt in an awkward position. Rachel didn't avoid trouble, but met it head on. He knew the trouble here and she didn't seem to know what to do about it. The other men were as curious as he and felt they deserved an explanation. Should he come out and say something?

He'd started liking Braddock today. He was a hard worker, not afraid to put his back into a task even when it was apparent he was unfamiliar with what he was doing. He also didn't brag. Hank couldn't stand a braggart, and when Braddock broke those horses so easy he never spoke a proud word. Yes, he seemed to be a nice young fella, but if Rachel needed help getting rid of him, he'd be happy to oblige. He knew where his loyalties lay.

Rachel noticed the men were unusually quiet and realized they were waiting for her to say something. She looked down at her plate and noticed she'd eaten without tasting a bite. Her gaze met Sin's and locked. A silent battle raged between them. His eyes burned into hers, challenging, defying.

Jace watched this exchange with growing anger. Damn

it, he wanted Rachel, and now this Braddock had an involvement with her that made her eyes spark with green fire. His own deep brown eyes narrowed as he watched. He threw his fork onto his plate with a clatter and pushed himself away from the table with such force that he moved the entire bench he and several other men were sitting on.

"Jace?" Rachel asked, startled by his action and grateful for the break from Sin's stare.

"I've got work to do," he announced gruffly, grabbed his hat, and slammed out the door.

Ben let out a long, low whistle. "Jeez, I ain't never seen Jace act that'a way. You, Stoker?"

"Nope. Never."

Rachel put her forehead in her hand. This was going to be another Rosebud night. She stood up and addressed the men.

"Mr. Braddock here is my new partner . . . temporarily."

Sin raised one dark brow and debated the wisdom of correcting her in front of the men. Instead, he rose and crossed to her side.

She could feel him standing next to her, and the hair on the back of her neck stood on end.

"He's not a working partner, so you'll still be taking orders from me alone."

"He worked today."

Rachel couldn't tell where the voice came from.

"What's that?" She waited. No response. Whoever said it thought better of repeating it.

She heard Braddock stifle a chuckle behind her and had to resist the urge to turn and knock him on his smug ass.

"Well, if no one has anything to say, or any questions?" She waited a moment. "All right then, good night." She turned and was about to leave when Sin touched her arm. She pulled back as though burned. "Yes?"

"There are some things we need to discuss."

"Not here."

"Of course not."

"Where?"

She thought for a moment. She couldn't face the office with the broken cabinet.

"The dining room."

"Very well. Ten minutes?"

She just nodded and left the room.

Sin saw her square her shoulders just before she went through the door. A frisson of regret passed through him at the sight.

4

"What the hell do you mean, we're broke?" Rachel demanded.

"Just what I said. There's barely enough money to make another payroll." He opened the ledger and shoved it across the table in front of her. "Look. If you'd have bothered to balance these figures you'd have seen it for yourself."

Rachel couldn't believe it. Below her father's rather scratchy numbers were the neat figures Sin had put there, bringing everything to balance. The outcome was bleak at best.

"How do I know those figures are correct? You may have entered things incorrectly for your own reasons."

"My God, Rachel, I know you don't trust me or want me here but what reason would I have for telling you lies about this?"

"I don't know yet." She slammed her hand down on the ledger. "But I'm damn well sure you've got your reasons."

"Just look at that ledger again, Rachel. You're not stupid. Even if you only look at your father's last entries, you can see you were in trouble then. All I did was balance everything for this month, subtracting the expenses I found in another ledger. As it was, I could only subtract fixed expenses. I have no idea what else there is to deduct. I won't know until I go through the rest of the paperwork." He could see the shadow of bewilderment cross her face. "How could you not know about this, Rachel?"

She lowered her eyes then raised them again defiantly. "My father did all the books for the ranch." She looked at the figures now, closely. "I helped him with the orders, but in the last few years he'd insisted on handling the paperwork himself." She could see that they'd been steadily losing money for quite some time. "I should have known," she whispered, as she felt the responsibility of her ignorance.

As she turned back the pages she could see that they'd had no actual income for nearly two years. She flipped some more pages. They'd just been living on the reserve cash in the bank. Cash, which she saw was replenished once by a deposit, but no reference was made as to the origin of the money. It didn't matter. The amount and date were the same as on the contract Sin possessed. The confirmation of the loan's existence caused her to bring her lips together in a grim line, an action not missed by Sin. But that didn't mean he was now entitled to half her ranch. Nothing could ever convince her of that. The money was now nearly gone. What this ledger didn't tell her was why. Their ranch, though not one of the biggest or most successful in Texas, had been supplying beef to slaughterhouses and feeding people from Maine to Florida in some of the finest homes and restaurants in the country. It galled her to have to ask, but she had to know and she felt certain Sin knew the answer.

"How did this happen?"

Sin felt a moment of pity for her, but it was swiftly replaced by intense anger. Anger that she'd known nothing about this. Regardless of the reasons, she'd had a responsibility to this ranch and the people who lived here to see to it that the place remained successful. Because of her neglect, this ranch, his last chance, might fail before he could save it.

"Your father was a fool with his loyalties."

"How dare ..."

"He stopped selling beef to any of the Northern buyers, effectively cutting off over half of your business with one act."

Rachel had of course known they'd been affected by the war. They'd been driving their cattle only to Southern cities for years. She'd known that their sales had been cut, but it was a hardship she felt they could endure for the war years.

"There were Southern buyers. We made regular drives."

"You've been supplying the Confederate army. An army that can't pay."

"Then why did we keep on shipping?" She knew the answer before she even finished her sentence. For all her father's pioneering ways, and the independence that brought him to the Texas territory and gave him the determination to build this ranch, her father had still been a Southerner at heart.

She pushed the ledger away from herself and stood up. She couldn't look at it anymore. Gone was any hope of offering to buy Sin out. She went to the liquor cabinet and pulled out a bottle of whiskey. "You want a drink?"

"Sure." Sin rose and walked to look out the front window. He didn't really see anything but it didn't matter, as his head was full of visions of a gentler time. A time of white mansions and green lawns. A time of too much food, too much drink, too much honor. A time when just living was enough. When every breath you took didn't hurt with the effort of staying alive. When the voices of lost loved ones didn't echo in the dusty whispers of a breeze on a hot day or scream out at you in the fierce crash of thunder when awakened from a sound sleep.

"Here."

He turned to take the drink and noticed the wound

on the back of her hand from the night before. He suppressed a desire to touch her.

"What are we going to do?" he asked.

"We?"

"Don't fight me, Rachel."

She knocked back her drink in one swallow, then looked up at him with lids lowered. Her lips were parted and moist from the hot liquid. "I've got no choice but to fight." She turned and put her glass on the table. Without looking back she headed through the house and out the back to saddle Roux.

She had no money and no plan. She was also full of guilt about her ignorance. She had to come up with not only a way to get rid of Braddock, but to save the Triple X and ensure a future for all the people that depended on her for their livelihood.

Sunday morning, the sun raised its head for another scorcher. Sitting in her normal pew in church, with Tish at her side, she continued to dwell on a solution to her problem. She moved slightly when a trickle of perspiration slipped down her back. Most of the women were fanning themselves, and Tish wiggled uncomfortably next to her.

"How much longer, Mama?" Tish whispered.

She listened to the sermon for a moment and decided the pastor sounded like he was about through. He'd better be, she thought, or he's going to lose some parishioners. "He's almost done, darling." She squeezed Tish's knee affectionately then looked past her to where Lena's head nodded sleepily.

During the long night, Rachel had tried to come up with a solution to her money problems. The only way she knew to get money fast was to sell something. But what? And to whom? Then, about three A.M., she got an idea. After church she was going to the Wagonwheel Hotel and Saloon to talk to Jon, the owner.

Jon was a big Swede. He'd moved to Mesa City about ten years before and made an instant success of the

Wagonwheel. He always teased Rachel about her being his only competition. Maybe he'd like to buy the Rosebud.

She took a deep breath as she left the church a short time later. "Lena, take Tish with you to the store. I have an errand to run. It shouldn't take me long."

"*Sí*, Miss Rachel. Come, little one." She took Tish's hand and led her away.

"Mama, can I have some candy?" Tish called after her mother.

Rachel waved a yes to her, then headed toward the Wagonwheel.

When she entered the saloon it took a moment for her eyes to focus in the dim light. She heard the giggle of some of Jon's girls as they saw her come in. Rachel never thought about the propriety of her presence there, especially since she owned her own bar, but apparently the whores weren't used to seeing women come into the establishment.

"Is Jon here?" Rachel inquired.

"Who wants to know?" A slim blond girl asked as she walked forward from the group.

"Tell him Rachel Walker would like to speak to him."

"I ain't his servant," the girl replied. "Tell him yourself."

Rachel let her gaze take in the girl's slovenly appearance. She was barely dressed in a dirty black chemise with a torn strap. One of her breasts was totally exposed and hung limply against her shallow chest. "I'd be happy to, if you will be so kind as to tell me where he is."

"He's up in his bedroom," the blonde announced with a singsong tone to her voice.

She's trying to embarrass me, Rachel realized. She almost laughed out loud. The little bitch. "Is he alone or will I be interrupting an orgy?" she asked bluntly as she headed for the stairs. She had the satisfaction of hearing the girl gasp.

"You can't go upstairs," another woman told her with a frantic note.

"Then I suggest one of you tell him I'm here."

A dark-haired girl ran up the stairs two at a time and called through a door at the end of the hall. Two minutes later Jon appeared at the top of the stairs.

"Rachel," his voice boomed down at her. "To what do I owe this honor?"

"We've got business to discuss."

Jon's brows raised with curiosity, and he started down the stairs.

Moments later, in his office, Rachel was once again feeling the desperation of having no solution to her problems.

"But you always said I was your only competition. I thought for sure you'd want to buy the Rosebud."

"I like the competition, Rachel. And like I told you, even if I wanted to buy you out, I don't have the money right now."

"But . . ."

"Besides, Rachel, I know you don't really want to sell that place."

He was right. The thought of selling made her physically ill, but she felt she had no alternative. She needed the money.

"You think about it, Rachel. Nobody needs money that quick."

She almost laughed. She hadn't told him the reason she needed the money, just said she needed some cash rather quickly.

"Really, Rachel. You think about it. Maybe the bank would give you a loan."

She stood up. The last thing she needed was another loan she couldn't repay. She wouldn't dig herself in any deeper. There had to be another solution. "I've got to be going, Jon. Lena and Tish are waiting for me at the store." She turned to the big man now standing in front of her and offered her hand. "Thanks anyway."

"You're welcome, Rachel. You come back anytime." He shook her hand, then walked her to the door.

Rachel made her way from the Wagonwheel toward

the general store. She could see that Jace and a couple of the other men were just about through loading the supplies that she'd ordered into the wagon. She knew Lena and Tish would be inside the store waiting for her. Tish would be eyeing the candy and Lena the fabric. Every Sunday was the same. Every Sunday but this one. And none would be the same from now on. She looked at the town around her. The same buildings and people surrounded her. The sky was just as blue as it had been a week ago and the air full of the same smells of tobacco, horse manure, hair tonic, and rose water. No, she thought defiantly. I'll be damned if I'll let one man change my whole life. She squared her shoulders and entered the store.

"Lena, are we ready? It's a long ride home."

Jace stopped loading the wagon and watched her disappear through the door. He wondered what business she'd had in the Wagonwheel. He had to get close to her again so she'd confide in him like she did when they were kids.

As Sin sat on the porch with his booted feet up on the railing, he thought of Rachel. He thought about the way she'd looked the night before when she'd told him she had no choice but to fight. He'd seen that look on countless Southern faces during this war, an inner defiance and strength as much a part of the person as the color of their eyes. Unfortunately, he'd seen that look change too often to a look of bewilderment and defeat. It was true the war wasn't over yet, but he could predict the outcome now and his beloved South was going to lose.

He didn't want a war with Rachel but she was ready to fight one, and though he wanted, no needed, to be victorious in their battle, he also didn't want Rachel's defeat. If only there was a way to make her see they could both be winners.

He'd spent the day going over the books more closely and then looking through more of Hyram Walker's papers. The fact that Rachel, Lena, Tish, and most of the ranch hands had gone into town for Sunday services gave him the perfect opportunity to really study the information in the files in the office. He discovered that the Rosebud was sitting on Triple X land and so was also partly his property. He'd examined maps of the region also, and got a good idea of how the ranch sat with reference to the open range and the other landowners in the area. He was satisfied to see the terrific potential for success that the Triple X possessed, if they could only solve their current problem.

The sound of an approaching wagon took his attention. He thought for a moment it might be Rachel coming back from town early, but when he squinted his eyes against the sun, he could see it wasn't a wagon coming toward him but a buggy. A buggy with four people that he was seeing more clearly as each minute passed.

In a few moments he could make out the figure of a large, buxom woman who appeared to be in her late forties. She was sitting in the front seat with the driver, a man he thought he recognized from town. In the back seat were a boy and a young woman. He squinted against the sun's glare. The young woman was Rachel. But no, it couldn't be Rachel. He looked again. She was younger than Rachel with a fairer complexion and strawberry hair instead of Rachel's deep wine locks. The family resemblance was remarkable, though. There was no mistaking the bloodline.

As the buggy pulled up to a stop he rose and descended the porch stairs, rather unsure of how to proceed. Rachel hadn't told him she was expecting a visit from relatives. And from the amount of luggage on the back of the buggy, these people planned on a long stay.

"Well, young man, aren't you going to help me down?" The older woman extended her hand toward Sin and awaited his attention. Her voice held the authority of one used to giving orders and having them obeyed.

"Yes, ma'am." Sin smiled as he helped her from the buggy.

"And who might you be?" the woman asked directly, while sizing him up with one glance. Then without waiting for his reply she began scrutinizing the exterior of the house and frowning.

"I'm Rachel's new . . ."

"Well, if the interior is half as bad as the exterior, I'm here in the nick of time," she announced to no one in particular. "Come, children. You were saying, young man? And where is Rachel? She was supposed to meet us at the stage today. Fetch her, please."

Sin stood next to this whirlwind of a woman and didn't know what to make of her. She turned to her children as they stepped down from the buggy and then began ordering the driver to assist them in the unloading of their luggage.

"Ma'am. I . . ."

"Are you still here? I asked you to fetch Rachel." Then to the driver, "Hand me that hatbox. Yes, the red one," once again dismissing Sin.

He took a deep breath. This woman was beginning to frustrate him. "Madam, Rachel is not here and I'm not the hired help," he stated loudly, placing his fingertips in his back pockets.

An intake of air from the young woman now standing near her mother took Sin's attention for a moment. Apparently no one questioned the older woman's authority. In that moment, as his attention was diverted, Sin was pleasantly surprised. The clear blue eyes that met his were fringed by golden lashes the same color as the sunlight reflecting off the strawberry-blond curls framing high cheekbones, turned-up nose, and a full-lipped smile. The resemblance to Rachel he'd noticed at first wasn't nearly as distinct this close up, but the women had to be cousins at least.

"I beg your pardon, young man?"

Sin's eyes were brought back to the older woman. She was staring straight at him with her back up, ready for a fight.

"I said, Rachel's not here. She, and nearly everyone

else for that matter, are gone. They're in town attending church services. And I'm not one of the hired hands. I'm Sinclaire Braddock, Rachel's partner. Now who, Madam, are you?"

"I, Mr. Braddock, am Mrs. Lucille Jacobs. I am Rachel's aunt. I wrote and notified her that we were coming and again to tell her when to meet us. I was also unaware that Rachel had married."

A brief look of surprise crossed Sin's face at the conclusion she'd come to. "I'm not married to Rachel. I'm her partner, and she said nothing to me about company arriving, today or any other day."

It was Lucille's turn to look surprised. She had lived forty-two years in Southern propriety and knew as well as anyone that men and women didn't own property together unless they were married. This didn't sit well at all. And there was another aspect to this that she didn't like. Another partner could cause problems for her and her plans as well. She glanced at her son, now pushing a small stone around in a circle with the toe of his shoe, and at her daughter who seemed to be standing a little straighter and not taking her eyes off Mr. Braddock.

"Well, it seems that there is a lot that needs to be discussed. Can we get out of this hot sun, please?"

When Rachel pulled the wagon team to a stop in the ranch yard, it was nearly dinnertime. Sunday evening meals were always light, and Lena stepped down from the wagon as soon as they pulled up to the house.

"I'll start getting things together, Miss Rachel."

"Me too, Mama. Me too." Tish jumped from the wagon to help Lena.

"Do you mind?" Rachel asked.

"Of course not, Miss Rachel. Come, little one. What shall we fix tonight?"

Rachel smiled to herself as she watched them walk away. She then scanned the ranch yard. Where was Sin and what had he been up to all day? Probably no good.

She pulled the wagon closer to the back of the house so the men could unload the supplies more easily and hopped down and headed toward the barn. She needed to talk to Hank but knew he'd gone to his sister's for Sunday supper.

She entered the cool shadow of the barn and walked to where Roux was standing in his stall. If only she had someone to turn to, to confide in, someone to help her through all this.

"How ya doin', old friend?" She rubbed his long smooth neck and glanced around the barn to see if Sin were perhaps somewhere nearby. Just then a shadow filled the doorway. The hair on the back of her neck stood up.

"Braddock?"

"No, Rachel. It's me, Jace."

She took a deep breath. "Jace, what can I do for you?"

"Well, Rachel, I've known you a long time." He clenched his fists at his sides, not sure how to continue. He couldn't stand feeling this way with her. They had grown up together, for Christ's sake, and now he didn't know how to talk to her. She made him so damned uncomfortable now.

"Yes?" She stepped from behind Roux.

He watched the way the fabric of the dress she was wearing moved around her legs. She always wore dresses on Sunday and he looked forward to it each week. But now what? What could he say to make her see that she didn't need to keep this distance between them?

She couldn't see his face. The light outside the door behind him was bright, leaving him just a dark silhouette.

He took a step toward her. Then another and another. He could see the concern in her expression. She was looking tired and nervous. More than that. He knew her well enough to know that something was terribly wrong. Taking another step closer still, he watched her face, hopeful of some sign of softening toward him.

She looked up into his chocolate brown eyes and was reminded of why she'd fallen for him when they were kids. She could see the shadow of his beard though he'd shaved just that morning. She'd just been thinking how nice it would be to have someone to confide in, but this was Jace. She'd promised herself she wouldn't feel anything for him. If only the heat from his body, so very close now, wasn't making her so warm. She had to tilt her head to look at him. His arms were close to his sides and his hands were clenched. She looked at the fullness of his mouth. For just a moment she was tempted. It would be nice to lean forward into the protective circle of his arms, to let her mind be free of its troubles, to be held in the warmth of another human being's arms for just a little while. She brought her hand up and placed it softly on his broadly muscled chest. The heat from his body warmed her hand as she felt his heart beating erratically.

"Rachel ..." Her name came from his lips in a whisper.

Rachel heard the need in his voice. This wasn't right. But the heat from touching him was traveling up her arm. She saw him tilt his head back with pleasure at her touch.

Jace watched her eyelids lower suggestively. Saw her wet her lips with the tip of her tongue. The corners of his mouth pulled up slightly. He was going to make things right between them. Then whatever problems she had, he'd help solve.

She watched the look of pleasure on his face and remembered how he used to smile at her while they were making love. She was losing herself in the feelings and memories. And some of those memories were so sweet. It seemed she'd slipped back into the past as his head descended and his lips touched hers. Oh, this felt so good. Gently, the tip of his tongue traced her lower lip. She felt his large hands on her back pulling her to him. Her arms slipped around his neck as she pressed her breasts tightly to him and opened her mouth to receive his kisses. It had been so long since she'd felt this way. Then she thought about why it had been so long. He'd left her when she needed him most. She began pulling away.

Jace must have sensed her distancing because she felt him holding her more tightly. She couldn't help the sharp intake of her breath as he molded her against the length of his fully aroused body. She wasn't surprised by the blatant desire he was feeling for her. She had been remembering what sex with this man was like, but again she brought herself up short. That's all it would be for her. She would never allow her heart to become involved again. She had to stop this. She tipped her head back to try to talk to him, but all the while his hold on her was becoming more intimate. He brought one hand between them to cup her breast. She groaned softly as his fingers found one nipple and teased it to a sensitive peak.

"Jace, please stop." Her voice was but a whisper.

"No. Rachel. Not now." He could feel her resistance but didn't want to stop. He'd finally started to make things happen the way he wanted to with Rachel. When she'd responded to him so quickly he'd nearly lost his control. He'd been with so many women since leaving years ago that he'd forgotten how sweet her surrender could be. She was very special indeed, and her response made him believe that they could go back. There was no reason not to. She'd never married, and with her father dead now, she needed his help.

The sensations he was causing throughout her body were making her lightheaded, and she had to admit she wanted him. But it was only physical. Jace was wrong for her. He had been wrong for her years ago, and he was wrong for her now. And her reason was purely selfish. He was Tish's father. So far he didn't know. He'd believed her story about a ranch hand passing through town shortly after he left, and she had every intention of keeping it that way. She was afraid that if he knew, he would make trouble for her. Make demands that she wasn't prepared to deal with. She brought her arms down and pushed away from him. "I said stop it, Jace." She pushed herself free.

Jace tried to reach for her again but she stepped back, once more putting up the walls that had been there before. He didn't know what had caused her sudden change of attitude, and he didn't like it. He felt he'd been coming so close to making a change in their relationship.

Rachel watched the hurt, then angry, expressions on his handsome face. She didn't want to hurt him. Maybe she should just ask him to leave the ranch. Letting him stay was giving him ideas about the two of them. Hell, her reactions to him just now had just about spelled out that she was ready to fall into bed with him. Damn it. Why did she keep making the same stupid mistakes?

"Jace, I think you should leave," she blurted.

She once again watched the play of emotions.

"I think you're right. I've got work to do anyway." He turned and left the barn. He didn't know what else to do. He couldn't figure her out no matter how he tried. He knew she wanted him, but she wouldn't let herself give in. Why?

Rachel watched him go. He'd misunderstood what she'd meant. She wanted him to leave the ranch but he'd walked away so fast that he'd startled her. Now she'd have to deal with him again later. Heaving a sigh, she rubbed her face with her hands and walked to the window only to see Sin walking away with an angry stride. Had he seen her with Jace? If so, how much had he seen? Breathing another sigh, she decided she didn't care.

Sin had done his best to make introductions between Lena, Tish, Aunt Lucy, and her children, then went out to find Rachel. He was totally unprepared for the sight of Rachel in Jace's arms. Something inside him swelled in rebellion at the sight of her with another man. Then he realized he was being ridiculous. He barely knew her.

He should have guessed she'd be involved with someone. She was, as he'd observed himself, a very healthy, attractive woman. It also made sense that she would find his own arrival on the scene poorly timed. She'd probably been waiting for the right moment to bring her relationship with Jace out into the open. The more he thought about it, the more it all made sense. The one thing that didn't make sense to him was the way he was reacting to seeing her with Jace.

He had no right to be angry, but he was. He had no rights at all where Rachel was concerned, but that didn't stop him from feeling what he was feeling. Before he did something he would regret, he turned back to the house.

"Damn it!" he cursed as he went.

Rachel was completely unprepared for the family reunion going on in her kitchen. Finding Tish on the floor laughing with a strange little boy, and Lena deep in conversation with two faintly familiar women threw her off guard.

"I ..." She didn't know what to say.

"Well, it's about time you came in." The older of the two women broke away from the others and came toward her with arms open wide.

"Aunt Lucy?" Rachel was pulled into a killing embrace.

"Of course, it's me. And I'm sorry it took me so long to get here. By the look of things around here, I've been needed for quite some time."

"But what are you doing here? I mean ..." Rachel pulled back from her aunt slightly. "How nice of you to visit."

"My dear, this isn't a visit. I've finally come to stay. Now don't try to thank me. It's my Christian duty. I'm only sorry I didn't come years ago, but I had no idea how much I was needed. Your poor father, my dear brother, rest his soul, was a brave man and didn't want to burden me with his troubles." She released a stunned Rachel and sat down at the table. "His letters, although few, were always so happy. He made it sound like you two were doing so well." She took a handkerchief from her sleeve and brought it to her eyes. "And all the time you were living like ... like this." She gestured around the kitchen with her free hand.

Rachel looked around the room and wondered what in the world the woman was talking about. She knew that her home wasn't fancy, but there was absolutely nothing wrong with the way they lived. She could also see a firmer set to Lena's jaw and knew she'd taken offense at Lucy's words. She knew she'd better say something quick. "Aunt Lucy, we're perfectly happy with the way things are. Lena takes excellent care of us." She smiled at Lena and received an answering smile.

"Nonsense, child, you're just being brave like your father." She wiped her eyes again and took a deep breath, raising her ample bosom. "But don't worry. I'm here now and things will be run correctly around here from now on."

"Look, Mama, cousin Jeremy gave me one of his toy soldiers!" Tish held up a tiny wooden Confederate soldier and grinned from ear to ear. "Isn't he pretty?"

Lucy answered before Rachel got a chance to respond. "Letisha, girls are pretty and men are handsome. Now, you two children take the toys into the other room to play." She stood and put her hand out to Rachel and pulled her in front of the young woman who had remained standing quietly beside Lena. "Rachel, this is my Lily. She's much younger than you, but I'm hoping you two can become the fast friends that cousins should be."

"I'm happy to know you, cousin Rachel." Lily curtsied ever so slightly.

Rachel looked at her cousin's perfect white complexion, heard the soft lilting drawl of a true-blue Southern belle, and groaned inwardly. What on earth was this useless creature going to do on a cattle ranch? She supposed it was really no concern of hers as Lucy probably had the girl's entire life already planned out for her.

"I'm pleased to meet you also, cousin Lily." She held out her hand.

Lily looked at her hand and then at her mother, bewildered.

Rachel realized a second too late that ladies didn't shake hands when meeting. She felt very much like she had just committed a huge social error, especially after the concerned looks Lucy and Lily exchanged. She dropped her arm to her side. "I'm going upstairs to freshen up before dinner. Lena, do you have everything about ready?"

"*Sí*, Miss Rachel."

"Good. Then if you'll all excuse me, I'll be right down." She left the kitchen without looking back at her aunt or cousin. She could hear Tish and Jeremy laughing out on the front porch. As she took the stairs two at a time, she wondered how she was going to get rid of all these people.

5

Rachel slammed the bedroom door as she went through and began to unfasten the high-necked bodice of her dress. She needed to cool down, and wiping off with a fresh washcloth sounded wonderful. She splashed some water into the basin and pulled her arms from their sleeves, letting the bodice hang loosely from the waistband. She unlaced the low neckline of her chemise and bent over the basin to cool off.

Then she heard a noise. Someone was moving around in the room next to hers. That was the nursery. The two rooms shared an adjoining door and no one should be in there.

The only person it could be was Sin, but she couldn't guess why he would be rummaging around in a room used mostly for storage now. If he wanted to talk to her about what he'd just witnessed in the barn, why didn't he come to her door? She crept quietly to the door between the rooms and listened. Someone was definitely moving things around. Maybe the children had come upstairs to play? No, she could still hear them on the porch below.

She decided to open the door just a crack and peek. Still holding the wet washcloth in one hand, she very carefully turned the knob, trying not to make a sound. Pushing the door open just a fraction of an inch, she peered in to see Sin's strong back as he bent to move a box. She couldn't make out just what he was doing, so she opened the door a tiny bit more. He seemed to be clearing out the stored boxes and making room for something. Then she realized, with a quick intake of air, that he was moving into the nursery! She scanned the room. Sure enough, there were his belongings piled at the end of the daybed.

Sin had heard Rachel slam her way into her room. He'd planned on being in the kitchen when Rachel came in, but the surprise of finding her in Jace's arms had caused him to head upstairs. He needed to think this through. If Rachel was planning on marrying Jace, his own place on the Triple X could become more of a problem. Of course, there was always the chance that Jace would see and accept his legal right in the whole thing, but somehow he doubted it. And now there was Lucy. She'd briefly explained her position to him, and although he could understand her motives, he could see very troubled waters ahead for all concerned.

He'd listened when Rachel came into the house, hoping that her Aunt Lucy wouldn't unravel her plan as soon as she came face-to-face with her. He'd heard no explosion so he assumed she hadn't. But the slamming of the door told him Rachel wasn't overjoyed with the prospect of houseguests.

"What do you think you're doing?" Rachel demanded from behind him.

Sin spun around to see her standing in the open doorway between the rooms. She was in a shocking state of undress, with the top portion of her dress down around her waist and her upper undergarment unlaced, exposing a good portion of her full white breasts to his gaze. His breath caught in his throat and he found he couldn't swallow, let alone answer her. She stood there waiting for his explanation, but all he could do was continue to stare. He could see the dark shadows of her nipples behind the sheer fabric of her chemise and noticed the droplets of water that still clung to her flesh where she'd splashed herself.

He took several steps toward her. How could she be so oblivious to how she looked? Didn't she know what this could do to a man, was doing to him? He felt himself responding on a purely physical level. The blood pounding in his temples was also pounding an echo in a lower region of his body. He moved even closer to her.

The look on her face was still one of impatience when she asked again, "What are you doing in here?" Then she noticed his expression. His lids had lowered seductively over coal-black eyes. She noticed how long and thick his lashes were and that there were tiny laugh lines at the corners of his eyes. His mouth was wide, with his lower lip being fuller than the upper, and right now one side turned up slightly. Damn it. She knew what he was thinking. She glanced down at herself and could see why. She reached up and closed the chemise with one hand, which only pushed her nipples harder against the fabric, causing Sin even more discomfort.

She looked down his muscular frame, and like the first time she saw him, found him lacking nothing. Right now she noticed even more. His desire for her was apparent within the confines of his snug trousers. She wanted to reach out and touch that desire. Yes, she, too, was at the mercy of physical needs. The encounter with Jace had left her dissatisfied, but she wouldn't give in to this kind of need with just anyone. Her feelings had kept her alone for a long time, but here within the space of a few days she was attracted to two men. Two men, who very obviously could satisfy her sexually, but who were threats to her in frightening ways. Why was her life becoming so complicated? Just months ago everything was on an even keel, no surprises, no difficult decisions to make, and no pressures from outside influences. Now everywhere she looked there were people making demands on her.

Sin stood right in front of her. She could feel his

breath on her face as she looked up into those black, dangerous eyes. It would be too easy to get lost in those eyes.

Sin watched her. Watched the subtle changes her emotions brought to her beautiful face. He was wondering again what kind of woman she was. Right now she was a most desirable one, and Jace or no Jace, she was standing half naked just inches from him. For just a moment he didn't want to think about consequences. He reached out for her with both hands.

Rachel's eyes opened wide when she saw him move. There was no way she was going to let this happen. Remembering the washcloth, she brought it up and slapped him across the face with it.

"Rachel!" he sputtered, any desire he'd felt now dead cold. She'd let go of the cloth and it slipped down to hang, dripping limply from the side of his neck. A black scowl covered his face as he pulled it down, then looked carefully at it in his hand.

Rachel watched him studying the cloth. One hand covered her mouth in surprise at her own actions. The way he was standing there not saying more was making her nervous. He wouldn't use the cloth on her, would he? She suddenly felt very silly. The wet area on his face and neck and the drops of water that spotted his shirt began to strike her as funny. Also, the incredulous look on his face. She could well imagine that Mr. Sinclaire Braddock had never been struck with a wet washcloth before in his life. She began to giggle.

Sin looked up at her in astonishment. She was laughing at him? What was so funny about this situation?

Rachel continued to laugh though she tried to stifle it with her hand. The look on his face was getting better all the time.

"I'm ... I'm ..." She tried to speak but was having difficulty through her giggles. "I'm ... sorry." She gave up and backed through the door into her own room. She continued to laugh as she shut the door between them, then turned and leaned against it as she allowed herself to laugh freely.

Sin still held the cloth as he listened to her through the door. Somehow this was hilarious to her. Then he felt the corners of his own mouth turning up into a smile. He supposed it was pretty funny. Rachel was definitely an interesting woman. He doubted that if he lived here for the next fifty years he'd ever figure her out ... or get tired of her.

Rachel looked around the dining table at all the new faces in her life. Directly across from her, at the foot of the table, was Sin. She'd informed everyone, Aunt Lucy in particular, that she was the head of the household and would continue, as always, to sit at the head of the table. She had endured disapproving glances from the older woman throughout the meal. Directly to Sin's right was cousin Lily, in all her Southern beauty. Next to her and on Rachel's left was Jeremy. On her right sat Tish, then Aunt Lucy.

The meal was about over. Lucy had been making small talk, telling her news about relatives that she'd never met. Somewhere, Lucy had come up with a little silver bell and tinkled it whenever she wanted Lena to appear. She did so now, and Rachel watched Lena come through the door with a very disgruntled expression. This was going to have to stop. Lena was nearly one of the family, not some servant to come running at the sound of a bell.

"You may bring in dessert now," announced Lucy.

Lena scowled and disappeared back to the kitchen.

"Aunt Lucy."

"Yes, dear?"

How was she going to say this? "I don't think Lena is happy with that bell." She gestured with one hand.

"Nonsense, child. Lena is the housekeeper. She must know her place. When she gets used to things being run correctly around here, she'll appreciate the order."

Rachel heaved a sigh. "Lena isn't just a housekeeper. She's more like family."

"I know you've allowed this improper relationship to develop because of your and your father's needs." She took her hankie from her sleeve and touched it to the corner of one eye. "I'm as much to blame for your sad situation as anyone, because I didn't come to your aid much sooner." She sniffed softly and tucked her hankie back into its place. "But I'm here now, and I'm going to make up for lost time and see to it that things are done correctly. It may take some getting used to, but I know in the end you will see that I'm right."

Rachel glanced from Lucy to Sin, curious about how he was perceiving this exchange. She frowned to see him totally engrossed in something Lily was saying quietly to him only. They hadn't spoken since the scene in the nursery and since then she'd learned of the changed sleeping arrangements. Lucy now occupied the large room Sin had used the past few days. Lily had moved in with Tish. Jeremy, much to his delight, was in a storeroom downstairs off the kitchen. He said it made him feel grown up to have such a room. And Sin was, of course, in the nursery next to her. She would have thought that Lucy would find it quite improper for her and Sin to have connecting rooms, then realized she probably didn't know about the door. She smiled to herself at the thought of Lucy finding out some time in the future.

Lily's light laughter and the deep resonance of Sin's responding mirth interrupted her own musings. She looked at them just in time to see Lily flirtatiously place her hand on Sin's arm. Rachel noticed that Lucy was watching her to see how she would react to this exchange. It still wasn't clear to Lucy just what her and Sin's relationship was. She smiled at her aunt, hoping to assure her that there was nothing "friendly" between them. In fact, she still had every intention of getting rid of him if at all possible. She took a sip of water and looked again at Sin and Lily, and frowned.

"Mama, may Jeremy and I take our dessert out on the porch?" Tish tugged softly on her mother's sleeve.

"Yes, of course, my darling." She reached out to tuck a stray piece of hair behind the child's ear, then caressed her soft cheek. "Don't forget to bring in your dirty dishes when you're through."

"Yes, Mama. Come on, Jeremy. Let's get our dessert from Lena and go outside!" She pushed back her chair with a scrape and rushed toward the kitchen.

"Slow down, little one," Rachel admonished with a smile.

A few moments later the children were settled on the porch, and Lena brought in the spice cake she'd made the day before. That and fresh coffee made a heavenly dessert as far as Rachel was concerned. She noticed, though, that Lily turned up her pretty nose a bit at the strong black liquid when Lena set a cup of it down in front of her.

"Is there a problem, Lily?"

"Oh, no, cousin Rachel, I'm fine. Really." She smiled and picked up her fork.

"Would you prefer something else to drink?"

"I wouldn't want to be any trouble."

"If you want something else just say so. It's no trouble." Rachel was finding Lily's attitude a little hard to understand. She'd been raised in this country to ask for what she wanted, to demand it if necessary. If Lily couldn't even say she wanted something else to drink, how could she make her other needs known?

"Rachel," Lucy interrupted. "It's just that we're not used to drinking coffee. You see, dear, ladies don't usually drink coffee, especially this strong. We prefer tea. It's my own fault for not informing Lena. I'll make sure we have tea from now on."

Rachel listened and once more found criticism in Lucy's words. This was twice in their first evening together that she'd been informed, though kindly, that the things she did were unladylike. It surprised her that it should bother her in the least. The women in town disapproved of just about everything she did, and it had never entered her mind to care about their opinions. She pushed those feelings abruptly aside. I don't have time for this sort of nonsense, she thought.

"That's fine, Aunt Lucy. You may ask Lena to prepare tea for you and Lily. I will still have coffee. Mr. Braddock, do you prefer coffee or tea?"

He looked at her, a bit surprised. For some reason this question seemed important to her. Before he could speak, Lily squeezed his arm and answered for him.

"Mr. Braddock is a gentleman. I'm sure he would prefer coffee."

"Very well. Now if you all will excuse me, I have things to do." Rachel stood, leaving her cake and coffee uneaten.

"Rachel, I need to speak to you, dear," Lucy called after her.

"Yes, Aunt Lucy." She had just about made her escape but turned with a sigh.

Sin could see what was coming. Lucy was going to tell her what she'd explained to him earlier, and Rachel wasn't going to take it well.

"Ladies, let's go out onto the porch." He stood and took the arm Lily offered. "We'll be more comfortable there."

Lucy rose and smoothed down the front of her skirt. "Very well, Mr. Braddock. If you wish."

Rachel wondered what was going on. Why was Sin being so friendly to her aunt? And what was so important that Lucy needed to talk to her about? Probably some other major household problem.

Once on the porch, Rachel had to remind the children to bring in their dessert plates. They'd begun running around the yard in a wild game of tag and left them piled on the steps. "Mama, after we take in our dishes, can I show Poco to Jeremy?"

"If Aunt Lucy doesn't mind."

"Of course not," answered Lucy. "As long as you don't try to ride him."

Rachel turned a curious expression to Lucy. "Doesn't he know how to ride?" The thought was absurd to her.

"Not very well, I'm afraid. We have been living in the city, my dear. We use buggies for travel. But this does bring me to what I needed to discuss with you." She sat down carefully on the rather rickety swing at one end of the porch. "Come, sit with me."

Rachel was getting suspicious. She looked to see Sin and Lily sitting next to one another on the two ladder-backed chairs at the other end of the porch. Sin was watching her, and she knew in an instant that he knew what it was Lucy was about to discuss. And he's worried about it, she thought. Taking a deep breath and bracing herself, she sat down next to Lucy. The old swing groaned under the weight of the two women.

"Rachel, dear." Lucy pursed her lips and took a breath, heaving her great bosom. "It's only been a month since your father's untimely demise, so it's difficult for me to speak of business matters now, but there are some things that need to be settled."

Rachel listened, waiting for the woman to get to the point. Her eyes narrowed almost imperceptibly. "Yes, Aunt Lucy?"

"Well, I understand that your father passed on without benefit of a will. Oh, this is so difficult to speak of." She took out her hankie and wiped perspiration from her upper lip.

Rachel's back had stiffened slightly. It was a very hot evening and even she was uncomfortable with the heat, but she could tell that Lucy was perspiring from nervousness. "How does my father having or not having a will concern you?"

"It's just that, well, if he'd taken the time to write a will I'm certain that we, Jeremy in particular, would have been included." She'd begun fanning herself with her hankie.

The truth was out. Rachel looked at her aunt, then at Lily and Sin. She could see in Sin's lack of expression that he was waiting to see how she'd react. She glanced back at her aunt. One more person, no, three more, had come to claim something that didn't belong to them: her home.

Her voice came out in a dangerous monotone. "Please continue, Aunt Lucy. I'm interested in just what it is you want."

Lucy misread her quiet response and smiled. She smoothed her already smooth skirt and continued. "I feel it's fair to assume that your father would have wanted Jeremy to be an heir to at least half ownership in the ranch. He is, after all, the only living male relative." She touched her hankie to her forehead. "It truly isn't proper for a lady to run a cattle ranch. I'm sure people will be forgiving with their gossip if it's understood that you're training Jeremy to take over the ranch one day."

Sin watched Rachel very closely. Lily was talking quietly to him, but she could have been naked and not gotten any more attention. The deadly look in Rachel's cool, green eyes was making him very nervous. In the past couple of days he'd been the recipient of the same look, and it hadn't been pleasant.

Rachel stood and turned to look down at her aunt. "First of all, I would like to establish one fact. I am not a lady." The tone of her voice was as harsh as the rattle of a snake, and Lucy stared up at her, aghast. "Secondly, I've never given a rat's ass what other people think, and I'm not going to start now." She heard Lily's shocked gasp and continued. "There is already an heir to this ranch, and her name happens to be Letisha Walker. She is only seven years old and can ride almost as well as I can. In another year or two I will teach her how to rope cattle and shoot a gun as well as any man on the place."

"Rachel!" Lucy tried to stand, but Rachel was standing over her and wouldn't give an inch.

"I'm not through yet, Aunt Lucy. This is my ranch, damn it! A few days ago Mr. Braddock here came riding in with a contract that supposedly gives him the right to half of it, and now you're here with pious propriety and some imagined family obligation on your side to claim another half." She was now including Sin in her speech. "Well, guess what, folks? There aren't enough halves to go around. Like I just said, this is my ranch and I'll be goddamned if I'm going to hand it over to you two or anyone else who happens to ride in here in the next few days."

"Rachel, I've never been so offended! Your dear father would turn in his grave if he heard such talk coming from his little girl's mouth." Lucy was huffing with each breath and fanning herself vigorously. "And I can't believe you'd take such a hard stand against your family. We sold everything to come here to help you."

Rachel looked down on her aunt once again. "I will not get into a discussion about your motives for coming here. I will give you the benefit of the doubt about your intentions being good. You say you sold everything to come here, which leads me to believe that you have nothing to go back to." Lucy shook her head. "I would never turn away family. You may stay, but we'd better get one thing straight right now." She glanced once more at Sin. "I am the boss." She headed toward the door. "Now, if you will excuse me, I have to change and go check on things at the Rosebud."

"The Rosebud?" Lily asked softly.

"It's her saloon," Sin answered.

"Her what?" demanded Lucy.

Rachel turned back as she went through the door. "That's right, Aunt Lucy, my saloon. You should come see it sometime. Oh, and by the way, my father's the one that taught me to swear, so I doubt he's doing any turning." With that, she closed the door behind her.

Sin looked from one shocked face to the other and had to stifle his laughter. Rachel had handled this better than he'd expected. She'd been angry with Lucy's demands, had even included him in some of her retort, but all in all it had turned out fairly well. He just hoped Lucy would be willing to accept things the way Rachel had left them. She seemed like the sort of woman not used to giving up many battles.

He thought about Rachel upstairs changing into her trousers and man's shirt and realized he'd like to talk to her over a drink. They still had the immediate problem of being nearly penniless. If he could begin to convince her to work together, they might think of a solution. He smiled to himself as he looked to Lucy, and Lily, now sitting by her mother, comforting her. He doubted too many people stood up to Lucy and won. "If you ladies will excuse me, I, too, have business in town."

A short time later, after kissing Tish and promising to check on her when she returned, Rachel was riding Roux toward the Rosebud. The sun was a fiery orange ball near the horizon, turning the ground into a glowing yellow field of long purple shadows. Tiny bats flew around her in their search for insect prey, and jackrabbits darted across the road in front of her.

This was her favorite time of day. This quiet time between light and dark, day and night. This was the time that rejuvenated her. She was able to ponder decisions, sort out emotions, scold and laugh at herself. As this day grew to its end, she had much to think about. Lucy's revelation had come as a shock. She leaned forward and patted Roux on the neck. "Can you believe the nerve of that woman, to just arrive here and announce to me that she believes it was my father's intent to give her son half the Triple X? Over my dead body."

She stood in the stirrups for a moment, stretching her back, then sat again. Roux seemed not to notice the action. She adjusted her hat lower over her eyes as the sun dipped. "At least she can't make some legal claim like this Braddock character is trying to do. Braddock. What am I going to do about him?" This was a tough one. No matter how hard she thought about it, after her meeting with Pete yesterday, and talking to Jon at the Wagonwheel that morning, she could think of no way, short of her original thought of murder, to get rid of him.

He might have his own good reasons for being there, but no matter what those reasons were, he didn't have the right to walk in and take half her life. "Half hell! He's moved into the next bedroom, for Christ's sake!" she shouted into the quickly settling night.

Riding in the near-dark quiet, she was able to hear a rider coming almost before she could see him. The plodding hoofbeats indicated the rider was in no hurry. As he got closer, she could make out the form of Hank, the foreman. He was returning to the ranch from his sister's. He pulled his horse to a stop next to her.

"Howdy, Miss Rachel. Goin' to the Rosebud?"

She smiled at him. "Ya, Hank. How was dinner?"

"Good as always." He scratched his whiskers. "I passed Jace just outside of town. He wasn't in a talkin' mood."

"Oh?"

"I think he was head'n for the Wagonwheel."

She frowned. Jace was another problem. "Thanks, Hank."

"What if he doesn't show up for work tomorrow?"

She knew that Hank could drink with the best of them, but he didn't hold with drinking on a work night. She also knew that he remembered a time when Jace was at the Triple X as much as his own place, and was probably wondering if she was going to play favorites. Thank God he didn't know any more.

"You're the foreman, Hank. Your decision."

He nodded, satisfied. "Right. Well, I guess I'll see you in the morning." He began to turn his horse.

"Oh, I just remembered, Hank. I wanted to ask you something earlier." She'd been formulating a plan, just an idea really. She had to come up with a way to make enough money to save the ranch, and so far she had only one possible solution. "Would you have any problem with driving the cattle north this year?"

Hank watched her for a moment. "What do you mean, a problem?"

"With loyalty?"

He looked down and chewed the inside of his lower lip for just a bit. "I reckon not. I've got relatives on both sides of this war, and they all gotta eat just the same."

"Do you think the other men will feel the same?"

He waited again for a moment before answering. "Well, Miss Rachel, Stoker might feel strongly about it. He had a brother killed by the Yanks not too long ago. But I don't think anyone else would care much, one way or another."

"Okay, Hank, thanks. I'll see you tomorrow." She pulled Roux around and headed toward town. She'd hate to lose Stoker, but she'd sure as hell hate to lose the ranch a whole lot more.

Night had settled in completely by the time she could see the lantern lights of the Rosebud in the distance. A little closer and she could hear laughter coming through the open door. It felt good to get there. Even as a child, when her mother was still living and made her wait outside in the buggy with her while Hyram went in to do his business, she remembered loving this place. After her mother died, when she was six, Hyram had started bringing her in with him, and it had always felt right. She could even remember the first drink she ever sold. She'd been about twelve, maybe eleven, and a big cowboy with shaggy red hair and a thick bristly mustache had slammed his fist on the bar and demanded a whiskey. Thank God, she'd had enough sense to pour him some of the good stuff. She smiled at the memory.

She tethered Roux and went into the bar. She was a little surprised to see so many people there on a Sunday night, but thought that the heat of the late summer night had made a lot of men thirsty.

"Hello, Vera." She raised a hand in the older woman's direction, where she was serving a drink at one of the tables.

Vera nodded at her, then turned to hurriedly take the money. She wanted to talk to Rachel, to tell her why the bar was so busy, to let her know that she'd been the topic of conversation all over town since her meeting with Pete. In Vera's mind it just wasn't right for folks to talk about Miss Rachel the way they did. She was a fine person and deserved better.

"Busy night," Rachel observed as she checked the till.

"Bunch of busybodies, if you ask me," Vera mumbled as she handed Rachel the money she'd just collected.

"What?"

"Some folks ain't got enough business of their own, so they gotta mind everybody else's."

Rachel smiled. "What on earth are you talking about?"

"These folks," she swept the room with her eyes. "They're here hopin' to see you and that new partner of yours. They're hopin' to see some kind of showdown."

Rachel glanced around the room. She noticed quite a few eyes on her. Vera was right. Damn Pete Bigley. She heaved a sigh. "Well, Vera, there's nothing I can do about it. You know as well as I do, you can't piss in this town without everyone knowing how big a puddle you make." She looked at the concern on Vera's face and smiled. "Don't let it bother you. I don't."

Vera shrugged and reached across the bar to grab an empty glass. "When am I going to get to meet this new partner?"

"Sooner than you think." Rachel had seen Braddock come through the door as Vera was speaking. She tapped her on the arm and gestured in his direction as he walked toward them.

"That's him?" Vera whispered. "He's quite a looker."

Rachel let her eyes travel up his body and stop at his eyes. She remembered how he'd looked with a dripping washcloth on his face and couldn't help but smile a bit. "He's got his moments, I guess."

"Well, I'd like to give him a few moments of my own," Vera whispered even more softly as he approached.

"Vera, I'm shocked." Rachel scolded in mock disapproval.

"You are not. But I will be if you haven't thought

about it yourself at least once." Vera nudged her with her elbow.

As Sin crossed the room, he wondered if he would ever get used to the way Rachel sized him up nearly every time she saw him. It was quite unnerving. Now the old woman he'd seen in here before was doing the same.

"Hello, Rachel." He touched the brim of his hat and nodded at Vera. "Ma'am."

"Braddock." Rachel acknowledged him. "This is Vera, my bartender." Was it his imagination, or did she emphasize the word "my"?

"Nice to meet you, Vera. I'm sure it will be a pleasure getting to know you." He held out his hand.

Vera looked from Sin to Rachel and back at Sin, then took his handshake. She couldn't help but respond to his warmth when he smiled at her, and felt a slight tug at her loyalties. It had been all over town, how Rachel had threatened to kill this new partner, how he'd ridden in with no warning to demand half ownership in the Triple X, and how he'd taken the sheriff to help make his claim against Rachel. And though there had been little sympathy for her, in fact many relished the situation, the picture Vera had formed of Braddock hadn't included broad shoulders, black hair, coal-dark eyes, an engaging smile, and enough charm to make her feel ten years younger. "Likewise, Mr. Braddock."

"I've got work to do," Rachel interrupted. "I'll be in the back room if you need me, Vera." She started toward the door behind the bar.

"Rachel, I came to talk to you," Sin announced quietly.

"Then you wasted a trip." She continued through the door, closing it behind her.

Sin took a deep breath. She wasn't going to make this easy. He started around the bar to follow her, but Vera blocked his way.

"Nobody goes behind the bar." She squared her shoulders and waited for him to back down.

Sin's eyelids lowered. He'd just met Vera and didn't

want to turn her into an enemy, but he was going to the back room, one way or another. "Vera, please get out of my way." It was a command, not a question.

Vera's head turned slightly as she sized him up, but she didn't move. "Miss Rachel says, no one behind the bar."

"And I commend your strict enforcement of the rules, but I am now your employer as well as Rachel. You wouldn't stop her from going back there, would you?"

She shook her head, getting a little confused by his reasoning.

"Then you won't stop me either, will you?" He touched her shoulder softly.

"Well, Mr. Braddock, I don't know." But it was too late. He'd already moved past her and was opening the door. She put out a hand to stop him, then decided better of it. Rachel was going to have to deal with this, not her. She would take a wait-and-see attitude. She had great respect for Rachel, but until everything was settled, it was best not to cause too much trouble. She hadn't lived this long and not learned a few very important facts, one being to look out for yourself first and others second. If this Mr. Braddock did stay around, it wouldn't do to be on his bad side. She picked up a damp towel and began wiping down the bar.

6

Rachel looked up from the desk when she heard the door open. "I'm sure as hell getting tired of you barging into places you're not welcome!" She closed the ledger in front of her and stood up.

"I told you that I came here to talk to you, and I'm not leaving until I do." Sin crossed the small room and faced her across the desk. "And, as for my not being welcome, well, Rachel, that's just too damn bad. I'm here and I'm staying," he sat down in a brown leather chair that faced the desk, "so you might as well sit down and talk to me."

Rachel looked down into his handsome face, set with determination, and decided to let him give his speech. If she listened, maybe he'd leave her alone, and she could get on with her own plans. She heaved an impatient sigh and sat down. "All right, Braddock. What do you want?"

His eyes narrowed as he recognized her acquiescence for what it was. He hesitated for a moment. "Rachel, we have to work together on saving the ranch."

"The ranch is my problem, not yours."

"That's where you're wrong. The Triple X is my only chance now," he spoke faster when she tried to interrupt, "and I'm not going to just sit back and watch it die if there's anything I can do to help. If you would only open your eyes to the fact that I may not be the burden you think I am, but perhaps a good partner for you, we might be able to come up with a viable solution."

Rachel leaned back in the chair and crossed her arms in front of her. "Are you through now?"

"Yes." Sin watched the stiff way she moved and knew that she hadn't really heard anything he'd said.

"Good. Will you please show yourself the way out, I have work to do."

"Damn it, Rachel. Listen to me!" His anger got the better of him as he stood, leaned over the desk, and shouted at her.

"Go to hell, Braddock!" She jerked herself out of the chair and met his glare with one of her own.

"I won't go to hell or anywhere else! And I won't stand by and watch while you let the Triple X die because you're too damn stubborn to accept my help."

"Why, you ..." Rachel hauled back her arm and swung.

Sin stopped her fist with his hand and pulled her off balance, catching her as she fell across the desk and against his chest. Both his arms went around her, and he held her there.

Rachel was shocked to find herself in Sin's arms, when her intent had been to knock him on his ass. She tried to straighten herself, but he held her fast. "Let go of me, you bastard!" she demanded and pushed against him. "I said, let me go!" The strength of his arms surprised her as she struggled to free herself.

Sin felt the heat of her fury in the way she fought against him. Like the night in her father's office, he was impressed with her strength, but she was no match for him. He looked down into her green eyes and watched the sparks there as she swore at him. He pulled her across the top of the desk, sending a wood paper-box and the ledger crashing to the floor, and set her on her feet in front of him. She'd grabbed his shoulders as she slid across the desk, and with her arms up, he found himself flush with the voluptuous curves of her body. His heart skipped several beats and it became difficult to breathe evenly. Reason left him, and before she could react he slid one hand down to the firm curve of her buttocks and pulled her even tighter against him. Her head came up in surprise, and as she opened her mouth to protest, his lips took hers possessively, demanding a response.

Rachel was stunned to find herself crushed against the strong length of Sin's body. His arousal was complete, hard, pushing against her abdomen like a brand. Her mouth was open to his kiss and she tasted him as he explored her with his tongue. Her hands found their way into the thickness of his hair and his kiss deepened as her own tongue moved in rhythm with his. She could feel him begin another rhythm as he moved his body slowly against hers in the pattern of lovemaking. She couldn't stop her own body's answering motion and tilted her head away from his kiss to savor the heat between their hips and legs.

Sin watched the way Rachel's breasts strained against the fabric of her shirt as she leaned her head back. He continued moving against her and brought one hand up to rub its palm across her hardened nipples, then cupped one breast, holding its weight, and caressed its hardened peak with his thumb.

Rachel gasped as a lightning sharp sensation shot through her body, finding its mark, centered deep within her.

"Miss Rachel ..." Vera stood in the opened door, taking in the scene. She winked at Rachel and quickly closed the door.

"Oh, my God," Rachel gasped as she pulled herself from Sin's arms. She couldn't believe what she'd just allowed to happen.

Sin was amazed as he looked at Rachel. He was still breathing hard, and he knew it would take a few minutes for him to regain control of his emotions. He couldn't remember ever being so aroused. He had been ready to make love to Rachel right here in the office. What surprised him even more was that Rachel had seemed just as eager as he was to consummate what he'd started. "Rachel?"

She held up one hand, gesturing him to silence. She couldn't look at him. Turning her back to him, she crossed the room and opened the door that led outside. She stepped into the doorway and leaned against the frame. Taking a deep breath, she looked out into the darkness. She was disgusted with herself for giving in to the attraction she felt for Sin, and she knew she'd done more than give in. Putting one hand under her hair, she rubbed the back of her neck. She shook her head, angry with herself.

Sin lowered himself to sit on the edge of the desk. He watched Rachel at the door and waited for her reaction. He was certain she would turn at any moment and hurl accusations at him about taking advantage of her. He could still feel the after effects of their embrace, and the memory of the way her soft body felt next to his brought a fresh rush of blood to his loins. Any recriminations were worth those moments.

Rachel finally turned around. She saw Sin sitting on her desk, saw the way his long legs stretched out in front of him, the way his shirt hugged his strong shoulders and arms. She let her gaze travel to his face and then to his dark eyes. She knew he was waiting for her to speak. "Well, Braddock, that solved nothing."

Sin's mouth dropped. "What?"

"I said that this little scene changed nothing between us. I still want you off my ranch, and I doubt you're prepared to leave just because I kissed you." She squared her shoulders. "Now, I better go talk to Vera. I'm going to have a lot of teasing to put up with for a while."

Sin couldn't believe it. She'd said nothing about blame. She hadn't demanded an apology, or accused him of sullying her reputation. She'd even admitted that she'd taken a part by kissing him.

"Rachel, I don't know what to say."

"Why do you think you should say something?" She closed the outside door and started toward the bar.

"I just thought you'd want me to apologize."

"For what?"

Sin rubbed his forehead. He wasn't used to this kind of honesty from a woman.

"I guess for nothing, Rachel. Never mind."

A loud crash in the bar startled them both. Rachel headed through the door into the bar with Sin right behind her.

Vera was bending over a customer with a wet towel pressed to his bleeding nose. Jace was standing above them with his fists clenched.

"Vera, what the hell's going on here?" Rachel demanded as she approached them.

"It's Jace here," Vera answered, "he's drunk as a skunk and came in looking for someone to punch."

Rachel looked at Jace and saw that he was swaying on his feet.

Sin wasn't sure what his role in all this should be. He was part owner of the Rosebud, and under different circumstances, would be happy to escort a drunk from the premises. However, seeing Rachel in Jace's arms earlier that day made him unsure how she would want him to proceed.

Rachel could tell that Jace was too drunk to reason with. He had a wild look in his eyes, a look she remembered from their youth. "Damn it, Jace. Get out of here and sleep it off!" She ordered him from the bar.

Jace was looking at Rachel through a red haze. He'd come in here to tell her he loved her. He'd already forgotten why he punched the man on the floor, and now Rachel was telling him to leave. He swayed toward her. "Rachel," he slurred her name. "I just want . . . want to tell . . ." He swayed back a bit. He focused his eyes on Sin, standing just behind Rachel.

Sin touched Rachel's arm. "Is there anything I should do?"

She jerked away from his touch. "I think you've done enough, don't you?"

Jace watched this exchange and though his brain was foggy from alcohol, he knew he didn't like Braddock touching Rachel. He squinted his eyes. She didn't seem to like it either. "Keep your hands to ... to yourself, Braddock." He was slurring badly, but the tone of his voice was deadly.

Sin straightened when he heard the challenge. He knew Jace was drunk, and he wouldn't take advantage of him, but a man Jace's size shouldn't be underestimated. "Calm down, Jace. You've got no argument with me."

"Don't ... don't tell me what to do." He tightened his fists.

Rachel could see trouble coming. "Jace, Braddock isn't telling you what to do." She planted herself more squarely between the two men. "But I am. Now get back to the ranch and get some sleep."

Sin watched the stiffness of her back and the squareness of her shoulders as she told this giant of a man what to do. He could see by the scowl on Jace's face that things were getting worse. He braced himself for what he felt was coming.

Jace didn't like Rachel telling him what to do any more than he did Braddock, and she'd been ordering him around since she hired him. He took a step toward her.

Rachel was prepared for this. She'd been handling bar fights for the better part of her life, but she wasn't prepared for Sin's reaction. From behind her, his arm went up and his hand stopped Jace cold.

A growl that turned into a curse erupted from Jace as he made a wild swing at Braddock. Sin had a handful of Jace's shirt as he sidestepped, taking Jace off balance when he did. The punch caught Rachel on the shoulder, sending her several steps back with a curse of her own.

Sin continued pulling on Jace, dragging him toward the door. Then Jace threw himself against Sin, bringing them to the floor with a crash as they hit a table on the way down. The man sitting there shouted as his drink spilled down the front of his shirt.

Vera scrambled up to stand next to Rachel. "Miss Rachel, are you all right?" She could see that she was holding her arm where Jace's punch had connected.

"Yes, I'm all right, but this has got to stop." She couldn't believe her eyes. Jace and Sin were brawling on the floor just inches from her. She looked around the Rosebud at all the curious eyes, watching with relish. "Well, I guess the busybodies got their money's worth tonight. But enough is enough." Sin was winning quickly because of Jace's drunkenness, but she could see Jace wasn't giving up easily. She pulled her gun and fired several shots into the ceiling. "Stop this, now!"

Startled, Sin stopped long enough to get hit square across the cheekbone. "Damn!" He got up above Jace and took one final swing, landing his punch like a brick against Jace's temple. The big man slumped. Sin grabbed his shirt front and dragged him to the door, stood him up, turned him around, and kicked him out into the street.

Jace hit the ground with a thud. The next thing he saw was stars. Tiny pinpoints of light in a deep black sky seemed to move around him. The only problem was that he couldn't tell if they were real or in his head. Then he saw Rachel's face above him and heard her disgusted "He'll live" as she walked away.

Inside the Rosebud, moments later, Rachel was straightening tables and chairs. "Give Sam another drink, on the house," she told Vera, who was holding a cool cloth to Sin's rapidly closing eye. "And Braddock can take care of himself."

Vera looked at Rachel suspiciously. The scene she'd witnessed in the office should have made Rachel talk a little softer toward Mr. Braddock. Rachel was sure a strange woman. "Yes, Miss Rachel." She went behind the bar to get the drink. "What were you drinkin', Sam?"

As she poured a whiskey for the disgruntled customer, Sin came up and leaned on the bar. He gestured for her to pour him the same. When she set the glass in front of him, he picked it up, turned to look at Rachel, and knocked it back in one swig.

"She's sure a tough one," Sin observed.

"She's had to be," Vera answered.

He remembered Lena had said the same thing. He was beginning to see why. This kind of life was hard.

Rachel had the mess pretty well straightened out so she went behind the bar and poured herself a drink. Her shoulder was stiffening up, and she could tell it would be sore for a few days. She winced a little as she moved her arm around to loosen the shoulder. She noticed Sin watching her and stopped.

"Is it bad?" he asked.

"No. I'm fine." She abruptly turned to Vera. "I'm going to call it a night. I'll see you in a day or two." She headed toward the door.

"Wait a minute, Rachel, and I'll ride back with you." Sin had noticed the way she avoided admitting she was in pain. It surprised him until he realized she would consider showing pain as a sign of weakness, a correlation most men would make.

She stopped. "Why?"

"Why should I ride back with you?"

She frowned and nodded.

He realized his mistake in time and smiled. "Because I'm afraid of the dark?"

Rachel looked at his smile, the way the corners of his mouth pulled up a little unevenly, the stark white contrast of his teeth against his dark skin. It irritated her that he was so darn good-looking, but she supposed he couldn't help it. Even now, with one eye half swollen shut, he was nothing any woman would turn away from a cold bed. "You understand that I'd just as soon you stay here in town?" she asked him.

"I understand. But you understand I'm coming, whether you like it or not. Right?"

"Right." She scowled at him.

"Then we might as well ride back together."

"Suit yourself." Rachel went out the door and straight to where Roux was tethered.

Sin shook his head and followed.

Rachel stared up at the ceiling of her room and stretched in her bed. She flinched as she tested the soreness of her shoulder. Jace could sure pack a wallop. Even drunk, he was more than a match for most men. Braddock had even had some trouble handling him. She smiled when she thought about the black eye Sin'd be wearing for a while. Served him right for interfering. If he hadn't butted in she would have calmed Jace down with no trouble. She felt a nagging suspicion that that wasn't entirely true, but she pushed it aside.

The sky was barely gray but dawn was coming quickly, and she had a full day ahead of her. The fence, forming the large corral they used during roundup, was just about repaired and she wanted to start the men gathering some of the cattle in the lower, more easily accessible regions of the range. She also had to go through her father's desk again, to find the addresses of the Northern buyers they used to supply. One sad truth about this war was that the South had no money, and money was what she needed to save the Triple X. She had to put political loyalties aside and sell her beef to the highest bidder, and if her father's ledgers were correct, the South had no bidders at all.

She had washed, dressed, and was about to pull on her boots when she heard Sin moving around in the next room. She tiptoed to the door to eavesdrop. She heard him splash water into the basin, then listened to the sounds of him getting dressed, holding her breath when she heard the jingle of his belt buckle. Swallowing, she slowly backed away from the door and began breathing again. During the long ride home the night before, they'd barely spoken, and as soon as Roux was taken care of, she'd gone to bed. But throughout the night she'd remembered Sin's kiss and the way her own traitorous body had responded. Realizing that Sin's tremendous appeal made him a more dangerous adversary, she was determined to keep a distance between them. She wasn't about to let him use sex as a weapon to soften her resolve to get him off the Triple X.

Sin had lain awake most of the night listening to the silence of the house and straining to hear Rachel. He'd even gotten up twice to listen at the door, hoping he would hear her breathe. Kissing her last night had changed something in him. The attraction he'd felt for her from the first had solidified somehow. It bothered him like hell to know that she didn't want anything to do with him. Oh, yes, she'd kissed him back all right, but she'd hated herself for it. He rubbed his hand over his jaw, then touched his lips with one finger, remembering how she tasted. He shook himself for being so foolish and practically growled out loud as he got up to wash, shave, and dress. A little while later he heard Rachel's boot heels on the wood floor as she left her room to go downstairs.

"Miss Rachel, I will not make this ... pastry, Lucy calls it, for hungry men. They need meat and potatoes and eggs in the morning, and tortillas!" Lena was fuming at her and holding a recipe book that Lucy had obviously instructed her to use.

"Now, Lena," Rachel looked around for Lucy, wondering how she could cause such a commotion and not stick around for the results, "I'm sure Aunt Lucy was just making a suggestion."

Lena shook her head and then the offensive book. "She told me to make this for breakfast." She pointed to a recipe for french puff pastry. "Do you know what the men would do if I put these silly little things on the table for them?"

Rachel almost laughed at the picture it conjured up

but knew better than to upset Lena any more. She took her responsibilities very seriously and prided herself on her cooking, which Rachel had to admit was excellent.

"Lena, you make the normal breakfast, and I'll deal with Aunt Lucy. She means well. She just doesn't know how men eat." She took the recipe book from Lena's hand. "I'll give this back to her. All right?"

Lena turned her head slightly, not sure that Rachel could deal with the overbearing woman. "All right, for now."

Rachel put her arm around Lena's shoulders. "It'll be fine. I promise. Now, I need a cup of coffee, please."

"Are you sure you wouldn't like tea? I have a whole pot made," Lena said sarcastically.

Rachel tried not to tighten her expression. "Coffee, please, Lena. And some steak and tortillas—I'm starving." She smiled at Lena and finally got a smile in return.

"*Sí*, Miss Rachel. It'll be ready in just a few minutes." She turned to the cupboards and began to grab ingredients.

"I'll be in my father's office for a while." She filled a coffee cup and left the kitchen. She could hear Lena talking to herself as she went through the dining room.

The half hour she spent going through her father's old papers wasn't as bad as she'd expected. The healing process had begun, and whether she liked to admit it or not, Sin's being there, forcing her to face things, was doing her some good.

More than once she felt like kicking herself for not being aware of the dire financial situation her father had gotten them into. When he was alive they'd fallen into a routine; he'd taken care of all the paperwork for the ranch, and she'd begun overseeing all of the outside work. It was an arrangement that suited her just fine. She had always hated paperwork. She was perfectly capable of doing it, but when given the choice of sitting inside at a desk or riding Roux to herd cattle all day, she had no trouble making her preference known. If only she'd questioned what Hyram was doing once in a while, maybe he'd have confided their situation to her, and the subsequent loan. But she knew that if he were alive today she'd still be going on blindly, happily content to let her life continue as it always had. She shook her head when she thought about all the changes that had taken place in her life in the last month.

"Miss Rachel, your breakfast is ready," Lena called.

"I'll be there in a minute," she answered. She'd found the names and addresses she was looking for and was just putting away the other papers when she heard a noise at the door and looked up.

"Tish, my darling, good morning." She smiled as the warm feeling of love filled her heart at the sight of her sleepy daughter.

"Good morning, Mama. What are you doing?" Tish padded into the room on slippered feet and crawled onto her mother's lap.

"Just looking for some important papers. How's my girl this morning?" She squeezed the tiny body pressed to hers and smelled the sweet scent of her still messy hair.

"I'm fine, Mama. I dreamt that I rode Poco all night. It was wonderful," she sighed.

Rachel marveled at how much her daughter was like herself. "Lena has breakfast ready. Are you hungry?"

"Oh yes! May I have two helpings of tortillas?"

Rachel laughed. "If you can eat two helpings."

"I can, I can." She climbed down from Rachel's lap and ran for the door, sliding on the rug as she went. "I'll race you!"

"Slow down, my darling. You'll fall," she called after her, but Tish was already gone.

She was still smiling with the glow of pure pleasure when she entered the kitchen moments later, and Sin's heart skipped a beat when he saw her. The look on her face hardened when she noticed him, and she glanced away. He lowered his eyes to his coffee cup.

"Your food is ready. Do you want it here or with the men?" Lena asked Rachel as she shoveled a huge steak and fried eggs onto a plate, then, "Tish, stop jumping around, *niña*. This pan is hot."

"But I am sooo hungry," Tish sang as she danced around Lena.

Rachel started laughing at her daughter. "I'll eat with the men, Lena. Tish, leave Lena alone so she can get your breakfast. Now, come here and sit down." She guided her daughter to the seat directly across the table from Sin.

He set his cup down and watched the exchange with a little envy and some amazement. Rachel was an entirely different person with Tish. Her normal abrupt manner was replaced by a softness she showed only to the little girl. There was a kind, even tone to her voice when she spoke, and her normal, deliberate, no-nonsense way of moving was replaced by a subtle, caressing way of completing tasks. He doubted she was even aware of the change herself, but it was obvious to anyone with eyes that Rachel loved her daughter more than anything or anyone else in her world.

Rachel felt herself under Sin's scrutiny and didn't like it much. She knew that if she met his gaze she would remember all too well the dizzying effect his kiss had caused. She'd been remembering and reliving those feelings all morning. Deliberately refusing to look his way, she crossed to the large dining area off the kitchen and, with the toe of her boot, kicked open the screen door connecting the two rooms.

"Mornin' Rachel," Hank greeted her as she entered.

"Mornin' Hank." She looked around the room at the men seated there and noticed Jace was missing. She sat down, picked up her fork and a tortilla and spoke quietly, "He didn't make it back?"

"Oh, he made it back all right. Came crashing into the bunkhouse madder 'n sin. Tried to start a fight with Stoker, but Stoker wouldn't have none of it." Hank took a drink of his coffee.

"Where is he now?"

Hank grinned. "Last I saw of him, he was headed for the outhouse, real quick."

Rachel smiled too. "Serves him right. You think he'll work today?"

"Will if he knows what's good for 'im."

Rachel heard the door from the kitchen open but didn't look up. She knew it would be Sin coming to breakfast.

"You got yourself quite a shiner there, Mr. Braddock," Hank exclaimed as Sin seated himself next to Rachel.

She looked up quickly then. She hadn't noticed how badly his eye was bruised because she hadn't looked squarely at him yet. She had to stifle a laugh. Sin's eye was indeed blackened and swollen nearly shut. It looked very painful. She stared back down at her plate of food, not wanting to comment until she heard his explanation.

Sin watched Rachel's reaction. She obviously hadn't had time to say anything to Hank about his fight with Jace, and it rankled him to see she was smiling at his expense. It also bothered him that she wouldn't look straight at him this morning. She was ignoring what had happened between them last night, and whether she was ready to face it or not, she was attracted to him, and he knew it.

He looked at Hank. "Yeah, I got it fighting a battle for Rachel last night."

Rachel nearly choked as she tried to swallow and talk at the same time. "You what?" She slammed her fork to the table. "You got that black eye because you stuck your nose in where it didn't belong." Rachel noticed the other men at the table had quit eating and were watching her with surprise. She didn't want to have an argument with Sin in front of the men, but this had to be straightened out. "If you hadn't been there I'd have calmed ... everything down a lot quicker." She glanced at Hank, then back at Sin.

"If I hadn't been there you might have been wearing this black eye instead of me," Sin countered.

"Don't be ridiculous."

"Ridiculous? How's your shoulder this morning?"

Rachel glowered at Sin. Her shoulder was indeed stiff and sore, but no one would have known it without his comment.

Hank's brow furrowed with concern. "You all right, Miss Rachel?"

"I'm fine, Hank. It's nothing more than a bruise, and an accident at that," she answered.

The creak of the outside door opening took everyone's attention. There standing just inside, with his hat pulled low over his battered face, was Jace. A very green Jace.

"Ho-ly cow," whispered Ben from across the room.

Stoker elbowed Ben in the ribs to silence him. In that moment everyone in the room knew what had happened the night before. At least everyone thought they knew. And Rachel didn't like what she could tell they were thinking.

"Good morning, Jace." She spoke directly to him. Facing him down should put some of the men's questions to rest. "Are you all right this morning?"

Jace looked at her, sitting there next to Braddock. He lowered his eyelids a bit. "Yeah, Rachel . . . Miss Rachel. I'm fine."

Sin could hear the slight edge to Jace's voice and didn't like it. This man was going to cause more trouble. He could feel it. Sin looked at Rachel as she sat smiling at Jace, trying to smooth things over with him and shook his head a little.

Rachel gestured toward the table. "Sit down and have some breakfast. There's fresh coffee in the pot."

Jace sat down at the far end of the table. He couldn't eat yet. His stomach recoiled every time he thought about food and the smell of the fried steak and sight of half-eaten eggs was making it nearly impossible to remain in the room.

"Ya' don't look too good, Jace," Ben teased from behind his coffee cup. The look Jace gave him kept him and anyone else from further taunts.

Sin watched the big man and wondered how to handle this. He supposed it was up to him to make amends, and though he didn't like doing it, he stood and crossed the room to stand at the foot of the table, opposite Jace.

Rachel watched as Sin held out his hand to Jace. She could see Jace hesitate a moment before he responded in a like manner.

"No hard feelings?" Sin asked.

"Nah, I guess not," Jace replied. He did have hard feelings, but now wasn't the time to show it.

Sin wasn't sure how sincere Jace was but decided to accept what he got. The handshake was brief. Sin touched his eye. "You pack quite a wallop." He offered a smile and tried to make the situation lighter.

"Jace hits pretty good, hey?" Stoker asked.

Jace rubbed his own bruised jaw and nodded. "You don't hit like a schoolgirl either, Braddock."

Ben snickered and the tenseness of the moment seemed to pass.

Rachel let out her breath slowly. She hadn't been sure how Jace would react to Sin when he saw him. Thank God, he decided not to cause any more trouble. Out of the corner of her eye she noticed Hank move and looked in time to see him take his hand from his gun. She raised her eyebrows to him. He just shrugged and drank from his cup again.

"I'm going to stay at the house this morning for a while, Hank."

He didn't answer, just waited for her to continue.

"My Aunt Lucy and her children arrived here yesterday, and I have to figure out what to do with them."

Sin walked back over to where she was sitting and poured himself another cup of coffee.

"They staying long?" Hank asked.

"Looks like forever."

Hank's brows raised. "That long, huh."

Rachel sighed. "Yeah, that long."

Hank set his cup down. "Time to get to work, boys." He stood and took his hat off its peg on the wall. "Jace, you help finish the fence today."

Jace looked gratefully at Hank. He was sure he'd have died if he'd had to herd cattle or break mares today. The pounding in his head was no better now than an hour ago, and he feared it wouldn't ease up for quite a while. He stood up slowly and passed Rachel without looking at her. He did, however, give Braddock a sideways glance.

7

When Rachel entered the kitchen a short time later, she was met with a sight like none she'd seen before. Lily was seated at the table, sipping tea, wearing some sort of filmy pink dressing gown that barely covered the white skin of her shoulders and more than half-exposed breasts. Her flesh seemed to glow in the reflected sunlight from the kitchen window and her hair, a mass of strawberry curls, was held, not too tidily, by a string of lace the same color as the gown. Yards and yards of fabric billowed around Lily, giving the impression that she sat naked in the center of a large pink cloud.

"Cousin Lily?"

"Yes, Rachel?" Lily looked sleepily at her cousin and yawned.

Rachel could think of nothing to say, at least nothing "polite" to say. She looked around the kitchen and found they were the only ones present. "Where are Tish and Lena?"

Lily sighed. "I couldn't begin to guess. They left when I came in. I even had to get my own tea."

Rachel's eyes opened wider. The girl was actually pouting.

"Do you think the maid will be back soon? I am getting rather hungry," Lily asked.

"Lena is not the maid. She's the housekeeper." Rachel didn't know why it all of sudden mattered to her what Lena's title was, but it did. "And I suggest that if you want to eat breakfast, you get up when it's being served."

Lily looked a little startled. "Are you angry with me, Cousin Rachel?"

Rachel wasn't angry with Lily. She just wasn't used to having a lot of people around the house. Not even one full day had passed since her relatives' arrival, and she couldn't expect everything to flow smoothly at first.

"I'm sorry, Lily. I'm not angry with you. It's just been a rough morning so far."

"Oh, how dreadful for you. Would you like some tea?"

"No, thank you. Where is your mother?" Rachel sat down across from Lily. She still had the cookbook to deal with.

"I haven't a notion where mother is." She took another sip of tea. "By the way, where is Mr. Braddock this morning?"

"In Hades, for all I care," fumed Rachel. She was still angry with him for the remark about fighting her battle for her and assumed he was now outside with the other men.

Lily gasped. "My goodness, you don't seem to care for Mr. Braddock at all."

Rachel looked at her sharply. "Why should I?"

"Well, he is your partner."

"Not by choice. I'd just as soon shoot him as look at him," Rachel answered heatedly.

"Excuse me, ladies." Sin pushed open the door. "May I come in?"

"Why of course, Mr. Braddock. Do join us," Lily gushed.

Rachel looked at the girl in amazement. Her skin had taken on a pink glow and her breath, coming in short gasps, was causing her breasts to nearly swell from their flimsy binding.

Sin walked to Lily's side. "You're looking lovely this morning, Miss Lily."

"Why, Mr. Braddock. I look positively horrid. I just woke up, and I always look like death first thing in the morning." She batted her eyelashes at him. "But whatever happened to your poor eye?" She reached up one delicate finger and gently touched the edge of the discoloration on his cheekbone.

Sin glanced at Rachel, then answered, "Just a minor misunderstanding. But even with only one eye to see with, you're as far from death as is possible, unless we are discussing heaven."

"Oh, Mr. Braddock." Lily breathed even deeper and turned her head to the side in false modesty.

Rachel had never seen such a disgusting display in all her life. She couldn't believe the way Lily was eating up the crap Sin was serving, and she couldn't believe how easily he did it. She stood up, scraping the chair roughly across the floor as she did. "You two enjoy yourselves, I've got to find Lucy and say good-bye to Tish before I go to work." She was out the door and headed upstairs before either one could react.

Upstairs, Rachel passed Tish's room and saw that Lena was helping her get dressed. She then found Lucy in her room unpacking her things and placing them neatly in the armoire.

Lucy looked up when she heard Rachel at the door. "Rachel, my dear. How are you this morning?"

"I'm fine, Aunt Lucy. How are you?"

"I suppose I'm fine."

Rachel could hear the implication that she wasn't at all fine. "What's the matter, Aunt Lucy?"

"Nothing to concern yourself with, I'm sure. I'll be fine."

Rachel resisted the urge to roll her eyes. "Aunt Lucy, I am concerned with your happiness. Now please tell me what's bothering you."

"If you insist." She heaved a great sigh and sat on the edge of the bed. "Come sit beside me, Rachel."

Rachel found herself drawn down to sit next to her aunt.

"You see, my dear, I was the head of a household with several servants for most of my life. Coming here, though the prudent choice because of the war, has made me feel like ... like a fish out of water, I guess. I had no idea how different Texas was from what I used to. I assumed that things would be very similar because your father and mother were both Southerners." She took a hankie from her sleeve and mopped her brow. "It's so very hot here. I do hope I get used to it. I barely slept last night."

Rachel looked at her aunt and felt a small stab of pity. The woman had come, making a ridiculous claim on the ranch, and gotten off on the wrong foot with her, but hearing Lucy talk like this was making Rachel realize how difficult it had been for her to leave her home, even though threatened by war. "Don't worry, Aunt Lucy. You're very welcome here."

"But what am I to do?"

Rachel's mind raced. What was she to do? Lena ran the household with enough efficiency to keep her and Tish happy, and it was obvious she didn't want interference from an intruder. The cookbook was evidence of that. Damn, the cookbook, she'd forgotten it downstairs. Oh, well. Right now she needed to deal with Lucy. But how could she tell this woman to live as a guest for the rest of her life? "Perhaps you could help Lena?"

"Help the help?" Lucy looked incredulously at Rachel.

"Well, yes. For a while. We do things differently here, as you said yourself. There are a lot of things you could learn from Lena." She smiled, hoping her aunt would agree.

"Rachel, some things may be different, but poor cooking and unkemptness are not acceptable anywhere." She had stiffened her back as she spoke.

"Lena is a wonderful cook," Rachel defended, "and the house is clean enough for me."

"That's because you don't know any better," Lucy puffed.

Rachel rubbed her forehead. This conversation was not going as she had hoped. "Aunt Lucy, if there are special meals you would like prepared, please feel free to ask Lena to learn how to make them, but don't interfere with what she cooks for the men or me. She showed me the cookbook you gave her. She won't be using it." Rachel raised herself from the bed. "And as far as you having something to do around here, please, by all means, try to fit in. Clean anything you wish to."

The sun was high in the sky and beating down with a vengeance by the time Rachel was on her way back from town. She'd gotten the telegrams to the Northern buyers sent and stopped in at the Rosebud for just a minute. Vera had been surprised to see her so soon again, and managed to inquire, with much innuendo, how Mr. Braddock was doing this morning.

"Roux, I shouldn't have snapped at Vera like I did."

The horse bobbed his head in response to the sound of her voice.

"You know, boy, sometimes I almost believe you really do understand me." She patted his neck, then stretched a little in the saddle. "God, it's hot today. I think this is the worst so far this season."

She could see the ranch buildings in the distance, could see one side of the huge corral, and even make out a few men on horseback on a distant ridge. This was her world. She always felt good when she rode home, especially when she was alone and could think out loud if she needed to.

"I wonder how long it will take the buyers to contact me in return?" The rhythmic beat of Roux's hooves echoed in her mind. "If we get roundup started a little early we could get top dollar for the beef, and the Triple X will be out of trouble." She wiped a trickle of perspiration from her cheek with one gloved fingertip. She was already feeling relief at having solved the money problem. If she could only solve her current people problems so easily.

Out of the corner of her eye she saw a horse galloping across the open range. She looked closer. It was one of the Triple X horses, she was sure. But who was riding a horse that hard in this heat? Then she heard the faint cry.

"Good lord, Roux. It's Jeremy!" In one movement she turned the horse and had him galloping in the direction of the screaming child. She was riding hard and fast and the sweat began pouring down her back and face, but she was oblivious to the discomfort in her efforts to save Jeremy.

"Faster, Roux." She spurred him slightly and bent low over his neck to pick up speed. Then she noticed another rider following Jeremy in an attempt to help stop him. It was Sin. They were riding intercepting courses toward the boy and only terrain could dictate which one would reach him first. Rachel heard Jeremy cry out again, and her heart lurched with concern. The poor child must be terrified, she thought, and spurred Roux again. "Sorry, old friend," she whispered.

Jeremy's course was taking him up a rise that had a sharp drop on one side, the side Rachel was coming from. She had to adjust her direction, pulling Roux to the left, closer to the path taken by Sin. This put her some distance behind Sin in their rescue attempts but she kept Roux's pace hard. She could see Sin was nearly even with Jeremy's horse and watched as he reached for the reins. The horse's eyes were wild when Sin pulled back to stop him. Rachel arrived in time to grab Jeremy from the horse's back as it reared and bit at the air in anger. Foam flew from its mouth, and its coat glistened white with lather.

"Get the boy away!" shouted Sin as he attempted to get control of the wild animal.

Rachel was already putting some distance between

them, holding Jeremy to her side with one arm. She could feel the wracking sobs of his body and wanted to get to a safe spot to examine him for injury. She pulled Roux to a stop and dropped the reins. Gently, she lowered Jeremy to the ground, then jumped down and knelt in front of him.

"Jeremy, are you all right?" She was inspecting his arms and legs for bites or bruises. Then she heard the laughter.

"Cousin Rachel. Did you see how fast I was going?"

Rachel looked up at the boy's face. What she thought were cries of terror had been shouts of glee. The sobs had been hiccups.

"I never knew horses could run so fast!" Jeremy was still excited.

Rachel couldn't speak. She was so angry she wanted to scream, to punch something, or someone. She looked at her young cousin. How could he be so stupid? He could have killed himself or the horse or both of them. As it was, he might have ruined the horse. She looked to where Sin finally had the poor animal under control and was walking him slowly to cool him down.

Sin felt Rachel's gaze and started her way. "How's the boy?" he questioned when close enough.

Rachel looked back at Jeremy who was covered from head to toe with dust but still had a huge grin on his face. Her anger hadn't subsided when she answered. "He's fine. The little shit did it on purpose!" She walked to Roux's side and picked up the reins.

"He what?" Sin wasn't sure he'd heard her correctly.

"I said, he did it on purpose," she repeated heatedly.

Jeremy ran to Rachel's side. "Are you cross with me?" He'd never been called a "shit" before, at least not by an adult. When he thought about it, he'd never heard a woman swear before. He liked it. He liked Rachel. In fact, in that moment she became his idol, and he didn't want her angry with him. "Rachel, I'm sorry." He still wasn't sure what he'd done wrong, but he wanted to make amends. He touched her shirtsleeve.

"Please, Cousin Rachel?" He wanted her to look at him and see how sorry he was.

Rachel took a deep breath. She turned to face the small boy. "Jeremy, tomorrow you start school. Every day after school you will have horse lessons." She saw his face light up. "Not riding lessons. Horse lessons." Bewilderment crossed his face. "Every day you will rub down the horses. You will feed them, clean their stalls, and help shoe them. After I am sure that you understand that horses are valuable, intelligent animals, you will begin riding lessons." She looked up at Sin and thought she saw a smile hidden beneath the firm line of his lips. "Hand Jeremy the reins to his horse."

"My horse?" Jeremy inquired in a quiet voice.

"Yes, your horse. You nearly killed him, now you can take care of him. His name is Brandy. Lead him back to the barn."

"Lead him?" Jeremy asked, disbelieving. Horses were to be ridden.

Rachel mounted Roux, then looked down on her small cousin. "First lesson. You overheated him. You cool him down."

Jeremy knew better than to argue further. He took the reins from Mr. Braddock and began walking his horse back to the ranch. He started smiling. His horse. His very own horse. He couldn't wait to tell his mother!

Sin rode up beside Rachel. "I thought for a moment there you were going to kill him."

"I thought for a moment I might. At least I wanted to."

"You handled it pretty well."

"Thanks."

"You handle most things pretty well."

Rachel looked at him from the corner of her eye. This conversation was making her uncomfortable. She didn't want compliments from Sin. "Thanks. I've got work to do." She turned Roux in another direction.

Sin pulled his own horse to a stop. "Rachel?"

"Gotta go." She called over her shoulder.

He watched her straight back as she rode away. Her hair was stringy with perspiration and sticking to her neck and face in wet curls. The dust from their ride was clinging to her clothes and streaked her skin where she'd rubbed away the sweat with her gloves. As she got further from him she adjusted her seat, patted Roux's neck and pulled her hat lower over her eyes. Sin couldn't remember ever being so impressed with a woman or ever thinking he'd seen one so beautiful.

Rachel circled around the corral and saw that they'd just about finished repairing the fence. She found Hank on the far side.

"Howdy, Miss Rachel." He untied his handkerchief from around his neck and wiped the sweat from his eyes.

"Hello, Hank. I sent word to the Northern buyers this morning. Should hear back fairly soon. Can you get the men started on roundup early?"

He took off his hat and rubbed the sweat from his nearly bald head. "Yeah, I can get our boys goin'. What about the other ranchers? If you start early, they should too."

"Yeah, I thought of that. When I hear from the buyers I'll discuss it with the other ranchers. I don't know how all of them will feel about selling to the Yanks, but I've got to make some money, and I'll bet I'm not the only one."

"Well, soon as you hear let me know and I'll tell the men. Some of them might leave, but I reckon most'll stay on."

"I hope so." She looked at the men working around her. Good men, every one. Then she saw Jace. He had stopped working and was watching her. She smiled at him, but he didn't return the smile. He must be angry about last night, she thought. She turned back to Hank. If Jace wanted to hang on to his anger, it was fine with her. Maybe it would solve the problem of what to do about his infatuation with her.

Jace could tell Rachel was thinking about him, even though she was no longer looking his way. He'd tried to tell her how he felt yesterday in the barn. He remembered how she'd returned his kiss, remembered how her soft body had melded with his for those precious moments before she pulled away. His hands ached with the need to once again feel the full curve of her breasts, and he longed to taste her sweet kiss. He couldn't remember how many times she'd lain with him in the tall grass by Leaver Creek when they were kids, but he did remember how she'd opened herself to him, giving all she had to give. He wanted that kind of surrender from her again. She was so distant now, so in control, but with the right set of circumstances he was sure he could get what he wanted. He just had to be patient.

Rachel glanced once more in Jace's direction before she rode away. He was still watching her, and she felt a slight chill despite the intense heat of the day.

As Rachel rode toward the ranch yard she could see a group of men gathered around a large tree. She couldn't see what was holding their attention, so she headed that way. When she got close enough, she stopped dead.

"What's the hell's going on here?" she demanded.

The gathering broke apart as the men were startled by Rachel's appearance.

"Cousin Rachel, do join us. I was just getting to know these lovely gentlemen," Lily invited.

Rachel surveyed the group. She could have called them many things, but "lovely gentlemen" wouldn't have been one of her choices. Stoker stood next to Lily, grinning sheepishly at Rachel. He actually had a small bouquet of wildflowers in one hand. Ben was holding his hat and had begun twisting it nervously.

"I suppose this means that you all have your work done for the day?" She looked from man to man, and none of them could meet her glare. "No one wants to answer?" She kept scanning the group for a spokesman.

"Now, Cousin, please don't be cross. I asked these gentlemen to join me. I was so lonely as I took my afternoon stroll, and they were kind enough to make me feel welcome."

Rachel let her gaze take in her cousin's attire. She was clothed from head to foot in white eyelet. Tiny pink rosettes adorned the low neckline of her gown and pink ribbon bound her small waist, then fell to the ground at her feet. Rachel became very aware of her own appearance. The fact that she wore men's clothing, usually her father's castoffs, had seemed only practical before. Right now she realized how terrible she must look to these men. Her lack of confidence lasted only a moment, though, then she brought herself up short. Her attire was practical. This was a cattle ranch and it was her duty to see to its smooth operation. It was her cousin Lily who was dressed inappropriately, however attractively, and she must make certain that she wasn't allowed to disrupt the work schedule, especially when they might be starting roundup so soon. "Stoker, you and the other men get back to work."

"Yes, Miss Rachel." He hung his head and walked toward the barn, with the other men going off in their own directions.

"Lily, we need to have a talk." She swung her leg across Roux's neck and jumped to the ground in her customary fashion. She saw the disapproving way Lily watched her.

"Yes, Cousin Rachel. What would you like to talk about?"

Rachel reached down and touched the fabric of Lily's skirt. She hadn't removed her gloves yet, and Lily grimaced as the leather left a spot of dust where she'd touched. "This is what I want to discuss. Your dress."

"What's wrong with my dress?"

"Absolutely nothing. In fact, it's quite beautiful, for a garden party or a tea social in the city." She took off her gloves and slapped the dust from them against her leg. "But it couldn't be more inappropriate on a cattle ranch."

"But, I . . ." Lily began to sputter.

"Don't interrupt me, please. The dress is lovely and if the occasion should arise that we have cause for celebration you should, by all means, wear it again. Until then, please wear something more practical."

"I don't know what you're talking about."

Rachel thought she'd made herself clear. "The dress is inappropriate for a cattle ranch. You're distracting the men. I need their minds on work."

Lily waved a dismissing hand at Rachel. "I know I'm a distraction. I don't know what you're talking about when you say I should wear something else. I don't own anything else."

Rachel frowned. Was it possible that what Lily said was true? Were all her gowns as frilly and useless as this? "I'm sure you have something else."

"No, Cousin. I do not. And I must say that my feelings are hurt. I am trying to get to know everyone here, trying to make myself presentable so you'll be proud to claim me as a relative, and instead of appreciating my attempt, you attack me for it." Lily took a small hankie from the fold of her skirt and touched the corners of her eyes.

"Lily," Rachel began, "I realize this must be a difficult time for you and I appreciate your attempt to ... make friends, but I really must insist you find something else to wear." She watched Lily as she spoke. "You will come to realize in time that living out here will be much easier for you if you're dressed properly, especially when you start finding things to do."

"What kind of things?" Lily whimpered.

Rachel sighed heavily. "I don't know. Maybe you'd like to learn to ride, or possibly help with some of the chores. Your mother has expressed an interest in cleaning things."

Lily gasped in shock. "You expect me to do chores?"

"Well, I ..." Rachel didn't know what to say.

"I'm truly insulted, Cousin Rachel. I don't do chores. That is something left for the servants, and I'm sure mother was only speaking of overseeing the cleaning. I suppose you'll want me to start wearing trousers and shoveling horse dung next!" She stood and started indignantly for the house.

Rachel shook her head and muttered, "It might, in fact, do you some good."

Lily's shriek brought the closest men running when she slipped and fell flat on her backside. "Goodness, I'm going to faint," she called to her rescuers.

Rachel started to laugh as three of her crew began to tussle over who was going to help Miss Lily stand up. In the end they each grabbed a part of her and started to pull. She was shrieking even louder by the time she was standing.

Rachel had walked closer, still laughing, to watch the scene.

"What ever did I slip on?" Lily questioned the group.

"Horse dung." Rachel supplied.

"Oh! Halifax!" Lily shrieked once again and began running to the house. "I'm going to hate it in this awful place."

Rachel was still chuckling as she mounted Roux. She'd been laughing so hard she had tears in her eyes. Sometimes there was justice in the world, and once in a while a person got to see it. She grinned as she headed for the swimming hole. "Come on, Roux. Let's take a dip."

The swimming hole in Leaver Creek sat just a little lower than the rest of the range. Surrounded by black willows and deep brush as it was, it provided privacy for the swimmers enjoying its coolness on hot days. As Rachel rode through the waving branches of a willow to get to the creek, she was completely hidden from view for a few moments. It always felt like entering another world to her, this transition from the heat and wind of the range to the soft protective breezes of this secluded spot. The few minutes she was able to steal for herself here from time to time meant a lot.

Today, she was still laughing to herself, picturing Lily falling on her butt in the ranch yard, when she emerged from the leaves and found Sin standing stark naked at the water's edge. He saw her in the same moment and dove head first under the water, but not before the startled expression registered on her face, and she got a good view of his more private, and, she noticed, well-endowed male parts.

"Holy shit," she exclaimed, and whistled to herself. Moments passed and Sin was still under water. She started to wonder if he was going to try to stay under until she left. "Hey, Braddock!" she called. She wasn't leaving, and he'd have to come up for air pretty soon.

Sin couldn't believe the timing. If Rachel had showed up one second later, she wouldn't have seen him until he was already in the water. Damn it, he thought, as he surfaced and shook the water from his eyes. He wasn't particularly shy, but he didn't like being on display for a fully clothed woman on horseback. Especially for one now having such a good laugh at his expense. "What's so funny?" he demanded.

"You are," she said through her mirth. "I thought for a minute there you'd be willing to drown yourself rather than come up for air." She was still sitting high on Roux, and it was obvious that Sin didn't realize how clear the water was. Even though he was standing chest deep, she could see his body almost as well as when he was standing on the shore.

"I'm not used to having an audience when I bathe," he answered, "especially a woman."

Her gaze traveled from the interesting aspects of his body under the water and focused for a moment on his shoulders and face. She noticed an angry, jagged scar just below his left shoulder. She was curious how he got it, but her gaze was once more pulled to the underwater scene.

"I suppose you're not used to being nude in public, but if you'd have started to drown I would have had to save you. Then I'd have gotten an even closer look at what you're trying to hide." She smiled down at him.

It was the first truly unguarded smile he'd received from Rachel, and his breath caught in his throat as he smiled back. "Why don't you get down and join me?"

"I'm thinking about it." That's not what she was thinking about at all. But she couldn't tell him the truth, that watching his body was having a very powerful effect on her.

Sin was surprised. She wouldn't really swim with him, would she? He doubted it. But something was keeping her here. He watched her eyes. Her lids were lowered slightly and with her hat low over her forehead, it was hard to see her clearly. He noticed that her breathing was becoming a little heavier, and her breasts seemed to push against her shirt more than a moment ago. He felt himself growing in response.

Rachel observed the change in his body and had a hard time swallowing. This peeping-tom game had gone a bit too far for her and as exciting as it was to watch the water playing with Sin's body, she couldn't sit there any longer.

"Rachel?"

"I guess I'd better get back to work. You were here first." She smiled again, this time it was forced.

"Rachel, you could swim with me ... if you wanted to."

She turned Roux. "I don't think that would be a very good idea." She started Roux back through the trees.

Sin didn't want her to go. He wanted to see her smile again. He wanted ... Oh, hell, he wanted her.

"Rachel!" He called her more loudly, now that she was no longer visible.

She heard him calling her and, despite her resolve, she wanted to go back. She wanted to undress and slide into the water next to him, but she knew that wasn't possible. If only he weren't a threat to her ranch. If only she'd met him under different circumstances. But she hadn't. And wishing for things didn't make them so.

"Rachel, what are you afraid of?" His voice carried through the trees.

She stopped Roux. She heard the challenge in his voice. Did he think he could goad her into making a mistake? She waited for a moment, listening for what he'd say next.

Sin waited too. He hoped, probably foolishly, he admitted, that she'd come back. "Rachel?" He called again, more softly this time, almost positive she could no longer hear him.

She did hear. She sat perfectly still and listened. She listened when he slapped the water in frustration. She listened when he swore at nothing in particular, and she listened when he emerged from the water. Throughout all his actions she pictured his nude body, powerful, muscular, and fully capable of satisfying all her needs.

"Damn him," she whispered as she quietly turned Roux toward the house.

Sin lay on his back on the soft grass at the water's edge with one arm thrown over his eyes. The breeze blowing across his nude body should have had a relaxing effect, but he was too keyed up after his encounter with Rachel. He could still see her in his mind, watching him. He would imagine the heat from her green eyes, and he would become aroused all over again. Memories of the way she felt in his arms at the Rosebud added to his arousal. Torturing himself wasn't doing him any good. He stood and threw himself into the water, hoping to cool the fire he'd built with his thoughts. I'm the biggest damned fool I've ever known, he thought bitterly as he swam.

Rachel watched for Sin to leave the creek, then waited until she was sure of privacy before she went to swim and cool off. It occurred to her, now there were so many people living with her on the Triple X, she'd have to be more careful about swimming nude. The hands never used the swimming hole until after work, so the days had been hers. Now things were different. Catching Sin the way she had proved that. She floated on her back and looked up at the sky through the leaves. She was certain that Lucy and Lily wouldn't even be tempted to swim—the thought made her laugh—but Sin and Jeremy could come upon her anytime. Yes, she'd have to think about her privacy if she wanted to preserve it.

A short while later, as she rode back to the house, Jace rode in the opposite direction from the creek. He'd thoroughly enjoyed watching Rachel as she swam naked across the creek. He watched her every move and knew that someday soon he'd make her see how things should be between them again.

8

I went back and swam," Rachel answered Sin's raised eyebrows when he saw her wet hair.

"Alone?"

She passed him as she took the three back steps in one jump and went through the screen door into the house. She glanced back over her shoulder as he followed, seemingly expecting an answer. "Of course alone. What business is it of yours anyway?"

Sin realized that if he didn't tread very carefully he would cause more problems between them than now existed. It had occurred to him as he rode back to the ranch that the swimming hole could be a very dangerous place for a woman alone. Especially one who swam nude. Anyone could surprise her, just like Rachel had surprised him earlier, but the outcome could prove to be terrifyingly unpleasant, if not fatal.

"Rachel, I'm just concerned about your safety."

They were now in the kitchen, and she stopped and turned to face him. "Listen, Braddock, I've been riding around this ranch, by myself, for the past twenty-seven years. I've had to shoot several rattlesnakes, chase off a couple of Indians and, in recent years, some deserters from the war. I've seen my fair share of wind storms, floods, hail, and even several tornadoes. But up until you arrived, I've felt completely safe." She turned from his startled expression and left the kitchen.

He caught up with her in the dining room. "Rachel, I'm serious. You shouldn't be out there alone."

"How the hell do you think I'm going to run this ranch if I can't go out alone?" she asked sarcastically.

"I don't mean out on the range. I have no doubt that you can take reasonable care of yourself there. I'm sure you'd kill anyone that threatened you." He glanced down at the gun strapped to her thigh, then back up at her eyes. "I'm talking about the swimming hole."

She paused for just a moment to ponder his concern. She had questioned her ability to assure herself privacy earlier that day, but she'd never doubted her safety and she still didn't. "Mind your own business," she stated flatly.

"You are my business. Everything on this ranch is my business." He saw her tense as he spoke.

"Nothing on this ranch is your business." How dare he tell her she shouldn't swim alone? How dare he tell her anything?

Sin watched the narrowing of her eyes and knew he was making no headway. Why couldn't she see how dangerous it was for her to be out at that damned swimming hole alone?

"Rachel, when you rode up while I was swimming today, could I have defended myself?"

She remembered how he looked just before he dove into the water and tried not to smile. "I . . . I don't know what you mean."

"Like hell you don't. I was standing there naked as the day I was born, and if you'd have been a . . . an outlaw, there would have been nothing I could have done to stop you from doing whatever you wanted with me."

She noticed his voice had dropped in pitch and realized he was thinking the same thing she was. "So, what's your point?"

"Well, unless I miss my guess, you swim just as naked as I do. And like it or not, being a woman, you'd be even more helpless than I was."

"So?"

He paused only a moment. "I already said, I don't think you should swim alone."

She looked him up and down. "So who should I appoint as my bodyguard? Which one of the men should I pull from their regular jobs to watch me swim nude? Any suggestions?" She was being sarcastic again, but she couldn't help it. He'd managed to put a small fear into her. She'd never been uneasy about swimming alone. In fact, it had always been a time she relished. Now, his concern had placed a small doubt in the back of her mind, and she knew she would never feel as comfortable in those moments again.

He listened and heard through the sarcasm. He'd finally gotten through, and she didn't like it. "As a matter of fact, I do have a suggestion."

"I'll just bet you do." She crossed her arms in front of her and waited for the inevitable.

"What about Jace?"

"Jace?" she nearly choked. "Why on earth would you think of Jace?"

Sin watched her reaction and was a little surprised by it. "I saw you in the barn with him yesterday and I thought, maybe, his behavior last night was because you'd had a quarrel or something."

So, he'd finally decided to let her know he'd seen her kissing Jace. "There's nothing between Jace and me. You misunderstood what you saw."

He frowned slightly. "If you say so."

"I do." She straightened, and wondered if she should offer more information to confirm her story. She needed him to believe her, for Tish's sake, and her own.

"It's just looked like ..." He didn't know how to continue.

"It was a mistake," she repeated. That was true, and her look dared him to pursue the issue at his own risk.

By the way she took her stance, and the upturned tilt of her jaw, he knew there was more to this thing with Jace than she was willing to share, but decided that this was not the time or place to argue about it. And, whether he liked it or not, he had to admit that her personal relationships really were none of his business. Right now he needed to solve the problem of who she should swim with. "So, if you don't want Jace to go with you, who do you want?"

"No one." Even admitting to herself that Sin had a valid concern couldn't make her think she needed a chaperone. She'd just make sure she stayed closer to her gun.

"Rachel, I insist you not go alone."

"Braddock, you're being ridiculous. I'm a grown woman, and I will do as I please."

"And you're just being stubborn. If you don't make some arrangement to keep yourself safe, I'll come with you myself!"

"Oh, you'd just love that, wouldn't you? You'd stand on the shore, brave, gun in hand, ready to protect my virtue, while you watched me swim around totally naked. I think not."

She was still being sarcastic but she really wasn't far off. He would protect her if need be. "Rachel, you know I wouldn't watch you undress, and once you were in the water you'd be hidden from my view. You might even enjoy the company."

She started for the door. Arguing with him got her nowhere. "It'll never happen, Braddock. Not in a million years." She turned back toward him just before she left the room. "Oh, by the way. There was a beautiful big trout by your left foot in the creek today. Didn't mention it then. Didn't know if you were squeamish."

Sin stood there with his mouth open for a full minute while what she'd said sank in. She had seen a fish at the bottom of the creek while he stood there, certain he was safely covered. He began to grin. She'd seen a lot more than a fish.

* * *

In her room, behind a locked door, Rachel stripped off her dirty work clothes and reached into the bureau for some clean trousers and a shirt, then tossed them onto the bed. The swim had done her some good, but Sin confronting her the way he'd done caused her nerves to tighten up once again. As she stood in front of the mirror, she noticed the large bruise on her shoulder from Jace's punch. Frowning, she thought about Sin seeing her in the barn with him. "I'm going to have to get rid of Jace," she told her reflection. "I can't take the chance of him causing more trouble." Once again, she admonished herself for hiring him in the first place.

She poured some water in the basin and sponged herself off lightly to remove any dust from her clothes. She then put on her wrapper and sat on the edge of the bed. Maybe I just need to lie down for a minute, she thought. She arched her back and rubbed her neck. She didn't usually stop working for the day until dinnertime, but she hadn't slept well lately and it seemed to be catching up with her. As she lay back on the bed, she thought, with satisfaction, about the telegrams she'd sent. It would be a few days, maybe a week or so, before she got any answers, but she felt confident that she'd be able to start roundup fairly soon.

She was curious as to which, if any, of the other ranchers would object to doing business with the Yanks. She remembered Hank's remark about the possibility of losing Stoker and maybe a few of her other hands. She frowned at the idea of being shorthanded at roundup. At the same time, she realized that as much as she disliked it, she'd probably need to keep Jace on until after the drive north. At least, if she sent him on the drive, he'd be away from the ranch for a while. Then, when he returned, she'd have the money to pay him in full and she could let him go.

The laughter of children broke through her dreams a while later. She sat up in bed and was surprised how long the shadows had gotten during the time she was asleep. She leaned over to the window and looked out through the curtains to see Tish and Jeremy playing tag in the yard. Tish was "it," and she squealed every time Jeremy let her get almost close enough to tag him. Rachel laughed at the sight. Tish stopped running for a moment to catch her breath and put her hands on her hips. "Jeremy, you stop running so fast. I'll never catch you if you don't slow down a little."

"That's the idea!" He teased as he danced around her.

"Oh, you brat!" Tish giggled and took off after him again.

Rachel leaned back against the pillows again and listened to the happy sounds below her. She was feeling a little guilty for stealing the time for her nap, but she had to admit that it had done her a world of good. She stretched and listened for sounds downstairs. She could tell Lena was in the kitchen preparing dinner from the rattle of pans, but she couldn't hear Lucy's or Lily's movements or voices. "I'm sure they're not helping with dinner," she said out loud. She wondered, with a devilish grin, how Lily's backside was after her slip in the yard.

Then she heard Sin's masculine voice in the yard below and once more peeked out the window. Coming toward the house were Sin and Lily. Lily had her hand resting lightly on Sin's arm as he assisted her walk across uneven ground. Rachel noticed how Lily looked up at him and leaned toward him a bit too much. Once again, Lily was wearing a totally unsuitable dress. It was a light green fabric that seemed to carry its own glow. A white collar and sleeves matched the slip that billowed from a parting in the front of the skirt. Rachel's eyes narrowed when she observed the amount of bosom the girl was showing. "My God, if she took a deep breath, her breasts would pop out in his face!" She pulled back from the window and stood up.

Sin noticed a movement in an upstairs window and looked just in time to see the lace curtain in Rachel's room sway slightly. He smiled, once again remembering her remark about the fish.

"So what do you think of my idea, Mr. Braddock?" Lily questioned softly.

"I'm sorry, Miss Lily. What was it?" Sin was having a hard time concentrating on the lovely creature at his side.

"My idea about the party," Lily pouted.

"Oh, yes, that. I think it's a splendid idea." He couldn't remember what she'd been talking about, which surprised him, because Lily was the kind of woman he'd been around his whole life. She was the kind of woman he would have married if the war had not taken Bessie. As he looked down at Lily, he realized he had to be kinder to Bessie's memory. Bessie had never been as obvious as Lily, but she had been more like Lily than Rachel.

He stole another glance at Rachel's window. When he'd come to Texas, looking for another chance in life, he'd never have guessed he'd meet anyone like Rachel.

"So you will help me?" Lily asked.

He realized he hadn't been listening again. "Of course." He hoped he hadn't just agreed to something he would regret.

"Good. Then we'll ask Rachel tonight after dinner. Don't forget you promised to help." She hugged his arm to her breasts and smiled conspiratorially at him.

"Lily, children, come in for supper," Lucy called from the porch.

Lily made a face as Sin extricated himself from her grasp. "Excuse me please, Miss Lily. I must wash up before eating." He released her hand, glanced once more at Rachel's window, and headed for the back of the house.

"Mama, you look so pretty!" Tish exclaimed as Rachel entered the dining room.

"My dear, you do look ... lovely." Lucy complimented her while Lily just sat there staring.

Sin looked up to see Rachel glance his way quickly, then look away. She did indeed look pretty and he couldn't help but assess her appearance. She was wearing a white cotton dress that buttoned down the front and fit snugly across the hips. Actually, it fit snugly all over. He noticed that she'd left the top buttons open, creating an enticing view of her breasts. It occurred to him that perhaps she'd had to leave the buttons unfastened for comfort. Her hair was brushed through and shining curls carressed her hips, while a portion was held up away from her face and secured with white ribbon.

As soon as she entered the room, Rachel wished she'd ignored the impulse to put on the stupid dress. She hadn't worn it in years, in fact it was a little too small, and though she'd admired her reflection upstairs, she now felt ridiculous. The only thing that kept her from going back upstairs and taking it off was that she'd have to explain her actions to the what seemed like hundreds of people that now inhabited her world. And, right now, she couldn't explain her actions to herself. Instead, feeling horribly self-conscious, she squared her shoulders and sat down at the head of the table.

"Cousin Rachel," Lily finally spoke, "I didn't think you approved of wearing dresses, except to church, of course."

Rachel could tell by the tone of her voice that Lily was still angry with her. "I never said that, Lily. I just think that there are appropriate clothes for certain times and places." Just then she felt Jeremy kick Tish under the table and heard him whisper, "I think your mama's beautiful."

"I agree." Sin said softly.

Rachel glanced up, startled, and felt the impact of his dark eyes. She looked away again, uncomfortable under his scrutiny. This is foolishness, she thought.

"Miss Rachel?" Lena asked as she brought in their dinner. "Is there a special occasion you did not tell me about?"

Lilly giggled behind her hand.

"No, Lena. I just felt like dressing up a little. Please

serve dinner." She could hear the abruptness in her voice but couldn't help it.

Lena rolled her eyes and shook her head as she set the covered platter she was carrying in the center of the table. "Things are changing more around here all the time," she muttered as she left.

Rachel was thinking the same thing as she began to dish up Tish's food.

Several hours later, Rachel stood alone on the front porch. The sun had nearly disappeared behind the sharp edge of the earth, and the dark purple shadows of evening were stretching their long fingers across the land. She could hear the children playing tag once again, this time in the kitchen, by the sounds of Lena's scolding, and she knew Lucy and Lily were upstairs where they'd gone right after dinner. A few of her hands were still out on this warm night, and she raised her hand in greeting as they rode by and tipped their hats in her direction. She saw their curious looks but supposed she couldn't blame them for noticing her dress.

"You should have told me about the fish." Sin's soft voice behind her caused her to jump.

"How long have you been behind me?" she asked and turned to face him.

"Not long," he lied. He'd been there quite a while, watching the way the hot golden rays from the sun shot through her hair, turning it to fire. He'd seen the warm kiss of light on her cheek when she turned her head, and he'd nearly touched her back when the last explosion of sunlight for the day had illuminated her figure through the thin dress she was wearing.

"You should have told me you were there." She frowned up at him.

"And you should have told me about the fish," he repeated.

She swallowed. He was standing so close, and his mention of the fish reminded her of the way he looked at the creek. "I suppose that wasn't fair of me."

"No." He continued to stare down at her.

She could see the corners of his mouth were turned up slightly. He was having fun with her. "Would you have told me?" she asked.

He thought about that for a moment and couldn't help but smile. "I suppose not."

She watched how his lips moved when he smiled and spoke, exposing the whiteness of his teeth. She remembered how those teeth felt against her tongue. He's so tall, she thought, looking up at him. He seemed to have moved closer, and she could feel the strength of him next to her even though they hadn't touched. She took a step back and saw him frown slightly at her action. "I should go in and tell Tish to get ready for bed." She started to walk around him, but he stopped her with a touch. Fire danced up her arm from the tip of his fingers, and she pulled away.

"You're one up on me, Rachel." He tried to continue the conversation.

"And I have every intention of keeping it that way." A breeze blew a stray curl across her face. Before she could brush it aside he took it gently from her cheek and wound it lightly around his index finger.

"I have a few intentions of my own." He moved toward her.

She felt caught by his gaze, lost in the dark depths of those black eyes. As his lips grew closer she felt her own body drawing nearer to him. She knew very well what his intentions were, but they all centered around her giving him half her ranch without a fight. She jerked back abruptly.

"Ouch!" She rubbed her head where her hair was pulled by her action. "Why didn't you let go?"

"Why did you jump back like a scalded cat?" He held up several strands of her hair, still wrapped around his finger, and let them fly free on the warm breeze.

"I guess I just don't trust your motives."

"Couldn't you try not questioning my motives?" He looked her square in the eye.

129

"Not while my ranch is at stake."

"Damn it, Rachel." He pushed both fists into the pockets of his black trousers. "I know this can work, if you just give me a chance. We could save this ranch together."

She felt a moment of smug satisfaction as she answered. "I have already 'saved this ranch,' as you put it."

He stood very still and watched to see if she was telling him the truth. He knew that the Triple X was ready to go under, and if she were bluffing and wasting precious time they could lose everything. "What have you done?"

She looked him over before she decided to answer. He stood straight, tall, waiting. His dark eyes were intense, fringed thickly by lashes the color of the coalblack hair curling softly over his forehead and around his collar. She knew that he wouldn't let her get away with not telling him anything. "I've sent telegrams to the Northern buyers we used to supply, letting them know were ready to start a drive north. I should hear from them in a few days."

Sin thought about her answer. "That was a good move. You ignored your father's loyalty to the South and did what was necessary." He was quiet for a moment. "Perhaps there are a few wires I could also send. I do have quite a number of contacts in the North myself."

"That won't be necessary. We'll be making the drive soon and, as you can see, I don't need your help with anything."

Sin looked down into her green eyes and took a step closer. "Don't you ever need help, Rachel? Don't you ever need anything? You're so busy being strong. Don't you ever need someone to share some of the burden?" His voice had become a whisper.

She took a breath and watched the pulse beating in his temple. "I . . ." She wouldn't let him get to her. "No, I don't need anything," she told him flatly.

Sin straightened. "Then you're one of a kind, Rachel,

because everyone needs someone or something. I just hope you don't realize it too late." He moved away from her and sat on the porch railing with one boot toe hooked through a crossbar.

She didn't like what he'd just said and watched him through narrowed eyes. "You're wrong, you know. Not everyone is needy. The people around here have learned to take care of themselves. They've had to. This land is hard, and the weak don't make it. If you had any idea how difficult it was for my father to create this ranch out of the nothing this land was when he came here, you might understand why I'm so damned infuriated at the idea that you have the right to walk in here and take half of what he and I worked so hard for. You don't deserve it." She turned her back on him, breathing hard, afraid that if she kept looking at him she'd kill him. A moment later, when he didn't respond, she walked quietly through the screen door into the house.

Sin did understand what she meant. He'd hoped when he arrived that she'd have accepted his presence gracefully, but after meeting her knew that wasn't possible. She didn't think he knew how she felt, but he did. He'd felt the same way about his home, his world, when it was all taken by the war. He didn't like having to cause Rachel this pain, but he had no choice. He wasn't stealing something that didn't rightfully, legally belong to him, and he truly believed that it would all work out, eventually. "But it's still a long road ahead," he sighed.

Tish and Jeremy burst through the door at almost the same moment. Jeremy was carrying a guitar. "Mama's going to sing to us, Mr. Braddock!" exclaimed Tish and danced around the porch.

"She is, heh? What's the occasion?" he asked the happy child.

"Me and Jeremy just asked her and she said yes!"

Sin looked up as Rachel joined them on the porch, followed closely by Lily and Lucy.

"Have you heard our Rachel sing, Mr. Braddock?" asked Lucy as she settled herself on the porch swing.

"Yes, as a matter of fact I did."

Rachel sent him a surprised look.

"I heard her sing in the Rosebud one evening," he elaborated. "It was the evening when I first arrived here. Remember, Rachel?"

She just frowned at him. So, he was there that night. It bothered her to think he'd been there watching her, and she hadn't known it. "Seems to me, I'm not one up on you after all."

"I think the circumstances were quite a bit different. Wouldn't you agree?" He raised one brow when he looked at her.

She knew he was referring to the fact that he'd been nude. "I suppose, a little."

"Whatever are you two talking about?" asked Lily. At the same time Lucy asked, "You actually sing at this saloon you own?"

Rachel looked from one to the other. "Yes, Aunt Lucy. I do sing at the Rosebud, occasionally, and Lily, I'll let Mr. Braddock explain what we were talking about."

"Well, I'm certain I don't approve," Lucy puffed.

Rachel didn't bother to acknowledge her aunt. She'd have been surprised if Lucy hadn't made a comment about her singing.

"Mr. Braddock?" Lily inquired.

Sin looked at Lily's pretty face and into her pale blue eyes and found himself tempted to tell her exactly what he and Rachel had been talking about, then thought better of it. He doubted that she'd find the topic amusing, and he was sure Lucy would have a fit of apoplexy if she knew Rachel had sat and watched him swimming nude that afternoon. Instead, he answered, "Oh, it was nothing of importance, really."

Rachel could see that Lily was disappointed by his lack of an answer but knew she was too much of a lady to question him further. Rachel took the guitar from Jeremy and sat down on the top step of the porch. "Now what do you want to hear, Tish?"

Tish jumped up and down and clapped her hands. "I want to hear 'Two Toe Joe.' Please, Mama? Please?"

Rachel smiled at her daughter. "All right, sit down and be still."

Tish sat down in front of her mother, and Jeremy plopped down beside her and waited for the song that sounded so interesting. Rachel watched as Lily arranged herself on one of the ladder-back chairs next to Sin. When everyone was seated she began to sing the song she'd made up for Tish's amusement.

Sin watched the way Rachel's face changed while she was singing to the children. Her eyes glowed with joy, and she laughed every time Tish squealed with delight at another of Two Toe Joe's mishaps. He found himself laughing, too, and Lily and Lucy joined in the fun by singing along when they'd learned the simple chorus. This was a moment he would remember forever.

Jace sat in the shadow of the barn and watched the happy scene on the porch. He watched as Lena brought out a lantern so everyone could continue to see when the last pink glow left the sky. He watched Rachel and her little girl laughing together, and his heart was filled with resentment. I should be on the porch singing with everyone, too, he thought. It was his right. He'd known Rachel long before these people became a part of her life. Even Tish. He wondered what Rachel would do if he just walked up and started singing. She wouldn't dare tell him to leave. He listened to Rachel's voice drifting across the yard. He wouldn't walk over there, though. He needed to talk to Rachel alone first. He'd almost made her understand when he'd kissed her. If he could just talk to her one more time. One more time, when she wasn't being the high and mighty boss-lady, when no one else was around to watch her. And next time he'd do more than kiss her. He was certain he could get through to her. Until then he'd wait and watch.

Rachel finished the song and told Tish to get ready

for bed. Lucy told Jeremy the same thing, then stood to scoot the children through the door when they showed their reluctance. Rachel could hear Jeremy protesting still as they went to their rooms. "I'll be up in a minute to tuck you in," she called to Tish.

"Okay, Mama." Tish called back, then scolded Jeremy for being a crybaby about bedtime.

Rachel's fingers gently strummed the strings of the guitar and she began to hum, almost unaware of Sin's and Lily's continued presence on the porch. She leaned back against the porch pillar and closed her eyes as she played.

Sin watched her and remembered the song she had sung in the Rosebud. It was the one she now hummed. Lily began to speak, but he gestured her to silence. He wanted to hear the deep, soft tones of Rachel's voice as she hummed this sultry song. He barely noticed when Lily left or when Lena came back out and handed him a cup of fresh coffee. He was lost in Rachel's voice and was barely breathing when she opened her mouth to sing the words. Her voice was having the same effect on him tonight that it had in the Rosebud. He felt as though she were singing to him, and each time she changed tones his skin tingled with the sound. Deep within his body her voice was touching places hidden from view. He felt his heart beating with the rhythm of her fingers on the strings, and the blood flowed powerfully through his veins in tempo with her words. Then, all too soon, the song was over. She opened her eyes, and when she did, she was looking directly at him.

Rachel saw the look in Sin's eyes. He was somewhere deep within her song, and she once more felt as though they'd connected in some way. Those black eyes were dangerous, but she found she couldn't look away. He moved slowly from the railing to sit directly in front of her on the step. She tried to back up, only to find herself against the pillar. He was trying to corner her again. "Braddock, excuse me, please. I have to go kiss Tish good night." She tried to stand but he was sitting on her skirt. "Please?"

"Why don't you kiss me good night?" he dared.

"Because I don't love you." she answered quickly and stood, guitar in hand, jerking her skirt free as she moved. "I don't even like you," she said over her shoulder as she went through the door.

9

Over a week had passed since Rachel sent the telegrams to the Northern buyers and, still, she hadn't received a single answer. As she walked across the street, from the general store toward the telegraph office, she was in a terrible mood, sure she would once more be disappointed by the lack of a response.

"Slow down a little there, Rachel," Sheriff Jamison said when she nearly ran over him.

"What? Oh, sorry, Frank, I didn't see you. I've got a lot on my mind."

"I figured as much. Anything I can help with?" he asked while chewing on a toothpick.

"No. It was nice seeing you." She started to walk away, anxious to get to the telegraph office.

"By the way, how's that young man, Braddock, doing at your place? He still alive and kickin'?" he teased, not ready to let her leave.

Rachel thought about Sin and the past week. He'd been helping Hank every day, learning all he could about a cattle ranch. "Yeah, he's fine."

"Well good, glad to hear things are working out." He laughed a little. "He thought you might kill him. Have to admit, I thought there was that possibility myself for a while."

"I thought about it a few times," she admitted, "but I figured I couldn't get away with it." Rachel knew Frank couldn't tell if she were joking or not. "Of course, people have accidents out on the range every day. You couldn't blame me for an accident, could you?" she goaded.

"Now, Rachel," Frank spit the toothpick on the ground.

"Don't worry," she interrupted, "he's not in any immediate danger. At least not from me." She started walking toward the telegraph office again. Frank followed. "I've got some things I've got to do now, Frank."

"There's something else I need to mention to you, Rachel." He caught himself staring at her too intently as she moved. Damn, she's a pretty woman, he thought.

"Yes?" She waited again. It was hot standing in the sun, and she wished he'd say what was on his mind so she could get going.

"It's Jace."

"What about Jace?" She hadn't seen much of him lately and had been hoping he'd gotten over the silly ideas he'd had about the two of them.

"He's been comin' into town after work a lot. He goes to the Wagonwheel and drinks too much. Then he starts talkin'."

"So?" Hank told her Jace had been drinking a lot, but as long as he showed up for work it wasn't her concern.

"It's you he's talkin' about, Rachel. He's saying crazy things about how you two should be together again." Frank rubbed his whiskered jaw. "Most of what he says doesn't make sense, but I thought you should know." He was dying to ask her if any of what Jace was saying was true, but Rachel wasn't the kind of woman you could ask that kind of question. He did notice that she had an odd look on her face.

"Thanks, Frank. I don't know what he's talking about, but I'll have Hank speak to him about it. I don't want any of my crew causing you trouble. I really have to go now. Thanks again, bye." She turned and walked away before he could say anything else. Damn Jace, anyway. Damn him to hell. Why couldn't he just leave things alone and keep his big mouth shut?

As she entered the telegraph office she was ready for the worst. "Nothing again today, right?" she asked Sam, the operator.

"No, Rachel, you got two today but . . ."

"Two!" she didn't let him finish, "Give them to me. I can't believe I got two answers today."

"But Rachel . . ." Sam didn't know how to tell her so he just handed her the telegrams.

She grabbed them from him and began reading. It took her only seconds to finish the first one and look at the second. "I don't believe it." She read them again. "I don't believe it. What am I going to do?" she asked no one and sank down onto a bench in the waiting area. It hadn't occurred to her that her offer would be turned down. She was so certain she'd solved all her problems. She suddenly realized it was very unlikely she'd get any other answers. The other people she'd contacted probably wouldn't even give her the courtesy of a response. She glanced down at the top telegraph, now crumpled in her hand.

RACHEL WALKER
TRIPLE X—MESA CITY, TEXAS. NOT INTERESTED IN YOUR OFFER—NOT IF ONLY BEEF IN COUNTRY—CONFEDERATE CATTLE INEDIBLE—FROM CONROY PACKING CO. U.S.A.

She looked at the other telegram again. It said pretty much the same thing. Confederate cattle? How could people be so stupid? Cows were cows, it didn't matter where they came from. Then she realized how ridiculous this war had become, probably every war. She leaned forward and put her head in her hand. What the hell was she going to do? Sin had asked her every day that she'd come to town if she'd gotten any word yet. And every day she'd told him it was none of his business. Now she was going to have to find some other way to solve this problem, and she knew that he was going to be determined to stick his nose in where it didn't belong. "Damn it!" she shouted as she stood up and slammed her way out of the office.

Sam cowered behind the counter as she left. "My goodness," he whispered. He pushed his glasses up on his thin nose, glad she was gone.

The ride home wasn't long enough. She needed more time to think about what to do next, but too soon she saw the ranch buildings and the tiny forms of the people in the distance. One of them, she knew, was Sin. He always met her with the same question. What was she going to say? He seemed to have accepted that she'd solved their, her, problem without his help and now it turned out she hadn't solved anything. And, for the life of her, she couldn't think of another solution. No drive meant no money; no money meant no payroll; no payroll meant no hands; no hands meant no ranch. She looked off into the distance at some of the cattle the men had started to round up. Money walking around on four legs. That's what they were, but how to get the money out of them? She shook her head. She didn't have a clue.

Riding into the yard a while later, she was grateful for Sin's absence. Ben told her he'd gone somewhere with Hank. She put Roux in the corral and watched as he walked to the trough to drink. Even talking to her old friend didn't help. She took off her gloves and set them on the fence post, then headed toward the house.

"Miss Rachel, I quit!" Lena burst through the back door when Rachel reached the bottom step. "I am going to my brother's home where I am needed."

"Lena, what's the matter? What are you talking about?"

"I quit, Miss Rachel. That woman makes me loco. My brother's house is full of children, and I am needed."

"Lena, I need you. You can't go. What woman?"

Lean's face was tear streaked and she was out of breath. "Your Aunt Lucy. She tells me I am dirty. All day she follows me while I am cooking and tells me to wash my hands. I wash so much, my skin is turning yellow like the soap. See?" She held up her hands for Rachel to look at them.

"Lena, your hands aren't turning yellow. You're just upset." If the situation weren't so serious it would have been funny. But she knew Lena meant what she said. She would leave if something weren't done about Lucy.

"*Sí*, I am upset. I am leaving!" She started toward the barn.

Rachel reached out and took her arm. "Please give me a chance to talk to her, Lena. I need you. What will I do without you? What will Tish do without you?" Rachel knew she'd hit a nerve when she mentioned Tish because Lena stopped tugging against her hand.

"I will miss my little Tish." Lena put her head down. "Miss Rachel, I don't want to leave, but that woman, she is making me loco."

"I promise I'll talk to her. I'll make her leave you alone. You do everything perfectly, as far as I'm concerned."

Lena raised her head a bit. "You will make her stay out of the kitchen?"

"Yes. I will make her stay out of the kitchen." Rachel knew this was a dangerous promise, but she had to try. If she failed to come up with a plan to save the ranch, this whole conversation would be for nothing, anyway.

"Than I will stay." She went back toward the house. "If you talk to her today."

Rachel sighed. "Yes, I'll talk to her today." And I'll talk to Braddock tonight, she thought. She followed Lena into the house and began looking for Lucy. She found her upstairs in the room that Tish and Lily shared. She was standing on a chair and taking down the curtains.

"Aunt Lucy, what are you doing?"

"Oh, Rachel, I'm glad you're here. Hold the end of this rod while I untangle this hook."

Rachel did as she was asked, then repeated her question. "What are you doing?"

"I'm taking down these old curtains, of course." Lucy looked at her as if she were addled.

"I can see that. Why?"

"Because they're filthy, like everything else in this house. I'd be willing to bet you, these haven't been washed since before your sainted mother passed on. Now help me down." She reached for Rachel's hand and stepped off the chair.

Rachel had to admit she couldn't even remember them being washed, but it hadn't seemed important.

"Goodness." Lucy coughed as dust billowed from the lace curtains. "I've never seen such a mess. How you and my dear brother ever stood living this way, I will never understand."

Rachel was reminded about her reason for finding Lucy.

"Aunt Lucy, sit with me a moment. I need to talk to you about something."

"My dear, I have to get these filthy things into a vat of hot water. Can't this wait?"

She wished it could. "No, Aunt Lucy, it can't." She guided her aunt to sit on Tish's bed with her, the curtains forgotten for the moment. "You see, there is a problem with Lena."

"I'd say there's a problem. The woman doesn't know the first thing about cleanliness. Do you know I even had to tell her to wash her hands while she was cooking today?"

"That's what I came up here to discuss with you."

"Good. It's about time you did something about her," Lucy stated with satisfaction.

"Aunt Lucy," Rachel began and swallowed, "it's you that something has to be done about."

"What?"

"You see, Aunt Lucy, Lena has been running this household for as long as I can remember ..."

"And very poorly!" Lucy interrupted.

"Anyway, she is like one of the family, and she threatened to quit today if you don't leave her alone."

"How dare she!" Lucy stood and shook the curtains, sending clouds of dust everywhere. "How dare that woman complain about me. She is the hired help and not much more than a heathen. I heard her telling Jeremy that her grandmother was an Indian. An Indian! And she has the audacity to threaten you with her intentions about leaving? Why, I'll fire her myself."

"You will do no such thing!" Rachel stood, nearly shouting over her aunt's ravings. "Lena is important to the running of this ranch, and as long as I own this damn place, she'll be here if I can keep her."

"I can't believe you would side with her against one of your own family." Lucy spoke coolly and gave the impression she was looking down on Rachel even though she was several inches shorter.

"Aunt Lucy, it's not a question of siding with her against you. It's a question of necessity."

"And just what does that woman do that I cannot?"

Rachel looked around the room for just a moment before she answered. "Have you ever cooked three meals a day for more than a dozen hungry men?"

"Well ..."

"I mean hungry, Aunt Lucy. Lena showed me the recipe you suggested for breakfast last week. Those men would have laughed at the joke, then asked for the real food."

"I was only thinking they might like a change."

"A change for them would be biscuits instead of tortillas. They don't want fancy, just filling."

"I only thought ..." She broke off and let her gaze travel to the floor.

"I know you were only trying to help, but I must ask you to stay out of the kitchen."

Lucy looked up sharply. "Stay out of the kitchen?"

"Yes."

"But the woman is unclean. Do you know I saw her gather eggs this morning and not wash her hands or the eggs before she began making breakfast. I, for one, don't like chicken droppings mixed in with my eggs!"

Rachel rubbed her forehead. "Aunt Lucy, I don't believe that Lena would be so lax in her cooking habits."

"But I saw . . ."

"It doesn't matter what you saw. It doesn't even matter if it's true. I need Lena to remain working here. Do you understand? I need her, so you will have to try to stay out of her way." She held up her hand when she saw Lucy begin to protest. "Do you understand?"

Lucy walked to the uncovered window, dragging the dusty curtain with her. "I suppose I don't have a choice if I'm to continue living here." She turned and faced Rachel. "But I will not put up with filth when I see it."

"Just don't look for it in the kitchen."

"I shall stay out of the kitchen whenever possible, but if I see something I cannot abide, I shall do something about it."

Rachel supposed that was the best she could expect from Lucy for now. "Very well." She started for the door, then turned back and smiled, hoping to smooth things over a little. "I do think it's wonderful of you to wash those curtains. I really had no idea they'd gotten so bad."

"Humph." Lucy grunted at her but wouldn't look up from curtains she was attempting to fold.

As Rachel descended the stairs, she hoped that Lucy's acceptance of the situation would last, and that Lena would be tolerant if Lucy occasionally got in her way. Right now she had more serious problems to worry about without having to keep peace between the two women. She just couldn't afford to lose Lena now.

Rachel left the house and went to the corral to get Roux. He saw her coming and trotted over to meet her at the gate. She let him nuzzle her cheek and she wrapped one arm over his neck and gave him a hug.

"How 'bout you and I go for a ride?" She opened the gate and mounted him. At the back steps she saw Lena emptying a bucket and rode over to speak to her. "I don't think you should have any more trouble with Lucy."

"Good. That woman, she is trouble."

Rachel stiffened in the saddle. "That woman is my aunt, and although I have told her to stay out of the kitchen, you will respect her wishes about the rest of the house."

Lena's eyes opened wide as she looked up at Rachel. "*Sí*, Miss Rachel."

"Lucy is used to living differently. This move has been a huge change for her. I want her life here to be as pleasant as possible," she pulled slightly on the reins to turn Roux, "and I would like your help to make her feel welcome."

Lena lowered her eyes ashamedly. "*Sí*, Miss Rachel. I will help."

"Thank you." she began to ride away, then stopped. "Lena, when was the last time the curtains upstairs were washed?"

Lena raised her brows and thought for a moment. "I don't remember. Why?"

"It's not important, I guess. I'll be back in time for dinner." She nudged Roux away from the house as Lena nodded.

Rachel rode around the Triple X, checking on the progress the men were making on the various jobs assigned to them. She looked to the horizon and saw a small herd being brought closer to the ranch and grimaced at the sight. What good was bringing them in going to do? They had no buyer, and it didn't look like she would find one in the near future. The North wasn't buying and the South couldn't pay.

She noticed the ranch wagon coming slowly across the range with a horse tethered to the back. Lily had commandeered the wagon during the week so she could take 'buggy' rides in the afternoon. The men had rigged up a canvas cover for it so her white skin wouldn't be touched by the 'horrible sun,' as she put it. Rachel remembered how her aunt had exclaimed that Lily couldn't be allowed to freckle. She shook her head at the memory. As the wagon drew nearer she recognized the tall form sitting next to Lily as Braddock. She had hoped to avoid him until this evening, but she noticed him turning the wagon in her direction.

Sin saw Rachel riding toward them and pulled the horses to the right to intercept her more directly.

"Oh pooh, Sin. Do we have to stop and talk to Rachel now?"

Sin looked down at the lovely face of Lily seated closely beside him. "I thought you wanted my help asking about the party." He felt her pressing her feminine curves against his side. "You've scolded me several times already this week for not mentioning it before."

"That's true, and I do think Rachel would be more apt to listen to you than me, but I was having such a pleasant time with you that I don't want it to end. Rachel is always so . . . cross. She acts like everything I do is silly." She fanned herself with a lace hankie. "She doesn't seem at all feminine, not really like a woman at all. She acts more like a man."

"Do you think so?" He looked at Rachel and could see nothing but a woman coming closer. The way her shirt hugged every curve and was tucked tightly into the snug trousers she always wore was causing him to feel things he knew were best not to acknowledge. There was something magnetic about watching the way she handled Roux by barely touching the reins or moving her legs, and the way she sat with her back straight and her eyes hidden beneath the brim of her hat were intriguing to him in a purely female way. It was curious that Lily had such a different opinion of her cousin.

"Are we enjoying our ride this lovely afternoon?" Rachel asked, her voice dripping with false sweetness, when they pulled next to her.

"Why, yes we are, Rachel." Lily wrapped her arm

145

through Sin's and looked up into his dark eyes. "Mr. Braddock was nice enough to drive me back to the house."

"I thought you were helping Hank," she directed bluntly at Sin.

"I was."

"You leave him to finish a job alone?"

"Of course not. He's on his way back another way." He noticed the tight set to Rachel's jaw and wondered about it. During the past week, although she was never pleasant to him, she'd seemed to be tolerating his existence. Today, she was being short and sarcastic again. Something was wrong. Then he remembered she'd gone into town. If she'd received bad news from the buyers, she'd be taking it out on everyone. And if it were bad news, their problems would be back full force. He glanced at Lily. Now was not the time to question Rachel. He would catch her later and find out what was going on.

"Cousin Rachel, Sin, and I have something to ask you," Lily squeezed his arm tighter, "don't we?"

Sin knew the timing was not right. "Perhaps later?" He hoped Lily would pick up on his thoughts.

"Nonsense, Sin. We've wanted to ask her for simply ages. We might as well do it now. Go on, you ask her."

Rachel looked from one to the other. Her eyes narrowed as she observed the lack of air space between them. "By all means, Sin," she emphasized the use of his name, "ask me."

"It really might be better if we waited."

"But we've already waited over a week." Lily pouted. "If you don't want to ask her I will."

"No, I want 'Sin' to ask me." Rachel sat Roux like a statue, waiting for whatever was coming. It was obviously some plot of Lily's that Braddock had gotten himself involved with, and she wanted the satisfaction of telling him no. She was in the perfect mood for it.

Sin could feel Rachel waiting for the opportunity to turn him down. He could sense her stillness and had the distinct impression he was being watched by a rattle-snake about ready to strike. "Lily, Lily and I, would like to throw a party." He watched the surprise register on Rachel's face. "We feel it would be a good way for your neighbors to get to know your family better."

Rachel didn't know what she'd been expecting, but a party was the furthest thing from her mind right now, especially since she barely had enough money to keep the ranch afloat. She certainly didn't have enough money to be giving parties. "I don't think a party is such a good idea. You met all our neighbors in church last Sunday."

Sin watched Rachel's reaction and knew it for what it was.

"Cousin Rachel, just meeting your neighbors in church wasn't enough. Mother and I want to get to know people. We want to make friends." Lily sulked.

"I'm sorry. A party now would be inconvenient. Perhaps in a few months." Her voice was firm but quiet, and she couldn't help but wonder if she'd still have a place to give a party in a few months.

Sin could see the worry in Rachel's face.

"But, Cousin ..." Lily began, only to be interrupted by Sin.

"Let's not discuss this anymore now." He put a finger to Lily's soft lips, quelling further protests. "Perhaps later, if we can make it more convenient. We'll work on it." He looked up at Rachel. "I'll see Lily back to the house, then I'd like to talk to you."

Rachel's eyes met Sin's and knew there was no avoiding a confrontation. It was going to be now or later. Either way he was going to cause her problems. "Why don't you let Lily drive herself back, and come with me now?"

It was Sin's turn to look surprised. Rachel never made an effort to speak to him, in fact, she avoided it.

"Sin promised to take me back to the house," Lily protested.

"I think you can make it by yourself," Rachel told her bluntly.

"But it's such a long way," she pouted.

"You didn't have any trouble driving out to find him. I'm sure you'll get home just fine." She turned Roux. "You coming, Braddock?"

Sin was already removing himself from Lily's grasp. "I'm sure you'll be fine, Miss Lily. We'll see you back at the house later."

"Oh," Lily hissed. "You are not behaving like a gentleman, Mr. Braddock. I can't believe you'd leave a lady alone out here in the middle of nowhere." She threw Rachel a hateful look, then gave Sin her most hurt expression.

Rachel almost laughed. She was getting used to Lily's histrionics. It was amazing to her that women actually behaved this way. How in the world did any work get done if they were continually pretending they were incapable of completing simple tasks?

She continued riding away, knowing Sin would catch up as soon as he was free of Lily. In a moment, she heard the creak of leather and the thud of hoofbeats as he drew near. She never looked at him, just accepted the feel of him riding next to her.

He had his horse moving at the same leisurely gait that was comfortable for Roux, and she was grateful he didn't break their silence during the ride. In a few minutes, they seemed to zero in on the swimming hole as their destination, though neither had consciously made that decision. Rachel led the way through the black willows and was reminded of the way she found Sin the last time she came through those trees. She had a smile on her face as she emerged, but it soon vanished when she remembered why she'd allowed him to accompany her now.

She jumped from Roux's back and dropped his reins, moving toward the water's edge, where she sank down to sit in the cool grass. Sin followed her lead and sat next to her, though not too closely. He knew she was going to need space if she was going to talk to him.

Rachel listened to the sounds around her. The leaves

almost tinkling as the wind blew through their tops and the gurgling water being strained by long grass at the bank usually had a relaxing effect on her, but today she wouldn't be afforded that luxury. Sin, sitting next to her, waiting, although patiently, was causing her nerves to scream and all the while a voice inside her head and heart kept asking; what am I going to do?

Suddenly Sin broke the silence. "Does this place have a name?" He gestured to their surroundings.

"The swimming hole?"

"Yes."

She knew he was biding his time, being patient until she was ready to talk. "Not this place. The creek has a name, of course."

He raised his brows in question.

"It's Leaver Creek."

"Was this ranch owned by someone named Leaver before your father got it?"

She smiled as she remembered the story of the creek's name. "No, this land was never owned by anyone else." Then the shadow of a frown saddened her eyes as she thought about losing the land her father had worked so hard for.

Sin saw the color of her eyes change from emerald to almost gray. "How then, did the creek get the name, Leaver?"

Pulling her thoughts away from the trouble they'd come here to discuss, she lay back on the soft bed of grass and watched a bluebird fly through the treetops. "The creek was named long before we got here. I suppose my father could have renamed it, but he loved the story about it so much that it probably never occurred to him to change it. You see, a trader that traveled through these parts many years ago used to take this route when coming back from the Indian settlements at the foot of some distant mountains."

"His name was Leaver?"

"No." She smiled. "Let me tell the story. His name was Lebeaux."

Sin's chest contracted at the sight of her unguarded smile. He moved closer to her and watched the rise and fall of her breasts against her shirt as she spoke.

"On one of his expeditions he'd traded some cheap silver earrings and a coffeepot for a beautiful palomino stallion. He brought the stallion with him to his last stop, the camp of a chief named Running Duck. Running Duck was a great warrior and when he saw the stallion he knew he had to have him no matter what the cost. He tried to trade skins for the stallion, but Lebeaux knew that the quality of the skins wouldn't bring the same price as the stallion, so he wouldn't trade. Then the chief's daughter, Little Deer, came to her father's side wearing a leather necklace with a huge gold nugget tied at the end. Lebeaux became very excited. He knew that the gold nugget was worth ten stallions so he told the chief he would trade, but only for the necklace his daughter wore. The chief was reluctant to trade, but the bargain was struck and sealed with the smoking of the pipe. Running Duck had the stallion led away and ordered a feast and celebration for the evening. Little Deer, still wearing the necklace, sat at Lebeaux's side throughout the celebration, which was fine with him. He knew the chief was true to his word, and he'd get the gold nugget before he left in the morning."

"Did he?"

Rachel began to laugh, a deep bubbling sound that wound around Sin's insides as he listened to her. "Oh, yes, but with Little Deer thrown into the deal."

"Little Deer?"

"Yes. It never occurred to Running Duck that Lebeaux would be so determined to trade the stallion for a mere necklace. He was certain the trader wanted his beautiful daughter, Little Deer."

"Was she beautiful?"

"I suppose, by Indian standards." Rachel was laughing again. "The story goes, that she was a fine healthy squaw, capable of bearing many sons."

"Which means?"

"That she was as big as a house." Rachel's laugh had turned more to a giggle as she lay there telling the story.

Sin had repositioned himself slowly. He looked down into Rachel's eyes. They were emerald again. "Did he clear up the misunderstanding?"

"He couldn't. Not without offending Running Duck. Would you want to offend a warrior chief?"

"Not really. But what does this have to do with Leaver Creek?"

"Just a minute and I'll tell you. Lebeaux set out at first light with Little Deer following close behind like a dutiful wife. All day long he tried to think of a way to explain Little Deer to the wife he had waiting for him back in town."

It was Sin's turn to laugh. "I can see where that would be a little difficult for him. Wives can sometimes be so narrowminded about those kinds of things."

"Yes," she turned on her side to face him, "and by the end of the day he'd come up with nothing. For two days he traveled like that. Little Deer followed faithfully along while he tried to think of a way to explain her to his wife. Then, at the end of the third day they came to this creek.

It was spring and the water was high and fast. As Lebeaux started to cross, he noticed that Little Deer was staring at the water with an expression of sheer terror. He tried to ask her what the problem was and finally discovered that she couldn't swim. He tried to convince her that he would help her across, but every time he pulled her to the water's edge she began to wail. Then it hit him; the answer to his problem. If she couldn't swim and wouldn't cross he'd leave her there." She paused and waited a moment. "Get it? Leave her ... Leaver Creek?"

Realization hit Sin. "You've got to be joking."

"Not at all." She defended, laughing.

He started to laugh too. "I don't believe it." But he did. It was strange enough to be true, and he could see why Hyram Walker never renamed it. It was wonderful.

He looked at Rachel, still laughing, enjoying the story she'd known most of her life. Her eyes were sparkling and her teeth shone white against the tan of her face as she smiled. She unconsciously licked her lips, and a sudden fire flared in his chest and traveled downward.

Rachel looked up just as Sin's head lowered to hers, and his lips touched the corner of her mouth. Her breath caught in her throat in surprise. "Braddock?" she whispered.

"Shh, Rachel." He touched her lower lip with his tongue, sending shivers through her he could feel.

Rachel felt herself slipping away. The heat from Sin's body was melting her resolve to avoid this kind of contact with him. The soft touch of his lips was becoming more demanding as he nibbled and tasted her mouth. She discovered herself responding to his kiss, and moved her head to have easier access to his lips. Her own tongue began to explore and taste as his was doing. This was so delicious. The breeze overhead seemed to sing a love song around them and she stretched languidly, pressing her body full length to his.

Sin's system felt the shock of contact with the female form next to him. She was firm, but soft. Strong but feminine. The combination was proving to be too much for him. Swallowing, he pressed her back onto the grass and made her feel the hardness she was causing. The rhythm she'd begun.

Rachel knew that sex with Sin would fulfill her needs. The pressure of the bulge between his legs and the memory of his nude body was reassurance that he was more than capable of performing the necessary act. She felt his hand begin to caress her breast. Her nipple hardened against his hand as sparks shot through her body, centering in her most sensitive areas. She matched his rhythm with an answering rhythm of her own.

He felt so good. It had been so long, too long since she'd accepted the pleasure of being in a man's arms. The kiss at the Rosebud had been more of a fight than a kiss and had surprised her more than anything else.

This was different. He wanted her. She could feel how much as he moved against her, and there was no denying that she wanted him. Her body was aching with wanting him. Perhaps this need was the culmination of all the pressures she'd been feeling for so long, but whatever the reason, she knew she wanted a release.

She opened her eyes and looked at Sin's dark face above hers. He had his own needs. Yes, right now one of them was sex, and whether she trusted his motives or not he was here, now, and able to satisfy something she'd all but forgotten existed. She closed her eyes again and gave herself up to sensation.

10

Sin felt her relax against him in surrender, but with Rachel he knew it would be much more than that, he knew instinctively she would be an involved lover. The thought of making love to Rachel, of culminating what they'd begun, brought a rush of blood through his body that nearly undid him. He heard a soft moan from her lips and claimed them once again, tasting the slightly salty sheen of perspiration along her upper lip. He licked the moisture there, savoring the taste that was Rachel's alone. Her lips were swollen, and he felt her bite gently on his lower lip as she kissed him. Each time she moved he was pushed nearer the edge of a precipice. Oh, Lord, he thought, no woman had ever affected him so.

Rachel lay with the hard surface of Sin's body pressing her onto the earth. Every nerve was attuned to his movement, his rhythm. He pushed his thigh between her legs and, straddling one of them, rubbed the heated passion of his arousal against her in a promise of possession. Her arms were around his neck, and her fingers twined into the thick curls at his nape. The soft hair twisting around her fingers felt better than she could have imagined, but she wanted more. She wanted to touch all of him.

Sin felt her arch her back as he let his hand roam freely over her breasts and massaged her nipples between his fingers, teasing them into heated buds. Slowly he took his mouth from the soft moue of her kiss and trailed a moist path to the hardened peak of one breast. He took it in his mouth, creating a wet circle in the fabric covering it.

Rachel felt Sin's large hand holding her breast up to his greedy mouth. His tongue, flicking her nipple, was sending spasms of pleasure through her body. She brought her own hand down to feel the muscles of his chest as he strained against her. She began to unbutton his shirt. She needed to feel the wet heat of his skin against her hand. After releasing a few buttons she slipped her hand inside to feel his heartbeat raging out of control. She cupped the muscles of his chest, roughing the dark hair there against her fingers. Softly, teasingly, she touched his nipple, curious as to his sensitivity. He let out a low moan in response, and she felt a moment's exhilaration before he bit down tenderly on her own nipple. She cried out from the sheer pleasure he was giving her.

Sin could wait no longer to feel her flesh. Raising on one elbow he quickly unbuttoned her shirt, freeing her full, dewy breasts to his view. He glanced to her face for just a moment. He wanted no hesitancy but would stop if she was feeling remorse. Her face was a beautiful picture of passion and desire. Her lips were swollen from his kisses and her eyes, half closed, were dark emerald and glazed with wanting. He brought his head down once more to savor the soft mounds of her breasts. Pushing them together, he buried his face between them, savoring the feeling of being lost in pure femininity.

Rachel held his head to her breasts. She felt as if she were growing fuller against the slightly rough texture of his cheeks. She caressed his face as he tasted and suckled first one breast and then the other. He raised up for a moment and she felt his hands at her belt and heard the jingle of the buckle as he released it, then repeated the process with her gunbelt. Pulling her shirt from the waistband to assist him as he unfastened her trousers, she felt a breeze against her bare skin.

His lips kissed her just under one breast, then nipped the smooth path of her stomach. She felt the heat from his hands as he explored her abdomen. Slowly he parted the opening in her trousers more and more and slipped his fingers lower, finding the soft hair protecting that most secret part of her. She arched upward toward his hand, ready to receive its invasion. He pushed against the fabric of the trousers, creating a space between them and her flesh. Then he touched her. Softly at first, he explored the moist folds of her body. Rachel thought she might die from the exquisite pleasure he was giving her. Then, without warning he plunged two fingers deeply into her. She gasped, moving even closer to him. More, she thought, I need more. She wanted to be filled by him. He began a slow rhythm with his hand. One that matched the rocking motion he was making against her thigh. Up and down, slowly, deeply he stroked. She had to touch him the same way, had to feel the heat and the pulse of his blood in her hand. She was becoming impatient.

Sin felt the remaining buttons of his shirt give way as Rachel ripped the fabric apart. Her need fueled his passion, and he drove his fingers deeper into her moist heat. When Rachel reached for his waistband he pulled back slightly, allowing her freer access to release him from the binding confines of the tight pants. He swallowed hard, almost exploding, as she found the head of his passion.

"Rachel," he gasped, "more, touch me, there." He guided her hand lower to grasp him wholly.

The throbbing heat of his body pounded through her hand and his voice was a mere rasp against her skin. She'd never felt a man like this before. Her experience with Jace had been the shy fumblings of a teenage girl. Jace had been quicker to satisfy himself, and though she'd loved him, and felt a tingling satisfaction, he'd never been patient enough with her to allow this kind of exploration.

She moved her hand even lower and caressed the soft globes, now pulled tightly against his body. "Sin?" she questioned.

"It's all right. So good," he moaned his answer. He was having a hard time maintaining his control. He'd known Rachel wouldn't be afraid of him. She was matching his curiosity with her own, but he didn't know how much more of this he could take. He'd wanted her from the first time he saw her.

She massaged him gently, then moved her hand back up to his heated shaft. It was hard to concentrate on what she was feeling with her hand, as he was continuing the sweet torture of her body as well.

"Sin, please?"

It took him only a moment to realize what she'd asked. He moved away from her just long enough to remove his boots, socks, pants, and gun, shaking off the torn shirt in just a second. He returned to her, naked, looking powerful in his need. He was glad she didn't look away, but instead, devoured him with her eyes.

Rachel had watched Sin undress, then come back to her. His arousal was complete, full, proud. The muscles of his body glistened with perspiration, and she thought how beautiful he was. The only flaw on his perfect body was the scar he carried below his left shoulder. She wondered how he'd been injured but couldn't speak to ask him.

She watched as he moved over her to remove her clothes. When he bent with his back to her to pull off her boots, she rubbed her hand softly between his legs and was rewarded by the shudder she saw run through him. It seemed like only seconds, and she was lying naked before him. He knelt over her, between her parted legs, and touched her lips with his own. She returned his kiss again and again, parting her lips and reaching deeply into his mouth with her tongue.

Sin looked at Rachel as he kissed her. He was poised

above her, ready to unite with her in a way that would change things between them forever. His manhood was barely a whisper from the dark heat of her soft body. He was ready, but he needed to see the acceptance in her eyes. She looked up at him, questioning his pause. The deep emerald of her eyes sparked, and she reached behind him to pull him to her. A tiny smile curled the corners of her mouth. This was what he'd been looking for. Swiftly, with one thrust, he was buried deeply inside the tight center of her body.

Rachel felt the thrust to her very core. It was what she'd wanted, needed. She moaned as he began to move within her. He was huge and hot and each thrust drove her closer to the release she so desperately desired. His rhythm was perfect for her, and she matched him move for move. She reached for his buttocks, wanting to feel his muscles tighten as he rocked against her. His breathing was becoming erratic as he grew closer to his release, and she held him tighter to her, pressing her breasts to his chest. She was losing herself in this man, in the power of his strong body.

Sin heard Rachel's soft gasps as he pushed himself deeper into her. He was dangerously close, but he wanted her with him. She was matching his thrusts, wrapping her legs around his hips tightly and he could feel the urgency in her hands as she cupped his buttocks. He could feel her moving perfectly with him. He knew instinctively she was ready, she was with him. He heard her cry out his name as he shuddered deeply within her, his release wracking him over and over again as never before. He felt the spasms moving through Rachel at exactly the same moments.

Rachel felt the deep pulsing of Sin's climax just as her own senses exploded. Wave upon wave of roiling heat throbbed though her. She held him tightly, digging her nails into his flesh. Each time he moved within her, it set off another burst of exquisite sensation. It seemed to go on forever. She was on fire and floating at the same time. She could hear him moaning her name over and over again as he pushed himself deeper into her, making the pleasure last even longer for them both.

"Rachel, Rachel," he whispered. He wanted to say her name a thousand times. Never before had he experienced a complete loss of awareness of his surroundings. He'd enjoyed the company of beautiful women, but until now he'd not known what ecstacy was possible in a woman's arms. He lowered himself to rest above her, braced by his arms so not to crush her. He pressed his cheek to hers, letting his breath mingle with hers.

Rachel accepted his embrace as she floated to earth. Small aftershocks tingled through her system, and she kept her eyes closed to savor every one. Sin's body was slick with perspiration as she massaged his back, enjoying the feel of his muscles under the moist skin. It seemed she enjoyed every part of him. She smiled to herself. He was the perfect lover. She doubted, if she lived to be one hundred, she'd ever find another that made her feel this good. She wished it were possible to remain this way forever, lying in the soft grass in his arms. But she knew that was a foolish dream. There were too many problems between the two of them. She still didn't want him on her ranch, and she still couldn't think of a solution to her money problem. Damn it, why did reality always have to come back?

Sin could feel Rachel's breathing becoming more regular. He knew she would open her eyes soon and smile at him. He couldn't believe the turn of events they'd just experienced. Maybe, just maybe, coming here was the best thing he'd ever done in his life. He knew he'd gotten off to a bad start with Rachel, but now things would be different, and he'd help with whatever was bothering her earlier. If it was bad news from the buyers she'd contacted, they'd think of a solution together. There were always his contacts in the North to be considered. He took a deep, satisfying, breath and felt her breasts move beneath him. He was startled to feel his body beginning to grow inside her again so soon. He smiled.

Only with Rachel would he feel this way. He looked forward to the long nights ahead.

Rachel felt him sigh. He was obviously pleased with himself. She supposed he should be. He was very good at what he'd just done, but she hoped he didn't read too much into it. Men were sometimes such dramatic creatures.

"Braddock?" She spoke.

Sin frowned at her use of his surname again. She'd just cried out his first name in passion. Why go back to "Braddock" now? "Yes, Rachel?"

"You have to let me up now. I want to get dressed."

He moved slightly to the side and looked down at her. "Do you want to swim first?" He leaned over and nibbled her jaw.

She thought about swimming with him. It might be nice to freshen up. Her body was covered with the essence of him. She probably should wash the after-effects of their lovemaking away before she went back to the house. "All right, let's go."

He rolled away and stood up, facing her unself-consciously, hand out, to help her up. She looked up at his nude body and took his hand. His fingers were strong as he pulled her to her feet. He tried to pull her against him, but she stopped the action and took her hand from his. She could see the confused expression on his face but turned her back to him and walked into the water a few feet before she dove under the surface.

Sin watched her swimming underwater and wondered if she were uncomfortable with what they'd just done. He knew it might take her a while to adjust to the change between them. Rachel, he'd learned, was not able to cope with change easily.

"That felt good but I have to get going," she announced as she emerged from the water and started wringing out her hair.

Sin looked at her with his mouth open. Had to get going? Was she crazy? They'd just made the most incredible love of his life, and now she was going to just "get going?" He dunked himself quickly under the water to rinse off, then climbed out of the creek. "Rachel, I think you should stay. We have a lot to talk about."

She sighed. She knew he was going to question her about the telegrams again, and she might as well get it over with. "All right. I got the answers from the buyers today and they were: No." She bent over and picked up her shirt, noticing the wet spot on the front where he'd kissed her breast. She walked to the water's edge and knelt to rinse out the shirt. When she stood up again, pulling on the wet garment, she looked at Braddock and found him staring at her with an incredulous look on his face. "Okay, so say something. Get it out of your system." She began buttoning the shirt.

Sin couldn't believe his ears. She was actually talking about the ranch at a time like this? Yes, they had problems that needed to be discussed, the lack of cattle buyers was nearly first on the list, but right now they needed to talk about the change in their relationship. Something wonderful had happened here today. Something that couldn't be ignored. Or could it? Was he the only one that this mattered to? He watched Rachel getting dressed. Was she capable of making love and not getting emotionally involved? His mind rebeled against this idea. She was a woman, for Christ's sake. A woman didn't make love to a man without it meaning something. At least not a woman like Rachel.

"Rachel, we need to discuss us, this." He gestured to the impression their bodies had made in the grass. "Then we'll discuss the ranch."

"You don't think for one minute that what we just did changes anything between us, do you?" She watched him with narrowed eyes.

"Of course it does. It changes everything."

She sat down to pull on her boots. "Not in my book." She gazed at his nude form. "You'd better start getting dressed."

Sin glanced down at himself. He was still damp and saw drops of water glistening on his skin. He'd completely forgotten his nudity in the face of her uninvolved attitude. He bent for his clothes. "I don't understand you, Rachel." He pulled on his trousers and shirt but couldn't button the latter because of her ardent lovemaking.

"Well, understand this, Braddock. What we just did was . . . fun. But it has nothing to do with the ranch or my desire to be rid of your claim to it."

"Fun? You'd describe it as fun?" he asked, unbelieving.

"I guess 'fun' wasn't a good word to use, but it didn't mean to me what it obviously meant to you. I'm sorry for that." She strapped on her gunbelt and started toward Roux.

"Just a minute, Rachel," he demanded. He took the few steps necessary to reach her and grabbed her arms, turning her to face him. "You're trying to tell me that this meant nothing to you?" She shrugged. "That I don't affect you? That you can just ride away from me and pretend nothing's happened or changed?"

She looked up into the black depths of his eyes. She could see how angry she'd made him, but it didn't matter. She wouldn't allow herself to succumb to the emotions he was trying to use against her. "That's exactly what I mean."

"You're a liar," he accused, then brought his mouth down to hers, savagely parting her lips and forcing his tongue into her mouth. He immediately felt her response as she stepped closer and opened herself to his kiss.

Rachel felt liquid fire screaming through her veins at the first touch of Sin's lips. He had the power to bring her body to life with a mere brush of his hand, but it was only physical. She had too much at stake to let it be more. She let him kiss her, then pulled back. "What was that supposed to prove? That I'm madly in love with you? Well, I'm not. Like I said before, Braddock, it was fun." She stepped away from him, freeing her arms from his grasp. Looking him up and down in a blatantly sexual way, she smiled. "You're a very good lover. That much I'll admit. But that's all."

Sin observed the stiffness of her movements as she mounted Roux. He couldn't believe that making love the way she had was just for "fun." It had been earth-moving for him, and he knew she'd felt the same. But had she? Was she capable of making love but not feeling love? Was it just sex for her? Lily's words rang in his mind: "Rachel's really more like a man." He could taste the bile as it rose in his throat. How many beautiful women had he had sex with and not loved? He tried to swallow. It was a bitter pill to be on the receiving end of typically male treatment.

"Rachel," he nearly choked as he spoke, "we still have to work together on this ranch."

"Don't worry about it. I'll come up with something else." She was surprised she sounded so sure of herself. She still didn't have a hint of a solution.

"I'm going to telegraph my contacts in the North. I should have done so sooner, whether you liked it or not." He rubbed his eyes. "I should have let some people know where I am before this, anyway," he said, almost as an afterthought.

"Waste your time if you want. I already know how the Yanks feel about Confederate cattle."

"Not all Northern people feel the same, Rachel. And I've been thinking about something else that might improve the Triple X. After we solve the immediate problem."

"What's that?" She didn't like him getting ideas about the ranch.

"I'll tell you later. Tonight if you like. Right now I'm going to finish getting dressed." He looked down to the torn buttons on his shirt. "I hope I don't have to explain this."

Rachel had the decency to blush. "I'm sorry about that."

"Don't be. It was fun," he used her word against her.

She tilted her chin upward a little. "Yes, it was. I'll see you back at the house. I want to hear this idea of yours."

As Rachel rode back toward the house her head was swimming with memories of Sin's body. He was an excellent lover and some of the tension she'd been feeling had ebbed, but now she was experiencing another kind of unease. She'd used him for her own satisfaction and assumed he'd done the same. There was no mistaking that his desire for her had been real. She smiled. "There are some things a man can't fake," she said out loud. But his attitude afterward kept nagging at her. He'd tried to act hurt about her reaction to their lovemaking. "What did he expect, Roux, that I'd stop wanting him off my ranch—just because he's one hell of a lover? Did he really believe that I could be so swayed by sex?" She shrugged. Once again, she experienced a wave of heat as she remembered his lips on hers and the way his hands felt as he explored her flesh. "Maybe that's exactly what he was hoping." Roux bobbed his head and snorted. She patted his neck, then straightened in the saddle. "Hell, he shouldn't be too upset, he enjoyed himself, even if his plan didn't work."

Sin dressed quickly. He was angry. Angry? He was mad as hell. How could he have been such a fool to think that making love to Rachel would change anything between them? She was a stubborn, mule-headed, aggravating, exasperating ... beautiful woman. He sat down on the grass where moments before he'd lain with her in his arms. He was flooded with thoughts of their shared passion. "Shit!" he exclaimed as he threw a stone into the creek. She had enjoyed making love to him. He now carried the small scratches that proved her involvement was genuine. But why had he hoped for so much? He knew the answer to his own question. He wanted Rachel's acceptance. This chance at the Triple X was important to him, and he couldn't help hoping for a good future here. He couldn't picture being here, years from now, and still putting up with Rachel's animosity. Someday, she'd have to realize that he was a part of her life, would be a part of her life, until death. It had seemed natural to him to hope for, at least, friendship with Rachel. When she'd responded to his lovemaking the way she had, he'd hoped for much more. Now he realized it had meant nothing to her. Nothing but good sex.

Something inside him refused to believe that. There had been more to it than that. He was sure he felt more from her, even if she didn't know it herself yet. Was he just being more of a fool? Was he reading more into her responses than had actually been there? He shook his head. How would he ever know? He stood up and walked to his horse. "I just can't believe she's as unaffected as she claims," he whispered. "She's not that cold." He mounted his horse and turned him to leave the swimming hole.

At the dinner table, several hours later, Jeremy kept up a constant stream of chatter about how he was going to be a cowboy when he grew up. "I'm doing real good with my horse lessons. Pretty soon I'll ride as good as Cousin Rachel."

Rachel had to stifle her laughter at Lucy's reaction, which had been one of horror. "Really, Aunt Lucy, it'll be good for him." She tried to get Lucy to accept the inevitable.

"I'm going to be a cowboy, too!" exclaimed Tish.

"You can't be a cowboy," argued Jeremy.

"I can so. Can't I, Mama?" Tish looked to her mother for confirmation.

"Of course you can. You can be anything you want. In fact, it's important that you learn every aspect of running the Triple X. One day it will belong to you." Rachel explained, hoping that it would be true.

"Humph," Lily grumbled from the other end of the table.

Rachel looked at Lily, glancing for only a second at the empty place Sin usually occupied. He hadn't come back to the ranch yet. "Do you have a problem with what I've said, Lily?"

"Of course not, Cousin Rachel. I'm sure you'll be pleased if Tish grows up exactly like you." Her tone implied an insult.

Rachel was getting a little tired of Lily's surly attitude toward her. It seemed the only time the girl smiled was when Sin was around; then she couldn't be sweet enough. Rachel sighed, deciding not to rise to the bait.

"So, Aunt Lucy, how did the curtains turn out? I haven't been upstairs to see them, yet," she inquired of Lucy, changing the subject.

Lucy pursed her lips. "I wasn't going to mention it until after dinner." She looked directly at Rachel. "But since you asked, they disintegrated, turned to mush in my hands as soon as they hit the hot water. It's because they hadn't been washed in years, you know. I told you things were a disgrace around here. Now they'll have to be replaced."

Rachel looked down at her plate for just a moment, then back up at her aunt. "I'll check on getting some new ones Sunday morning after church." She knew she couldn't afford the expense of new curtains, or even the fabric to make some, but she didn't want to let anyone, especially Lucy, know about the money problems she was dealing with. Everyone might find out soon enough, the hard way, she thought.

"Very well," Lucy answered. "In the meantime I'll check on the condition of the other curtains and drapes in the house. They'll all probably need to be replaced."

"That won't be necessary, Aunt Lucy. We'll just replace the ones you ... that fell apart, for now. I'll think about getting new ones for the rest of the house at another time."

"But they're disgraceful!" protested Lucy. "Why on earth would you want to put off refurbishing this dusty old house now that I'm here to help?"

Rachel stared hard at her aunt. She had the great desire to ask the woman if she was prepared to help financially. It was amazing to her that Lucy had descended on the Triple X, complete with a family, and expected to be taken in and fed just because they were relatives. "Aunt Lucy, I appreciate your concern, but the curtains are not a high priority with me right now. I will replace the ones destroyed, but that's all for now." Her tone of voice brooked no argument. She glanced once more at Braddock's empty chair. "I have things to do now," she stood, "so if you will all excuse me, I'll be in my father's office for a while." She looked down at Tish, staring up at her mother, brown eyes wide with curiosity. She smiled at her daughter and cupped her cheek. "And you, little one, finish your vegetables so you can have dessert. Lena made pie." She bent to brush Tish's forehead with her lips, then straightened and left the room.

Rachel had no real business to attend to in her father's office. She just sat behind his desk with her eyes closed and breathed the memories filling the room. She still felt the betrayal of not being told about the loan, or their loss of income, but she couldn't deny the need to feel close to her father. "Oh, Pa, I wish you were here. I keep making mistakes." She leaned forward and rested her head in her hands, her elbows on the desk. "I guess you made some mistakes, too, though. If you hadn't, my life would sure be a lot simpler now." She sighed and looked around the room. Every corner held another memory, but no solutions. "Damn it, what am I going to do!" she hissed, frustrated.

She glanced at the still broken gun cabinet. Her father's guns, loaded, hung there as they had for as long as she could remember. She was reminded of the night, such a short time ago, when she'd charged for those guns, bent on killing Braddock. "And now I've had sex with him." A charge of liquid fire coursed through her at the memory. Here, in the quiet of this room she could remember, uninterrupted, the different textures of his skin. She swallowed and felt her heart rush at the thought of his body in her hands, the way he shuddered at her touch. She wanted him again, now. Shaking her head, she pushed herself away from the desk and stood up. "Jesus, I must be the biggest fool around." She left the room and headed for the front porch. "Maybe I'll go for a ride," she whispered.

Once on the porch, she scanned the ranch yard. There was always activity. Men working, or, like now, right after dinner, standing around visiting, exchanging stories of the day. She sank down onto one of the chairs and leaned forward, elbows on her knees. She listened to the busy sounds around her: laughter, the creak of leather, the jangle of spurs, and the low bawling of cattle in the distance. Familiar sounds, every one. But tonight they filled her with melancholy. What would she do if she lost the ranch? This was the only life she knew. This was the only place she'd ever lived.

She watched the men passing her in the yard. She returned their smiled greetings but wondered how many of them would be smiling when she couldn't pay them their monthly wages. Probably not many. Yes, there would be some, like Hank, who would stay on for a while, out of a sense of loyalty. But sooner or later even Hank would have to look for a paying job.

She wondered if any of her neighbors were in the same predicament. There were several she knew of, who, like her father, had stopped driving their cattle north when the war broke out. They had to be hurting, too. The Triple X couldn't be the only ranch in trouble because of this war.

Leaning back in the chair, she balanced it on its back legs and hung her thumbs through her belt loops. She let her gaze scan the horizon, curious about where Braddock had gone.

Sin sat at the bar of the Wagonwheel Saloon. He'd been drinking for more than an hour, but after the burn from the first whiskey had died down, he'd switched to beer. He looked through the bottom of the glass as he let the last of the golden liquid slide down his throat. He focused on a red-haired woman in the corner. If he squinted just a little, and continued looking at her through the glass bottom, she looked a bit like Rachel.

He slammed the glass on the bar. "I'll have another," he announced to the startled bartender. He swiveled around and looked at the redhead again. Who was he trying to kid? No one looked like Rachel. No one was Rachel. For the millionth time since he'd held her at Leaver Creek, he remembered. Remembered the fullness of her breasts against his chest. Remembered the way she'd touched him and called his name as he entered her. "Hell," he muttered. It seemed he'd been on fire since then. And so far, the liquor hadn't dampened the inferno one bit.

He threw his money onto the bar and started for the door.

"Mister, I noticed ya lookin' at me. Ya wanna' buy me a drink and let me show ya a good time?" The redhead stopped him halfway across the room.

He looked down into her face. Her eyes were a true hazel and he supposed she was pretty, in her own way, but she wasn't Rachel. No sparks flew from her eyes, and no fire was lit deep within him when he looked at her.

"Not tonight, miss." He brushed past her.

"Ya don't know what yer missin'," she called after him.

"I'm afraid I do," he muttered to himself as he stepped out onto the sidewalk. He rested his hand on the butt of his gun and scanned the street. He thought about going to the Rosebud; Rachel might be there. But then he thought better of it. "She probably wouldn't want to see me anyway." He adjusted his hat and decided to head back to the ranch. It was already late, and she'd be sleeping by the time he got back. He'd have to tell her about the telegram he'd sent first thing in the morning. He hoped his friend John Wright could help him once more.

As he rode up to the ranch everything was dark. If he hadn't known where the house was, he might have ridden into it.

Rachel heard Braddock coming half an hour before

he got close. She'd gone to bed, only to get up again when she couldn't sleep. Sitting alone in the dark on the front step, she'd continued the stream of thoughts that had kept her awake. Now, here he was, the reason for her sleeplessness.

"Well, I see you found your way back," she stated as he rode closer.

Sin hadn't seen Rachel sitting on the step so her voice surprised him. It also excited him. "Rachel?"

"Yes, it's me. Where've you been?"

He squinted, trying to make out her form. "In town. Where are you?"

"Down here, on the step." She could barely make out his shadow as he dismounted.

"I thought you'd be sleeping when I got back." He tethered his horse to the porch railing and walked toward her.

"Couldn't. Got a lot on my mind."

He sat down next to her, then realized she was wearing only a nightgown of some kind. The blood rushed through his veins. "What?"

"I said, I've got a lot on my mind." She was aware of his body next to hers. It was amazing that although he was at least a foot away she could feel him as though he were touching her.

"Me too," he responded.

"What?"

"Have a lot on my mind." He realized they were speaking in circles. She was as affected by him as he was her, but he doubted she'd admit it. He sat there next to her, not knowing what to say.

Rachel listened to him breathing. They couldn't just sit here all night. "Why did you go to town?" she finally thought to ask.

Sin took a deep breath. He didn't want another fight with Rachel, but he'd had to do something about the ranch. He was angry with himself for not doing something sooner. "I sent a telegram to a friend of mine in the North." He waited for a moment. "He may be able to do something to help us."

Rachel listened to what Braddock told her. Her eyes narrowed as her heart rebelled against this man helping save her ranch. It rankled her that he insisted on interfering in her business. But at this point, with no plan of her own, she supposed it didn't matter if he found out on his own what she'd discovered for herself. Yanks didn't want Confederate cattle. "Was that the plan you mentioned earlier?" she asked.

Sin noticed a quiet, foreign tone to Rachel's voice. "Part of it. I was hoping to discuss my ideas for the ranch with you some other time."

"Why not now?"

He waited, wondering if he should be honest with her. "I don't want you to turn the ideas down just because they're mine."

She sighed and bent her head down over her knees. "You're probably right. I would do that. But I'd still like to hear them."

He heard her voice muffled slightly by her position. "Well, Rachel," he hesitated for a moment, not sure if there was any point in continuing, "I was thinking that the addition of thoroughbred horses to the Triple X might increase income in the future."

She raised her head. "Thoroughbreds? To herd cattle? That's the silliest . . ."

"Not to herd cattle," he interrupted, "to sell. Do you know how much money you can make with a good bloodline?"

"No, but it really doesn't matter. If I can't come up with a solution to the immediate problem, there won't be a ranch to raise anything on." She started to stand but stopped when he reached out and touched her arm.

"What will you do if we lose the ranch?"

Her breath caught in her throat. "I don't know."

"Maybe we could get a loan. Just to tide us over until the war is over. The end is very close, Rachel."

"A loan? You want me to get another loan? And just

what would I use as collateral, my half of the ranch—or yours?" Her voice had risen in pitch.

"Calm down, Rachel. I have banking contacts. I'm sure I could arrange something suitable."

"I'll just bet you could. Something suitable to you, no doubt." She jerked her arm free of his touch. "Get this straight, Braddock. I won't have another loan against this ranch. It was a damn loan that got me into this mess and saddled with you to boot!"

Sin grimaced as she spoke. "Rachel, I wouldn't do anything to hurt you—or the ranch."

"Forgive me if I don't believe you." She stood up.

"Someday you'll have to believe me."

"Don't bet on it, Braddock."

Sin heard the screen door close behind her as she went into the house. "Someday, Rachel. Someday you'll believe in me," he whispered.

11

The weather grew still the following Saturday, and Rachel found herself watching the sky for storm clouds. The fact that she continued to see clear blue troubled her. The calm before a storm, she thought. The wind that had been ripping across the open range for weeks previously, suddenly quieted. Even the puffs of dust, raised at the hooves of the horses and cattle as they moved, died in small heaps before they became airborne.

Rachel took off her hat and wiped the sweat from her brow with her shirtsleeve. She blew on her wrists between her gloves and the cuffs of her shirt. "What I wouldn't give for a blue norther right now, Roux," she told the horse as she put her hat back down firmly on her head. Roux nodded at the sound of her voice. "Let's head back to the house." She turned him in the direction of the ranch buildings and let him make his own pace. It was too hot to go much faster than a slow walk.

Rachel had been at odds with herself about what to do about the ranch. She'd pondered her problem and examined it from every angle. So far she still couldn't think of a solution, and more than once she'd cursed her luck, Braddock, her aunt, the war, her father, and even herself for being responsible for her predicament. But all the cursing did nothing to help.

Braddock said that the war was about over, but she certainly couldn't hang the future of the ranch on one man's opinion. It could go on for years yet. It had already lasted longer than anyone had predicted. It also seemed that he was convinced the South was going to lose. If that were true, the South wouldn't have any money for who knew how long.

As Rachel got closer to the house, she saw a horse tied to the porch rail. It took a few minutes for her to recognize it as Frank Jamison's. She nudged Roux to a faster gait, curious as to why the sheriff would be making a visit.

"Frank?" Rachel called as she went through the screen door on the front porch. "What's the problem?"

Frank was sitting in the dining room, holding a forkful of pie. "Nothing's wrong, Rachel. How're ya doing?"

She frowned. "I'm fine." She looked to where Sin was sitting, acknowledging his presence with a nod, and crossed to sit down opposite Frank. "What brings you out here on such a hot day?"

Sin watched Rachel sit down, and his expression hardened. Since the day they'd made love, Rachel had put up a wall between them. A wall of indifference. Although he hadn't appreciated her anger before, he found he preferred it to her latest attitude.

"Well, Rachel," Frank addressed her with a mouth full of pie, "I've been meaning to come out and see how you've been doing for a while now." He pointed at Sin with his fork and grinned. "Wanted to see for myself how this young fella was getting on." He continued chewing. "Anyway, Sam told me he had a telegram for Captain Braddock, so I decided to bring it out."

"Captain Braddock?" Rachel looked at Sin, surprised. "Captain of what?" she asked.

"Eleventh Cavalry, under Lee," Sin answered and watched the display of emotions that crossed her face as she realized what he was talking about.

"I didn't know you'd fought in the war." Her eyes were a deep green as they locked with his.

"There's a lot you don't know about me, Rachel. You never bothered to ask."

"Why are you here now? The war's not over yet."

Sin saw the frown that weighted her brow as she waited for his answer. "It's a long story. I'll tell you some other time. Some time when you're interested."

"Did I hear correctly? Sin is a captain?" Lily exclaimed as she entered the room.

"That's right, miss," Frank confirmed.

"Hello, Sheriff Jamison. How are you this afternoon?"

"I'm fine, Miss Lily. And yourself?" Frank inquired.

"Just wonderful. Will we be seeing you in church again tomorrow?" Lily asked politely.

Frank took another big bite of pie and nodded, grinning.

Rachel continued to watch Sin with narrowed eyes. She was still trying to digest the fact that he'd been an officer in the Confederate army. It had never occurred to her to ask about his past. His claim on the Triple X had labeled him a gold digger to her, so she hadn't cared whether he thought he had good reason or not.

This new information made her curious. Why would a captain stop fighting just as the war seemed to be coming to its end? Then she remembered the scar he carried. Had he been wounded? Why though, when he was healed, hadn't he returned to the fighting?

"Captain Braddock. How romantic that sounds," exclaimed Lily.

"I really prefer Mister, if you don't mind, Miss Lily," Sin told her gently.

"But why ever would you want to drop your title? I'm sure you must be very proud to have served under our courageous General Lee," Lily questioned.

How could he make her understand his desire to separate himself from a time in his life that held many bitter memories? He looked at Rachel, still watching him, and realized she, too, was waiting for his answer. "My feelings on this are very private. I would appreciate it if you all just respect my wishes without question."

His voice came out in a quiet, even tone, but the look in his eyes was anything but serene. Rachel tried to read his expression, and for the first time since she'd met him, she wanted to know about his past. The look in his black eyes told her that all she had to do was ask. She also saw the challenge there. The dare. Would she take the step? She could tell he didn't think so. He was correct, at least for now. She wouldn't question him in front of anyone else. If she decided to ask him personal questions it would be in private. He knew it. And privacy with him was what she'd been avoiding.

"So, was the telegram anything important?" Frank asked, breaking the silent battle between them.

Rachel looked at Frank and then again at Sin. She'd almost forgotten the telegram with the discovery of Sin's rank.

"Yes, as a matter of fact. It was exactly what I was hoping for. Please forgive me if I don't share its contents. Suffice to say, it was good news." Sin smiled at Frank. "Thanks again for bringing it out to me."

"Not at all, Sin. It gave me a chance to sample another of Lena's pies." He pushed himself away from the table and stood. "I think I'll go tell her how delicious it was." He picked up his empty plate and headed for the kitchen. "Maybe I'll even talk her out of another piece." He laughed a little as he went through the door.

Rachel could hear Frank's voice in the kitchen and Lena's laughter. Lily was now seated in a chair next to Sin and she was talking a blue streak about how wonderful it was to know he had been, not only one of their gallant men in gray, but a captain, too. Rachel heard all this through the blood rushing with her heartbeat to her ears. Her eyes locked with Sin's again as she tried to fight the feeling of trepidation that seemed to hold her in her chair. He'd said the telegram held news that he'd been hoping for. The only telegram she knew he'd sent was concerning the Triple X. Had he received favorable news of a buyer? She swallowed and pulled her eyes from his. She couldn't stand to sit there another second. "I've got to see to Roux. Tell Frank good-bye for me." She stood and walked for the door.

"Rachel?" Sin tried to stop her.

"Sin?" Lily questioned. She'd been talking to him, and he was ignoring her.

Rachel kept going. There was something inside of her afraid to know what the telegram said. Afraid to find out that he'd succeeded where she failed.

"Rachel!" Sin spoke louder and rose to go after her. He heard Lily's protests but didn't care.

Rachel heard the demanding tone to Sin's voice behind her as she crossed the porch and descended the few steps in one jump. She grabbed Roux's reins and started to lead him across the yard toward the barn.

It took only seconds for Sin to catch up to Rachel. She was looking straight ahead, refusing to meet his eyes. "Rachel, I have to talk to you."

"You have nothing to say that will interest me. Now leave me alone. I have work to do."

"Rachel, slow down. I know you've figured out what the telegram says, and we need to discuss it." He grabbed her arm when she continued to ignore him. "Damn it, Rachel. Listen to me." He clamped down hard on her arm.

Rachel tried to jerk free but couldn't loosen his grasp. She stopped walking and turned to face him. "Let go of my arm, Braddock, or I swear to God I'll shoot you where you stand," she said through clenched teeth.

Sin slowly loosened his fingers but continued holding her. "I've solved our problem, Rachel. Why won't you listen?" He could see the gray cloud over her eyes but couldn't understand her reluctance to hear good news.

Rachel didn't want to hear that he'd solved their problem about money. She didn't want to admit that he'd succeeded. She remembered how she'd so smugly told him that no Northern buyers would appear and wanted to shrink inside herself. The hardest part of this was that if he had truly solved their problem, she'd have to accept it. She was in no position to tell him what he could do with it. Her responsibility to the ranch, and the people it supported, put her in a very vulnerable position. "All right, Braddock, talk."

Sin saw the anger on her face. The pure willpower she was using to stand still before him. He tried to analyze her feelings but couldn't figure out why she'd be so upset about having her problem solved for her. Then it hit him. That was exactly what was bothering her, the fact that he'd solved the problem, not her. "Rachel, how can you be so narrow-minded?" He spoke softly.

"What the hell do you mean?" she demanded.

"You don't even care that your precious ranch is saved, you're just angry that I was the one to do it," he accused.

"Don't be ridiculous. I . . ." But she couldn't continue. He'd guessed the truth and it wasn't easy to have to admit to something so petty about herself. Instead of appreciating what he'd done, she didn't even want to talk about it.

Sin took the telegram from his pocket and shoved it into her hand. "Here, read this." He let go of her arm and walked away.

Rachel held the folded paper and watched him enter the barn, his dark head bowed. Slowly she held up the paper and read.

SINCLAIRE BRADDOCK,
TRIPLE X, MESA CITY, TEXAS. GLAD TO HEAR YOU'RE DOING WELL. CAN HELP SELL CATTLE. WILL CONTACT FRIEND STARTING RANCH IN COLORADO. WILL BE IN TOUCH SOON. SORRY ABOUT YOUR FAMILY.
          JOHN WRIGHT, PHILADELPHIA, PA.

Rachel read the telegram three times. This man, John Wright, knew someone needing cattle to start a ranch in Colorado. This was good news for her, if he could convince this person to allow the Triple X to supply the cattle. But the part of the telegram that kept jumping out at her was the reference to Sin's family. Had he lost family members to the war?

She stuffed the telegram in her pocket and took Roux's reins with both hands while she led him to the barn.

"Braddock?" she called as she entered the dark interior. "Where are you?"

"I'm over here, Rachel," he answered from his horse's stall.

She put Roux in his stall, then walked to where Sin stood, brushing the animal. She watched the deliberate movements of his hands as he stroked the length of the horse's coat. Something about his rhythm reminded her of the way he'd stroked her own body by the creek. She took a deep breath and tried to think of something coherent to say. She took the telegram from her pocket and held it out to him. "I brought this in to you."

"You didn't have to. It's as much to you as it is to me." He could see she was uncomfortable and wasn't going to make it easy for her. She was being selfish in her need to be the one to save the Triple X. She should be jumping for joy right now, not hating him for being the one to give her hope.

"I ..." she swallowed. "I ... there's a personal message. It's yours."

"About my family?"

"Yes."

"That's not personal, just a fact."

"You lost someone?"

He stopped brushing and looked at her. She still held the telegram and he could see pity in those green eyes. He didn't want pity from Rachel. He wanted an honest chance. He wanted her to accept him for what he was. A man that would work hard to be an asset to the Triple X. A man that would be an asset to her, if she'd let him. "Yes, I lost someone." It was all he would say for now.

"I'm sorry." Rachel lowered her eyes, and her voice was only a whisper. She didn't know what else to say.

"Don't be. It doesn't concern you." His tone was harsh, and he noticed her head come up with a start.

"Fine." Rachel's voice became just as harsh. She'd only been trying to be polite. She couldn't force him to accept her sympathy. "Do you think this friend of yours can really help sell my cattle?"

"Our cattle," he corrected. "Yes. He wouldn't have given me false hope. If he says he can get us a buyer, he will."

Rachel decided to let his remark about 'our cattle' slip by. Things were tense enough between them as it was. "All right, then I suppose all we can do is wait until he contacts us again."

"Yes. I'm sure it'll be soon. He knows we're in a financial pinch." He could see the stiffness in Rachel's stance, and how she set her jaw with a defiant tilt. "Rachel, I think you can start to relax now. Things are going to get better from now on."

She continued to hold her stance. It was bad enough to have him to thank for the probable solution to the ranch's problem. She didn't need the nagging pity she felt when she thought about the message in the telegram, nor the incredible surges of heat that coursed through her every time their eyes met. It seemed that things were getting much worse, and more complicated. Not better. Of course, he was talking about the ranch's financial situation, not her emotional status. "I suppose you're right, Braddock. If your friend can help sell the cattle, I should be grateful." She turned her back on him and, seeing the telegram still in her hand, put it on the crossbar of the stall. "I'll have Hank get roundup going full swing. We should be ready when your friend contacts us again."

"Right." He wanted to say more but wasn't sure what it should be.

Rachel glanced at him over her shoulder. His black eyes were examining her. She could feel him studying her and was shocked when her nipples hardened against her shirt in response to his gaze. She was glad that her back was to him so he wouldn't see the effect he had on her body. She couldn't help the quick exploration her own eyes did of his tall frame or the way her lids lowered slightly as she did so.

Sin felt the heat of her gaze and saw the way she unconsciously wet her lips. His response was swift and sure. In this darkened building he didn't think she would see what her perusal was doing to him, and he frowned at his quick reaction. He had to remember Rachel's comments about making love to him. It had been "fun" to her. He wanted more. And until she was ready for more, he wouldn't give in to the desire in those emerald eyes.

Rachel shook herself. What was she doing? She knew she'd made a mistake when she'd made love to Sin, and now here she was, staring at him like this, ignoring all her good intentions about avoiding this type of contact with him. Damn, when would she ever learn? "I'll see you back at the house, later," she offered as she pulled her gaze from his. She started for the door.

Sin watched her go. He stood completely still until she'd left the barn, then he took several deep breaths to relax. He closed his eyes and leaned back against the stall railing. "Rachel, what am I going to do about you?" he whispered and heard Roux snort from his stall.

Lily turned dinner into a party that night. She'd told her mother about Sin being a captain in the army, and though he'd indicated he would prefer to forget his commission, she decided it was an occasion to celebrate. Lena had obliged them with whipped cream to top their dessert and some candles in a candelabra in the center of the table.

Rachel watched Sin from across the table and had begun counting the number of times Lily touched him on the arm and leaned over to him, exposing as much of her breasts as was possible without dumping them into his plate. She was curious about why Lucy didn't object to this kind of behavior. Perhaps it was the way all Southern belles behaved, so was considered acceptable.

"Rachel, dear, would you care for more dessert?" Lucy asked.

"No thank you, I've had quite enough of everything." She looked directly at Lily when she spoke. She couldn't help but notice the girl's attire once more. She frowned as she wondered how Lily had managed to bring so much fabric with her in the few trunks they'd brought with them from their home.

"So, Captain Braddock, you think we should have the party for our neighbors now?"

Lily's singsong voice broke through Rachel's musings. "The party?" she questioned.

"Yes, Cousin. Captain Braddock thinks it would be a good idea to give the party now," Lily happily explained.

"Oh he does, does he?" Rachel spoke to Lily but looked at Sin.

He stared back at her, unflinching. Her reason for not wanting to have a party would soon no longer exist, and it had suddenly sounded like a good idea. He would like to celebrate. He needed some light-hearted fun. It had been a long, long time since he'd felt like dancing, or had anything to dance about. Now, even though things between him and Rachel weren't perfect—might never be perfect—he had decided it was time to become more a part of the town and its people. Lily was right. They needed to get to know their neighbors, especially now that he knew he was going to be here for a while. "Do you have a strong objection, Rachel?" he asked quietly and waited.

The children had begun a rapid stream of excited squeals at the mention of a real party, and Rachel noticed the delighted look on Lucy's face when Lily made the announcement. She didn't have the heart to disappoint everyone. "In light of the news your telegram brought today, I think a party is a good idea." She put her napkin in her plate and stood up. "Lucy, Lily, would the two of you please coordinate with Lena and take care of the preparations. I'm sure you know more about giving parties than I do. Make it as fancy as you want."

"Mama, can I have a new dress for the party?" Tish asked.

"Yes, of course." Rachel looked down at her daughter's beautiful face. "We'll see to it you get the prettiest dress in town."

Tish clapped her hands together. "Oh, thank you, Mama."

"Rachel, I'm so thrilled," Lily gushed. "Mother and I would love to plan the party, wouldn't we, Mother?"

"Certainly. Oh dear, I must get this house in order. Rachel, your mother's parlor is a disgrace. It must be cleaned." She worried her napkin in excited thought of all that had to be done.

"Tish, honey, I'll help you find a pretty dress, if your mama doesn't have time," offered Lily. "Goodness, I'll need to look through my things to see if I have anything suitable. I may need a new dress myself."

"Yes, dear, you may. Heavens, what will I wear?" Lucy joined in the dress discussion. "Rachel, do you have a dress?"

Rachel was still standing at the head of the table. She was in awe of the excitement caused by the impending party. "I'm sure I'll find something, Aunt Lucy. Don't worry about me. You all have enough to do." She glanced at Sin, only to find him once again watching her.

"Do you have a dress, Rachel?" he asked.

Her breath caught in her throat for a second before she answered. "Like I said to Lucy, I'll find something. Don't worry about it. This party is really for all of you, anyway." She backed away from the table and left the room.

Sin couldn't help but feel a little sorry for Rachel. She was giving in on this party because she was feeling trapped, and he hated to see her defeated.

Rachel went outside and walked around the yard for a while before she came back and sat on the bottom step of the porch. She could still hear the excited chatter of voices in the dining room. Lena's voice was now among them. She also heard laughter. Her aunt and cousin finally had something to do.

She went to the barn to get Roux. This was a Rosebud night.

In the two weeks that followed, the house became a constant hub of activity. Curtains and drapes were taken down and washed, rugs were taken out and beaten, wood floors were polished and, true to her word, Lucy cleaned the parlor. Rachel couldn't remember the house ever being so shiny. What surprised her most was that she'd never noticed it needed cleaning before. So many changes were taking place in her life, changes she was having a hard time keeping up with. She decided to let things with the house run their course. If planning this party made everything run more smoothly for a while, so be it.

Another telegram from Sin's friend John had come, so roundup had begun in earnest. Rachel had been surprised and grateful to find out that the buyer they were supplying was a Southern man and his family. This had alleviated any problems with the hands and the question of their loyalty to the South.

Rachel spent every day on Roux, overseeing the roundup, helping wherever she could. The hours were long and the dust choking, but at the end of each day she was satisfied, and fell into an exhausted, dreamless sleep.

Another thing Rachel was grateful for was that Jace had seemed to give up the notions he'd had about her. She saw him watching her on several occasions, but he'd made no more advances and Hank told her that his nightly drinking trips to the Wagonwheel had stopped.

The only thing that nagged at her now was Sin. He was helping with roundup and putting in long hours right along with everyone else. Some of the men had even started looking to him for answers when she wasn't around. He was earning his way and that bothered her.

She couldn't get over the feeling that this was still her ranch and that he had no business being here. The fact that it was his contact with John Wright that had saved the Triple X did little to dispel these feelings.

Rachel sat astride Roux on a small hillock and watched Ben herding a group of cattle toward the corral. She smiled to herself when she heard him swearing as one of the cows veered off in the opposite direction. Sometimes cows were obstinate creatures. She turned her attention to the activity at the corral gate. The men were pushing cattle through, trying to get them to the other side to make room for the cattle coming up behind them. Hats were being waved, and whistles and shouts could be heard above the bawling of the animals. The scene was one she loved.

Stretching in the saddle, she rubbed her thighs where the heat from the sun was beating with a vengeance. The weather was the only thing making this roundup a little more difficult than some others. The wind had still not returned, and though she sometimes cursed the biting sand it wielded, it also provided a vehicle for the dust raised by the hooves of so much activity. As it was, she and the hands were continually working in an enormous cloud of choking dust.

Right now, as she sat a distance away, Rachel noticed quite a few of the hands had pulled their handkerchiefs over their faces. It made it difficult to identify all of them easily, especially through the dust. She scanned the group, looking for Sin. He was one figure she could usually pick out, no matter how dirty he was or how many of the other men were around him. She couldn't find his tall frame among the men in view. Frowning, she turned Roux, angry with herself for looking for him.

Jace stood on one of the gate posts and watched Rachel. She was heading away from the corral now but he'd seen her sitting there for quite a while. His eyes narrowed as he pulled the handkerchief from his face. "Miss Rachel, high-and-mighty boss lady," he whispered.

185

In the last couple of weeks he hadn't been able to get a free minute with her. The roundup was taking everyone's time, but he knew that even if he'd had time, she wouldn't have had time for him. She didn't even look at him anymore. It seemed that she'd forgotten he even existed. She used to know he was around. It even seemed she was softening toward him, until Braddock showed up.

Braddock—even thinking his name made him spit. He remembered how Braddock had beaten him in the Rosebud, and his heart filled with hatred. "Just you wait, Braddock. I'll meet you when I'm not drinking, and we'll see who gets the better of who."

"You talking to someone, Jace?" asked Ben, who now had the cattle walking through the gate.

Jace looked up at the younger man. "No, Ben. Just thinkin' out loud." He continued thinking as Ben rode away. The desire to meet Braddock sober was what had stopped his nightly trips to the Wagonwheel. He knew that his chance would come. And, maybe, if Rachel saw him beat her new partner, she might once again have time for him. She'd see who the better man was, and he, Jace, would finally be allowed back into his rightful place. He'd finally get Rachel where he wanted her, back into his bed.

"You gonna stand around daydreaming all day, or are you gonna help get these cattle through this gate?" demanded Hank.

Jace, startled out of his thoughts, pulled his handkerchief back over his face. "I'm workin', Hank. I just needed a break."

"Then get down off the gate and let someone else get up there 'til you're ready to get back to work. I need someone who's gonna help get these cattle through here now, not in ten minutes when you're through restin'"

"I'm through," Jace growled.

"Good." Hank rode away.

Jace knew that Hank had been more than fair with him when he was drinking, but that didn't give the old man the right to ride him now. He just might have to do something about him one of these days, too.

As Rachel walked from the barn to the house late that evening she heard the thunder. She looked up to the darkened window of Tish's room and hoped it wouldn't wake her with nightmares. Another clap rolled across the open range like a deep growl, and she felt it as much as she heard it. She looked to the horizon, but in the darkness couldn't see the clouds. The weather had been bothering her for several weeks, and she was afraid they were in for some bad storms. Late summer had the potential for tornadoes, and the strange calm they'd been experiencing had given her cause for worry.

"Did you hear that?" Sin's voice was soft as he saw Rachel climb the porch steps.

Rachel hadn't seen him sitting there in the shadows and jumped a bit. "Yes, I heard it."

Sin felt her unease. "Bad weather ahead?" he asked her opinion.

"Hope not, we've got too much to do." She debated about whether to go on into the house or to sit down and talk to him. She found herself sitting on the porch rail.

Sin was more than a little surprised that she decided to join him. She'd been avoiding him, and he'd started wondering if she would do it forever. He waited to see if she would reveal the reason for this change.

The silence between them was like a black space waiting to be filled. Rachel couldn't see Sin's face in the shadows but could feel him watching her. She turned her head slightly and gazed out across the yard toward the large bulk of the barn, standing in darkness. She took a deep breath. She wanted to ask him questions. Questions about his past. Questions that had been nagging her for days. Questions she thought about at night when she lay in bed, listening for sounds from his room before she fell asleep. She took another deep breath and chewed the inside of her lower lip. Somehow, talking to

Sin, really talking to him, seemed more personal than having sex with him.

Sin watched all her subtle moves of unease. When she turned her head, he could see the silhouette of her face against the night sky and saw that she was frowning. Still, he waited.

"Were you wounded?" Rachel's tentative voice broke the silence.

Sin took in a shallow breath. So this would be her first question. "You saw the scar."

"Yes." She remembered the jagged red that scored his left shoulder. "You were shot?"

"Yes." He straightened in the chair, unsure of how much to reveal. "In a small battle in South Carolina."

Rachel digested this information. It was hard to picture Sin in a battle. It was even harder to imagine him lying in the dirt with a bullet through his shoulder. "Why did you quit fighting?" He obviously hadn't been crippled by his injury so she could think of no excuse for his absence from the war.

Sin heard a slight change in her voice. Was it the tone of accusation? He waited for a moment, deciding what to tell her. "I was asked to stop fighting."

"By your superiors? That would be ridiculous." She answered her own question, then continued. "By who?"

Sin breathed deeply. "By the North."

Rachel sat silently, waiting for what he'd said to make sense to her. "What do you mean, by the North?" she finally asked. "The Yanks just asked you, a captain of the Confederacy, to quit fighting and you did?"

Sin knew she didn't understand. She didn't know the circumstances of his decision. "Rachel, there was more to it than that."

"I should hope so." Rachel found herself becoming angry with him. She realized it was her Southern heritage rebelling against the idea that he deserted the war because some Yank asked him to. "There has to be a good explanation."

Sin leaned forward in the chair, putting his face in his

hands for a moment, remembering the months he'd spent in hell. "I was in prison." His voice came out stilted.

Rachel waited.

"I was captured when I was wounded and spent seventeen months in a Northern prison." He grimaced with pain at the memory. "I didn't know it had been seventeen months until I was freed." He looked up at Rachel, her silhouette against the sky. "You have no idea how quickly you lose track of time in a place like that."

Rachel had heard stories about the prison camps. The conditions and treatment were inhuman. Did Sin agree to stop fighting to get away from the horrors of prison? "So, Braddock, you agreed not to fight anymore to get out of prison."

The shock of her assumption gripped his heart. "You think so little of me, you'd believe that?"

"Am I wrong?"

Sin narrowed his eyes, realizing how quickly she'd jumped to the wrong conclusion. She was eager to believe the worst about him. "Yes, Rachel. You're wrong."

"So tell me what happened. Explain it to me so I understand it."

"I don't know if you'd ever understand it, Rachel. You'd have to understand some other things first. You'd have to understand how a man feels when he learns he's needed at home by an ailing father. You'd have to understand what it's like to fight a battle between loyalty to country and loyalty to family. You'd have to understand what it is to feel normal human emotions like concern and love. These are things you'd need to understand first, and frankly, I wonder if you ever will." He stood and looked down at her. "Rachel, you're so busy being strong and right about everything that you don't give yourself the time to be human."

Rachel was scowling when she stood. "Braddock, you and I have different definitions of what being human is. I sure don't think being human means being weak."

"And you think I do?"

"It seems that way. Every time you don't like the way I react to something you accuse me of being too hard. Well, don't let this come as a great shock to your delicate system, but I don't care what you think. If you want a woman that swoons every time some little thing goes wrong, you should start spending more time with Lily. I'm sure she'd be thrilled to get your attention. In case you haven't noticed it, her nipples get hard every time you enter the room. Now, leave me the hell alone." Rachel brushed past him and went into the house.

Later that night, as she lay in bed, Rachel remembered the remark Sin had made about his father. Something about him being ill. She realized that she still didn't know the reason Sin had left the war, but she knew instinctively he wasn't a coward or a deserter. She shuddered as she fell asleep thinking about what it must have been like in the Northern army prison. In her troubled dreams, the distant thunder sounded like cannon fire and gunshots. She awakened several times with a start, soaked in sweat, remembering the nightmares that woke her, and wishing morning would come and end this torturous night.

12

Damn it, what am I going to wear?" Rachel grumbled as she kicked her green dress under the bed. She'd worn that same dress to church every other Sunday for the past two years. Her light pink dress, the other church garment, was lying crumpled in a heap on the floor by her nightstand. "Why didn't I think about this sooner?" she berated herself.

The party was but a few hours away, and she was standing in her room in a chemise and pantaloons trying to figure out how she was going to manufacture a party dress in the remaining time. "Oh, hell!" she cursed loudly. She'd managed to get a lovely dress for Tish, and had even purchased a new one for Lena, but had overlooked the importance of her own attire until now, when it was too late.

"Is something the matter, dear?" Lucy inquired through the door.

"No, Aunt Lucy. I'm fine, really." What a liar I am, she thought.

"I heard you ... exclaiming. Are you sure there isn't a problem?" Lucy persisted.

Rachel crossed to her door and opened it a crack. "I was just trying to decide which dress to wear." She smiled at her aunt, hoping the woman wouldn't guess what was wrong. Everyone had asked her, at least twice, if she had a proper dress, and she'd assured them she had. Now, here she stood, in her underwear, with no dress.

"Well, if you're sure there's nothing wrong I'll go check with Lena about the food." Lucy was wearing a tiny frown of concern.

"I'm fine, really. You go ahead. I know you have a lot to do." She smiled again and used her sweetest tone of voice. She could tell Lucy was suspicious.

"Very well. Call me if you need anything."

"Oh, I will, Aunt Lucy. I promise." She closed the door gently, then crossed to sit on the bed. "Damn it!" she whispered.

The problem was that she had so few options. She owned two dresses, if she didn't count the white dress she'd worn to dinner that one evening. Even if she did count it, it was unsuitable. Not only was it a day dress, it really was too small. The other two dresses were old, well worn, and suitable for Sunday services, not a party and dance.

Rachel kicked herself mentally. "Why the hell did I allow this stupid party in the first place? If I had stuck to my guns I wouldn't be going through this now."

She leaned up over the headboard and looked out the window. Below her, in the yard, the hands were finishing up their work early so they could get cleaned up for the party. Everyone was invited and very excited. All the neighboring ranchers were coming and most of the townspeople. "Hell, the place is going to be overrun with people that don't even like me."

She turned over on her bed and pulled her hair out from under her shoulders. It was still damp from the washing she'd given it in the creek a short time before. She wasn't sure how she was going to comb it. Lily had explained in great detail how her own hair was to be arranged, and it had seemed like a lot of importance being set on something foolish. Now she wasn't so sure.

She heaved a heavy sigh just as she heard a soft knock on her door.

"May I come in, Mama?" Tish asked as she stuck her blond head into the room.

"Of course you may come in, if I can have a big hug and kiss." She held her arms open, and the little girl flew to join her mother on the bed.

"I'm so glad we're having a party, Mama."

"It'll be a lot of fun for you, won't it, my darling?" Rachel smoothed the hair from her daughter's forehead.

"Yes, but that's not why I'm glad."

"All right, why are you glad?" Rachel inquired, sure the answer would be something simple, like because she would get more dessert, or because she would be allowed to stay up late.

"I'm glad because the party made you stop work early. I haven't been seeing you enough, Mama. You've been working so much lately that I miss you." Tish's earnest brown eyes gazed up into her mother's.

Rachel pulled her daughter even closer to her. "My darling girl, I love you so much. I miss you too. But sometimes mamas have to work." She leaned back and took Tish's chin in her hand, looking into her eyes again. "You understand, don't you?"

"Yes, Mama." The child answered seriously. "But I'm glad we're having the party."

Rachel smiled. "Me, too," she said, then wondered at her own lie. She wasn't happy about this party, but she was glad that Tish was enjoying herself. "Are you about ready to get into your party dress?"

"Aunt Lucy says I can't put it on until right before the party." She stuck out her lower lip.

"She did? I think that's silly. Run and get it, and I'll help you put it on."

"Really, Mama?" Tish's eyes opened wide. "Aunt Lucy will get angry with us."

Rachel grinned. "Let her. I want to see you in your dress now, so run along and get it. Go on. Hurry up."

She helped Tish up off the bed and shooed her out the door.

Turning around once more to face her own dress dilemma, she had about decided to go to the party in her trousers and shirt with her gun strapped to her thigh. "That would send Lucy into a fit, if anything could." She laughed at the thought.

"I'm back, Mama." Tish rushed through the door carrying a bright pink dress with more ruffles than either one of them had ever seen before.

"All right, let's slip it over your head." She lifted the dress and dropped it over her daughter's wiggling form. "Stand still. Put your arms through the sleeves. Yes, that's it. Let me fasten you up. Now, turn around and let me see." Rachel's eyes filled with unaccustomed tears at how beautiful her precious little girl looked wearing the frilly dress.

"Am I pretty, Mama?" Tish asked.

"Oh, my Letisha. You are beautiful." She pulled her daughter to her in a strong hug.

"Mama, you'll wrinkle me," Tish admonished.

Rachel started to laugh. "You're right, I'm sorry."

"That's all right, Mama. You can hug me again." Tish giggled and threw her arms around her mother's waist.

Rachel obliged her and kissed the top of her head.

"Now you have to put on your dress, Mama."

Rachel's heart was seized by a moment of panic. What was she going to do? She released her daughter and went over and picked up the discarded dresses. She held them up for Tish's examination. "Which one?" She was just going to have to put up with being inappropriately dressed. It couldn't be helped.

"Mama?" Tish asked. "Don't you have a pretty dress to wear?"

Rachel took a deep breath. "I'm afraid not, my darling. One of these will have to do."

"But, Mama, they're your church dresses. You need something fancy, like me."

"I'm sorry, Tish. This is all I have. It will have to do."

She could barely stand to look at the fallen expression of her daughter.

"But, Mama!"

"It's all right, darling."

"But everybody got a new dress. Even Jeremy."

"Even Jeremy got a dress?" Rachel smiled.

"He didn't get a new dress, Mama," Tish frowned at her mother's attempt to make this funny, "but he got new trousers and a new shirt. He even got a black tie."

"I know, but I've been too busy to worry about a dress." That wasn't exactly true. She'd had time, she just hadn't wanted to think about the party.

"Oh, Mama." Tish hung her head. "Lily got a new yellow dress with satin rosettes."

Rachel knew that Tish had no idea what "satin rosettes" were, but Lily had been talking about her dress so much that everyone, including some of the hands, knew what it looked like. "I know, but it really doesn't matter, Tish. Honest." She tried to get Tish to lift her head, but she wouldn't.

"But, Mama, you're prettier than cousin Lily. Now everybody is going to think she's prettier."

Rachel sank down onto the bed. She felt she'd let her daughter down. It didn't matter to her what anyone thought, but it obviously mattered to Tish, and she should have thought of that while she was ignoring the impending event.

"Don't worry, little one. I'll think of something."

Tish's head came up just a little as she looked at her mother. "Really?"

"Really. Now run along, and don't worry about it." She had no idea what she was going to come up with, but she was determined not to disappoint her daughter. "And don't get dirty, Lucy would skin us both if you did." She tickled her daughter and sent her toward the door in a fit of giggles.

"Yes, Mama." Tish danced out of her mother's room, happy that her mama was going to be the prettiest lady at the party.

Rachel continued to stare at the door of her room after Tish had bounced through it. "What the hell am I going to do now?" she asked herself. "I don't have the slightest idea where to get a dress on this short notice." She shook her head and once more fell back on the bed. "Right now I could use a mother, myself," she whispered.

It had been so long since her own mother's death that she seldom thought about her, but she remembered that her mother always seemed calm. "What would you do in this situation, Mother?" she whispered. She rubbed her hands over her face. "You wouldn't have gotten yourself into this mess in the first place. You were always so prepared for every occasion." Rachel sat up very slowly. "You were always prepared," she whispered. A thought had occurred to her. She grabbed her wrapper and, pulling it on, left her room, heading for the attic.

"Where is it?" she exclaimed a short time later as she rummaged through boxes for her mother's things. Rachel thought that most of her mother's possessions, including her clothing, was still stored in the attic. If she could find the box, and if the clothing was still intact, and if anything fit her, and was suitable for a party, her problem would be solved. A lot of "ifs" but it was her only chance.

Finally, in the very back corner of the hot dusty attic, she found a box containing what looked like dresses. She pulled the box over and around years of accumulated junk and lifted it to carry it down to her room.

Moments later, she was almost afraid to start looking through it. Tentatively at first she pulled a dress from the top. It was a deep burgundy brocade, with a high collar and fur trim on the sleeves. She also found a matching muff. "Well, this one won't do." The second dress was a deep green, similar to the first, only with matching gloves and hat instead of the muff. "Didn't you own any summer things, Mother?" she mused, certain she'd get to those in a moment.

Several dresses later she began to worry in earnest. All of the garments in the box were dark colors and heavy material. Rachel knew that this was the only box of clothing in the attic because she'd looked in all the rest. She continued pulling dresses from the box.

She came across a black satin gown with a lace insert from the bodice to the high neckline and long lace sleeves. Huge black flowers adorned the breast area and hung limply around the hemline. "God, Mother, did you actually wear this awful thing? It looks like a party dress you'd wear to a funeral." She plucked at one of the flowers that rested along the shoulder, and it fell off in her hand. "Horrible." She dropped the dress and flower onto the pile and continued looking through the box.

Only minutes later she made the discovery that there was nothing suitable in the box. She sat down on the bed and surveyed the pile of dresses. "Now what am I going to do?" She heaved a sigh and kicked at the pile. The dress that caught on her foot was the black satin. She picked it up and angrily began pulling the huge ugly flowers from it. "Damn it!" she hissed. She pulled another flower off and dropped it to the floor. Another and another followed suit. Pretty soon all the flowers were off the bodice, and she moved on to the hem. It took only a moment more for the idea to form. If this dress was the only chance she had, she'd make the best of it.

She laid the dress out on her bed and tried to think of a way to make it not quite so grotesque. The fact that it was black couldn't be helped. She was going to be out of place in a black dress at a summer party, but the color was the least of her worries.

A few of the flowers wouldn't come off gracefully so she grabbed some scissors and cut them free. After all the flowers lay in a macabre bouquet on the floor she wondered what else she could do. Rachel was not a seamstress. She'd never made a dress in her life, and the closest she'd ever come to mending was when she fixed the seam on her saddle. She knew this was going to be difficult. Somehow, she was going to have to make this dress as presentable as possible and do it with scissors alone.

The next things to go were the sleeves. Rachel cut the lace away carefully, without cutting through the seams that held the dress together. She threw the sleeves to the floor with the flowers. It was at this point that she realized she didn't even know if the dress would fit her. "Please let this fit? Please?" she begged, her eyes skyward, as she pulled the garment over her head. As she pulled it down she found that her mother's figure and hers were very similar. Rachel's bust was a bit fuller and her waist just a little smaller, but the dress would be fine. If she could make it presentable.

After she took it off, Rachel cut away the lace that created the high neckline. For a few minutes she was worried that this would cause the new neckline, created by the satin bodice, to be too low. She didn't allow herself to worry too long. She had no other options. By the time she was through cutting and ripping, the dress she held only vaguely resembled the one she'd started with. Only the reaction of others would tell her if she looked ridiculous.

She only hoped Tish would think she looked pretty. "I know I can't compete with Lily's yellow rosettes," she mused, "but maybe this will do." She put the dress over her arm and carried it downstairs to iron.

Sin greeted guests, arriving by wagon and on horseback, from the front porch. Everyone was laughing and talking, and a sense of excitement filled the air. All of the ladies were dressed in their finest summer gowns of the palest hues, and he was reminded of the glorious picnics and barbecues held at his family's plantation during his youth.

The men who'd agreed to play the music for the party had begun a lively tune, and several couples had already started dancing. Sin wondered if Rachel would dance with him later. He hoped so, even though she'd barely spoken to him since their discussion on the porch about his past.

"Captain Braddock, how are things going out here?" Lily asked as she came up behind him and put her hand through his arm.

He turned and looked down at her loveliness. The pale yellow of her dress set off her white complexion perfectly, and he noticed just a hint of rouge on her cheeks and full lips. She leaned forward the tiniest bit as she spoke to him, giving him a good view of the deep cleft between her breasts. He remembered the remark Rachel had made about Lily's nipples and nearly laughed. He managed to control the urge as he answered her question. "Everything's going well. The people already here are enjoying themselves, and more are arriving every minute."

"Wonderful." She batted her lashes up at him. "You will save me a dance later, won't you, Captain?"

Sin had given up trying to stop her calling him Captain. "Yes, of course, Miss Lily. I would have insisted if you hadn't mentioned it," he assured her.

She coyly turned her head. "Until later, then. I must go help Mother."

Sin watched her go and was relieved. Why wasn't it Lily who made his blood race, who caused his body to harden with desire each time she was near? "Because life isn't fair, and you're a fool," he whispered as he looked around for Rachel. She still hadn't made her entrance.

Upstairs, Rachel stood in front of her mirror, assessing her appearance. The dress had turned out better than she'd expected, once ironed, but she was certain she would be the only woman in black at the party, and she felt self-conscious about how low the neckline had ended up being. It was true, she'd seen Lily with as much breast exposed, but that was Lily. She tugged at the fabric trying to cover herself but realized, for the tenth time in as many minutes, that it wasn't going to stretch. "Oh well, if I don't bend over too far, maybe no one will notice."

She patted her hair and frowned. It was still damp. After rummaging through the dusty attic, and finding a spider's web in her curls, she'd had to wash it again. There was no way to get it dry in time, so she was going to have to go to the party with it wet. She'd pulled it up with a piece of the black lace she'd cut from the dress. Damp curls wound wildly around her face and fell in ringlets down her back, with several lying coolly against the bare curve of her breasts. She had no fancy jewelry or adornment and so was certain she was barely presentable. "If Tish thinks I look beautiful, that's all that matters," she told her reflection. Taking a deep breath, she headed toward the door and the party.

Sin saw Rachel slowly descending the stairs, and his breath caught in his throat. "My God," he said in a whisper. Rachel looked more beautiful than he'd thought possible. The very starkness of her attire gave her a radiance unmatched by any of the other women in their pale finery. The shining black satin caused her skin to glow in creamy contrast, and as she noticed him, he could see a pale pink blush start up over the smooth mounds of her breasts and travel to her cheeks.

Rachel was coming down the stairs when she discovered Sin watching her. She'd never felt so self-conscious in her life and had to resist the urge to dash back up the stairs and put on her trousers. Then she noticed the approval in his black eyes and the desire. She felt herself blush and frowned. She was definitely out of her element here. Straightening her shoulders, she reached the bottom step as Sin came forward to meet her.

"Rachel, you look . . . beautiful." His voice was raspy when he spoke.

She turned her head slightly, still not sure he wasn't just being polite. "Thank you. Where's Tish?"

Sin couldn't take his eyes off her. He noticed her hair was damp and longed to touch the cool curls that caressed her shoulders and breasts. No artificial color graced her cheeks or lips, but her own natural pigment made it unnecessary. The light tan of her face and pink glow on her cheeks accented the deep green of her eyes and the darker, moist pink of her full lips. He was assailed by memories of their lovemaking and wanted to take her again, to pull her from the party, out into the darkness and to bury himself deeply within her.

"I said, where's Tish? Have you seen her?" Rachel repeated when he didn't answer.

"I think she's outside helping carry food to the tables," he told her. "Rachel, will you dance with me later?"

She was surprised that he'd made it a point to ask her now. She was even surprised he'd asked her at all. They hadn't been on the best of terms for quite a while. Actually, if she thought about it, they'd never been on the best of terms. It seemed the only time they'd ever had any kind of agreement was at the creek the day they'd made love, and even that had ended badly when she'd hurt his feelings.

She supposed he was making an effort to get along because of the party. It wouldn't do for them to have an argument in front of everyone. Well, if he could call a truce, so could she. "I suppose I'll dance with you, Braddock. Now I have to find Tish, if you'll excuse me?"

Sin watched her back as she went toward the door. His heart was beating erratically, and he wondered if he'd get through the night without making a fool of himself.

Once outside, Rachel glanced back over her shoulder, through the screen door, to where Sin was standing now, talking to Hank. She watched while Hank introduced Sin to his sister, Selma.

Rachel narrowed her eyes as she examined the way he was dressed. The black trousers Sin wore fit snugly over the muscles of his thighs and buttocks. She swallowed as she remembered the feel of those muscles under her hands. He was wearing a white shirt and a thin, black bolo tie with a silver and turquoise conch.

His hair was curling softly over his forehead and the back of his collar. She closed her hands into fists to stop the tingle she felt, remembering the texture of those curls.

As Rachel walked around the yard, looking for Tish, she heard several exclamations about her appearance. It was obvious from the remarks that the men found her attire quite lovely while their wives disapproved. Sighing, she realized that things seldom change.

"Rachel, I'll bet you're glad to have a man around the place to help run things again." Emily Bigley's voice broke through her thoughts.

"I'm sorry, Emily, I was thinking. What did you say?" Rachel turned and looked at Pete's wife and felt a pang of pity for the little man. Emily was a large, dark-haired woman with broad features, and, according to gossip, a terrible temper.

"I was only saying how lucky you must be feeling to have a man around the place again," Emily repeated, giving Rachel's appearance a distasteful once-over.

"Why would I be feeling lucky?" Rachel's eyes sparked.

"To help you run the ranch, of course."

"Why would I need help running the ranch? I've been running it most of my life." The challenge in her voice was obvious. It was then that she noticed several of Emily's friends standing in the background listening to their conversation.

"I only meant that any woman would be happy to have a man around to do the jobs that aren't proper for a lady." Emily's patronizing tone sealed her fate.

"That's not what you meant at all, Emily." Rachel's stance had changed, and her voice carried the quiet threat. "You meant to insult me and put me in my place, and from the look of your audience," she gestured toward the other women, "you're not the only one who wanted to see me squirm. Well, I hate to disappoint you all, but it takes a lot more than a bunch of mealy-mouthed busybodies sticking their noses in my business

to make me dance a jig. I suggest you pay more attention to your own problems and less to mine." She looked
around to find Pete standing across the yard, talking in
a very animated fashion to her cousin Lily. Perfect, she
thought. "You may have problems you don't even know
about yet." She pointed at Pete. "See, Emily," she
looked the woman up and down, "of course, I can't say
I blame him."

"Why you . . ." Emily sputtered. "Pete! Come here at
once," she called as she stomped away.

Rachel let out a deep breath and turned to see the
other women had dispersed quickly. Shaking her head,
she continued to look for Tish. It was exactly this kind
of confrontation with some of the townswomen that
she'd hoped to avoid. She only hoped the rest of the
evening would go more smoothly. "Tish, there you are!"
she called when she saw her daughter running after Jeremy toward the barn.

"Mama! You're beautiful!" Tish clapped her hands
together when she saw her mother.

Rachel knelt down and kissed Tish's soft cheeks. "So
you approve?"

"Oh, yes, you're the prettiest lady here."

Rachel grimaced slightly at the term "lady." She'd just
been informed, once again, that she wasn't a lady. She
smoothed a stray piece of hair from her daughter's eyes
and kissed her lightly on the tip of her nose. "Thank
you, my darling girl. You make me feel pretty."

"Wow!" Jeremy exclaimed as he ran over to them.
"You look wonderful, Cousin Rachel."

Rachel stood and placed her hand on his shoulder.
"Thank you, Jeremy. What are you two up to?"

"We're just playing hide-and-seek with some of the
other children." He was tugging gently on Tish's dress,
trying to get her to go with him.

"All right, you two have a good time and stay together. It's awfully dark out by the barn," she warned.

"Yes, Cousin Rachel. Yes, Mama," they said in
unison.

Rachel leaned over and kissed Tish just before she ran off giggling with Jeremy. As she watched them go, Rachel thought about how nice it was to have Jeremy around for Tish. She startled herself with this thought. So far, she'd considered her relatives not much more than a nuisance.

Jace saw Rachel with her daughter and Jeremy and was gripped by jealousy. Rachel had so much love for some people and none for him. He wanted her love. He wanted . . .

He looked at the way she was dressed, and a heated pulse beat in his temples and throughout his body. He stepped back into the shadows and took a deep breath as he watched the swell of her breasts above the neckline of her dress. He wanted to reach down the front of her gown and pull her breasts free, to taste them, to feel their peaks harden against his tongue. Lord, he was getting hard thinking about her. He didn't want to go on yearning for Rachel. There was no reason she should deny him. She'd loved him once, he could make her love him again. He growled angrily as he stepped back out of the shadows. He wouldn't be put off any longer. He'd do something about Rachel tonight.

When Rachel entered the kitchen a few minutes after leaving Tish and Jeremy outside, she was met with a surprising sight, Lucy and Lena were bent over a casserole on the table, laughing about which seasoning should be added. "You two seem to be getting along," she observed when she joined them.

"Oh, yes. We are just fine," said Lena, smiling.

Rachel was puzzled about how these women, who'd been at continual odds over how things were to be done around the house, now seemed like fast friends. She couldn't remember anything specific happening to change things. They'd been working together on the preparations for the party, but this went beyond mere cooperation. "I'm glad to see everything running so smoothly. Do you need help?" she asked.

"Heavens no, Rachel. You just run along and have

fun. Lena and I have everything under control," answered Lucy.

Rachel felt like one of the children being told to go out to play. "Are you sure?"

"Of course I'm sure. We've just about got all the dishes outside on the tables, and many of our neighbors are bringing more. We'll be ready to have a feast in just a little while." Lucy heaved a satisfied sigh. "Now run along. Enjoy yourself."

Rachel left the kitchen feeling a little like a stranger in her own house. She looked at the miraculous changes all around her. The floors and other woodwork glowed with fresh coats of wax and lemon polish. The new white curtains gleamed at the windows, and the house was dust free for the first time she could remember. It seemed that some time during the past few weeks, while she was busy with roundup, and trying to ignore the upcoming party, things had begun to change. Even Lucy and Lena had changed under her very nose, and she'd never even noticed it until now.

"Cousin Rachel, you look ... very nice," Lily stated flatly, when they met in the hall. "How ... interesting of you to wear black."

"Thank you, Lily." Rachel answered her offhanded compliment, then looked at Lily's beauty. She couldn't deny the girl's attractiveness. "And you are definitely the most beautiful girl here. Your dress is lovely." She could tell that Lily thought her own dress was ghastly, but it didn't matter, Tish thought it was pretty.

"Do you think so?" Lily gushed. "I hope Captain Braddock likes it."

Rachel looked at the girl's exposed cleavage. "I'm sure he will." She was sure that every man around would enjoy the view.

"Oh, here he comes!" whispered Lily excitedly. "He's probably going to ask me to dance."

Rachel turned to see Sin approaching them through the crowd. She stepped back as he reached them, giving him a clear path to talk to Lily. She had just started wondering what Lily would do if she knew about her and Sin's lovemaking when she felt him touch her arm.

"Captain . . ." Lily raised her hand to him.

"Rachel, will you honor me with this dance?" His voice interrupted Lily.

Rachel looked up, surprised at his request. She heard Lily's quiet intake of air and knew the girl was stunned. She looked at Lily's flushed face, then up into Sin's black eyes, watching her intently. "Well, Braddock, I . . .," she looked once more at Lily. Her jaw was firmly set, and a feral gleam showed in her eyes. Rachel raised her chin and met the girl's stare, "If you will excuse me, Lily?" She took Sin's arm as he led her out of the house to where the dancers were turning slowly to the music.

There was something in Lily's expression that had irritated Rachel. She hadn't wanted to hurt her but the challenge in Lily's eyes caused her to react, perhaps foolishly. She didn't care if Lily thought herself in love with Braddock. In fact, she'd prefer it if he lavished his attention on the younger woman all the time. If she was lucky, maybe they'd marry and leave the Triple X to start their own ranch somewhere else. She looked up to see Sin watching her curiously.

"What was that all about?" Sin asked as he took Rachel into his arms.

Rachel felt the heat from his body as he pulled her closer. She saw the erratic beat of his heart in the pulse at his temple, and she felt the immediate rush of her own blood as her body responded to his nearness. Damn, she thought. "What?"

"What was going on between you and Lily? She looked ready to kill. Are you having problems with her?"

Only since you became her target, she thought to herself, and I started acting like a fool. "No problems," she lied and continued gliding with him to the music. "Why didn't you ask Lily to dance?" she questioned him a moment later.

Sin looked down into her green eyes and was caught

by their emerald glow. "I told you earlier that I wanted to dance with you. You agreed."

Rachel didn't like the way he was looking at her or holding her. She didn't like the way her body was heating up at his touch, or the way people were watching them. She saw Emily standing at the edge of the dance area with a smug look on her face. "Well, now I've danced with you, so thanks." She tried to pull away, but he held her fast.

"What's the matter, Rachel? The dance isn't over yet."

"I just don't think the truce is a good idea."

"What truce?" He frowned at her.

She thought for a moment and realized they'd said nothing about a truce. She'd gotten the idea on her own when he mentioned he wanted to dance with her. "That's what this is," she stated.

He stopped dancing. "You agreed to dance with me because of some imaginary truce you dreamed up?" His voice was incredulous.

"I only thought . . ."

"No, Rachel, you didn't think. You never do," he interrupted her.

"May I cut in?" Jace questioned at that moment.

"By all means, Jace. She's all yours."

Rachel was stunned by Sin's reaction. He walked away without so much as looking back and she found herself in Jace's arms, being led around the dance area, surprised at the turn of events.

"I'm so glad I got this chance to dance with you, Rachel," Jace told her. He looked down at her breasts and swallowed his desire.

"Yes, Jace. This is nice," she said absently.

"I've wanted to talk to you for a long time."

"Is that right?" she asked while wondering why Braddock had gotten so angry.

"Yes, Rachel. I want to start courting you. I'd ask your father, but since he's dead I suppose I just have to ask you."

This finally got through her thoughts. "You want to what?"

"Rachel, I know we can work things out between us. I've given this a lot of thought and I want to do this right, so you'll take me seriously. That's why I'm asking to court you proper."

He was talking fast, and Rachel noticed a nerve jumping in his jaw. Was he crazy? She'd tried to show him that there was no hope of a future between them. Now he was talking about courting her like she was some virginal schoolgirl. The man had no idea how ridiculous he sounded. "Jace, I . . ."

"Don't say anything yet, Rachel. Think about it."

"Jace, I don't have to think about it. It's impossible."

He held her hand tighter. "No, Rachel, it's not impossible. Don't say that it is."

Rachel had a hard time not flinching from the pressure he was putting on her hand. "Jace, you're hurting me. Let go."

"Not until you agree to think about it. Please, Rachel?"

She could see the desperation in his eyes and knew that she could no longer put off firing him. She glanced at the crowd around her and decided to wait only until morning. If his absence meant she'd be shorthanded for the rest of roundup and the drive, so be it. "All right, Jace. I'll think about it." Her voice was a monotone, but it was the best she could do.

"You really will?" He didn't trust her. She might only be agreeing with him so he'd let go of her hand. He squeezed it even harder to make sure she knew that he meant what he said.

"I said I would." Rachel didn't like feeling cornered. Her first instinct was to turn and fight. "Either you believe me or you don't. But if you don't let go of my hand right now you'd better be prepared for all hell to break loose when you do."

He watched the green sparks of anger in her eyes and felt the stiffness of her back under his other hand. He slowly released her. "You just remember what you're supposed to be thinking about, Rachel."

"I know exactly what I'm thinking about." She'd thought about it and decided. This man would be off her ranch by noon tomorrow, or he'd be dead. She walked away and realized that this was the first time she'd ever felt fear when confronting Jace. He had changed oddly, and it gave her an uneasy feeling of dread.

Before Rachel could get back to the house she was confronted by Stoker.

"Would you please dance with me, Miss Rachel?" He held his hat in his hand, twisting it nervously.

She looked at him as though seeing him for the first time. His brown hair was damp and combed securely in place. He had a thick mustache that curled at the ends, and she noticed his eyes were a deep gray. She was amazed that he was really quite attractive when cleaned up. "I'd be proud to dance with you, Stoker." She smiled at him and let him lead her back out onto the dance area.

Once there, he didn't know what to do with his hat. Rachel tried not to notice, he was already so obviously nervous, but as he stood there, looking bewildered, she decided to solve his problem. "Here, let me have that." She took the hat and tossed it to a hay bale not far away. "All right?"

He smiled sheepishly at her. "All right."

The band was playing a waltz and Stoker wasn't the best dancer she'd ever been with, but they made it around the dance area a few times without mishap. Rachel was starting to relax after her meeting with Jace, and she smiled at Stoker.

"Miss Rachel?"

"Yes, Stoker?"

"I . . . I wanted to talk to you about something."

She could tell he was having a hard time broaching something with her. "Yes?"

"It's about Miss Lily."

She saw him gulp and felt sorry for him. "Miss Lily?"

"Yes, ma'am. Do you think . . ."

"Yes, Stoker?"

"Well, do you think she'd be interested in the likes of me?" He hung his head in doubt.

Rachel found his lack of confidence touching. She suddenly realized how lucky Lily was to have a man like Stoker thinking he was in love with her. "Stoker, if the girl has an ounce of sense she'll be more than interested."

"You really think so?" His eyes were wide with surprise.

"Yes, I really think so."

"That's wonderful, ma'am. That's just wonderful." He wore a grin a mile wide as he continued to swing her around.

"Why don't you go ask her to dance?" Rachel asked, her head tilted, smiling.

"I wouldn't want to be rude, ma'am. Our dance isn't over yet."

"I won't mind. Go on, ask her."

"Really?"

"Hurry, before the song ends."

"Yes, ma'am!" He turned away from her, then turned back. "And thank you, ma'am."

Rachel just grinned at him as he left. She hoped Lily was smarter than she acted most of the time and would appreciate Stoker's attention. She hoped the girl's infatuation with Braddock wouldn't cause her to be cruel to a good man. Then she frowned, remembering that only moments earlier she'd been hoping Lily and Braddock would wed and leave the Triple X. "Just wishful thinking," she muttered. She heard her stomach growl and knew she was ready to eat a large portion of the banquet that filled the tables in front of the house.

13

Rachel surveyed the food and couldn't remember ever seeing so many good things to eat. She noticed Tish and Jeremy had found turkey drumsticks and were gnawing away at them with a vengeance. She waved at them and received greasy-fingered waves in return.

"My goodness, Miss Rachel ... you look ... beautiful," stammered Frank Jamison when he came up behind her.

"Thank you, Frank."

He gulped as he looked at the fullness of her breasts above the low décolleté. "I ... ah ..." He struggled for something to say. "Did you ever see so much good food, Rachel?"

"No, Frank. I don't think I ever have. Are you enjoying yourself?" She tried not to notice his gaze.

"You bet, Rachel. Are you?" His eyes still wandered over her curves.

"Of course." She didn't sound very convincing. Leading the way by picking up a plate, napkin, and silverware, she watched Frank follow suit and move farther down the table, selecting his dinner. She sighed, grateful that his attention was finally diverted to the food. She saw Emily not far away, with her husband, Pete, close by her side. In the distance, she could see Jace leaning on a fence post watching her, and Sin and Lily were deep in conversation near the house with a forlorn-looking Stoker watching them. She suddenly wasn't quite as hungry as she had been only moments before. "I knew this party was a bad idea," she mouthed, as she reached for a thin slice of turkey.

"Rachel, you've got to be eating more than this," Lucy insisted, as she came closer. "That much wouldn't keep a sparrow alive. Now pile some food on that plate. Try some of Lena's pie, or Selma's. Hank told me she bakes a wonderful apple pie."

Rachel was taken aback by her aunt's manner. She was bustling around like a bee in heat. "Aunt Lucy?"

"Yes, dear?" Lucy looked at Rachel and touched her handkerchief to her upper lip. "Was there something you wanted?"

"No, I guess not." She took a little more food so Lucy wouldn't nag, and moved off to sit by herself on the porch steps.

The food was delicious, but everything that had happened so far had finally caught up with her. She looked to where she'd seen Jace, only to find him gone. She scanned the crowd of people at the tables and couldn't see him there either. She didn't relish the fact that she had to fire him in the morning, but the time had come once and for all.

She set her plate down beside her, and putting both hands behind her neck, stretched and twisted to relieve some of the stress she was feeling. She needed to get away for a while. She stood, taking her plate with her, and went into the house. Looking around to make sure no one was watching her, she ducked into her father's office. She just needed to be alone.

Crossing the dark room, she set the plate down on the desk and lit the lamp. She kept the light dim and went around to sink slowly into her father's chair. "Oh, Pa," she breathed, "I wish I knew what you were thinking now." She leaned back in the chair and closed her eyes.

"Now that you're in heaven, do you know everything? Do you know about Jace? Do you know what I did with Braddock? Do you now know how stupid I am sometimes?" Crossing her arms in front of her, she hoped he didn't know everything. Could he forgive her for all her faults? Then she smiled. He'd always forgiven her when he was living, why would he be any different now?

Rachel heard the door open and looked to see who was intruding on her moment of privacy. "I should have known it would be you," she said, when she saw Braddock.

"I saw you come in the house. When you didn't come back out right away I decided to come check on you," he explained.

"How very thoughtful of you to stick your nose in my business once again."

Sin's black eyes narrowed. "Forgive me for being concerned, Rachel. It won't happen again."

"Forgive me if I don't believe you," she returned.

Looking around her father's office, she was reminded that he was the one that got her into the position of having to accept Braddock as a partner. "You know, Braddock, I almost wish it was me that was thrown from my horse instead of my father." She could see Sin's puzzled look. "Then it would be him stuck with you now, not me."

Sin sucked in air as her words hit him. "You still don't think I belong here? Even though I'm the one that was able to find a buyer for your dirty cows? Even though I've been sweating right alongside you every day on this damned, dusty roundup?" His voice dropped a note, "Even though I'm the one that made you feel like a woman by Leaver Creek?" His eyes had become hooded with the lowering of his lids. "Rachel, why won't you just accept the fact that I'm here to stay? It's foolish to keep fighting me this way."

Rachel listened to his words, then spoke quietly. "Braddock, whether you think my feelings are foolish or not doesn't really matter. I can't accept your ownership of my ranch. It goes against everything I was raised to believe. I was taught that you work for everything you get in this life, and that wrong is wrong no matter how you twist it. I was also taught that this land, the Triple X, was special; that if I worked it hard and gave it everything I had, it would take care of me and my children and grandchildren for generations. I know that the ground where my parents are buried will, one day, hold my body, and Tish's, and so on. I'm part of this land, Braddock. It's not a possession. Do you hear what I'm saying? I, Tish, and my father before me, belong here. You do not. You could work here for the next twenty years and never belong here. This place is mine, not yours, and it never will be."

Sin still stood in the doorway when she finished. There was a quiet finality to her voice that hadn't been there before. She no longer seemed angry, and the absence of that anger made him see how futile his dreams were. He finally believed she would never accept his presence on the Triple X. He ocouldn't swallow the lump in his throat. All his work and good intentions didn't matter. The fact that he'd fallen in love with Rachel didn't matter. He backed out of the room without saying anything. He could think of nothing to say.

Rachel watched him go. She'd seen the hurt in his eyes and felt a pain in her middle for being the cause, but what she'd said was true. And sometimes the truth hurt.

She stood and went to her room. She needed to get out of this dress and into her trousers. She'd had enough of this party and was going to the Rosebud.

When Rachel went out the front door to find Tish, Lucy was the first to meet her. "Aunt Lucy, where's Tish? I need to say good night to her before I leave."

"But where are you going? And why are you dressed like that?" Lucy questioned as she inspected Rachel's attire.

"I'm going to the Rosebud, and I'm dressed like this

because this is how I'm comfortable. Have you seen Tish?" She pushed her hat lower on her forehead, then leaned over to tie the strap from her holster around her thigh.

"Oh, dear, yes, I saw her with Jeremy a minute ago. They were running around back of the house. I believe they were playing tag." She fanned herself nervously.

"Don't worry about me, Aunt Lucy." She bent and kissed the older woman on the cheek, an action that surprised them both. "I'm just not what you're used to."

"No. You're not," Lucy agreed, her brow wrinkled. "Will you be late?"

It was so strange to have someone ask about her plans. "I don't know," she patted her gun, "but I can take care of myself." She smiled at Lucy and walked into the darkness toward the back of the house. She just had to say good night to Tish, and she'd be on her way.

"So, the party was a success," Vera confirmed after Rachel had told her all about it.

"Yes, and like I said before, you should have come. We might as well have closed up tonight, anyway. Everyone was out at the ranch."

"Oh! I'm sure your aunt, and all the other ladies at the party, would have loved it if I'd shown up," Vera scoffed. "I can just imagine the introductions; Mrs. So-and-so, this is my bartender, Vera Blade. And by the way, your husband used to pay for her services."

Rachel burst out laughing at Vera's words. "It would have been worth it, just for that!"

"Miss Rachel, sometimes I think you look for trouble," Vera scolded, laughing along with her boss.

"Maybe I do," Rachel agreed. "You go on home now, Vera. I'm going to clear the till and check the supplies and the ledgers before I head back to the ranch."

"Is there anything I can help with?" Vera offered.

"No, you call it a night. Get a good night's rest, and I'll stop by again in a couple of days." She walked the older woman to the door and locked it behind her.

Yawning, she walked back behind the bar to count the till. A knock at the door startled her. "Did you forget something, Vera?" she called as she went back to reopen the door.

When she'd turned the key, the door pushed open against her, forcing her back hard. "Vera?" she said the name at the same time she recognized Jace. "What do you want?" she demanded.

"I want a drink, Rachel."

She watched him close the door behind him. "You can leave that open, it's stuffy in here."

"I said I want a drink, Rachel." He ignored her request about the door.

"We're closed."

"You're open now."

Rachel didn't like the look in Jace's eyes. He looked sort of crazy, out of control. "I suppose you can have one drink." She went behind the bar and pulled out a bottle of rotgut whiskey.

"I want the good stuff, Rachel. I've decided I'm going to have only the good stuff from now on."

She heard the double meaning in his voice. "Jace, you can have one drink, then you have to go. I've got work to do."

"Still trying to tell me what to do, Rachel?"

Rachel watched as he knocked back the drink she'd poured. He never took his eyes off her, and something in his manner made the hair on the back of her neck stand up. The longer she watched him, the more certain she became that something was terribly wrong. The knowledge that her gun was strapped securely to her thigh, and fully loaded, made her feel relatively safe. She wouldn't enjoy killing Jace, but she'd do what she had to. "I've got a lot of work to do here, and I need to be alone to do it. If you're set on drinking yourself into a stupor, I'll let you take the bottle with you when you go."

"You don't get it yet, do you, Rachel?" He reached

across the bar, picked up the whiskey bottle, and poured himself a drink. "I'm not going anywhere."

"Why is that, Jace?" Rachel watched him swallow the whiskey in one gulp.

He poured another shot into his glass and, picking it up, looked at her through the liquid. "Well, I thought about the way you acted when we were dancing, and I figured you were just trying to put me off."

"That's not true. I told you I'd think about your proposition, and I will."

He took a sip of the whiskey. "I don't believe you, Rachel." His voice was quiet, deadly. "You know, when I came to you all those months ago, asking for a job, you were the only thing I had left."

"I gave you a job. You didn't ask for more."

"I wanted more."

"That was your mistake, Jace. We can't relive the past. Nobody can."

"You see? I knew you'd already made up your mind to turn me down. You lied to me, Rachel." He finished his drink and poured another.

"I think you've had enough. Now get out." Rachel reached for the bottle in a show of force, but it was a fatal mistake. Jace grabbed her wrist and slammed her hand on the bar, pinning it there. "Let go of me," she hissed through clenched teeth.

"No, Rachel. I'm not going to do what you, or anyone else, tells me anymore."

She tried to pull her hand free, but he held her fast. Damn it, how could I be so reckless as to let him grab my right hand, she thought. She couldn't reach her gun with her left because he was holding her arm so tightly that she was forced against the bar. "Jace, listen to me. No one wants to tell you what to do. How can I even consider letting you court me when you behave like this?" Maybe she could still talk her way out of this.

Jace began laughing. "You must think I'm stupid. It's too late, Rachel. I know you're a liar."

His laughter cut through to her soul. He was truly mad. She swung with her left hand and punched him as hard as she could across the bridge of his nose.

"Damn you!" he shouted, as blood began spurting down his face. He grabbed her left hand and twisted it viciously.

Rachel cried out with pain as she continued to fight him. If it was the last thing she did, she was going to kill this bastard. "Let go of me, you crazy son of a bitch!" she demanded.

Jace heard her ordering him to let her go. She was never going to order him again. He didn't even try to stop the blood that covered his face and rapidly soaked the front of his shirt. He began pulling her across the bar.

Rachel grimaced as her hip bones scraped over the edge of the bar. Her gun belt got hung up for a second, but Jace jerked her hard and it freed itself. Her arms felt as though they were being pulled from their sockets and her hands were getting numb, he was holding them so tightly. "You're making a big mistake, Jace. Stop this now, and I'll forget it." Like hell she would. The first chance she got, she'd grab her gun and blow a hole through his heart. "Let me go, Jace. We'll talk."

He was laughing again. "The time for talk is over, Rachel." He pulled her against him and pinned her arms behind her back. "Feel that?" He pushed his erection against her abdomen. "You're gonna love it, just like you used to."

Vomit rose in Rachel's throat. She didn't fear rape. What she feared was his insanity. She had to get to her gun. "You're right, Jace. Let me help. Let me have my hands, and I'll help."

"You're the one who's stupid, Rachel. You think I don't know that you'd shoot me the second you were free?" He rearranged her hands behind her so he could hold them both with one of his. He then slid her gun from its holster and brought it up to her face. "See how cool it feels on your skin, Rachel." He stroked her cheek with the barrel.

She tried to bring her knee up to his groin, but he jerked her arms back and avoided the blow.

"That was a mistake, Rachel." He raised one boot and scraped it down her shin and onto her instep. "You keep making mistakes." He continued the pressure on her foot as he traced her lips with the gun barrel. "Do you know what would happen if I pulled the trigger now, Rachel? I'd blow your pretty head off."

Rachel swallowed and fought the urge to spit in his face. The blood that still flowed from his nose had soaked the front of her shirt, and the smell of it drying on her flesh was adding to her nausea.

"Yes, if I pulled the trigger now, you'd be dead. You'd be dead, and your bastard brat would be an orphan."

Rachel stiffened. His mentioning Tish terrified her.

Jace felt her response. "You don't like me talking about your brat, do you?"

"It's fine." She was breathing as shallowly as possible, trying to convince him what he said about Tish didn't affect her.

"Do you know how much it hurt me to come back and find out you'd had a bastard child with some cowboy right after I left?" He pulled her even tighter against his body. "Didn't I mean anything to you, Rachel? Wasn't making love to me special?"

"Of course it was, Jace. Things just happen," she tried to convince him.

"You're a lying slut, Rachel." He gave her arms another vicious jerk. "You never loved me, or you'd have waited for me."

Rachel listened to his insane arguments. "You were gone for nearly eight years!" she shouted. "Do you think I should have waited for you for eight years?"

"You didn't wait eight years. You didn't wait eight months. You fucked the first man that came along!" He bent her backward and once again pushed his erection into her body. "Were you so hot that you couldn't wait even a week?"

"I . . . it just happened, Jace." She felt as though her back were breaking, and the pressure from where he still ground his heel into her foot was sending a shooting pain up her leg.

"It just happened, Jace," he mimicked in a whiney voice. "What was his name?" he asked as he straightened a bit.

"What?" She'd never had to come up with a name before. Her father had never questioned her.

"I asked you what his name was."

"I . . . it was . . ."

"You don't even remember his name? Was he so memorable, Rachel? Or was there more than one? Did you become the town slut after I left? Did you screw all the hands, too?"

"I never screwed anybody," she denied, and tried to turn her face away from where he still held her gun against her cheek.

"Don't try to move, Rachel. I still may pull the trigger and make your brat an orphan."

At that moment something snapped in Rachel. She jerked violently and felt sharp agonizing pain in her shoulder. "Let go of me, you bastard! Let go of me or pull the fucking trigger!" She saw his eyes widen with surprise. "Yes, I said pull the trigger, or haven't you got the guts? That's your problem, isn't it, Jace? You haven't got the guts to do anything. That's why you left all those years ago. You were afraid. Afraid to accept the responsibility of loving me. And afraid of taking over your family's ranch. You're a coward, Jace. A stinking, lowly coward. Now go ahead and pull the trigger, or let me go!"

Jace growled and threw her gun across the floor. "I'll show you who's a coward. I'll kill you, all right. But I'll do it with my bare hands, and I'll have some fun with you first. By the time I get through with you, you'll be begging me to kill you."

Rachel watched her last chance escape as her gun slid across the floor and stopped under a table on the other side of the room. She'd never get to it now, and her bravado of a moment earlier was gone. She'd hoped to shock and anger him into letting her go long enough to give her a break. Now she saw death in his eyes.

"It's too bad you didn't take me seriously sooner, Rachel." He cupped her face with his free hand and lowered his mouth to hers.

She could taste the blood on his mouth and began gagging. She tried to turn her head, but he held it fast. He'd turned her around a little, and she could feel the bar pressing hard into her back. She never thought she'd die in the Rosebud.

Jace continued kissing her. He could feel her revulsion, and it spurred him on. He'd show this bitch what a real man was capable of. If she'd slept with every man in town, he'd make sure she'd remember him. Of course, she'd only remember as long as it took him to kill her afterward. He slipped his hand down to her throat. "Such a pretty neck. Maybe I'll squeeze it a little. Is that how I should do it, Rachel?"

She tried to struggle, but her movements didn't seem to faze him. She cringed as she felt his hand slide down from her throat to her breast.

"Remember how you used to like this, Rachel?" He rubbed his hand over the soft mound of flesh, then reached to the collar of her shirt and began to unbutton it. "I remember a lot of things about making love to you, Rachel."

"This isn't making love. This is rape," she hissed.

"Don't talk now, Rachel. You'll spoil everything." He reached inside her shirt and held her breast in his hand. He began to knead it gently. "If you relax, this part of our evening can be very pleasant." He laughed a little.

"Nothing about this is going to be pleasant. In fact, it wasn't that pleasant all those years ago, only I was too naive to know it then."

"Shut up, Rachel. You're only going to make it harder on yourself."

"I don't care. You're going to kill me anyway so what does it matter how?"

"Shut up, Rachel!" he demanded.

"No! I won't shut up, and I won't make this easy for you." She tried to pull away again, but he only held her tighter. Her hands had lost all feeling but the pain in her shoulders and back had increased, making it difficult to breathe evenly. She felt herself getting lightheaded and prayed she wouldn't lose consciousness. She had to stay alert for any chance to escape. Then she felt him give her breast an angry twist. She bit her lip to keep from crying out but was almost grateful for the sharp pain. It brought her senses back.

"When I tell you to shut up, you listen to me, bitch."

"Or what? You'll hurt me? You're already doing that. Maybe you'll kill me? So what, you're going to anyway. So why should I shut up?" she goaded.

Jace twisted her breast again and smiled when he saw her flinch. "Yes, I'll hurt you, Rachel. I'll . . ."

The blow from behind came so suddenly that neither Jace nor Rachel saw it coming. "You bastard!" growled Sin. He'd come in just seconds before and was horrified at what he saw. Hatred filled Sin's heart as he crossed to where his blow had sent Jace sprawling, unconscious. He then turned back to Rachel. She was bent forward slightly and rubbing her arms.

"Rachel? Are you all right?"

She looked up to see the concern in his eyes. "Yeah, Braddock, I'm fine. You arrived in the nick of time."

He reached up and touched her face. "Are you sure? You're covered with blood." His heart was still pounding with anger.

She smiled. "It's Jace's. I punched him."

An animal-like howl pierced the air as Jace flew across the room. All three of them hit the floor with a crash. "I'm going to kill you both!" promised Jace. He came up swinging, catching Sin across the cheekbone, just as he'd begun to rise.

Rachel lay dazed where she'd fallen with the weight of the two large men on top of her. She didn't see Jace reaching for her, but Sin did. He swung his fist and punched Jace in the stomach, then followed with an uppercut to the jaw. He couldn't remember ever wanting to kill with his bare hands before. Even in the war, during hand-to-hand combat, he'd never felt the blood of murder coursing through his veins.

Jace wasn't ready to give up yet. Sin was a good fighter, but no match for him, he was sure. He swung with both fists doubled up, and hit Sin square across the chest. He heard the wind get knocked out of him and grinned. Now he'd finish him, and then Rachel. He glanced to where she was starting to sit up. He'd still have fun with her tonight. "Ouuff." Sin's fist caught him in the stomach again.

Sin punched Jace as hard as he could. He punched him again. Sin staggered to his feet, his head aching and his chest throbbing. He caught Jace with a forceful blow to the side of his head and kept punching.

Jace was startled and dazed. Sin had caught him off guard when he'd looked at Rachel, and now his head was spinning. Rage boiled in his brain, and he tried to stand up.

Sin saw Jace trying to get to his feet and struck him across the back of his neck to knock him back down. With Jace on all fours, he began to kick him. Over and over he kicked. Each time he heard him grunt with pain, he remembered the sight of Jace holding Rachel against the bar, with his hand in her shirt and the fear on her face, and he would kick him again. Finally, he stopped. He was breathing hard as he watched Jace puke blood. He picked him up and pulled him toward the door.

Rachel's voice stopped them. "Jace," she was holding her side, "believe that you're getting off easy," she took a deep breath and winced, "if I ever see you again, I'll kill you."

Jace looked back at her through a haze of blood, holding his ribs, and vowed he'd get revenge.

Sin shoved Jace out the door into the dark night. "Get lost, Jace. If she doesn't kill you, I will."

Jace stumbled to where he'd left his horse. "I'll see you burn in hell, Braddock," he called back. "And Rachel, too."

Sin turned away from the door and looked at Rachel. She was sitting on the floor, surrounded by puddles of blood. "Why?" he asked.

Rachel felt the spinning in her head begin to slow. "He wanted me to love him." She shook her head, trying to clear it.

"He's got a great way of courting."

Rachel tried to smile. Sin had no idea how close he'd come to the truth. "He was angry when I wouldn't love him like I used to." She turned her neck and stretched her back. She was sore, but surprisingly that seemed to be all. She'd somehow gotten away with only bruises. She re-buttoned her shirt.

Sin was intrigued by what she'd revealed. "So, there was something between you two." It was a statement.

Rachel looked at him, startled that she'd given away so much. "It was a long time ago. It was over a long time ago."

"Apparently, he didn't think so."

"No." She stood up and started righting chairs that had gotten knocked over during the fight.

"Because of the kiss I saw you give him in the barn?"

She looked at him a little surprised, then sighed, "Yes, I suppose." She surveyed the damage to the Rosebud. She'd gotten off very easy. Nothing was broken. Just a lot of blood around, luckily all Jace's. She then looked back at Sin and noticed a cut running along his cheekbone. "You better take care of that." She pointed at the cut.

Sin touched his face and flinched when he felt the gap made by his separated skin. "Shit," he sighed. "Can I get a towel from you?"

"Sure." Rachel went behind the bar and grabbed a damp towel and tossed it to him.

He held it to the cut, trying to apply pressure, but only succeeded in causing it to bleed even more.

"Here, let me," Rachel instructed, when she saw the mess he was making. She came back around the bar and, sitting on a stool next to him, reached up to take the towel.

"You don't have to." He pulled back.

"Don't be brave, Braddock. You're bleeding all over my bar."

"I'm not being brave. I just don't want to trouble you."

"Braddock," she sounded strained, "it's no trouble. You were injured while trying to help me. It's the least I can do." She looked into his eyes. "And, by the way. Thanks."

"You're welcome." He let her take the towel from him and leaned forward so she could see better.

Rachel touched the cut gently at first, getting the edges to come together, then pressed harder, to stop the blood flow. She'd done this kind of ministering several times in her life. Men got injured frequently on a ranch, and with the doctor miles away in town, she was usually the one responsible for their care. "You're going to have a pretty scar from this." She glanced up into his eyes again. This time she saw something there that bothered her. "Why did you come here tonight?"

"I followed you." He looked deep into those emerald eyes he'd grown to love.

"Why?"

"I had something to tell you, actually two things."

She pulled her eyes from his and looked back at the cut. The bleeding was slowing. "It couldn't wait until morning?"

"No, at least I didn't want to wait until morning."

"I think you can hold this now. Just be gentle." She let him take the towel and leaned back. "All right, so what did you want to say?"

"That I'm leaving."

She wasn't sure she understood what he meant. "What are you talking about?"

"I'm saying, Rachel, that you've won. I'm leaving the Triple X. Your speech tonight finally convinced me."

"But I don't understand. You said you were staying, no matter what."

"I guess I underestimated you, Rachel. I really thought I could convince you that I'd be good for the ranch. I couldn't, and what you said tonight finally got through. I wanted to let you know that I'll be leaving in the morning."

"So soon?" Rachel's thoughts were in a jumble. She never thought she'd see Braddock leave, and now that he was going, she was confused.

"Yes. Now that I've made the decision I thought it best to go quickly."

She cast her eyes downward. "Yes, I suppose you're right. There's no point in hanging around."

"No." Sin's heart was aching with his decision and her easy acceptance of it.

"What about the drive? Your friend arranged it. Won't he be curious?"

"I'll explain it to him."

Rachel looked down at her hands and started trying to rub the blood away. "I feel I owe you something."

"I'll be in touch. After the drive we'll settle up. I will need a stake."

"Where will you go?"

"Why? Does it matter?"

"Surprisingly, it does. I still don't need your help on the Triple X, but I'm curious about where you'll be. You told me you had nothing left but my ranch."

He sighed. "Don't worry about me, Rachel. I'll find something."

She sat there beside him and didn't know what else to say. The elation she expected to feel if she ever got rid of him didn't come. She began to stand up, then remembered he'd had two things to tell her. "What was the other thing you wanted to tell me?"

He could feel the bleeding had stopped and took the towel from his face. He laid it on the bar and turned to look at her. He sat there, staring, trying to memorize every curve of her features, every expression he'd ever seen cross her face. "I wanted to tell you ..." He stopped, wondering if he should continue. What difference did it make now? He reached up and touched a stray curl of her hair, winding it around his finger, as he'd once done on the front porch of the house.

Rachel felt his intense perusal. His black eyes seemed to see through her, to her soul. Her heart was beating erratically, and the soft touch of his hand when he took her hair in his fingers sent sparks racing through her body. Waiting for him to continue, she frowned, letting him see her confusion.

Sin leaned toward her slowly, giving her the opportunity to pull back. She didn't. He bent and touched his lips to hers. She didn't move. He tenderly traced her lips with the tip of his tongue. This would be the last. The last time he would be able to touch Rachel the way he wanted. If she let him.

Rachel could feel his hesitancy. Was it because he was unsure she'd respond? Or was it because she knew he'd read more into it than was there? She waited. He had to want this. He had to show her that he understood her terms. He'd told her he was leaving in the morning so there would be no tomorrows after that. If they made love, he had to understand that she expected and wanted nothing beyond this night.

Sin did understand. Except for her interest in where he might end up, she'd showed no weakness in her desire to have him off her ranch. His decision to go was what she'd wanted all along, but she was willing to accept his sex. He sighed. How could he have fallen in love with a woman like Rachel? He knew it was exactly her honesty, with herself and others, that had caused him to love her. He wanted this night, even though it would be their last. He deepened his kiss, sending her the message she'd been waiting for.

Rachel opened her mouth to receive him. She tasted his lips and tongue with her own and reached up behind him to pull him closer. He would be gone tomorrow. The memories of this night had to last her a lifetime. "Braddock," she whispered against him.

"Say my name, Rachel." He pulled back and looked into her eyes. "You always call me Braddock. Say my first name."

"Sin," she whispered.

He breathed deeply and smelled the womanly aroma of her body. She possessed the sweet fragrance of the outdoors. Of wildflowers and hay, of soft breezes and clean water. She had a fragrance all her own, and it drugged him. Standing, he pulled her up with him, needing to feel the length of her body against his. "Rachel, Rachel," he breathed into her hair.

She gasped as his strong body melded with hers. The strength in his arms, as he pulled her to him, nearly forced the air from her lungs, but she didn't protest. She wanted to be as close to him as possible.

Sin couldn't get enough of her. His lips took hers once again in a fierce possession. He felt her lips part in invitation as he explored with his tongue, feeling the softness of her response and the sharp edges of her teeth. His lips left hers and kissed her face, her eyes, her cheeks, the tip of her nose.

Rachel loved the way he felt. She moved with the rhythm he'd begun against her, remembering the first time she'd lain beneath him, the perfect union of their bodies exquisite. He was her sexual match, the other half of her desire. She slid her hands downward along his back to the firm muscles of his buttocks. Pulling him ever closer, she reveled in the evidence of his need, pressing its message against her body.

Sin began a path of kisses from the soft curve of her cheek to the erotic pulse beat in her throat. He brought one of his hands up to the throb there, and touched it tenderly. Her heart was beating as fast as his was. His lips covered the pulse and continued downward. He parted her shirt and let his fingertips find the hardened peak of her breast. He heard her sharp intake of air as he teased the sensitive tip between his fingers.

A million tiny stars seemed to explode behind Rachel's eyes as she felt him playing with the hardened bud of her breast. Her head fell back, allowing him easier access to those sensation-filled areas. She moved back slightly, taking her hands from behind him, and reached to her shirt, pulling it apart, freeing her breasts from the fabric.

Sin's eyes devoured the sight of her breasts, full against her chest, like the ripe fruit of passion. He bent his head to bury his face in the soft creation of femininity. "Rachel," he moaned into her flesh.

Rachel wanted to feel him, to touch and taste every surface, to explore the different textures that were his body. She swallowed. "Sin?" She saw his dazed expression as he raised his head. She began to unbutton his shirt.

Rachel's hands were hot as she touched his chest. He took deep gulps of air as she tugged gently on his nipples. The feel of her hands was driving him mad. Her head came forward, and he could feel the tip of her tongue touch first one hardened nipple and then the other. "God ..." he groaned. He didn't know he could feel such an explosion from the erotic kisses he was receiving. Slowly she circled his nipples with her tongue, back and forth. He could barely breathe as she began a trail from his chest downward.

Rachel slowly lowered herself to her knees in front of him, tasting the saltiness of him as she went. She stopped to circle his navel, then went further. Parting his legs slightly, with her hands, she laid her face on the target of her passion. The heat came through the fabric of his trousers to her cheek. "Sin," she mouthed against his passion.

Sin felt her fingers at his belt. His heart was rushing

blood to his ears in a pounding rhythm. "Rachel," her name came out in a guttural moan. The release of pressure as she slowly, deliberately unbuttoned his trousers sent electric shocks through his nerves to his brain. Then he was free, incredibly free. Rachel's hands were on him and it seemed she possessed some secret to his innermost needs. Slowly she stroked him, smoothed the heated flesh in her hands. He felt, if he looked down at the exquisite torture she was exacting, he might lose control, but he had to watch, to see her fingers touching him. As he lowered his eyes he felt her tongue. A shudder ground through him, nearly sending him to the floor. "Rachel?" he groaned.

Rachel had never felt anything like this. She leaned forward and put her cheek against his throbbing shaft. She'd felt what her first taste had done to him and knew she wanted more. She had to experience as much as possible. This was her only chance. His hands were in her hair, as he held her head to him. She pulled back ever so slightly and began again the exploration with her tongue.

14

Sin felt Rachel's hands sliding his trousers lower as she explored his body. "Rachel, I don't know how long I can take this." He was breathing hard.

"You'll take it," she whispered against his thigh. She smiled when she felt him shudder. "Come down here." She pulled on one of his hands, guiding him to the floor beside her. "Touch me."

He claimed her lips in a deep possession. Never before had he felt as one with another person as he did now with Rachel. The bittersweet edge was, that after tomorrow, he'd never again hold her, or feel her gasp under his touch.

Rachel arched against him. She needed him to do more. She desired the release his body promised. Taking his hand in hers, she guided it to her breast, and felt the ecstasy when he then followed the movement with his lips. Each nibble, each tender bite, sent shock waves through the surface of her skin to deep within the core of her soul.

Sin watched Rachel's expression as he teased her breasts with his kisses. The smoldering green of her eyes showed him her pleasure, as did the low moans escaping her lips. He moved his hand lower, along the firm plain of her stomach. Lower, under the waistband of her trousers, he gently explored the mound of her femininity. She purred under his caress. He brought his hand upward again, and unfastened the trousers, freeing her body to a more intimate invasion.

Rachel loved the way he touched her. He seemed to know just what to do to send sparks coursing through her nerves. She bit down on her lip to control the spasms she felt herself so near. "Sin, wait."

He hesitated, looking to her face. "Why?"

"I want to be more comfortable. Let's go into the office. There's a cot there."

He smiled, not sure they would be more comfortable on a cot, but willing to move if it pleased her. He pulled off his boots, then rose, and stepped out of the trousers that still circled his ankles. He shrugged out of his shirt, and reached down to pull her up.

Rachel had watched him stand, mesmerized by the perfect form of his muscular body and the arousal that gave evidence of his need for her. She let him help her to her feet, then led him around the bar to the office. There was a small cot in one corner that she used once in a while when she stayed at the bar all night. Now it would strain under the weight of two bodies.

Before Rachel could sit on the tiny cot, he pulled her to him. He lost his hands in the wild mass of her hair, and claimed her once again with his kiss. "Rachel, Rachel," he breathed into her mouth. "I . . . want you." He caught himself just in time and kept from saying that he loved her.

"I want you, too." She pulled her shirt from her shoulders and let him tug down her trousers. "Let me get my boots off." She kicked them across the room, then leaned back into him, laying her face against his chest. "How did this happen?" she asked, as her fingers traced the scar that was so close to her cheek.

He heaved a sigh. "I was shot in battle."

"I know, you said that much before. But from the look of the scar, it wasn't taken care of very well."

He took her by the shoulders and pulled her away from him slightly. "Rachel, I don't want to think about that now. I don't want to think of anything but how you feel, and how I'll feel when I'm deep within you." He watched the green fire ignite in her eyes and pulled her down to the cot.

Rachel lay under the weight of Sin's body and felt the heat of his passion between her legs. They were both ready. She opened herself to him and felt the union of their bodies as he possessed her. Over and over he lost himself within her silken depths. Over and over she rose to meet him, once again realizing their rhythms matched perfectly, their desire rising to the same heavenly peak.

Sin could feel Rachel begin to shudder beneath him as he reached the moment of ecstasy. Grinding his teeth together, as spasm upon spasm jerked through his loins, he released the heated fluid of his love. He heard her crying his name, and it rang in his ears as a love song.

Rachel absorbed his passion as it mingled with her own. Wave after wave washed over and through her as she lost all sense of time and space, aware only of the feel of Sin inside her, part of her. They seemed to be as one person. After what seemed like an eternity of flight, they began their descent from the heavens, back to the plain of reality.

Sin lay still, holding her to him, listening to her breathing becoming more regular. He adjusted his weight slightly and turned his head into her hair. He wanted to inhale her fragrance all night. He wanted to feel her beneath him forever. He closed his eyes, and fell into a deep, exhausted sleep.

Rachel heard his heart beat slow, and knew he was asleep. This man had the ability to make her feel things she'd never felt before, and somehow knew she'd never feel again. Tomorrow he'd be gone forever. She lowered her eyelids, wondering where life would take him after this. Just before she dozed off, she heard him mumbling in his sleep. She leaned closer to listen, then wished she hadn't. She didn't want to hear that he loved her.

* * *

Rachel lay in the dim gray light that preceded dawn, listening to the thunder. It rumbled across the range and vibrated the rafters above her head. The storm had finally hit. Sin moved slightly in his sleep, and she took the opportunity to free herself from his grasp. She carefully sat up and looked back at his sleeping face. He'd whispered that he loved her. She hoped he wouldn't remember saying it.

Another growl of thunder caused her to jump. She wanted to get back to the ranch. This was tornado season, and the cattle got restless during a bad storm. She needed to make sure everything was all right. She didn't want to wake Sin, so making as little noise as possible, she gathered her clothing, and went out into the bar.

As she began to dress, she noticed the scrape down her right shin, ending in a dark bruise across the instep of her foot. "That bastard," she whispered, when she thought of Jace. "He doesn't know how lucky he is to be alive today," she said quietly. She finished dressing, grimacing as she pulled on her right boot. "He better be a hundred miles from here by now." She straightened and headed out to where Roux was waiting, standing by a water trough. "Come on, boy. We're going home."

By the time Rachel could see the Triple X in the distance, the dust swirling around was nearly blinding her. The wind was howling and forcing the earth to writhe under it as though in agony. She squinted across the range and saw the undulating grass and whipping fingers of dirt that raised up to strike the clouds. "Roux, this is a bad one." She spurred him a little. "Let's get going."

The clouds were hanging like a blanket of black wool overhead as Rachel rode into the yard. Large drops of water had begun pelting the ground, rapidly turning the dust into mud.

As she passed the house, headed toward the barn, Lena and Lucy came running out the front door in their nightgowns and wrappers. Lena's face was a mask of anguish, and Lucy had tears streaming down both cheeks. "Lena what is it?" she demanded as she stopped

Roux and jumped from his back. She glanced at Lucy, sobbing beside them.

"It's Tish," Lena answered.

Terror gripped Rachel's heart. She tried to pass the women, and go into the house. "What's wrong with Tish?" She imagined her daughter lying upstairs, injured. "What's happened to her?"

Lena grabbed her arms to stop her.

"Are you mad? Let me go!"

"No! She's not in the house, Miss Rachel."

Rachel stopped. "Where is she?"

"We don't know." Lena began to cry loudly. "Oh, Miss Rachel. We don't know where she is. And now this storm . . ."

Rachel looked first at one woman, and then the other. Why were they just standing here crying? "What do you mean, you don't know where she is? Is she lost in the storm? Why was she out?" Why weren't these women out looking for her? Her precious little girl was lost in this storm.

Lucy finally spoke. "Jeremy said, she told him she was going to check on Poco. She was worried about him being afraid of the storm."

That sounded like Tish. "But what happened to her? She didn't try to ride him, did she?" Rachel asked.

"We don't know for sure. Poco is gone, but one of the hands said he saw her talking to Jace. After that, no one's seen her. Oh, Rachel, where could she have gone?" Lucy cried.

Rachel's heart had stopped beating. She couldn't breathe, couldn't swallow, couldn't move. Nothing in her life had prepared her for the paralyzing terror that gripped her at that moment.

"Rachel?" Lena asked. "Are you all right? You look odd. Maybe you should sit down for a moment."

Rachel didn't hear Lena. She could hear nothing but the blood pounding in her ears. She threw back her head and screamed. "Tiiissshhh!" She felt as though her heart had been ripped from her chest, and she'd been left with

235

a gaping, bloody hole. "Tiiissshhh!" She screamed again. She mounted Roux in one leap and jerked his reins hard to turn him. She looked down at Lena and Lucy, staring up at her in horror. "If I don't find her, I won't be back," she told them. She spurred Roux toward the barn and found Poco's tracks, then with one vicious kick, had him at a full gallop. She could hear Lena and Lucy calling after her, but the hounds of hell could have been trying to stop her, and she wouldn't have even slowed. She had to find Tish before that animal killed her, or worse.

Sin opened his eyes and immediately felt Rachel's absence. Memories of their lovemaking flooded his mind as he realized he'd been hoping she'd have a change of heart and ask him to stay. "Braddock, she told you once it was 'fun.' Why don't you ever learn?" he asked himself. Sighing, he raised up on one elbow and looked around the office. It seemed awfully dark, but he knew it must be late into the morning. Then he heard the thunder. "Holy shit, that's close," he muttered. He knew he was in for a wet ride back to the ranch. It didn't take him long to get dressed, and soon he was riding through the rain, back to the Triple X. "For the last time, Rachel," he said out loud. "You're finally rid of me."

As he rode close enough to the ranch to make out the buildings, he was surprised to see so many people out in the yard in this storm. "What's going on?" he called as he rode up. He then noticed Lena and Lucy sitting on the porch, crying in each other's arms.

Stoker rode over to him. "We're going after Rachel."

"Rachel?"

"Yeah, Tish is missing, and Rachel took off like a bat out of hell to find her."

"Tish is missing? How?" he asked urgently.

"Lena told us, Rachel thinks Jace has her. None of us knows what to make of it, but we're going out after Rachel. You wanna come along? We're just about ready to leave."

Sin didn't even hear the last of Stoker's statement. He rode to where Lena and Lucy were sitting, sobbing. "Which way did she go?!" he demanded.

"She's not coming back," wailed Lena.

"Damn it, woman. Which way did she go?"

Lena took her arm from Lucy's shoulder and pointed east. "That way, toward the mesa. But she said, if she didn't find Tish, she wouldn't be back. Find them, please!" Her head fell back against Lucy's shoulder.

Sin was headed out of the yard before she shed another tear. He knew what Jace was capable of, and he knew that Rachel would die trying to save her daughter. He spurred his horse violently as a shudder ran through him.

The storm seemed to be on Jace's side as it ripped at Rachel's clothing. Lightning frightened Roux several times, and it was all she could do to hold on to the reins and keep him under control. The rain that had simply fallen from the sky earlier, now seemed to zero in on her, stinging with its force, even raising welts where it struck. But nothing was going to stop Rachel from continuing on this course.

Jace had taken a trail, not traversed often because of the unsure footing, to the top of the mesa. "Come on, Roux, we've got to catch up with them," she urged. She knew how frightened Tish would be by now, and each breath she took was another vow to destroy the man who was doing this. She cursed the fact that she hadn't killed the bastard the night before. The vision of his bloody body lying under her boot was a pleasant picture.

Hatred such as she'd never known possible burned through to her soul. "Just hang on, Tish. Mama's coming." She felt hot salty tears mingle with the cold raindrops on her face and blinked, trying to stop their flow. "I'll be there as soon as I can, darling," she called into the wind, but her words were swallowed instantly by its howling.

Sin followed as quickly as he dared. The trail was treacherous. He didn't want to end up on foot and not be able to get to them. Shale and sand made the footing deadly, sending his horse scrambling several times. He knew Rachel wouldn't slow for anything, and he prayed she'd be safe until he could get there.

He thought about Tish, and Jace's reason for taking her. He'd done it to hurt Rachel, not necessarily to hurt the child. It was, perhaps, a foolish hope, but one he had to hang on to. He couldn't imagine a world without the laughter of one little girl or the fiery passion of her mother. He knew that if Tish were gone, Rachel would die. Either at the hands of Jace, or from a bullet from her own gun. Tish was her life. "Lord, please help me get to them in time," he prayed. He looked to the sky, just as another bolt of lightning ripped apart the heavens, and he wondered if his prayers would be answered.

Rachel felt the hail begin with the pain of it hitting her back. Roux reared again, and she was barely able to hang on. "Damn it, why?" she screamed. The sand under Roux's hooves was giving way, and there was nothing she could do about it. "Lord, no. Please. I've got to get to my little girl! Please!" Her scream was but a whisper in the storm. Another, huge, renting bolt tore across the sky. Roux bolted sideways, and Rachel felt them begin to fall. "No!" Down and over they went. Rachel saw the bulk of Roux's body coming over on her and leaped to the side, just in time to avoid being crushed.

"Roux, get up!" She scrambled to where he still lay, struggling in the sand. "Come on, we've got to get Tish." Then she noticed his leg. "No, Roux. Not this, too," she whispered. Rachel fell to her knees and examined the broken leg of her friend. Tears coursed down her cheeks as she drew her gun. "I can't do anything for you, Roux. I've got to keep going. You understand, don't you?" The big horse lay very still, looking at Rachel, his large brown eyes dazed with pain. He seemed to be waiting. She brought the barrel of her gun level with his head. "Good-bye, old friend," she whispered as she pulled the trigger.

Sin heard the gunshot and fear shook his heart. Was it Jace or Rachel? He rode harder, terrified at what he'd find when he caught up to them. And who would he be catching up to? Rachel and Tish? Jace alone? He couldn't let himself think about the options.

Rachel knelt in the sand beside Roux's body for only seconds. Her aim had been true, he hadn't suffered. Rachel shoved her gun back into its holster and wiped her face with the back of her sleeve. She took the rifle from Roux's saddle, and pushing herself to her feet, started to run, still following Jace's trail. She would catch up to them, or die trying.

Sin continued, as quickly as he could force the horse, up the trail. The hail was beating the ground, and everything around him, to a pulp. Plants that lined the trail seemed to disintegrate as he watched. His horse shied at each bolt of lightning, and he wondered how Rachel was doing. It was then that he saw the dark bulk of a horse just below the trail ahead. "Rachel!" he called. He was terrified that he'd find her broken body beneath the heavy animal. As he rode nearer, he was relieved to see that Rachel was nowhere around. He was saddened to see the dark hole behind Roux's ear and knew she'd had to kill him. He noticed the horse's damaged leg. He closed his eyes for just a second and shook his head. "Dear Lord, how much more must she take?" He spurred his horse back up to the path, certain he'd find Rachel very soon.

Rachel hadn't slowed her pace for a second, and her lungs felt like they were on fire. Each breath was agony, but she didn't slow. Her shoulders and back ached from the pounding hail, but she didn't slow. Her vision was blurred with tears and sand, blown there by the wind, but she didn't slow. Then she heard the rider behind her. She dove for cover, cocking the rifle as she fell. She thought it might be Jace circling around to catch her from behind. When she saw it was Sin, she stood up, running out in front of him.

Sin saw Rachel jump in front of his horse just in time

to stop him. "Rachel? Are you all right?" He'd never seen anything like her. She was soaking wet and covered with mud and sand. Her hair was a mass of tangled dirt and twigs, and yet, it wasn't the filth that covered her that he noticed. It was her eyes. They were wild with hatred, sunken and haunted.

"Braddock, get off your horse," she ordered, her chest heaving with every breath.

"What? Rachel, what are you talking about?"

She raised the rifle and aimed it at his heart. "I haven't got time to argue. Jace has Tish. Now, get off your horse, I need it."

Sin could see she was nearly insane. "No, Rachel. You need my help. Climb on behind me."

"Two people won't move as fast. Get down!" She pinpointed her aim.

"No, Rachel. You need my help, whether you know it or not. If you want this horse you'll have to kill me."

Rachel looked into his eyes. He meant what he said. She began to squeeze down on the trigger. "Rachel?" he whispered.

"Damn you, Braddock!" She lowered the barrel of the rifle, reached up, and jumped on the back of his horse. "If you slow me down, or get in my way, I will kill you," she promised. "Get going!"

Sin spurred them on. The added weight of Rachel behind him did slow the horse a little, but it couldn't be helped. He knew that Rachel needed him. Jace was more than a match for her.

Rachel hung on to Sin with her left hand and held the rifle in her right. She'd come close to blowing him out of the saddle, but something had stopped her. She could feel his muscles straining as he fought with the horse, and hoped she'd made the right choice.

ZING!! The bullet narrowly missed Rachel's head, and she and Sin dove from the horse's back at the same moment. "Rachel, are you all right?" Sin shouted above the storm's bluster.

"I'm fine." She frowned, noticing she'd dropped the

rifle when she'd jumped. "Where did it come from?" she shouted back, trying to scan the small clearing ahead.

"Over by those rocks."

Rachel looked where he'd indicated, and saw the edge of Tish's nightgown showing below an outcropping of boulders. "Tish! Letisha, are you all right?" she screamed.

"Your brat can't talk right now, Rachel," Jace called back.

"Why not?" Rachel felt as though she'd died and gone to hell. "Jace, if you've hurt her I'll kill you!" Rachel screamed.

"You talk pretty big, Rachel. But I hold all the cards now. You'll do anything I say."

"What do you want, Jace?" Sin called.

"I see Rachel's got you doing what she wants, Braddock." Jace laughed.

"Not exactly, Jace. I'd have come after you myself."

"Why? Rachel's brat means nothing to you."

"That's where you're wrong, Jace. I love that little girl, and if Rachel doesn't kill you, I will. Now let her go." The threat in Sin's voice was a tangible thing. "If you let her come out here to her mother, now, I might kill you fast. If I have to come get her you're going to regret it."

Rachel looked over to where Sin lay in the sand and was surprised at the truth ringing in his words. "Let her go, Jace. Now!" she shouted. She saw movement behind the rocks, and prayed she'd see Tish's beautiful little form come running to her. Instead, what she saw horrified her. Jace carried Tish's limp body in front of him, like a shield, as he stepped out from behind the rocks.

"Tish!" she screamed and stood up to run to her daughter.

"No, Rachel!" Sin shouted, but it was too late. Jace had her in his sights.

Jace smiled as he raised his gun and aimed it at Rachel. "That's close enough, Rachel."

She stopped just several feet from them. "What have you done to her?"

"Nothing really. Nothing that will hurt her."

"What?" she demanded.

"Just made her drink a little whiskey. I got tired of hearing her tell me how her mama was going to kill me." Jace looked past Rachel. "You get out here, too, Braddock. Now!"

Sin had been hoping for an opening to shoot Jace, but when Rachel jumped up she'd stopped right in front of him, blocking a clear shot. He stood slowly and walked toward Jace.

"That's close enough, Braddock. Gee, I'm a lucky man. I get to kill the three people I hate most. All in the same day."

Rachel saw the crazy light in his eyes and knew she had to do something. "What do you want from us, Jace? Surely, not to just kill us in cold blood. Just gun us down? There's no challenge in that."

"You don't get it, Rachel. I'm not looking for a challenge. I'm looking for revenge. I want to hurt you, Rachel."

"Why?"

"Because you hurt me!" he shouted, his face contorted with rage.

Sin watched Jace's control slipping away with each passing minute. He just hoped he'd get a chance to do something before it was too late. He waited for his break.

"I never meant to hurt you, Jace." Rachel argued. "You went away."

"But I came back. I loved you, Rachel. I loved you, and you didn't care."

Rachel's reserve was cracking. This man was a lunatic, and he had her daughter. "So what!" she shouted. "Life doesn't always work out the way we want. You don't have to do something stupid now. You could go on from here, Jace. Think about it and let Tish go!" She knew that if he let Tish go, she'd still kill him. This animal didn't deserve to live.

Jace saw the lie in Rachel's eyes. "No, I'm going to kill you. But first I'm going to kill your bastard child. You see, I've figured out how to hurt you, Rachel."

Rachel watched, horrified, as he changed the aim of his gun from her to Tish's head. "No, Jace. Please!" she begged.

"Hurts, doesn't it, Rachel?" Jace taunted.

Sin could see his chance slipping away. If he tried anything, Jace's gun could go off accidentally, killing Tish.

The world seemed to slip into slow motion for Rachel. The horror of watching Jace's finger squeeze down on the trigger clawed at her heart and throat. She had to do something, but what? "Jace, no! You don't know what you're doing."

"Yes, I do, Rachel. I'm winning."

"No, Jace. She's your daughter!"

Jace's head snapped up. Rachel was lying again, trying to stop him from killing her brat.

This was the chance Sin had been waiting for. The aim of Jace's gun had changed when he looked at Rachel. Hopefully, it was enough. He leaped across the short distance, and tackled Jace and Tish. The gun went off with an explosion, and Sin felt the bullet bury itself deeply within his chest. Darkness engulfed him as he hoped he'd given Rachel a chance to save Tish.

"Noooo!" Rachel heard herself scream as the gun went off. In a split second she saw that Tish was all right and drew her gun on Jace. He tried to get up and grab the gun that had fallen from his hand. "Hold it, Jace!" she ordered. He knelt between the bodies of Sin and Tish and grinned up at her.

"At least I killed Braddock." He smiled as Rachel's bullet shattered his face.

Rachel sank to her knees in the wet sand. She crawled to the body of her daughter. Tish was breathing evenly, and the smell of whiskey on her breath confirmed Jace's claim about getting her drunk. She stood and picked her up, carrying her to the shelter of the rocks. The rain was still coming down fairly steadily, but the storm seemed to have hit a lull.

She then went back to where Sin had fallen. The dark circle of blood that stained his shirt caused her heart to wrench in her chest. She knelt beside him and placed her hand on his forehead. "I'll give you a good burial, Braddock." Then the tears started to spill. She fell forward, crying, putting her head on his shoulder. "Damn it, Braddock. Why'd you do it?" she sobbed, wracked with pain. "Why'd you go and get yourself killed?" But she knew the answer. He'd whispered it in his sleep. He'd loved her.

Then she heard a groan. Not even a groan, it wasn't loud enough for that. She looked frantically at Sin's face. He was alive, but just barely. "Oh, my God ... Braddock?" She leaned over and put her ear to his lips. He was breathing. She ripped open his shirt and looked at the bullet hole in his chest. Dark, thick blood oozed from the burned edges of flesh. She swallowed, and her nostrils flared as she fought back the bile that rose in her throat. "I've got to get this bleeding stopped, just hang on," she told him.

She glanced back at Jace's lifeless form and reached for the buttons of his shirt. It took only seconds for her to remove it and begin tearing it into a bandage. Hopefully, she'd be able to staunch the flow of blood from Sin's wound well enough to get him back to town and to the doctor.

"Mama?" Tish's small, weak voice carried from the rocks.

"Stay there, darling." Rachel didn't want Tish to see the gaping hole where Jace's face used to be. "Just stay there, and I'll come get you in a minute," she called. Her hands worked feverishly to pack the wound in Sin's chest and wrap him tightly with strips of Jace's shirt.

"I don't feel well, Mama. I think I'm going to be sick." Tish's voice quavered.

"I don't doubt it." Rachel muttered, knowing her daughter was suffering her first hangover. She suppressed the urge to spit on Jace's corpse. "Just lie still, darling. You'll be fine," she instructed, then felt a wave of realization and immense gratitude. Tish would be fine, all because of Sin. A new flood of tears threatened to blind her. She tied the last knot over the wound and hoped that she'd get him back to town in time to save him.

She stood and glanced quickly at Jace's body. She should probably take it back to town, too, although she couldn't think of anyone who'd care. She heard a slight gasp from Sin and knew she wouldn't waste even one precious second of time on Jace's body. She'd send someone back for it when she got back to town.

Rachel found two long branches nearby and, with the blanket from Jace's saddle, made a travois for Sin. As carefully as she could, she pulled his body up onto it, and tied him securely. She saw that blood had already soaked through the makeshift bandage. "Damn it, Braddock. You're going to bleed to death before I can get you back." She pulled her own shirt up, and tore off a section, then, kneeling beside him, stuffed it under the ties of the bandage. "Please hold on," she whispered.

"Mama, I need you," whimpered Tish.

"I know, darling. I'll only be another minute." She knew how awful Tish felt, but Sin needed her more right now.

Once Sin was ready to move, she turned Jace's body over, and went for Tish. She found her lying near the rocks, shaking and rather green. "I don't feel so good, Mama."

Rachel wrapped her arms around her little girl and reveled in the feel of her tiny body. "You feel wonderful to me," she murmured into her hair. She lifted Tish and, cradling her closely, shielding her view of Jace, she carried her to Sin's horse.

"What happened to Mr. Braddock, Mama?" Tish asked, worried when she saw him tied to the travois.

245

"He was injured, darling. We've got to get him back to town as fast as we can."

"Is he going to die?"

"Not if I can help it." She'd tied the travois to Jace's horse and then tied the lead to her saddle horn. She climbed up behind Tish, and started down the trail.

"Mama, don't forget Poco!"

Rachel looked around but couldn't see the small horse. "Where is he?"

"I don't know. Mr. Jace hit him when we stopped. I don't know where he went. We can't leave him out here, Mama. He'll die."

"If Jace slapped him, he's probably already halfway home by now. He's a smart horse, Tish. He'll be fine." She spoke in a soothing tone but felt a stab of remorse as she thought about Roux.

The trail seemed even more treacherous going down, and Rachel realized it was because so much damage had been done by the fierce wind and rain. She kept looking back at the travois, hoping against hope that Sin was doing all right. She feared he'd be dead before she got him back to town, and she'd never be able to tell him . . . Tell him what?

"Mama, I'm going to be sick!" Tish coughed. "Let me down, please."

"We don't have time. Just lean over my arm. I'll hold you." She held her daughter's heaving body, and then pulled her close to stop the shivers that followed. "We have to get him back, Tish."

"Yes, Mama," Tish said quietly.

After a few more painfully slow minutes passed, Rachel heard her daughter's voice again. This time she was asking how Mr. Braddock got hurt. Rachel felt a twist of pain in her chest as she tried to answer. "He was shot . . . helping us."

"How?"

"He saved us from Jace."

"Oh."

Rachel kept the horses at a steady pace down the trail

and across the open range. She made her way toward town as directly as possible, and cursed under her breath each time they crossed a wash or mound that made the course more difficult. She found herself holding her breath at every bump.

Tish began to shiver, so she had her pull her feet up under her nightgown, and tried to shield her from the cold that had invaded their world so swiftly. Rachel hadn't thought about Tish being cold. She, herself, was sweating.

"We're almost there, Tish. Look, there's the Rosebud." She nudged her daughter when they got close to town. The Rosebud was the closest building, and she knew she had to get Sin inside as soon as possible. If he was still alive. It seemed like it had taken them an eternity, and she was almost certain, and terrified, that Sin was already dead.

"Good Lord, we've been so worried!" shouted Vera, as she ran out of the bar to meet them. "Lucy sent word to the sheriff. Nearly the whole town is out looking for you. Oh my . . ."

Rachel jumped to the ground with Tish in her arms, and handed her to the older woman. "Take her inside, send someone out to help me! And send for the doctor!" She ran to the travois, practically falling on Sin, to listen for his breathing. "Please, please." She heard a faint rasp. "Thank God," she whispered.

"What can we do, Rachel?"

"Get him inside. Take him into the office," she instructed the men who had come out to see what was going on. "And be careful!" she warned.

"Yes, Rachel." "Of course, Rachel," they mumbled.

Once inside the office, she had them put him on the cot she and Sin had slept on just the night before. It seemed like a hundred years ago, now. "Leave me alone with him. And someone get word to the ranch that Tish and I are all right. Where is the doctor?" She barked out orders and demanded.

When everyone left the room, she ripped the bandage

from his chest and looked at the wound again. It was just a little to the left of his heart and continued to ooze dark red. When was that damn doctor going to get here? Just then the door opened and Dr. Wilson came rushing in, his bag in hand.

"Vera told me Mr. Braddock has been shot." He set the bag down and looked at the wound. "Oh, dear," he muttered. "Rachel, you'd better leave while I look at this." He began rolling up his sleeves.

"No."

Dr. Wilson looked up at her, surprised. "Rachel, I think it best if ..."

"I don't care what you think. I'm staying. Now save him."

Rachel watched as the doctor took a long silver instrument out of his bag and began to probe the wound. A thick clot of blood slid from the hole, and slipped down Sin's chest and side to the floor. Rachel had to swallow hard.

"I told you to leave, Rachel," the doctor told her when he noticed her pallor.

"I'm fine, just keep going." Rachel wiped the beads of sweat that threatened to blind her, and at the same time realized she was shivering. She grabbed the edge of the cot to steady herself and continued to watch.

She was certain the doctor was going to push the probe clear through Sin's body and out the other side before he was done. He slowly pulled the instrument back out, and laid it on a white gauze he'd taken from his bag. He leaned back and wiped the sweat from his brow with his handkerchief. "It doesn't look good, Rachel. The bullet's too close to his heart."

Rachel braced herself. "What does that mean?"

"It means that I probably can't get it out without killing him."

"And?" She waited.

"And he'll die for sure if I don't try."

Rachel looked at the still form lying on the cot. She could barely see the rise and fall of his chest, and noticed how pale he was. His lips were becoming an ashy color, as was the area around his eyes. She looked at the cut along his cheekbone, put there by Jace the night before, and remembered how they'd made love afterward. "I'll help you do it, Doctor."

"He may die anyway, Rachel. Probably will."

"I'll help you get out the bullet. What do we do first?"

"Rachel, did you hear what I told you? I don't want you to get your hopes up. This young man is probably going to die, no matter what either one of us does."

Rachel stared hard into the soft gray eyes of the doctor and saw his concern. "He's going to live," she told him. "Just tell me what to do."

15

Rachel stood at the door of the office. "Vera, tell Tish to come here, please."

Tish had been sitting on a bar stool with a cup of coffee warming her hands. She heard her mother's words and, setting the cup down, ran to see what she wanted. "Yes, Mama?"

Rachel knelt down to her daughter's level and took her into her arms. "I'm going to stay here awhile, and as soon as someone from the ranch gets here, I'm sending you home."

"But I want to stay with you." Tish hugged her mother hard.

"I know, but you need to go home and get cleaned up and dressed. Lena is frantic with worry over you, and Aunt Lucy will probably scrub you raw." She smiled and ruffled Tish's already messy hair. Then she leaned back and looked seriously into her deep brown eyes. "Mr. Braddock is very badly injured. I need to stay here until he gets well enough to bring back to the ranch. You understand, don't you?"

"How long will you be here?" Tish inquired.

"As long as it takes. But you can come see me whenever you want to. I'll tell Hank to have Stoker or Ben

250

bring you, all right?" She held Tish's chin in her hand
and watched her reaction.

"All right, Mama."

Rachel kissed her daughter's smudged nose, then her
eyes and cheeks. She tried to swallow the lump in her
throat and found it difficult. If it hadn't been for Braddock, she might never have kissed this dirty little face
again. Blinking back tears, she hugged Tish to her. "You
go finish your coffee and wait." She looked at Vera.
"There's plenty of milk in her cup, right?" Vera nodded
at her and winked. "All right then, let me know when
someone gets here from the ranch."

"Yes, Rachel." Vera watched the slump of Rachel's
shoulders as she walked back into the office. She shook
her head and said a prayer for Mr. Braddock and an
extra one for Rachel.

The doctor had his instruments ready, and was pouring alcohol around the wounded area, when she knelt
down beside the cot. "What do I do?"

"Well, Rachel, you're sure you won't change your
mind about this?"

Rachel sent him a look that left no room for doubt.

"Very well. Roll up your sleeves and pour this alcohol
over your hands."

Rachel did as she was told, then watched as the doctor
began to cut open the wound. She saw Sin flinch a little,
but knew it must be reflexive because he was still very
much unconscious.

"Rachel, hold some gauze there, where it's bleeding,
but don't move him," the doctor instructed.

She held the gauze in place and watched him cut even
deeper. She noticed him frowning and wondered if there
was anything else she should be doing. "Doc?"

"Shhh," he hissed.

She took more gauze from the stack and tried to catch
the blood as it spilled. The wound was larger now, and
Rachel wondered how long it would take to get to the
bullet. She glanced up at Sin's face and also wondered
how long he could hang on. His color was getting worse.

"Oh, Lord, no. Damn it," the doctor whispered.

"What?" Rachel asked urgently.

"Damn," he said again.

"What?!" Rachel saw the look of dread on the doctor's face. Something was wrong. She watched as he dropped the instrument and put his fingers inside Sin's chest.

"The bullet nicked an artery. When I moved it he started to hemorrhage. Damn it, Rachel, I can't save him!" He pulled his hand away. "Damn, damn, damn," he cursed.

Rachel watched in horror as blood began spurting up out of the wound in steady beats. "Do something!" she shouted. "There's got to be something you can do!"

"I told you the bullet was too close to heart, Rachel. I warned you that he'd probably die."

Rachel frantically tried to sop up the blood that ran down Sin's side. "Do something!" she shouted again. "Sew him up!"

"Rachel, I can't . . ."

"Do it!" She grabbed him by the front of his shirt, her bloody hands staining the white fabric, and pulled him close. What she demanded seemed logical to her. "Sew him up!"

"I . . ." The doctor seemed bewildered. He wasn't skilled enough to try what Rachel was suggesting . . . but Braddock was dead if he didn't try, and fast. He looked at the amount of blood that had formed a puddle on the floor under the cot. "He'll probably die anyway."

"Shut up and do something!" Rachel ordered.

"All right, Rachel. But you'll have to help me."

"Anything. Just tell me what to do."

The doctor reached inside his bag and pulled out a small leather pouch. From it he took a curved needle and some thread. "Are you ready?"

"Yes, yes." She looked at Sin, willing him to live.

"Put your fingers into the wound and hold it open so I can get to the artery. And be ready with gauze, if you can."

Rachel took a deep breath and stuck the first two fingers of each hand into the hot, bloody flesh of Sin's chest. She pulled open the wound and had to lean back to keep from getting squirted with the blood that began shooting upward.

As Rachel watched, the doctor pushed gauze into the hole and then felt for the artery. He began sewing the edges of the torn artery together, slowing the bleeding with each stitch. "Rachel, I've never done anything like this before. I don't even know if it will work."

"It has to work. Just keep going."

When the massive bleeding seemed to stop, she saw him continue the process with other damaged tissue around the hole. Gradually, he worked up through the wound until he asked her to remove her fingers once again. Soon after that, he sewed the muscle tissue and finally the skin together. He then covered the wound with a loose bandage.

"If he lives it'll be a miracle," he said, as he leaned back on his heels and looked around the room at the mess they'd created.

"He'll live," Rachel told him with certainty.

"You believe in miracles, Rachel?"

"No. I don't believe in giving up."

The doctor stood up, stretched his back, and began gathering up his instruments. He knew that the odds of Braddock making it were a million to one, but he wasn't going to argue with Rachel. "He'll be unconscious for quite a while, but when he does wake up," if he wakes up, he thought, "he's going to hurt like hell. I'll leave some laudanum here for you to give him, if you can."

"If I can?"

"Even if he's not unconscious, he may be out of his head. If infection sets in, well, never mind."

"What about infection?"

"Rachel, there's such a slim chance of him making it, anyway, that if the wound becomes infected you won't have to worry about giving him anything for pain. He'll be dead."

"Thank you, Doctor." She turned her head away from him. He was so ready to pronounce a death sentence on Sin that she didn't want to look at him anymore. Sin would live. She'd make him live. "Is there anything I can do in the meantime?" she asked over her shoulder.

"Just keep him warm and comfortable for now. If he does show signs of recovery, try to give him liquids. I'll check back tomorrow." He shook his head, knowing Rachel was wasting her time. Braddock would be dead by morning.

Rachel continued to stare at Sin long after the doctor left. "You're going to make it, Braddock. Do you hear me? You're going to pull through his," she ordered him quietly.

A knock at the door startled her. Vera stuck her head in and told her that Hank and Stoker were outside. "Good Lord, look at this mess," she exclaimed, when she saw the bloody room.

Rachel looked around. "I know, don't let Tish in here." She glanced down at her own appearance. "Tell Hank to come in."

"Yes, Rachel." Vera looked at Sin, lying on the cot, covered with blood. "The doc told me he's still alive."

Rachel looked Vera in the eyes. "Yes."

"He didn't sound too hopeful, though."

"The doctor has a big mouth. Braddock is going to be fine."

Vera looked skeptical as she went back to the bar.

Rachel grabbed a clean piece of gauze and tried to wipe her bloody hands, then rolled her sleeves back down. She knew she probably still looked like death herself, but it couldn't be helped. Her suspicions were confirmed by the look Hank gave her.

"Are you all right?" he questioned.

"Yes, Hank. I'm fine, just a little tired."

"Vera told us Braddock was shot. How's he doin'?" The older man looked down at the unconscious form on the cot.

"He'll make it," she told him, then noticed the skeptical look on his face. She sighed. "Anyway, I want you to get Tish back to the ranch, and keep on with roundup. I've got to stay here for a while."

"Right, Rachel."

"Hank, there are a couple of things I need you to do."

"Yeah?"

"Someone has to go get Jace's body. I didn't have time to deal with it."

"Jace's body?"

"Yes, I shot him."

"Jace did have Tish?"

"Yes. And he shot Braddock." She waited for his reaction.

Hank paused only a moment before answering. If Rachel shot Jace, he needed shooting. "We'll get him, Rachel. What should we do with him?"

She hadn't thought about that. What should they do with him? She knew he had no family left in the area. She thought for a moment about letting him rot, but then remembered his parents. The Coopers had been good people. She'd played at their place as a child, and remembered that Mrs. Cooper had doted on Jace. Her attitude, that he could do no wrong, probably caused him to turn out the way he had, but she couldn't pass judgment on parents for loving their child. "I guess you could take him out to his family's old ranch. I know his parents are buried out there."

"Yeah, I know where it is. We'll take care of it. What else did you need done? You said there were a couple of things."

Rachel looked at the floor, then back up. "I need you to get my saddle and bridle."

Hank gave her a puzzled look.

"Roux's dead. Broken leg. I need my saddle." Her speech was stilted, and she knew Hank could see the tears that threatened to fall.

"Sure, Rachel. We'll get it for you. I think I'll have the boys bury the carcass while we're out there.

Wouldn't want to attract any scavengers to the area," he told her.

Rachel knew he was telling her he'd give Roux a good burial. "Thanks, Hank. Ah, mark the spot. Just in case I ever get back that way again." She couldn't look at him as she spoke.

"I intended to, Rachel," he told her quietly. He donned his hat. "I'll see you later."

"Right. Oh, and Hank, if Tish wants to come see me while I'm here, would you or Stoker, or possibly Ben, see that she gets here safely?"

"You bet."

"Thanks."

Minutes after Hank had gone, she once again knelt beside Sin and listened for his breathing. It was shallow and thready, but it was there. She wondered what she should do. She'd never tended anyone this seriously injured before.

The doctor had told her to keep him warm and comfortable. He looked neither. She got some scissors from her desk and cut away the rest of his shirt, leaving the back portion under him. She unfastened his gunbelt and belt buckle, letting them hang loosely to the floor. Deciding to cut his trousers away sounded easier than it turned out to be. She struggled with the scissors as she tried to cut the heavy material. When she finally got to his legs, she had to stop, and gently remove his boots, before she could cut the trousers free.

Rachel looked at him. Even lying on a cot, with a bloody hole in his chest, he had the ability to make her heart race. His legs were straight and strong, and the rippled muscles of his stomach reminded her of the way she'd kissed his body the night before. "Stop it," she told herself.

She covered him with a blanket from the waist down and decided she better clean him up. Going to the door, she asked Vera for some fresh water.

"How's he doin'?" Vera asked.

"All right, I guess. I want to clean him up, he's a real mess."

"Yeah, I could see that when I peeked in. Do you need any help?"

"No, just some water."

As she wiped the blood from Sin's body, she was amazed at how much he'd lost. The basin was red with it long before she had him clean. How much blood could a person lose and survive?

She noticed the bandage over his wound was getting redder and worried that he was still losing too much blood. What would she do if he didn't stop bleeding soon? The doctor didn't seem to think he had much of a chance so she felt it was up to her to get Sin through this. Damn it, why did he have to go and get himself shot? She pulled a chair to the side of the cot and sat down next to him. Rubbing her hand over her eyes, she remembered that split second after Jace's gun went off when she thought the bullet might have found Tish. "Dear Lord." She took a deep breath to quell the terror that filled her heart at the memory.

She leaned back in the chair and studied Sin's face. He looked awful. The cut on his cheekbone was clotted over, puckering his skin, and the color around his eyes was pale gray. She noticed his eyelids fluttering spasmodically and wondered if he had any sense of his surroundings. She hoped not. She didn't want him to suffer. He'd saved Tish's life, and probably her own if she were truly honest with herself. A single tear slipped from the corner of her eye. "Damn," she muttered, wiping it away. She remembered how he'd told her that someday she'd find out she needed someone. "Why the hell did it have to be you, Braddock?" she whispered.

"I figured you'd be gettin' hungry about now," Vera explained as she came through the door with a dinner tray.

Startled, Rachel swiped at another tear. "You know, I forgot that I hadn't eaten since ..." she had to stop and think, "since last night." She remembered the party.

Was it only last night? How could so much have happened in one day? She reached for a dinner roll and stuffed it in her mouth.

"Do you really think he'll make it?" asked Vera as she looked him over.

"Yes," Rachel stated bluntly.

"The doctor didn't seem to think he had much of a chance."

"The doctor's wrong. Thanks for the dinner." She dismissed Vera, knowing her tone was rude, but couldn't help it. Braddock was going to pull through this. He had to.

Hours later, as Rachel slept uncomfortably in the chair next to Sin, she thought she heard something. Sitting up, she tried to rub the kinks out of her neck, and listened. She heard it again. A moan.

"Braddock?" She turned up the lamp and knelt beside him. "Oh, my God," she exclaimed when she felt his forehead. He was burning up. "No! The doc said you'd never make it through an infection, Braddock. Fight it," she ordered.

Sin writhed on the cot, tossing first one way and then another. Low moans escaped his dry lips, and his hands clutched the edges of the cot.

Rachel knew that if he kept on throwing himself around he'd probably tear open the stitches the doctor had put so deeply within his body, and she'd have no way to mend them. She threw herself across his chest and saw a grimace of pain cross his face. "Braddock, hold still." She held him down as well as she could, surprised at his strength. "Braddock, can you hear me? I said, hold still. You're going to kill yourself." She continued to hold him, knowing she had to try to get his fever down.

Somewhere from a distance Sin heard the soldier telling him to hold still. He knew he'd been shot, and he wondered why they didn't finish him off. "Yeah, we got us a Reb. And a Captain no less. Should I shoot him, Sir?"

"No, we'll take him to the hospital in the prison."

"Hold still, Reb." The voice kept telling him to hold still. He couldn't breathe. He was on fire. His skin burned, and his chest carried the weight of death. Why didn't he die?

Then he saw eyes. Green eyes. Who had green eyes? He couldn't remember. Oh, he hurt. It hurt to breathe. Rachel had green eyes. Rachel, I have to get out of this prison and back to you. But you're not waiting for me. Who ... Bessie. No. Bessie is gone. He should go see Bessie. He tried to hear the voices calling him. They kept telling him to lie still.

"Braddock, hold on. Please hold on," Rachel begged as she saw his eyes open. He focused on her for only a second, and she could tell he was delirious. He tried to talk but only mumbled. She couldn't make out what he was saying, but heard the word "prison," and knew he was reliving some terror from his past. "I'm here, Braddock. It's Rachel. You're here at the Rosebud and you're safe, just lie still." She pushed his shoulder down when he tried to lift it. "Lie still, Braddock."

She fought with his struggling for what seemed like an hour. Her muscles ached and sweat dripped from her brow and down her neck. She knew she had to get his fever down, but was afraid to let go of him. "Damn it!" she cursed. Leaning away from him for only a moment, she took off her shirt and threw it across his shoulders, carefully avoiding the wound on his chest. She then reached under the cot and pulled the sleeves together and tied them in a knot. He was still moving too much. She looked to where his belt had nearly fallen to the floor from his tossing and pulled it free. Wrapping it around his legs, she buckled it, securing his lower body as best she could. "Now to get some water," she told him.

The pump was behind the bar so she left the door open between the two rooms and filled the basin. As quickly as possible, she returned, and began sponging Sin's burning skin. Over and over she mopped his brow and chest, and let water dribble through his lips. "Come on, Braddock. You're going to make it, damn it." She continued to try to cool him down. Some time later she realized the water was doing little good.

Rachel ran from the Rosebud, wearing a bar towel tied across her breasts, and took the steps to the doctor's apartment, over his office, two at a time. When her knocking didn't raise him fast enough, she pulled her gun and used the butt to bang loudly on the wooden frame. "Doctor! Wake up. It's me, Rachel. I need your help!"

"Rachel?" Dr. Wilson looked incredulously through the window at Rachel. He was rubbing sleep from his eyes and couldn't believe what he was seeing. "What are you wearing?"

Rachel looked down at the bar towel across her breasts. "It's a towel," she answered, sure that the answer had been obvious.

"You can't dress like that in public," the doctor scolded.

Rachel couldn't believe this line of conversation. He was lucky she had anything on at all. In fact, she'd run from the bar half naked, then realized it and gone back for the towel. "Doctor, forget about me! I need help with Braddock."

"Is he dead?"

Rachel frowned at him again. "Of course not, if he was dead I wouldn't need you. Now, please come quick."

Doctor Wilson was surprised. He would have bet Braddock wouldn't have made it two hours, and now Rachel was here demanding he come help her. Braddock was probably going through death throes, and she didn't recognize it. "What seems to be the problem, Rachel?"

"He's feverish. I've been sponging him off, and it doesn't seem to be doing any good."

The doctor's shoulders drooped a bit. He had to say he was sorry that Braddock was going to die like this, but with infection set in, he didn't give the man half a chance in hell. "Well, Rachel, I warned you this could happen. I'm sorry."

"Sorry? Don't stand there telling me you're sorry. Come do something."

"Dear, what's the matter?" Mrs. Wilson came to stand behind her husband, then saw Rachel. "Oh, my . . ."

"Rachel's friend is dying," he explained to his wife.

"He's not dying! Not if you get your ass over to the Rosebud and do something!"

"Now, Rachel, I know you're upset, but I won't have you talking like that in front of my wife."

The condescending tone of the doctor nearly did her in. "Doctor Wilson, your dear wife isn't going to wither and die if she hears me swearing on her front step, but Braddock will if you don't stop wasting time arguing with me. Get your bag and come on!" Rachel could see Mrs. Wilson peeking out at her from behind her husband and wondered what it would be like to be so sheltered.

"Rachel, if infection has set in, there's nothing I can do."

"You won't even try?" It was sinking in that she wasn't going to get him to help her. He'd already given up.

"I'm sorry, Ra . . ."

"Never mind, Doc. You probably wouldn't know what to do anyway, right?" Her tone of voice was as insulting as she could make it.

"Now, Rachel, I don't think that's necess . . ."

"Don't worry about it," she interrupted. "I know someone who's not afraid to at least try." She turned on her heel and bounded back down the stairs.

"Vera! Wake up." She pounded on the door until Vera answered.

"What is it, Miss Rachel? Do you need my help? My goodness, what are you wearing?"

"Never mind. I need you to watch Braddock for me for a couple of hours. I have to get to the ranch and bring Lena back." She took the older woman's shoulders in her hands. "Can you do it, Vera?"

"Of course I can." She reached for the door, closing it behind her, and started for the bar that minute.

Rachel watched Vera pull her wrapper tightly around her ample frame as she walked and felt a surge of love for her. There were some people she could always count on when she needed them, and Vera was one of them. She was suddenly reminded again how right Sin had been when he'd told her she needed people.

When she and Vera went into the office, Sin lay, still fighting the bonds Rachel had put on him. "See, Vera, I need you to keep him as cool as possible while I get Lena."

"What about Doc?"

"I already tried him. He won't help."

The expression on Vera's face told Rachel that she understood Doc's reason for refusal. He didn't believe Braddock had a chance.

"He's going to make it, Vera," she stated bluntly.

"I know." Vera lowered her eyes, hoping Rachel couldn't see her disbelief.

Rachel took Vera by the arms and looked her square in the eyes. "I know you don't think he's going to make it either." She glanced at Sin's body, twitching in the cot. "But you have to promise me you'll keep wiping him down until I get back. Do you promise?"

Vera looked directly into Rachel's worried eyes. "I promise I'll do the best I can for him."

Rachel dropped her hands and her eyes. "All right, then I'll be back as soon as I can." She heard Sin moan and flinched at the sound.

"Rachel, you really should go to my place and get something to put on."

Rachel looked down at herself and saw that she still wore a bar towel. "I suppose you're right." She glanced back up. She hated to leave Sin for even a moment, but she had to get Lena. She was the only person Rachel knew that might be able to help. "Thank you, Vera."

Vera scoffed and gestured toward the door. "You'd better get a move on. You've got a long way to go."

Rachel didn't wait any longer. She dashed out the door and went straight to Vera's little house behind the bar. Going inside, she lit a lamp, and searched for something to put on. Everything was miles too big, but after just seconds she pulled on a dark green wrapper, discarding the towel. She pulled the garment around her and secured it with the belt. Even tied as tightly as it was, it hung loosely, with most of her breasts exposed. Still, it was better than a bar towel.

She ran from Vera's house, slamming the door behind her. Suddenly she felt as though she'd been hit in the stomach. She'd been running toward the hitching post, toward Roux. She was choked as emotion filled her throat. "Oh, Roux, what am I going to do without you?" she cried. She looked wildly around her, but there wasn't another horse in sight. Hank must have taken Sin and Jace's horses with him when he left. Then she ran for the livery stable. "I hope I don't get hung as a horse thief," she muttered, as she mounted one of the horses in the corral. Within minutes she was riding hard for the Triple X.

"Lena!" she shouted as she rode into the yard. She jumped from the horse's back and ran through the back door. "Lena, wake up!" She raced to Lena's room and found her just rising.

"Miss Rachel? What's the matter? Mr. Braddock isn't . . . ?"

"No, but he will be if you don't come help me."

"What can I do?"

"Oh, Lena, he's burning up with fever. You have to do something." Rachel knelt by Lena's bed and watched as she got up and started to get dressed.

"Of course I will come. You go put on a shirt, I will gather what I need."

Rachel ran up stairs and threw on the first shirt she came to, then ran back down. Lena was bustling around the kitchen. "Can I help?"

"Yes. Get me a flour sack from the pantry." Lena had her head buried in a cupboard. "Get some ashes from the stove, and some yeast. Let me think." She emerged from the cupboard with several small jars and bottles in her hands.

"What's going on here?" Lucy asked, sleepy-eyed, from the doorway.

"I'm going with Rachel to help with Mr. Braddock," Lena informed her. "You'll have to fix breakfast for the hands."

"Oh, dear," Lucy exclaimed.

"You can do it. Just make pancakes and steak. Have Lily help you, and Stoker; I think he knows how to cook."

Rachel watched this exchange with some wonder. It wasn't too long ago that Lucy would have bristled at Lena giving her instructions. Now she seemed to accept it without a problem, even though she was unsure about preparing the meal.

"How is Mr. Braddock?" Lucy asked her after a moment.

"He'll be fine," she insisted.

"I think I have everything," Lena informed them.

"All right, then let's get going."

Outside, Rachel headed toward the barn. She needed to saddle a horse for Lena and decided to saddle one for herself as well. She would return the horse she borrowed as soon as she got a chance.

She led the horses out of the barn to where Lena was waiting with her flour sack of ingredients.

"Is Mr. Braddock still bleeding much?" Lena asked.

"He seems to be. I'm not sure how much is bad. His wound is very deep," Rachel answered.

"Then I will need one more thing." Lena turned back to the house.

Rachel said a prayer of thanks as she watched her go. Lena's ancestors had been Indians, and she'd learned much about healing from her grandmother. She almost smiled when she remembered Lucy calling her a heathen. At this moment she was grateful for the heathen in her. It was all that stood between Sin and death.

"I am ready now," Lena announced as she returned. "Let's hurry. If Mr. Braddock has infection, we need to get there as quickly as we can."

"Right, can I help you up?" Rachel was used to seeing Lena riding in the wagon.

Lena smiled at Rachel, secured the flour sack to the saddle horn, and swung herself gracefully up into the saddle. "No thank you, Miss Rachel."

Rachel once again felt the glow of gratitude. "Then let's go!" She jumped into the saddle and, leading the horse she borrowed, headed for town.

Rachel had traveled this road between her home and the Rosebud more times than she could even guess, yet this time, it seemed to take forever. She signaled Lena that she was going to try to speed up the horses a little more. Lena nodded in response. Rachel huddled low over the saddle and spurred her horse, urging him on. Each second she was away from Sin was dangerous. She felt that if she could stay near him, she could will him to live. She knew it was foolish but couldn't help the thoughts that raced through her head.

Finally, they could see the Rosebud in the distance. As soon as they pulled the horses to a stop in front of the building, Rachel was off her mount and helping get Lena down. "Hurry, Lena. This way."

Lena looked at the horrible color of Sin's flesh as she entered the room and shook her head. *"Dios mío,* he has lost a lot of blood," she said to no one in particular.

"What do we do?" Rachel asked, wringing her hands.

Vera was now standing at the foot of the cot, giving Lena room to work. "He kept trying to get up," she told Rachel. "And he kept mumbling about prison, and someone named Bessie."

"Bessie? Did he say anything else?" Rachel wondered if Bessie was one of the people John Wright's first telegram referred to when he said he was sorry about Sin's family.

"Nothing I could make out. Except he called for you a few times."

"He did?"

"I just kept telling him you'd be back as soon as you could. I don't think I got through to him, though. His mind would just wander off somewhere else."

Rachel watched as Lena uncovered the wound and swallowed at the sight of the gray tissue, swollen, stretching against the doctor's stitches. "What's the matter, Lena? Is he going to be all right?"

Lena kept shaking her head. "I don't know, Miss Rachel. The infection is deep and the stitches, they are holding it in."

"Then cut them open," Rachel instructed.

"He may begin to bleed again. He is very near death."

"Can you stop the bleeding if it begins again?"

"I can try. If we don't get the infection out, he will die for sure," Lena told her sadly.

"Then cut the stitches. I'll help."

Vera put a hand over her mouth. "I don't think I can stay in here while you do this."

Rachel could see that she looked a little pale. "Go wait in the bar. Lena, is there something she can do?"

"Sí." She turned to Vera. "Get a fire going and heat some water."

"Yes," stammered Vera. "I can do that."

When Vera was gone, Lena took the scissors from the desk and began to carefully cut away the stitches the doctor had put over the wound.

Rachel watched as the flesh seemed to explode as it was freed, pulling back from the wound, swollen and infected. "What now, Lena?"

Lena looked up into Rachel's eyes. "I think I need to open him more. The infection runs very deep."

"Do what you have to."

Lena leaned over Sin's body and inserted the tips of the scissors into the wound. Slowly, she cut through the threads that made tiny stitches inside his body.

"Rachel!" Sin cried out. His eyes were open wide for a second, then rolled back, lids lowering, fluttering.

"Lena? Is he all right?" Rachel knelt closer to him, taking his feverish hand in hers.

"*Sí, sí.*" Lena kept working. "He is out of his head."

Rachel wasn't so sure. He'd looked directly at her when he'd called her name. Don't die on me now, Braddock, she thought.

Sin saw Rachel above him as the fiery spear shot through his chest. Then there was Bessie again. Somewhere he heard someone cry out and knew he was in hell. All around him were the faces of men he'd seen die in prison. "Hold on, boys," he tried to tell them. "I'm coming." But each time he got close, something pulled him back. The pain. It tugged at him and tore him in two. Where was Rachel? Why wasn't she here? He wanted to see her face one more time before he went away. He was leaving the Triple X. She'd won. She wanted him to go. But why did she love him like no one else? Why did she burn in his mind and loins like an inferno? "Rachel, where are you?" he tried to call her, but his mouth felt like it was full of week-old bread. "Rachel?" he whispered.

Rachel felt the fire in his skin and watched as pus and blood drained from the hole in his chest. She'd begun wiping him down again as Lena worked, trying to help cool him.

"I must make a poultice to draw the poison," Lena told her as she stood. "You stay beside him, and keep him still."

"Yes, Lena." She was breathing hard and wiped sweat from her forehead with her sleeve. "Please, Sin. Keep fighting," she whispered through her teeth.

Lena returned with a blackened mess in an iron skillet.

"What is that?" she questioned.

"It is a poultice to draw the poison. Help me put it in the wound." Lena knelt down and placed the pan on the floor between them. "Like this, push it into the hole."

Rachel watched in amazed silence as Lena forced the

filthy looking concoction into the open wound. She trusted Lena's knowledge, so she dipped her fingers into the mixture and began helping apply the poultice. Once the wound was full, Lena took some fabric from the flour sack and placed it over the wound. "We must keep this moist and hot," Lena told her.

"How do we do that?"

"I have a mixture waiting on the stove. You hold this bandage in place while I get it." Lena stood and headed for the door.

While she was gone, Rachel held the fabric and watched Sin's eyes. His lids continued to flutter. Where are you? she wondered.

Lena returned with a wet sack of pungent herbs. She placed it directly over the bandage and pressed it tightly, forcing some of the liquid to mix with the poultice. "That is all we can do for now. We must keep this wet and hot, and wait."

Rachel looked at Lena and saw the tired lines around her eyes. She wondered what time it was, and how long they'd been tending Sin. "Lena, why don't you try to rest? I'll stay here with him."

Lena looked around the room and could see no place to lay or even sit comfortably.

"Go tell Vera that I said you two should get some rest. You can go to her house and lay down on her sofa."

"What about you?" Lena asked.

"I'll be fine. I'm going to stay here and watch him. I'll keep the poultice wet, and I'll call you if there's any change. Go on, now, take Vera and go."

Within minutes the two women had left the Rosebud for the comforts of Vera's small house. Rachel continued to sit beside Sin's body, willing him to live.

16

Rachel watched the slight pulse beat in Sin's throat. She'd tried to keep an eye on the rise and fall of his chest, but found the time between his breaths was sometimes so long that she would jump from the chair and place her hand over his mouth, frantic that he'd stopped breathing. Watching the pulse spot at the base of his throat had proved to be a more reliable way for her to keep track of the life within him.

"Keep breathing, Sin," she whispered once when he seemed to gasp a bit. Damn, she thought, what will I do if he stops breathing? She wouldn't allow herself to even think he might die, she just wanted to know what to do to curb any symptom seemingly headed in that direction.

Hours moved by slowly. It had been near dawn when she'd sent Lena and Vera to bed, and now, with morning upon her, she could see that the storms were not over. The room remained gloomy in the lamplight, and she could hear distant thunder rumbling across the mountains. She continued her vigil, keeping the poultice hot and wet as Lena advised. She knew this was going to be a very long day.

Yawning, she stretched her back and tried to twist the kinks from her neck. It was time to check the poultice again and she leaned over Sin's body, gently raising a corner of the herb sack. She looked up at his face and was startled to see him looking at her. "Braddock? Are you all right?"

"So, Bessie, you did wait for me." His speech was slurred and slow, but audible.

Rachel felt her heart in her throat. Sin was still delirious and thought she was someone named Bessie. She wondered for a moment about correcting him, then decided it would probably be best to let him have his fantasy. "Yes, Sin, it's me," she answered.

"Oh, Bessie, they told me you were dead. I went to your grave and cried for so long."

Rachel swallowed hard at the emotions threatening her composure. "I'm here, Sin," she whispered.

"Did you know that Father is dead? And the bank and my home are gone?" He closed his eyes, and a tear slipped from one corner. "I never got to say good-bye to him, you know."

"Oh, Braddock." Rachel lowered her head, guilt flooding her heart.

"Rachel? Is that you?"

Rachel looked up, startled. "Braddock, are you awake?"

"Don't worry, Rachel, I'm leaving. You've won. I know I don't belong here."

His voice was getting softer, and Rachel had to lean closer to hear. "I . . ." she didn't know what to say. He was leaving, and it was what she wanted, but right now, with him lying near death because of her, she was so confused. Confused and tired.

She looked at his handsome face, now scarred and discolored, and she was overwhelmed by the greatest feeling of gratitude she'd ever experienced. "If it weren't for you, Braddock, Tish and I would be dead." It was unbelievably difficult for her to admit it, but it was true. "I'll get you through this, Braddock. I'll take you home to the Triple X and make you well and strong again. Then we'll talk." She could tell he'd slipped back into an unconscious state and nearly smiled. "You always wanted to talk, didn't you?"

Lifting the herb sack, she rose and went into the bar to dip it in the scalding water. She had to keep herself from leaning on the hot stove as she held the sack over the iron pot. The steam rising from the pot caressed her face and made her even more tired. She heard Sin begin talking again and squeezed out the excess water quickly so she could get back to his side.

"I'm here, Braddock," she called, as she entered the room, but when she neared the bed she saw that he was just rambling again. She fixed the bandage, pressing the herb sack in place, and lowered herself onto the chair once again. She rocked it on its legs and listened to the thunder, and to Sin. Somehow, the two became intermingled in her mind. Her head fell forward, and she slipped into a troubled sleep.

Jace had Tish! Rachel's heart was racing as she tried to run. Why wouldn't her feet move quicker? She could hear Tish crying and Jace laughing. She reached for her gun. It was gone. Why didn't she have her gun? This wasn't right. The wind tore at her clothes and burned her eyes. Lightning ripped apart the sky and hailstones beat the ground around her, turning it into an angry white mire. Tish! She tried to scream, but no words would come. Jace lowered his gun to point at Tish. Her heart stopped. Where was Sin? He'd saved her before, where was he now? She remembered; she'd made him leave. He was gone. Tish! Jace pulled the trigger and Rachel could see the bullet leave the barrel of the gun, heading straight for Tish's head. Sin, I need you! Tish! Tish! The bullet was nearly at her head. Sin, where did you go? Tish! Noooooo!

Rachel sat upright in terror. Her body was covered in sweat, and her heart was racing. She took great gulps of air, trying to grasp reality and escape the nightmare. She turned and looked at Braddock. He was twitching and moaning on the cot and looked like hell, but he was still alive. She leaned back in the chair, breathing hard. It took several minutes for her heart to slow to normal.

"Hell," she muttered when she finally felt free of the dream. "I need a cup of coffee." Rising, she touched Sin's forehead and grimaced at the heat she still felt there. I wonder if there's anything else Lena can do, she thought. She went to the bar and made up a pot of coffee, setting it on the stove. She stoked the fire and went back to the door to look at Sin. He looked the same. Suddenly needing some fresh air, she crossed the room and opened the back door.

The scene was a violent gray. Black clouds scudded across the sky, threatening to vent their fury on an unsuspecting earth. It was still early enough in the morning that few people ventured out, and those that did, did so quickly, not wanting to get caught in the impending storm.

Life went on. Rachel frowned, thinking that this scene would have been just the same had she and Tish been killed. The people at the ranch would have been affected, but life would have gone on.

She glanced back over her shoulder at Sin. If he were to die ... life would go on. It was the first time she allowed these thoughts to enter her mind. She didn't like thinking like this. She wouldn't let him die. A small voice asked quietly, "but what if he does?" I won't allow it, she answered. "But life would go on," the voice told her. She couldn't picture life without Braddock. In fact, she tried to remember her life before he and her relatives showed up and couldn't. She frowned up at the gloomy storm clouds. Why couldn't she remember how wonderful her life had been before she was descended upon by all these unwanted people?

A vicious bolt of lightning announced the arrival of the storm's force. She squinted against the glare and stepped back into the room. "Well, Braddock," she turned toward the cot, "it's time I started seeing some improvement in you. Start fighting, Captain Braddock," she ordered. Leaving the door open to the storm's fury, she crossed the room and knelt beside him. Taking his hand in hers, she leaned on the cot and stroked his fingers. "Come on, Braddock," she whispered, "I know you've got fight in you. I've seen it, remember?" She took a deep breath. "You saved my little girl, Braddock. And you saved me." She swallowed. "I don't know what the future is going to bring. And I won't make any promises. I'm still not sure how I feel about you, and I can't say I want you on the Triple X, but fight your way through this and we'll see. All right, Braddock? We'll see." She let his fingers drop and pulled herself up into the chair again. It would be a few minutes before the coffee was done. She'd just have to wait. She'd have to wait for several things.

"Miss Rachel? Wake up." Lena's voice was soft.

"What?" Rachel rubbed her eyes and sat up in the chair. "Braddock?" she asked, looking at him quickly.

"He's alive," Lena told her. "But just barely. We have to fight the infection from the inside, too."

Rachel was angry with herself for dozing off. "Should I have been doing something?"

Lena saw her fear. "No, Miss Rachel. He needs something to help him fight the infection, and he needs rest." She put her hand on Rachel's shoulder. "You are tired. Go eat something. Vera has breakfast ready at her house. I will prepare a potion for Mr. Braddock, and call you when it is ready."

Rachel looked from Lena to Braddock. "I'm not leaving him, Lena."

"But, Miss . . ."

"No, Lena. He's here because of me. I'm going to stay. I'll just get coffee from the bar. I'll be fine." She touched Sin's forehead, smoothing back some black curls, and remembered when she'd run her hands through the thickness of his hair such a short time ago.

"You won't be fine if you don't eat," Lena scolded. "I'll have Vera bring you a tray." She left the office by the back door, which still stood open, and headed for the house.

Rachel watched her go until she was out of sight. What would she have done without Lena's help? She shuddered as she looked back at Sin and realized the answer. He would probably have died by now, just as the doctor had been so quick to predict.

Forgetting about the coffee, she picked up the cloth she'd used earlier to wipe him down with, and dipped it in the basin of water still beside the cot. She began wiping his skin, starting with his face and the muscles of his shoulders. Lena would be back soon, with something to give him for the infection.

Sin felt the cool touch of hands upon his fevered body. Was he in heaven? No, he couldn't be. The pain in his chest was too intense for him to be dead. He wanted to open his eyes and see who was cooling him with such a gentle touch, but try as he might, the weight of his eyelids was too great. Trying to speak also proved to be too much of a strain. All he could manage was to lie there and keep breathing. Breathing was difficult enough without adding movement, too. But still, who stroked him? Who brushed the hair from his face and touched his lips with the moist tip of a finger?

Rachel traced the planes of Sin's face with her hands. Touching his eyelids and lips with water to cool them, she watched as he seemed to be trying to wake up. She was grateful he didn't. She knew his pain would be severe.

She lowered her ministering to his shoulders and chest, then to his stomach, then lower. She raised the blanket slightly, and slipped her hand and cloth across his abdomen, then down his thighs. She finished by rubbing his legs and feet. If this wiping down did nothing for his fever, she at least felt like she was doing something. She couldn't help the fact that her blood raced as she touched him. Shaking her head at her own folly, she dropped the cloth into the basin. "Braddock, you've sure made an impression."

"I'm back," called Lena as she came through the door.

"I have the liquid for Mr. Braddock. We must get some into him."

"How?" Rachel asked. She looked at Sin. He hadn't come out of his unconscious state long enough to give him anything. She doubted there was any chance in getting him to sit up and swallow.

"I have brought this." Lena held up a short piece of stick, hollowed through the center like a tube. "We will pour the liquid down his throat. You must help me."

Rachel watched as Lena approached Sin and pulled down on his chin, opening his mouth. "Miss Rachel, tip his head back and hold it," she was told. Kneeling at the head of the cot, she took Sin's head in her hands and held it back as Lena slid the stick a little ways down his throat. She was amazed he didn't gag. Lena poured a very little bit of liquid through the stick at a time and watched to make certain he had no problems with it. "What is it, Lena?" she asked.

Lena looked up for only a second. "Yarrow, mugwort . . ." she frowned as some of the liquid dripped down the side of the stick. "Some other plants that have a healing effect." She finished pouring the liquid down Sin's throat. "Now we will wait." She gently took the stick from his throat and watched as Rachel allowed his head to lower. "We will wait," she repeated and nodded.

Rachel sighed. More waiting. She reached for the herb sack. It was time, once again, to heat it. She wondered how long this would go on. She could see Lena examining the wound now that the sack was removed. "How is it doing?"

"We will need to cut away some of the dead flesh. It is causing the infection to spread."

Rachel couldn't help the shudder that passed through her. "I'll do it," she stated flatly.

Lena looked at her with dark eyes. "I'll get a knife."

When Lena returned with the knife, Rachel could see she'd held it in the fire of the stove for a while. She could feel the warmth still in the handle when she took it. Waiting for just a moment, she breathed deeply. It must be done, and she was the one to do it. Slowly, she began to cut away the dead, gray flesh at the edge of the wound. Each cut she made exposed more vulnerable tissue and caused her to dread the next cut, but she continued until the job was done. When she finished, she leaned back on her heels and took a deep breath. She was covered with her own sweat and saw that her hands were shaking slightly. "Do we use more of the poultice now?" she asked Lena, ignoring her own emotions.

"*Sí*, I will get it."

Rachel took several deep breaths while Lena was gone. "Thank God you didn't wake up then, Braddock," she whispered to him.

Lena returned and they covered the wound with the black, messy mixture as they had done before. Again, they began the watching and the waiting and the reheating of the herb sack. The day stretched out before them in a replay of the night before. Lena left several times during the day, but Rachel left only once to use the outhouse, and only then when she became so uncomfortable that she couldn't bear it another second. Vera came and went, bringing Rachel food she barely touched, scolding when it wasn't eaten.

The front door remained locked, as they'd begun using the back door exclusively, and Vera told everyone that inquired that Braddock was doing as well as could be expected, and that the Rosebud was closed until further notice. Hank sent word that roundup was going fine and that they'd taken care of Jace and Roux as Rachel had asked.

Tish didn't come to see her that day, and Rachel knew she had Lucy to thank for that. She knew Tish was safe, and she was in no condition to visit with her daughter. She hadn't eaten much, or bathed, or even brushed her hair in two days, and she was exhausted from lack of sleep. She mused once about Tish's opinion that she was "pretty." Right now, though she hadn't bothered to look in a mirror, she knew she probably looked nearly as bad as Braddock.

Rubbing her eyes once again, she squinted down at him. "It's going to be a long night, Braddock. You up to it?" she asked.

Sin's fever didn't break, and his delirium continued. He floated in and out between bouts of thinking he was still in the war, to thinking she was someone else, to utter silence. Rachel tried to watch every move he made and wiped him down several times. She dozed only lightly, and sporadically, hoping to see a change for the better. Dawn found her slumped in the chair, head tilted at an awkward angle, staring at Sin's still feverish body.

"What do I have to do to get your fever down?" Her voice was a rasp, filling the room. "Lena's done everything she knows how. I've watched you every second and helped as best I can. What else should I do?" She closed her eyes, wracking her brain for something, anything, that might give him a fighting chance. Suddenly it occurred to her there was one thing she hadn't done.

At this hour during the week the church was locked. Rachel banged on the pastor's door loudly. She could see the dim light of a lamp being lit through the window and continued pounding. "Open up, please!" she shouted. "I've got to get into the church."

"Rachel Walker? What are you shouting about at this time of the morning?" Pastor Wheaton opened his door and glared at her through red-rimmed eyes. He pulled his robe around his middle.

"I'm sorry to waken you, but I've got to get into the church."

Impatiently, he responded, rubbing the sleep from his eyes. "Rachel, the church is locked now. Can't this wait until Sunday?"

"No! Why is the church locked, anyway? Churches should be open all the time. People don't always need to pray only on Sunday." Rachel's tone was accusing.

Pastor Wheaton was finally waking up. He took in Rachel's appearance and was astonished. Her hair was a matted mess of snarls and what looked like mud. Her face was smudged and her clothes were filthy. He wrinkled up his nose when he realized the offensive odor he'd begun smelling was coming from her. "Rachel, are you all right?" He had, of course, heard about Mr. Braddock's unfortunate accident, had even been told by the doctor that his services would probably be required to perform a funeral, but he couldn't figure out why Rachel was in such a state. When he'd been told that she was trying to nurse Mr. Braddock, he'd pictured her gently ministering to his needs. Nowhere in his imagination did he picture this hellion, so full of wild anger and insistence. "Rachel, did Mr. Braddock pass on?" He thought perhaps this was the reason for her distraught appearance.

"No, damn it! And I'm tired of everyone thinking he's going to die. I won't let him!" She paused and pushed a bunch of hair from her face. "But I've got to get into the church. You see, it's the only thing I haven't done . . ."

The pastor could see she was nearly at the end of her endurance and shook his head. "You poor child, I'll unlock the church at once. Should I get you the doctor, too?"

"No, he won't help Braddock. I already asked him," she sighed.

"I meant for you." He raised the lamp he was holding so she could see herself as he spoke.

She looked down at the filth that covered her and smiled. "No, Pastor. I just need a bath. I don't think I want the doctor doing that. But I do need to get into the church."

The pastor shook his head at her implication, but appreciated her need to be close to God now. "I'll get the key."

The church was cool and quiet as Rachel sat in her normal pew and looked around in the dim light from the lamp the pastor had left for her. It seemed strange to be here alone, at this time of the morning, but she needed to do this. Slowly sliding to her knees, she clasped her hands in front of her and began to pray. "Lord ..." she didn't know how to start. "I know I don't talk to you enough. Most of the time I'm pretty busy." She stopped and rested her chin on her hands, her elbows on the pew in front of her, thinking. "I guess that's not entirely true. I come here every Sunday, and I listen to Pastor Wheaton give his sermons, but I don't talk to you much myself. I think it's because ... well, it's because I've always felt I could handle everything myself." She stopped and sighed. "And I guess it's been true ... until now. Lord, I don't know what else to do for Braddock. I won't pretend to understand why things happen the way they do, but I can't believe it's his time to die." She looked up at the cross behind the pulpit and felt the burn of tears in her eyes. "Please don't let him die, Lord. Please don't. I ..." she sniffed, "I ... oh, hell!" She wiped a tear from her cheek with the back of her hand. "Just don't let him die. Help him. I know you can." She raised up and slid back into the pew. She lowered her head and let her hands rest in her lap. Over and over she prayed, "Please don't let him die. Please don't let him die." It became a silent chant as sleep pulled at her with strong fingers. Before long she was lying in the pew, and the lamp sputtered and went out.

"Miss Rachel, wake up. Come quick, girl!" Vera shook Rachel hard. She'd been looking for her for nearly half an hour and never thought she'd find her in the church.

Rachel sat up, startled. "What is it?" She grabbed Vera's arm and saw her flinch. "What's wrong?" Fear gripped her heart.

"Lena says, come quick. Mr. Braddock's awake, really awake."

"Good Lord," she exclaimed, then looked at the cross and made a silent apology and a quick thank you. "Come on, Vera. Hurry!" She pushed the older woman from in front of her and began running toward the bar.

She could hear Vera puffing behind her, trying to keep up.

When she went through the back door of the Rosebud, she was met with a wonderful sight. Braddock was awake, and Lena was spooning liquid into his mouth. She went to the foot of the cot and smiled. "It's about time you woke up. How do you feel?"

Sin looked up when he heard Rachel's voice. Lena had told him that she and Tish were fine, but he needed to see it for himself. "I feel ... like I have ... an ax in my chest. But ... other than that ..." He tried to shrug but only ended up wincing.

"Don't try to move. You're going to be all right now. You just need rest."

"And more of my medicine," announced Lena, holding the spoon up to his mouth again.

Rachel watched as he grimaced but took the foul liquid into his mouth. "You listen to Lena, she saved you."

Lena shook her head. "That is not true. We saved you."

Sin looked up at Rachel and their eyes locked. He could see the exhaustion in her face and knew, from what Lena had already told him, that she'd barely left his side since she'd brought him back to the Rosebud.

"Who did the saving isn't important. The fact that you're finally awake is what counts. Now we can start thinking about getting you back to the Triple X to recuperate," she told him.

Something inside Sin dropped a little when she said "to recuperate." She still wanted him to leave or she would have said otherwise. In his first moments of consciousness he'd hoped she'd feel differently. That she'd now feel like he belonged at the ranch. That he'd more than made himself a part of it by what he'd done for her and Tish. He didn't regret what he'd done. He really had no choice because of his feelings and would do it again, but he couldn't help wishing it had made a difference to Rachel.

Rachel noticed a change in Sin's expression. It was a

very subtle change, and she doubted anyone else would have noticed it, but it was there just the same. She frowned slightly at him, curious, but he looked away. "Braddock?"

"I'm tired, Rachel." He closed his eyes.

"He needs to sleep now, Miss Rachel," Lena told her. "And you need a bath."

Rachel bit her lip to keep from laughing. She had to admit she agreed with Lena. She looked back at Sin's sleeping face. Something was wrong, or was it? Maybe she was just tired and reading things into his expression that weren't there. She'd be able to tell when he was stronger. "All right, Lena. I'll go use Vera's tub. If that's all right with you?" she asked as she turned to face Vera at the door.

"Please do," Vera insisted.

"I think I've just been insulted!" laughed Rachel. Now that Braddock was on the mend she felt decidedly lighthearted.

In the two days that followed, Rachel kept a close eye on Sin's recovery. She insisted on feeding and bathing him and wouldn't even let anyone else empty his bed pan when his body began functioning again.

The second afternoon, Rachel laughed when Tish came bouncing through the bar door with more energy than three adults, and Hank came in behind her, obviously out of breath. "She too much for ya, Hank?" she asked.

"I think so. Where does she get the spunk?" Hank answered and handed Rachel a covered basket, then headed toward the office to see Sin.

"What's this?" Rachel started to lift the cover.

"Lily sent biscuits that she's baked herself," said Tish.

Rachel took one and bit into it. She was surprised that they were actually edible. "Did Lily let you help with the biscuits?" she asked Tish, certain the child was already a better cook than her prissy cousin.

"No. She wouldn't let me and Jeremy in the kitchen when she and Mr. Stoker were cooking."

Rachel's eyes snapped open wide. "Stoker helped her make these?" She held up a biscuit.

Tish had seated herself at the bar and was busy tying a ribbon in her doll's hair. "Yes. She told us that if we bothered her we wouldn't get any." She giggled. "Jeremy said he didn't want any anyway 'cos she's a terrible cook, and so she yelled for Aunt Lucy, and she came and told us not to be pests." She turned the doll over. "So we went out to the barn and jumped off the hay."

"Well I'll be," mused Rachel. She was glad that Stoker had gotten the chance to spend time with Lily.

"You'll be what, Mama?" Tish looked at her mother with questioning eyes.

Rachel grabbed her daughter and pulled her into a bear hug. "It's just an expression, my darling." She kissed the top of her head. "I'm bringing Mr. Braddock home tomorrow," she said into her hair.

"I know—Hank told me. Aunt Lucy is making a place for him in the parlor. I heard her tell Lily it isn't proper for him to be in the room next to you." Tish leaned away from Rachel and looked up at her. "Why isn't it proper, Mama?"

Rachel lowered one corner of her mouth. "That's only Lucy's opinion. He will be in the room next to me. I'm the one taking care of him so he needs to be close." She played with a strand of Tish's hair. "I'll send word back with you and Hank."

"Oh, Mama! I almost forgot. I drew a picture for Mr. Braddock." She pulled a folded piece of paper from her pocket. She opened it and pushed it at Rachel. "See, Mama, it's me and Poco."

Rachel examined the childish drawing and exclaimed at its beauty. "Should I give it to him?" she asked her daughter.

"May I give it to him, Mama?"

Rachel thought for a moment. Sin still looked pretty bad. She was concerned about Tish being frightened by the sight of him, then decided that she was going to see him the next day anyway. "All right, just give me a minute with him first." She went to the office door and heard Hank giving Sin an account of the roundup's progress. She realized that no one but she knew of Sin's decision to leave. "Are you decent?" she called as she entered.

"Probably not," Sin said quietly and winked up at Hank. He didn't have much strength yet, but the time he was awake he made the most of.

"I have a little girl out in the bar that has a 'get well' gift. Can I bring her in?"

Sin glanced down at the blanket that covered his naked form and nodded slightly. He wanted to see Tish, to make sure she was really fine.

Very quietly, Tish took little steps into the office. Her mother had told her that Mr. Braddock had some bad injuries and didn't look too good. She was a little afraid to look at him, but when she did she smiled. He didn't look so bad. He had a cut on his face and a big bandage on his chest, but that was all. "Mama, Mr. Braddock is still pretty."

Hank guffawed loudly at that, and Rachel giggled behind her hand. "Yes, Tish, he is," she agreed. Her concern over Tish being frightened had been for nothing.

"Wait 'til I tell the boys you're still pretty." Hank slapped his hat on his thigh and laughed again. "That's a good one."

Sin smiled up at them from the cot. He was getting very tired again, but he could enjoy the humor in Tish's remark. "Your mama says you have something for me?" he whispered.

"Yes," she pulled the paper from behind her back, "here it is."

"Hold it up for me to see. I can't move much yet."

Tish obediently held up the picture for him. "See? It's me and Poco."

Sin smiled. "Do I get to keep this?"

"Oh, yes, it's a present. To help you get well."

"Thank you, Tish. I'll keep it always. It'll remind me of you when I leave."

283

Rachel sucked in her breath, surprised he would bring up leaving now.

"Where are you going?" asked Tish.

Hank asked the same thing.

"I told Rachel a few days ago that I'd decided to leave."

"But why?" Tish's little face was pouting. "I don't want you to go anywhere."

Hank rubbed his whiskers. "I don't get this," he muttered. He knew that Rachel and Braddock had a hard time when he first came to the ranch, but now things were different. Leastways, they should be.

Rachel didn't like the way this was going. If Braddock wanted to tell people he was leaving, why did he start with Tish? Damn it, she could see the tears in her eyes right now. "Don't cry, darling. Mr. Braddock has decided to leave, but it won't be until he's recovered. You'll have lots of time with him before he goes."

Tish's chin quivered as she tried not to cry. "Yes, Mama."

Sin looked up at Rachel. She'd once again failed to say she wanted him to stay. When was he going to give up hoping and face reality? Maybe never. Once a fool, always a fool.

"I'll sure hate to see you go," said Hank. "I've grown real fond of you, Braddock."

"Thanks, Hank. I appreciate it, but it's something I have to do."

Hank put on his hat then. "Well, Miss Tish, we best be gettin' on back to the Triple X. It's almost suppertime."

Tish hugged her mother and started to leave the room, but stopped. "May I give Mr. Braddock a hug good-bye?" she asked Rachel quietly.

Sin's breath caught in his throat at her request. He'd hoped he would be able to feel the warmth of the little girl he'd saved.

Rachel saw the expectant gaze in Sin's eyes. "I suppose. Just be very careful of his bandage. He's very sore there."

Tish tiptoed next to the cot and slowly lowered herself so her face was parallel to Sin's. She gently put her tiny hands on his shoulders and squeezed. Then leaning over a little more, she pressed her cheek to his and whispered, "Don't leave us, Mr. Braddock. We need you."

It was all Sin could do not to cry. The tender warmth of a little girl had more power to undo him than all the gunfighters in the west. He nodded silently and fought back the tears.

Rachel watched the exchange but couldn't hear what Tish had said. She could see, however, that whatever it was had caused Sin some discomfort. "Tish, you'd better go now. And Hank, I need you to tell Lucy that Braddock will remain in the room next to mine. I don't care if she thinks it's improper. It will be convenient."

Hank looked at her incredulously. "You expect me to tell her that?"

Rachel grinned. "I guess not. Just tell her I said he was to stay in the next room, and to see me if she has a problem with it."

"Yes, ma'am." Hank knew that even that was going to give him trouble. "See ya tomorrow, Braddock."

"Later, Hank," Sin answered, then "Bye, Tish. I'll see you tomorrow, too."

Tish was wriggling beside her mother, anxious to start the journey home. "Yes, sir. Maybe I'll draw you another picture."

"You do that." Sin smiled, then closed his eyes. He was so tired. The last thing he heard as he dozed off was Hank once again laughing in anticipation of telling the men that he was "pretty."

"CAREFUL!" Rachel ordered the men lifting Sin into the back of the wagon. "Can't you see he's in pain?"

"Sorry, Miss Rachel. We're tryin'."

Rachel looked at the hands Hank had sent to fetch Sin home and shook her head. Ben was there with several others. They were terrific cowboys but terrible on their feet. "Just lift him gently," she instructed.

She saw the tight set to Sin's jaw and knew he was gritting his teeth against the pain. She'd wanted to give him laudanum before the trip, but he wouldn't allow it. He'd told her that he'd spent enough time out of his head and wouldn't induce that feeling again for anything.

"There, we got him in," announced Ben when they finally had the cot situated in the wagon.

Rachel breathed a sigh of relief. "Good. We can get started." She turned back to Vera, standing in the doorway to the office, and squinted against the early morning light. "Thanks for everything."

"I didn't do much,' Vera told her. "Lena's the one who really helped." She gestured in the direction of the ranch, where Lena had headed at first light.

"You were here when I needed you."

"Well, of course." Vera's tone was dismissing.

"It means a lot." Rachel pulled on her leather gloves. "I won't be back for a few days. Take care of things for me."

"I should do a great business for a while." Vera smiled. "After all that's happened, the busybodies will be out in force."

"You're probably right," agreed Rachel. She jumped up into the seat of the wagon and picked up the reins. She turned to Braddock, "You ready to go home?"

"Yes, I'm ready to go home," he answered, wishing it were true.

Rachel waved at Vera and flicked the reins, starting the wagon forward. She heard Braddock gasp once when they began to move, but she kept going. This was going to be a slow trip as it was, she couldn't stop every time he made a sound. He'd probably make plenty before they were home.

Sin winced as the wagon's wheels crossed a rut. It was amazing to him how rough this road seemed. He'd traveled it often on horseback and never thought about its condition before. Now he felt every bump and dip. His chest felt as though he were being split in two, and he questioned the wisdom of turning down the laudanum. Right now, being unconscious sounded pleasant. He winced again as the wheels found another reason to balk.

Rachel did everything she could to keep the ride even. Whenever she saw a rut in the road she would pull the horses left or right to avoid the worst of it. She knew Braddock was suffering, and every time she heard him try to stifle a moan her grip on the reins tightened and her heart beat faster.

"You doing all right, Braddock?" she asked over her shoulder. They'd been traveling for over an hour and she was concerned about his stamina.

"Yeah." He did his best to be heard.

"Good. We'll be there soon, but if you need me to stop for a minute, let me know."

"All right," he whispered.

"What was that? You want me to stop?" His voice was so soft she couldn't tell. She pulled on the reins and turned back toward Sin. She was shaken by his ashen color and the dazed look in his eyes. "Jesus," she cursed and climbed in the back with him. "Why didn't you ask me to stop sooner?" She didn't wait for his answer but reached for the canteen under the seat.

"What's the matter, Miss Rachel?" Ben rode back to the stopped wagon.

"I need to stay back here with Braddock. Tie your horse to the wagon and get up here and drive the team."

"Yes, ma'am."

Rachel maneuvered herself so Sin's head rested in her lap. She carefully poured water into his mouth and held him while he drank. "All right, Ben. Let's get going."

17

It took some doing to get Sin up the stairs and settled into his room. Rachel shouted orders and directed the process with impatience.

"Rachel, calm down. They're doing the best they can," insisted Lucy, after one particularly caustic remark she'd made.

Rachel just glared her response. "Am I the only one who understands how much pain he's in?" she asked. "Ben, be careful!"

"Yes, ma'am." Ben was leading the way into Sin's room and had nearly bumped him against the door while going through.

Sin lay helpless on the cot, listening to Rachel's orders and remarks, and wondered why she was being such a harpy. He knew the men were doing the best they could. Why didn't she?

Lucy pursed her lips as they settled Sin on his bed. "Really, Rachel. I still find this arrangement unseemly. Isn't there something else we could do?"

"No." Rachel answered flatly. "I'm the one taking care of him. I have to be able to hear him if he needs me in the night." Rachel glanced up at that precise moment and saw Ben wink at Willie. Frowning, she continued firmly. "I don't care if it seems improper to the whole world. Braddock is my responsibility." She directed her next statement toward the men. "Is that all right with you, Ben?"

"I ... ah ... yes, ma'am," Ben sputtered, embarrassed at being singled out.

"Very well, then, if you will all leave us alone, I'll check his bandage and see to his needs." Rachel dismissed them but saw the disapproving look on Lucy's face as she left.

Rachel was still shaking her head when she crossed to Sin's side. She looked down at his face, eyes closed, and knew he was awake. Lord, you got him this far, keep going, she prayed. "Braddock?" she whispered. "Can I get you anything?"

He opened his eyes slightly. The rough ride to the ranch in the wagon had taken a lot out of him. He was taking his time breathing, trying to regulate the breaths to ease the pain that sliced through him. "Rach ... el ... I just ... need to sleep."

Rachel gritted her teeth against the sympathy she felt at his obvious pain. "Should I give you some laudanum?"

"Maybe ..."

Her heart lurched at his acceptance of the drug. At the Rosebud he'd been adamant about not taking any. She knew he must be suffering horribly now. "I'll get it." She left the room quickly, heading down to the wagon, where the sack of medication was still stuffed under the seat. When she reentered the room he was breathing more evenly, and she could see his eyelids had stilled. "Thank God," she whispered. He'd fallen asleep.

In the many days that followed, Rachel ran herself ragged trying to run the ranch and take care of Sin. Several of the hands dropped in to see how he was doing. Lily glanced in once, but was so put off by his weakened condition that she never came back, giving all her attention to Stoker, who beamed with happiness. Tish and Jeremy bounded in on several occasions to say hello and bring him wildflowers. But no one, except Lena, had any ideas about how to help him recuperate. Rachel knew it was up to her to get him through this.

The numerous trips up and down the stairs made her legs ache, and she slept little, listening for his breathing all night. Several mornings she woke in the chair she'd placed beside his bed, after falling asleep there, afraid to leave his side. One such morning Lucy cornered her in the kitchen.

"Rachel, I need to have a word with you." Lucy's hands were folded under her heavy bust, and she carried her customary hankie.

Rachel poured herself a cup of coffee and turned her head, trying to twist out the kinks. "I'm sorry, Aunt Lucy. I don't have time right now. I've got to feed, bathe, and shave Braddock before I get to work, and I'm already running late." She grimaced as she burned her tongue on the hot liquid.

"That is precisely what I need to discuss with you. You are doing too much."

Rachel leveled her look at her aunt. "Oh, really?"

"Yes, and as for you bathing him, well, it just isn't proper. It's been bothering me for a long time. I should have said something sooner to make you stop."

Rachel set her cup on the counter and rested her hands flat next to it, leaning forward, closing her eyes. "So you think I should let him lay in his own sweat?"

"Rachel, really!" huffed Lucy. "That's not what I meant at all, and you know it. I just think you should find someone else to do it."

Rachel opened her eyes and studied her aunt. "And who do you think would like to have the job? Hank? Stoker? How about you?" Rachel watched the shocked expression cross Lucy's face. "Don't you get it, Aunt Lucy? There is no one else. He's my responsibility until he's well. I will do whatever it takes to see that end, and unless you have some constructive ideas on how to bring that about sooner, I don't want to hear your criticism."

Lucy gasped, hurt. "I only thought . . ."

Rachel was sorry she'd been rude. Things were so complicated right now. And she was so tired. She rubbed her hand across her eyes. "Aunt Lucy, I know you mean well. This is a temporary situation that can't be helped. After Braddock is well, he'll be leaving anyway, so none of this will even matter."

Lucy's voice was soft when she spoke. "Is he really going?"

"He hasn't said otherwise," Rachel answered, and left the room. She went out on the front porch, ignoring the fact that she was already late for work, and sat down hard on the swing, causing it to creak loudly under such abuse. Sighing, she leaned her head back against the wood and closed her eyes. She'd been thinking a lot about Braddock's decision to leave. It was what she'd wanted all along, still did, but . . .

"Hell," she whispered. She pictured Braddock, lying upstairs in bed, wounded because of her, and was gripped by a feeling of guilt, an emotion she'd come to know very well as of late. She raised her head and massaged her temples. He was getting his strength back more and more every day. Soon he'd be riding away, forever.

Pushing herself up, she stretched, then went in to get his breakfast. She had too much to do to sit around all morning.

"Just a little more, Braddock." She held up a forkful of eggs for him.

He shook his head. "That's enough, Rachel." His appetite had started to come back, but just a few bites of food seemed to fill him.

She wanted him to try and eat more, but this was an argument she'd already lost on several occasions. "All right, then it's time for your bath and shave." She set the plate and fork on the bedstand and reached for the basin of warm water she'd already brought upstairs.

Sin watched Rachel move. He'd started feeling a lot better in the past few days and was appreciating his surroundings. Especially her. He watched the way her breasts pushed against the fabric of her shirt as she bent for the basin. If only his chest didn't hurt like hell every time he moved, he'd reach for her right now. He started thinking about what she'd done to him their last time together and realized his thoughts were causing a reaction he didn't want her to discover while bathing him. "Ah ... Rachel? I don't think I need a bath today."

She looked at him, confused. "Of course you do. You're still not able to get around. This bath is important."

He looked at the soft curls of hair that had escaped the braid she was wearing and knew his health was improving greatly by the way he was feeling. "No, really, Rachel. It's all right. I don't want you to go to all the trouble today."

"Don't be silly." She looked into his black eyes and tried to figure out what he was up to. Did she look so bad that he thought she was doing too much, too? She squeezed the excess water from the cloth and ran it over his face. "See, doesn't that feel good?"

Sin thought it felt good all right. Too good. And he knew that the more she did, the better it would feel. He closed his eyes and tried to concentrate on something else.

Rachel continued with the routine she'd established in the days before. She wiped down his neck and then his shoulders and chest, taking extra care around the wounded area. She re-wet the cloth and started to push the blanket down so she could do his stomach. She was startled when Sin grabbed her hand.

"Don't, Rachel." His voice was but a rasp.

"Braddock?" She could see the perspiration on his upper lip from the pain holding her hand was causing. "Let go of me. Are you crazy?"

"Not crazy," he whispered, dropping her hand. "Just don't do anymore." The pain of moving had quelled the desire he'd been feeling, but he knew it would rise again if she continued. He was in no condition to deal those emotions yet.

Frowning, Rachel agreed, dropping the cloth back into the basin. "But I don't get it," she told him. She picked up the basin and the dirty dishes and left the room. "I'll be back in a little while to check on you," she called over her shoulder.

Sin heaved a sigh of relief. If she'd continued the way she was going, she'd have discovered something that would have embarrassed them both. "Why do you do this to me, Rachel?" he whispered. He knew the answer of course. He'd known for some time.

Steadying his breathing, he tried to think of other things. Hank had told him about the roundup. He said they were just about ready to start the drive to Colorado, and he wished Sin was going with them. Hank had also asked him to reconsider his decision to leave the Triple X.

Sin examined the ceiling of his room for the millionth time this week and thought about what Hank had asked. He hadn't thought about much else for days. There was no way he could just announce to Rachel that he'd decided to stay. Things had to be different between them. She had to want him to stay, and it didn't look like that was going to happen. He sighed at the way things had turned out. He'd come to the Triple X looking for a chance to rebuild his life, and instead, he'd fallen hopelessly in love with a woman too stubborn and independent to love him in return.

As Rachel rode over the range that day, she wondered at Braddock's behavior during his bath. "He was acting squirrellier than a horse with a new bit," she said out loud. She glanced down at the horse beneath her and felt a pang of loneliness for Roux. Her new horse was a black mare named Chelsea. She was young and spirited and, Rachel couldn't help thinking, not half the horse Roux was. "Well, Roux, you were special," she whispered to the heavens. "I'm going to miss you."

She pulled Chelsea to a stop on a ridge and surveyed her land. "So, Chels. What do you think? What was wrong with Braddock this morning?" Chelsea pricked her ears back at Rachel. "Do you think he was feeling worse this morning and didn't want me to know it?" Rachel thought about the way he'd grabbed her hand. She'd felt the strength in his fingers, even though the movement had caused him a lot of pain. Her eyes narrowed as she thought about it. "I just can't figure it out." She pulled her hat lower over her eyes and nudged Chelsea toward the main corral. She had to check on some things with Hank before she headed back to the house and Sin.

Sin could hear Rachel coming up the stairs slowly. Her speed meant that she was carrying his food tray, and he wondered what kind of soup Lena had prepared today. His stomach growled. He needed something more solid, but so far all he got was soft eggs for breakfast and soup for lunch and dinner.

"Here we are, Braddock. Nice, hot beef broth," Rachel announced as she came through the door.

"Mmmmm." He sounded less than enthusiastic.

"What's the matter?"

"Do you think you could get Lena to fry me a steak?"

Rachel looked at him. He was serious. "You couldn't eat more than two bites."

"I know, but I'd sure enjoy those two bites."

"I think you'd better stick to soup for a while." She sat down and balanced the tray on her knees. Picking up the spoon, she started feeding him.

"Rachel, let me try."

"What?" She didn't think he could manage.

"Let me try. I'm getting a lot better, and if you ever want to get rid of me, I'll have to start doing for myself again." He stared hard into her green eyes, challenging her to argue his point.

Rachel could feel her heart begin to race. Sin's eyes held the moment, daring her. But daring what? "Are you sure you want to try?" she asked quietly, her emotions a confused jumble.

Sin regretted his statement but wouldn't back down. "Yes, help get me propped up."

A few minutes later, Rachel watched as Sin struggled to feed himself. She reached for the spoon once, but he frowned at her, stopping her action. Now that he's made his decision to leave, he's obviously in a hurry, she thought. Then she remembered that the night he told her he was going, he'd planned on leaving the next day. If it weren't for her and Tish, and his injuries, he would have already left. "Tish is going to miss you," she blurted.

Sin stopped eating, the spoon in midair. "I'm going to miss her."

"So, you're planning on leaving as soon as you're well enough?" She didn't know what she was expecting him to say. They hadn't discussed his decision since he'd been shot, but she had no reason to think he'd changed his mind.

Sin studied her through narrowed eyes. "I guess that's my plan. Yes."

"I never did thank you for what you did." She lowered her eyes to the bowl of soup.

"You're welcome."

"I mean it, Braddock. If it weren't for you, Tish and I would probably be dead." She couldn't meet his gaze. "I'm more grateful than you'll ever know."

"How grateful are you, Rachel?" His voice was a low, vibrating growl.

Her eyes finally shot up to meet his. "What do you mean?"

Sin was angry. It was obvious that Rachel wasn't going to ask him to stay, she was probably thrilled he'd be gone soon. Damn her—she just wanted a clear conscience when he left. "I mean, what is your life worth, Rachel?"

Rachel raised her chin defiantly. "What do you think it's worth, Braddock?" she asked in a level voice.

Even in anger, Sin admired her. She never backed down from a fight. "I think it's worth one night of sex," he informed her.

Rachel's eyes opened wider, but she refused to give in to her shock. "You don't set too high a price on my life."

"I'll be the judge of that," he nearly whispered, letting his eyes roam her curves.

Rachel's heart was hammering in her chest. "In your condition, you couldn't handle it."

"You're right—for now. But I'm getting stronger every day." He watched as Rachel squared her shoulders.

"All right, Braddock. I'll pay my debt, just as soon as you're up to collecting." She stood and picked up the tray. Taking the spoon from his hand, she dropped it loudly into the bowl and left the room. It wasn't until after she'd put the dishes in the sink and went out to get Chelsea that her heart had returned to its usual rhythm.

Rachel watched Sin's progress with a different eye after that. He pushed himself harder every day and had managed to stand by the end of the week. "Braddock, you're overdoing it," she told him, when he insisted on going down to the outhouse.

"I don't think so. I have a reason to get well, remember?" His voice was a silken ribbon.

"Right." She turned her back on him, leaving him standing in the middle of his room. "But if you fall down the stairs from all your stubbornness, you'll never collect!" She was getting so damn mad at this new attitude of his. She slammed her way out the front door and crossed the yard toward the barn. It put an edge on her already frazzled nerves when she heard him laughing through the open bedroom window.

How did all this come about? She brushed Chelsea and tried to remember when he'd changed. She could only remember trying to thank him that day, and somehow he had seemed to become angry, and twisted everything into this stupid debt he expected her to pay before he left.

Her stomach tightened every time she thought about "the debt." She brushed Chelsea harder and took a deep breath. All during the time she'd taken care of Sin, she'd seldom thought of him in a sexual way. She'd been so concerned about his care that his nudity had stopped affecting her. Well, nearly, she amended. And now, it seemed that all he did was remind her of their future appointment, and stare boldly at her breasts and backside. This strange new behavior had her baffled.

Sin pulled himself back up the stairs. His chest felt like he had a hot dagger thrust through it, causing him to experience waves of nausea every time he pushed himself. Right now, the beads of sweat that lined his upper lip and forehead showed the effects of his trip to the outhouse. He'd stopped on one step to rest for a moment and gather his strength when he heard the rustle of fabric above him.

Looking up, he saw Lily descending the stairs. She was, as usual, surrounded by yards of lace and ruffles. "Well, Miss Lily. I haven't seen you for some time. You're looking lovely," he complimented.

"Why, thank you, Mr. Braddock." she answered, flustered.

Sin lowered one brow in response to her formal use of his last name, and that she no longer called him Captain. He also noticed that she could not meet his eyes and was having a hard time looking at him at all. He remembered Rachel had mentioned that Lily had begun keeping company with Stoker, but that shouldn't warrant this drastic change in her behavior.

"If you will excuse me, sir?" she attempted to pass him, pulling her skirts aside so as not to brush him.

"Of course." He could see her discomfort as she passed and puzzled at it. Rachel's observation, that Lily's nipples got hard in his presence, was no longer true. In fact, she couldn't wait to get away from him. He continued on to his room. It wasn't until he passed the bureau mirror that he guessed at the reason for her embarrassment. He was barefoot and shirtless. His relaxed attitude around Rachel had caused him to completely forget the proprieties. "Damn," he muttered. It seemed like everything he did, and everything he'd become, was somehow due to Rachel. "If I'm going to get out of here, it had better be soon," he told the ceiling as he lay back on the bed.

Sin pushed himself even harder in the days that followed, and Rachel found herself curious about his hurry to leave. She watched the progress he made with amazement. His will was like iron, never giving in to the pain he so obviously felt.

She also noticed his attitude toward her took another slight shift. The sexual innuendos continued but were now mixed with a fair dose of anger. "I guess he's got reason to hate me," she mused to Chelsea. "I'm the cause of his leaving." She gazed out over the herd grazing below her. Tomorrow the drive would begin. When she and the men returned, Braddock would be gone. A small frown touched her brow at the thought.

"Come on, Chels. Let's go swimming." She turned the horse from the open range toward the swimming hole. Glancing in the direction of the house, she noticed a rider. Something about him caused her to look closer. "Hell's fire, it's Braddock." She spurred Chelsea in his direction. "What does he think he's doing?"

Sin saw Rachel out of corner of his eye. "Damn it!" he spat through clenched teeth. He thought she was out working the cattle and wouldn't find out he was gone until she came in for dinner. He'd thought about it long and hard and decided the best thing to do would be to just disappear. He couldn't stand the thought of tearful good-byes to everyone, especially to Tish. And he had no idea what to say to Rachel.

His plan for making her pay him a debt for saving her life was something he'd said in anger, and knew he couldn't carry it out. He'd given in to desire at the Rosebud and all it had done was give him false hopes. He wouldn't do that to himself again. Rachel didn't love him. She just liked his sex. It was a fact he had to accept. And just sex with her wasn't enough anymore.

"Braddock, what the hell do you think you're doing?" she demanded as she brought Chelsea abreast of his mount.

"I'm leaving, Rachel." His black eyes searched hers.

"You're what?" Rachel couldn't believe it. She glanced at the bedroll behind him. He'd given no hints that he'd planned on going today.

"You've known I was leaving. Why are you looking so surprised? It's what you've wanted."

"Yes, but ... you're not well enough yet."

"I'll be the judge of that."

"But ..." Rachel could think of nothing to say. This was what she'd wanted all along, and now that the reality was upon her she didn't know how she felt.

"Anyway, good-bye, Rachel." Sin kicked his horse's flanks and left Rachel behind. His chest was nearly bursting with emotion. So this is it, he thought, I just ride off and she gets her way.

Rachel couldn't believe he was really going. She saw the stiffness of his back and rode after him. What could she say? This seemed so anti-climactic. One day she was nursing him from injuries he received while saving her life, and the next day, he was gone. "Braddock," she called, "what about my debt?"

"Forget it, Rachel," he called back to her. "It was a joke."

Suddenly, she didn't want to forget it, and she didn't care if it was a joke. She wanted to feel him next to her. She was filled with an urgency to complete something that seemed unfinished between them. She remembered the night in the Rosebud, when she thought he was leaving the next day. She'd had that same feeling then, too. She needed to be close to him one more time. She didn't understand why, or care. She just needed it. "What's the matter, Braddock? Still can't handle it?" she goaded.

Sin heard her challenging tone. What was she up to?

Did she really want him to stop riding this horse and have sex with her before he left? Was this to be their final hurrah? "What are you up to, Rachel?" he asked as she rode next to him.

"I just don't want to be accused of not paying my debts. I've already made arrangements, through the bank, to see to it you get half the money from the drive. I don't want this hanging over my head, so let's settle up."

Sin's brows raised at her answer. He'd had no idea she intended him to be paid for the drive. They'd never talked about it. And now she wanted to finish "settling up." He pulled his horse to a stop and turned to look at her. Her eyes gleamed a deep emerald as she dared him to deal with her. "All right, Rachel. You want everything square. That's the way we'll part company, square. Now where do you want this payment to take place?"

She hadn't thought about it. She only knew she had to touch him one last time. Looking around, she saw the trees at the swimming hole. How appropriate. That's where they'd had sex first, it would also be the perfect place for their last. "Over there." She gestured with the reins and started toward the trees.

Sin followed Rachel, watching the way her body swayed in the saddle, and felt the beginnings of desire stirring his blood. He hadn't wanted this, had decided against it. But maybe, he thought angrily, he could get her out of his system by making love to her one last time. He started thinking about the way he would take her and felt himself growing in anticipation.

Rachel led the way through the trees to the water's edge. She swung her leg over Chelsea's head and jumped to the ground, waiting. She could see the tight set of Braddock's jaw and the fever-bright blackness in his eyes. Her heart pumped wildly as he dismounted and walked toward her. She devoured the sight of him. One last time, her brain chanted, one last time. She let her eyes scan his body from top to bottom. Dark, thick, black hair; piercing black eyes; full lips; strong jaw; broad shoulders and chest; narrow waist; muscular thighs; straight, long legs. Her eyes came back up to stop at the evidence of his desire, straining against the fabric of his trousers.

Sin could feel Rachel's gaze as a touch. He felt on fire, and she was holding the match. If this is what she wants, she can have it, he thought. She was the most beautiful woman he'd ever known. And the most confusing. He saw her wet her lips and took a step closer. He swallowed hard as her hand came out to stroke him.

Rachel loved the feel of him, the power encased in tight fabric. She slowly began to unfasten the trousers and free him to her touch. She stroked him gently at first, then rougher, as she could sense his need building.

Sin reached for her, pulling her closer, pressing himself against her. His mouth descended upon hers like an eagle claiming its prey. "Rachel ... Rachel ..." he whispered against her lips, in her mouth, as he plundered and tasted her sweetness. Nowhere would he ever find another woman like her. He raised his hands to her breasts, cupping, caressing, teasing their already hardened peaks to further tightness. This wasn't enough. He reached for the front of her shirt and ripped the edges apart, exposing the firm mounds of her flesh to his eyes and lips.

Rachel thrilled to his touch. Her heart hammered in her chest so that she was sure he must hear it as he suckled her breast. "Sin," she sighed. He caused her body to shiver with expectancy. "Please," she whispered. She was reaching a fevered pitch so quickly. "Make love to me," she asked, needing to feel him inside her, molding to fit her.

Sin's head came up at her words. "What?"

Rachel's passion-dazed eyes looked into his. "I said, make love to me." She pulled down on his shoulders, wanting him to lay down with her and finish what they'd started.

A cold hand seemed to clutch his heart. This wasn't

making love. Love wasn't what Rachel wanted. She wanted cold-hearted sex, nothing more. Somehow, he'd forgotten that. He felt himself going limp. "I don't think so, Rachel." He pulled away from her and began fastening his trousers.

Rachel's mind was still in a desire-drugged state. Her breasts tingled from his touch, and her lips were already swollen from his kisses. She couldn't understand what he was doing. "Braddock?"

"Not this time, Rachel. I've had enough." He was more angry and disgusted with himself than with her, but it was her he was going to take it out on. "I'm finally through. I can't service your needs and just ride away. Find some dumb cowboy to do it for you."

"What are you talking about?" Rachel couldn't understand the hostility in his voice. It was true, she'd goaded him into this "settling," but he'd been enjoying it as much as she was.

"I'm talking about sex, Rachel. You just asked me to make love to you, and that's not what you want. You just want me to satisfy your sexual needs before I go. Well, I won't give you stud service anymore."

"How dare you!"

"Can you deny that all you wanted was a roll in the hay, or in this case, grass, before I left?" He pointed to the ground. "Well, can you?"

Rachel couldn't understand why he was attacking her this way. She looked at the angry furrows around his eyes and the firm set to his jaw. "No, I won't deny it. I told you once before, you're a good lover. Why wouldn't I want it one more time before you were gone? Hell, Braddock, any woman can tell you, there's nothing much better than a strong back and a hard cock!" The only thing keeping her from swinging her fist at him was the nagging memory of his wound, not yet completely healed. "Just don't go blaming me because you can't handle the truth!"

Sin watched the green sparks flying from her eyes, and his own anger died. She was right. He couldn't handle the truth. Not her truth. Her truth was causing him to leave the Triple X. He turned away from her and walked to his horse. Picking up the reins, he mounted slowly, looking back at Rachel. She still stood, with her breasts exposed, chest heaving from anger. He wondered what she would do with a little truth herself. "You know something, Rachel? You're right about me not liking the truth. But I know you don't know the real reason I stopped this." He watched the expression on her face change slightly. "It's because . . . I love you."

Rachel saw the light in his eyes fade and heard the rasp in his voice. She blinked, not sure she'd heard correctly. He turned his horse and headed through the trees. He was soon out of sight, and she could hear the hoofbeats fading as he rode away. The last thing he had said to her was that he loved her. He loved her. It just wouldn't sink in.

She stared at the trees where he'd disappeared, then lowered herself to the grass, absentmindedly pulling her shirt closed in front of her, tying its ends together under her breasts. He loved her. The hoofbeats were farther away, barely discernible in the distance. He was finally gone, and he loved her.

She lay back in the grass and looked at the leafy roof overhead. Her heartbeat was erratic, and her mind was a jumble of emotions. He was gone, and she knew he was never coming back. She listened to the water, bubbling over rocks at the bank. She heard the birds singing in the trees. She could even hear the cattle lowing in the distance. She realized she couldn't hear his horse's hoofbeats any longer.

She looked around her and remembered. Remembered his touch, his kiss, his anger. She could still feel the heat of his kiss on her lips, and the tender tips of her breasts throbbed from the memory of his fingers. Everything around her seemed to reverberate with memories of Sin.

She glanced back at Chelsea. She was grazing peacefully a short distance away. Why did she suddenly feel so all alone?

She thought about going back to the house but didn't want to have to go upstairs and face Sin's empty room. Sitting back up, she wrapped her arms around her knees. She looked around her again. The quiet sounds of the creek seemed to mock her. She no longer felt comforted by the solitude she'd found here just weeks before.

Frowning, she tried to remember the peace she'd felt before Sin had come barging into her life. It bothered her that she could only remember the time since he'd come with any clarity. Of course, she could bring up memories of her life before. She had wonderful, loving memories of her father and Tish. But when she thought about herself, all she could remember were endless days that all seemed to run together. Why did her life suddenly seem so different than what she thought she remembered?

Her heart had begun to pound loudly in her ears. She swallowed, trying to calm the panic that threatened to claim her. She was alone. Alone.

"Oh, my God," she breathed when the wave hit her. She felt as though she'd been kicked in the chest. "My God," she repeated. If she'd been standing, she'd have fallen down. The truth made her weak. "Braddock!" she shouted, as she raced for Chelsea. She leaped into her saddle and spurred the young horse into a gallop. "Come on, girl, we've got to catch him."

Rachel leaned far over the saddle horn and Chelsea's neck, running her as fast as she could. She could see Sin in the distance. "Braddock . . . Sin, stop!" she screamed. "Please stop!" Her hat blew off and the wind caught her hair, blowing it into a wild mass. "Damn it, Sin. Can't you hear me? Stop!" Her throat hurt from screaming. "How could I be so stupid, Chels? Why did it take me so long to understand?" she whispered before she shouted again. "Braddock! Stop!"

Sin thought he heard something. Someone calling him? He turned in the saddle and saw Rachel riding hard to catch up to him. What did she want now? He was leaving. What more could she want? She certainly wouldn't try to seduce him again. He listened. She was screaming something at him.

"Sin, wait, don't go!" She could tell he'd seen her, but he hadn't slowed. "Damn you, anyway, Sin. Stop! I love you!" She leaned even lower and spurred Chelsea again. "Do you hear me, Sin? I love you!" She was screaming loud enough to wake the dead, why couldn't he hear her?

Sin pulled back on the reins. What had she said? He waited and heard it again. She loved him? What kind of trick was this? She rode closer, and he could see her hair flying behind her and the deep cleavage of her breasts where her shirt gaped open.

Rachel could see he'd finally stopped. She slowed Chelsea. Suddenly she felt timid. Now that he was close enough to talk to, she was afraid. What if he denied her? She walked Chelsea closer to him and stopped at his side. "I have something to say."

Sin had heard her screaming but knew it couldn't be true. His eyes narrowed suspiciously. "Yes?"

Rachel squirmed. These feelings were so foreign to her, she didn't know how to deal with them. She looked at Sin, sitting stiffly in the saddle. He was so handsome, even with the scar forming across his cheek, that her breath caught in her throat. How could she have taken so long to see the truth? Why hadn't she understood the reason her body responded to him the way it did? "I . . . I love you." Her voice was a whisper. She waited for his response. She wouldn't blame him if he rode away just to hurt her.

Sin saw the uncertain way she sat, the way she fidgeted with the reins in her hands. This was a different Rachel, an unsure Rachel. Was it possible she meant what she said? His heart ached with wanting it to be true. "Rachel?"

"Sin . . . I love you. Please don't leave me." She felt the heat of tears in her eyes. "I don't want to be alone anymore." She raised her chin and met his gaze straight on. Hot, salty tears slipped down her cheeks. "Damn it, Sin . . . I need you," she said defiantly.

Sin couldn't believe this sudden change in her, yet the tears she was fighting showed him her honesty. She was having a hard time with this. "Can you deal with it?" he asked. "Can you stand to need someone?"

"I don't have a choice anymore. If you leave me I'll die inside." She pushed Chelsea closer and reached out with her hand. "Sin?" she asked quietly, waiting.

Sin leaned over and brushed her hand aside. Grabbing her by the arms, he pulled her onto his horse with him, ignoring the pain still throbbing in his chest. "Oh, Rachel, I love you." He took her lips with his. "I love you so much." He could taste the tears on her face and kissed them away.

Rachel gasped as she was planted firmly against the heat of Sin's lap. She wrapped her arms around his neck and twined her fingers in his black curls. She reveled in the kisses he showered on her, giving back what he gave her. Her heart opened up and touched his. For the first time in her life, she knew what it was like to be truly in love.

"I think we should head back to the creek," Sin groaned into Rachel's hair.

"I think you're right," she purred against his neck.

"I think we'll have to stay there for a long while."

"Mmmmm." She rubbed her bottom over the hardness between his legs.

"We may even have to put off starting the drive for another day," he whispered into her ear.

"Yes, anything." She arched against him as he tickled her breast under her shirt.

He looked down into her sparkling emerald eyes. "Are you always going to be so agreeable?" he asked, smiling.

"Don't bet on it." She grinned up at him and winked.

EPILOGUE

Damn it, Rachel. Why is Jessie on that horse? She's not even three yet." Sin ran down the back steps of the house and jumped up on the corral fence next to Rachel. "Get her down. She'll hurt herself."

Rachel looked across the corral to where Tish and Jeremy sat on the fence opposite and laughed. "Are you kidding? She's showing off for her big sister. You'll never get her down. Besides, she's a natural. She rides better than she walks—just like most cowboys," she added for spite, trying not to smile.

Sin rubbed his brow. "I somehow hoped she'd be more than a cowboy," he told his wife and grabbed her from behind, pulling her from the fence, falling with her into the dirt.

"Sin!" laughed Rachel as she landed. "You ..." Her statement was cut short by his kiss.

"What time are Lily and Stoker going to be here?"

Rachel looked up at the sun. "Any time now. Lena's just about got dinner ready. Why?"

"I was hoping we had time to go to the creek." He rubbed her hip suggestively.

"We can't go now, but I'll meet you there at midnight," she whispered.

"You've got a date, pretty lady."

The creek of wagon wheels drew their attention. "Stoker, how are you?" Sin stood up, raising Rachel with him, and called to his friend.

"Just great. Howdy, Rachel. How's the family?" Stoker spied Jessie's tiny form on the back of a horse in the corral. "Holy cow. She sure takes after you, Rachel."

Sin pulled Rachel tightly to his side. "A little too much."

"Sin," Lily's voice scolded, "you know you wouldn't have it any other way. Now someone help me down."

"Gee, honey, I'm sorry." Stoker quickly assisted his very pregnant wife from the wagon. "I keep forgetting you can't move too well right now."

Lily smiled down at Stoker's handsome face. "It's all right, dear. Rachel, is Mother in the house?"

"Yes, she's helping Lena. Come on, I'll go in with you. I know our husbands want to look at those thoroughbred colts, anyway. I've already looked at them fifty times today." She linked her arm with Lily's and started for the house. "Oh, Sin," she called back, "you get to take your daughter off her horse."

"Thanks a lot, Rachel." Sin knew removing his green-eyed little girl from the back of her horse was going to cause a temper tantrum. Jessie might have inherited his black hair, but the eyes and temper were all Rachel's. "Tish, do you think . . ."

Tish jumped from the fence. "Not me! The last time I tried to get her down she scratched me. Jeremy and I are going in the house. Jessie is all yours."

Sin watched his stepdaughter and Jeremy run for the house. "Cowards!" he yelled after them. He walked toward the fence and the little girl he loved so much. He could hear Stoker laughing behind him and knew that life couldn't get any better.

JULIE GARWOOD

PRINCE CHARMING

❦

*Time and again, Julie Garwood
has delighted critics —and millions of
readers—with her exquisitely romantic love
stories. Her bestselling novels have inspired
such outpourings of praise as "destined to be a
classic...a treasure" (<u>Romantic Times</u>), "belongs on
my 'hands off or die!' shelf" (<u>Rendezvous</u>), and, simply,
"another gem from Julie Garwood" (<u>Affaire de Coeur</u>).
Her hardcover debut, SAVING GRACE, hailed by
<u>Rendezvous</u> as "a wonderfully romantic and memorable
story," was an instant <u>New York Times</u> bestseller.
Now she brings us a very special new love story...*

❦